CELL

ROBIN COOK

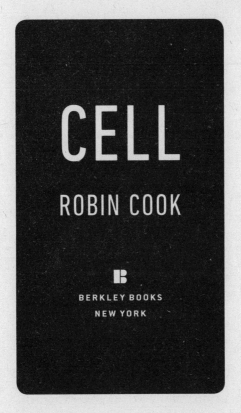

BERKLEY BOOKS
NEW YORK

THE BERKLEY PUBLISHING GROUP
Published by the Penguin Group
Penguin Group (USA) LLC
375 Hudson Street, New York, New York 10014

USA • Canada • UK • Ireland • Australia • New Zealand • India • South Africa • China

penguin.com

A Penguin Random House Company

CELL

A Berkley Book / published by arrangement with the author

For information, address: The Berkley Publishing Group,
a division of Penguin Group (USA) LLC,
375 Hudson Street, New York, New York 10014.

ISBN: 978-0-425-27385-2

PUBLISHING HISTORY
G. P. Putnam's Sons hardcover edition / February 2014
Berkley premium edition / December 2014

PRINTED IN THE UNITED STATES OF AMERICA

10 9 8 7 6 5 4 3 2 1

Cover design by Andrea Ho.

This book is dedicated to the democratization of medicine.

PROLOGUE

The insulin molecules invaded like a miniature marauding army. Rapidly infiltrating the veins, they rushed headlong into the heart, to be pumped out through the arteries. Within seconds the invasion spread throughout the body, latching on to receptors on the cell membranes and causing the cellular gates for glucose to open. Instantly glucose poured into all the cells of the body, resulting in a precipitous fall of the glucose level in the bloodstream. The first cells to be adversely affected by this were the nerve cells, which cannot store glucose and need a highly regulated, constant supply of the sugar to function. As minutes passed and the insulin onslaught continued, the neurons, particularly those of the brain, rapidly became starved of their lifeblood glucose and their function began to falter. Soon they began either to send errant messages or to send none at all. Then they began to die . . .

Kasey Lynch lurched awake. The nightmare had been a bad one, filled with progressing anxiety and terror. She was disoriented, wondering where she was. Then she remembered; she was sleeping in the apartment of her fiancé, Dr. George Wilson. She'd been staying at George's place two or three times a week for the past month, whenever he wasn't on call as a third-year radiology resident at the L.A. University Medical Center. He was sleeping next to her now. She could hear his soft, rhythmic, slumber-infused breathing.

Kasey was a graduate student specializing in child psychology at L.A. University, and for the past year she'd been volunteering in the pediatric department at the medical center. It was there that she met George. When she brought her pediatric patients into the radiology department for imaging studies, she immediately took note of George's easy confidence and his way with patients, particularly children. The handsome face and crooked smile didn't hurt, either. He was warm and personable, qualities she liked to think were part of her own personality. Just a mere four weeks before, they'd become engaged, although they still hadn't set a specific date for the wedding. The proposal was a pleasant surprise, perhaps because of her careful nature in all things "permanent," due to the reality of her health issues. But both she and George had been smitten, and they joked that the rapidity of their relationship was because they'd been unknowingly searching for each other for years.

But Kasey was not thinking any of this at 2:35 in the morning. Instead she knew instantly upon waking that something was wrong, very wrong! This was far worse than just a bad nightmare, especially because she was sopping wet with sweat. Having had type 1 diabetes since she was a child, she knew all too well what it was: hypoglycemia. Her blood sugar was low. She had experienced it on a number of occasions in the past and knew she needed sugar, and needed it fast.

Kasey started to get up, but the room began to spin. Her head flopped back against the pillow as a brief overwhelming dizziness engulfed her and her heart pounded rapidly. Her hand groped for her cell phone. She was always careful to have it within reach and had left it charging on the bedside table. Her thought was that she would speak with her new doctor for reassurance while she ran to the kitchen to get some orange juice. The new physician was incredible, available even at this hour.

As her dizziness lessened she sensed this episode was worse than usual, probably because she had been asleep, giving the problem a chance to progress much further than it would have had she been awake and able to recognize the earliest symptoms. She always kept some fruit juice on hand for just this kind of an emergency, but she had to get it. She tried again to get up, but she couldn't. The symptoms were progressing with horrifying rapidity, draining the strength from her body. Within seconds she was helpless. She couldn't even hold on to her phone. It slipped from her fingers and landed on the carpet with a dull thud.

Kasey quickly realized she needed help and tried to reach over to wake George, but her right arm seemed to weigh a ton. She couldn't even lift it off the bed, much less across her body. George was lying so close, but facing away from her, completely unaware of her swiftly deepening crisis. Using all her energy, she tried again, this time with her left arm; all she could manage was to extend her fingers slightly. She tried to call his name, but no sound came out. Then the dizziness came back with a vengeance, even worse than it had been moments earlier. Her heart continued to pound as she struggled to suck air into her mouth. It was getting harder and harder to breathe; she was being progressively paralyzed and suffocating as a consequence.

At that point the room started to spin faster, and there was ringing in her ears. The sound kept growing louder as darkness descended around her like a smothering blanket. She couldn't move, she couldn't breathe, she couldn't think . . .

George's smartphone alarm went off a little after 6:00 A.M., rousing him from a peaceful sleep. He quickly turned off the alarm and slipped out of bed intent on not disturbing Kasey. It was their routine. He wanted her to sleep to the last possible moment, since she frequently had trouble falling asleep. He padded over to the bathroom, taking his phone with him. As with most people nowadays, the device never left his side. Ensconced in the tiny room, he showered and shaved in just under his usual ten minutes. He was proud of his self-discipline; it had served him well throughout his seven years as a medical student and resident—a grueling endurance race in which "survival of the fittest" was much more than just an abstract turn of phrase.

Six twenty A.M.! Time to wake Kasey. He opened the bathroom door while briskly drying his hair and noticed that her eyes were open, staring up at the ceiling. That was unusual. Kasey was a heavy sleeper; it often required several attempts to rouse her.

"Been awake long?" George called, still drying his hair with his bath towel.

No response.

George shrugged and went back into the bathroom to brush his teeth, leaving the door ajar. He wasn't surprised that Kasey was in a kind of trance; he'd seen it before. When she was really concentrating on something, she had a tendency to zone out. Over the past couple of weeks she'd been consumed in a struggle to come up with a topic for her PhD thesis. So far she hadn't been successful. They'd just had a long talk about it last night before George had nodded off to sleep.

He walked back to the bedroom. Kasey hadn't moved a muscle. Odd. He approached the bed, still brushing his teeth, trying to keep from drooling on himself.

"Kasey?" He half gurgled. "Still worried about the thesis?"

Again, there was no response. She was staring upward, unblinking, with what looked like dilated pupils.

A shiver of fear shot down George's spine. Something was wrong; something was terribly wrong! She was much too still. Panicked, George yanked his toothbrush out of his mouth and bent over the bed. Was she having a seizure?

"Kasey! Can you hear me? Wake up!" He grabbed her shoulders and gave her a firm shake, sensing an abnormal stiffness in her body. That was when he realized she wasn't breathing!

"Kasey, honey! Please, please, God . . ." George leaped onto the bed, searching for a pulse in Kasey's neck. The coldness of her skin unnerved him. He fought back a growing dread as he tore back the covers to start CPR. On the very first attempt, he sensed an unusual resistance and noticed her eyes were not just open, they were frozen that way.

"My God . . . Kasey!" George shrunk back in horror. She was going into rigor mortis. She was dead! His fiancée—his world—had died during the night and he, a doctor no less, had slept right through it!

George collapsed onto the floor, his back against the wall, and wept. It was twenty minutes before he could manage to call 911.

BOOK
ONE

1

It was George's last day as a third-year radiology resident at L.A. University Medical Center. Tomorrow would mark the beginning of his fourth and final year in the hospital's residency program, and then he could start making some real money. After all his years of medical training and two hundred thousand plus dollars' worth of debt, the light at the end of the tunnel was finally visible. His focus on moneymaking was his way of surviving the devastating loss of the woman he loved, the only woman he had really loved. Although he knew it wasn't exactly the healthiest way to begin the healing, it was all he could come up with at the moment. Getting paid, and paid well, would at least be a vindication that all his years of education had been well spent, and he could begin to pay back the money he owed. At least his professional life was on track.

Over the past three grueling months, George had pretended an amenable camaraderie with his coworkers, but the truth was that he had become a hermit. Anyone who tried to dig under the genial surface scraped up against a strongbox in which he kept his feelings. It was what held his demons at bay, or so he had thought. Actually he knew that he was going back on a sacred promise he had made to Kasey. When he had asked her to marry him, she had demurred, saying that it was unfair for him to tie himself down with someone with substantial medical issues. To George's consternation, she had been extremely serious and had agreed to marry him only when he had finally said that if something were to happen to her, he would not shut himself off from his friends and would ultimately find another relationship. Kasey had even made him give her a written statement to that effect.

George sighed. He was exhausted. The previous night he had not been able to fall asleep until almost morning, overcome with guilt at having broken his promise and for the greater guilt at having slept through her death. He would never know if she had suffered or if she had died in her sleep. That was a question that would haunt him for the rest of his life. It kept him from sleeping well since her death, and his insomnia was getting worse.

He looked at his watch. It was 8:35 in the morning. George was in the MRI unit, supervising second-year resident Claudine Boucher. The radiology department in general and the MRI unit in particular were large revenue generators, and their reward from the administration was an excellent location on the center's ground floor immediately adjacent to the emergency department. Claudine had been on her current rotation under George's tutelage for the past month, and at this point George's presence was superfluous.

George was sitting off to the side, glancing through a radiology journal. Every so often he'd look up at the monitor as the computer generated image slices. He was too far away to see any detail, but all seemed in order. He continued sipping on a cup of his favorite Costa Rican coffee. He loved coffee. The taste. The smell. Its stimulative and euphoric effect. But he was highly susceptible to caffeine; his body didn't seem to metabolize it like those of other people. One cup in the morning was his limit. Otherwise, he would be bouncing off the walls into the early-morning hours with a crash-down throbbing headache rounding out the ride. In his present state of mind, indulging himself with even one cup was life on the edge. But George didn't mind since he felt as if he had already fallen off.

A large thermo-paned window let the doctors see into the adjacent room, where the enormous MRI machine did its work. Only the legs of the current patient were visible as they protruded from the multimillion-dollar testament to advanced technology. A highly efficient radiology technician, Susan Fournier, was monitoring the progress of the scan. All was going smoothly. Claudine was seated next to Susan, looking at the horizontal slices of the liver as they appeared. Except for the muffled clunks of the machine coming through the insulated wall, the room was

quiet. Inside the MRI room itself, the noise level was horrendous, requiring the patient to wear earplugs.

The patient, Greg Tarkington, was a highly successful
forty-eight-year-old hedge fund manager. All three of the
medical professionals in the room were aware of this
patient's history of pancreatic cancer. They were also well
acquainted with the details of the extensive surgeries and
chemotherapy he had undergone. The surgeries had made
the man diabetic, while the side effects of the chemo had
caused his kidneys to fail temporarily. At present, he was
relying on dialysis to stay alive. Tarkington's referring
physician, an oncologist, was particularly concerned with
making sure the liver was normal.

"How's it look?" George asked, breaking the silence.

"Good to me," Susan responded softly. Even though
there was no chance the patient could hear, the doctors
and technicians tended to whisper when a procedure was
under way.

"To me, too," Claudine said, turning to George. "Take
a peek?"

George heaved himself to his feet and stepped closer
to the monitor. He took his time, staring in silence as the
images emerged. Susan was rerunning the film starting
at the base of the liver and moving cephalically, or toward
the head.

"Stop there," George suddenly ordered. "Freeze it."

The technician paused the frame as instructed.

"Let me see the previous slice," George said, leaning
in for a better look. Most people, George included when
he had first started, thought radiology was a hard science,

meaning the sought-after lesion was either there or not there, but over the previous three years George had learned differently. There was a lot of room for interpretation, especially with small irregularities.

George sensed something abnormal in the image, just to the right of center. He rubbed his eyes and looked again.

"Give me the slice one centimeter lower!" He studied the requested image and suddenly he was sure. There were two small irregularities present. "Go back to the original image you had up, the one that's still being formed."

"Coming up," the technician responded.

The irregularities were in this image, too. George took a laser pointer from the pocket of his white coat and lit up the irregularities.

"That doesn't look good," he said.

Claudine and the technician studied the frame. Out of the various shades of gray they could now see the two lesions.

"My goodness," Claudine said. "You are right."

"It's pretty damn subtle," Susan said.

George stepped over to a hospital computer monitor and called up Tarkington's previous MRI, quickly locating slices from the same location in the liver. They had been normal. The lesions were new. George paused a moment to think about what that could mean. On one level, their discovery meant George was doing his job well. But to the anxious man in the adjacent room with his head stuffed into a 3.0-tesla-strength magnet—a magnetic field 60,000 times the strength of the Earth's—it meant something quite different. The incongruity of such a situation never failed to discomfit George. It also brought up his raw emotions about Kasey's sudden death. The image of her face in its mask of death—its frozen pallor, the staring eyes, the dilated pupils—confronted him.

"You okay?" Claudine asked, eyeing him.

"Yeah. Fine. Thanks."

But he wasn't. Burying a problem only made it fester. The clarity with which Kasey's death face appeared in his mind's eye scared him. In the wake of her death he had discovered she'd just been diagnosed with very aggressive stage-four, grade-three ovarian cancer found by a CT scan she'd had at Santa Monica University Hospital. The test had been performed on the Friday before her death, which was early on a Monday morning, so she hadn't even been told yet. Since the hospital was a sister hospital to George's, he had used his resident's access code to view the study. It had been a violation of HIPAA regulations, but at the time he couldn't help himself. He was lucky he hadn't been prosecuted, due to the circumstances, yet he had been worried.

"Let's finish the study," George said, shaking himself free of his disturbing thoughts.

"There's only fourteen minutes to go," Susan said.

Returning to his chair, George forced himself to go back to flipping through the radiology journal, trying not to think. For a time no one talked. No other abnormalities were found besides the two small lesions, which were undoubtedly tumors, but the implications of that finding hung like a miasma over the control room.

"I'm afraid," Claudine said, breaking the silence and giving voice to what they were all thinking, "that, with the patient's history, the lesions are most likely metastases of the patient's original pancreatic tumor."

George nodded, and said churlishly, mostly to Claudine, "Okay, now, quick reminder: We do not say or indicate in any manner anything to the patient, beyond mentioning that the test went well, which it did. The material will be read by the senior radiology attending, and a report will be sent to the patient's oncologist and primary-care doctor. Any 'informing' will be done by them. Understood?"

Claudine nodded. She certainly understood, but the admonishment and its tone came across harsher than George had intended and created an uncomfortable silence. Susan looked down, busying herself by arranging her paperwork just so.

George realized how he sounded and launched into a little damage control. "I'm sorry. That was uncalled-for. You're doing a great job, Claudine. Not just today, but in your whole month of rotation." He meant it, too. Claudine relaxed visibly and even smiled. George sighed as the previous awkwardness dissolved. He needed to get a grip on himself.

"What's our schedule for the rest of the day?" he asked.

Claudine consulted her iPad. "Two more MRIs. One at eleven, the other at one thirty. Then, of course, whatever comes in from emergency."

"Any trouble with the two scheduled MRIs, you think?"

"No. Why?"

"I have to step out for two or three hours. I want to go to a conference over in Century City. Amalgamated

Healthcare, the insurance giant and our hospital's new owner, has a presentation planned for would-be investors. It's something about a new solution they have come up with to end the shortage of primary-care physicians. Can you imagine: a health insurance company solving the primary-care shortage? What a stretch."

"Oh, sure! An insurance company solution to the lack of primary-care physicians," Claudine mocked skeptically. "Now, that sounds like a fantasy if I ever heard one, especially with Obamacare adding thirty million previously uninsured into a system that was already functioning poorly."

"You sure the presentation isn't being held down at Disneyland?" Susan said as she prepared to go into the imaging room to see to the patient, who at the moment was being slid out of the MRI machine by an attendant.

"Might as well be," George said. Even though they were making light of the situation, it was a serious issue. "I'm really curious what they are going to say. It would take a decade, at the very least, to train enough doctors to fill the gap, provided they can talk doctors into practicing primary care, which isn't a given. Anyway, I'd like to go hear what they have to say, if you don't have any problem."

"Me?" Claudine asked. She shook her head. "I don't have a problem. Knock yourself out!"

"Are you sure?"

"Very sure."

"Okay. Text me if you need me. I can make it back in about fifteen minutes if I'm needed."

"No prob," Claudine said. "Gotcha covered."

"We'll review them when I get back." He paused. "You sure you're okay with this—my leaving?"

"Yes, of course. I'll be working with Susan again. She doesn't need either one of us."

Susan grinned at the compliment.

"Okay, great. Let's all go in and talk with the patient," George said, motioning them toward the door.

They put on game faces and entered the imaging chamber. Tarkington was sitting on the edge of the bed, smiling nervously. He was obviously eager for some positive feedback.

The doctors were all careful not to divulge the bad news, knowing that it would most likely mean more chemotherapy, despite the man's tenuous kidney function. Claudine spoke as reassuringly as she could while George and Susan nodded.

Then, as the attendant and Susan got the patient onto his feet, George and Claudine retreated back to the safety of the control room. Talking with a patient destined to receive very bad news underlined the fragility of life. There was no way to be detached about it.

"That sucked," Claudine said, sinking into a chair. "I hate not being forthright and honest. I didn't think that was going to be part of being a doctor."

"You'll get over it," George said with a casualness he didn't feel.

She looked at him, stunned.

"I didn't mean it like that. But you *will* get over it." George didn't know why he had just said that. He hadn't gotten over anything of the sort. He hedged a little. "To

some degree, anyway. You have to, or you won't be able
to do your job. It's not the 'not being honest' part that
bothers me as much as the shitty situation itself. We just
had a conversation with a very nice man in the prime of
his life, with a family, who will in all likelihood soon die.
That will always suck." George busied himself with the
files of the upcoming cases so as to not have to look
directly at Claudine. "But you have to compartmentalize
your feelings so you can continue to do your job, which
will help save the lives of those who *can* be helped."

She looked at him.

George sensed her gaze and felt bad. Repeated exposure
to such cases had not deadened his own feelings. He looked
up at her. "Look . . ." he said, searching for the right
words. "It's part of why I went into radiology. So there
would be a buffer between me and the patient. I figured if
I could deal with the images rather than the patient, I
would be better equipped to handle my job." He motioned
to the adjacent room, where they had just left Tarkington.
"But as you can see, the buffer has holes in it."

They both sat silent for a moment, then George moved
to the door. "Well, I have to get a move on—"

"Me, too," Claudine said softly.

George looked at her quizzically: Me, too, what?

"It's why I went into radiology. And thanks . . . for the
honesty."

George gave her a melancholy smile and left the room.

2

As George walked into the presentation, he felt like a fish out of water. It was obvious to him that the event was primarily for prospective investors in Amalgamated Healthcare. The room was filled with "people of resources." In other words, people unlike him. George was immediately struck by their custom-tailored business suits, four-hundred-dollar haircuts, and general air of superiority. He was aware that Amalgamated had recently acquired a number of health care companies and hospitals, including the medical center where he worked. The prospect of offering health insurance on a national scale rather than on a state-by-state basis had been part of their acquisition strategy. George assumed the company had thoroughly combed through the 2,700-plus

pages of the Affordable Care Act—aka Obamacare—
determined to exploit all of the changes mandating health
insurance for everyone.

George pushed through the crowd at the back of the
room, thankful he had left his white coat back at the
hospital. As it was, he wouldn't have been surprised if
someone attempted to order him out, thinking he was
crashing the party. As he walked down one of the aisles,
someone handed him a fancy prospectus filled with
spreadsheets and financial data. He felt a rush of déjà vu.
It was as if he were glimpsing an alternative life he had
turned his back on. When he first walked into Columbia
University as an undergraduate all those years before, he
had already narrowed down his career choices to going
either into business or to medical school. By the end of
his first year he had veered toward medicine, a choice
Kasey had made him come to understand. Had he taken
the alternative, he would have felt at home here. This
could have been his life. He might even have some money
in the bank rather than a mountain of debt. He tried to
shut off such thinking; that was another life, another
world, another dream. He forced himself to focus on the
moment.

There was seating for several hundred people in the
room. He noticed several IT barons representing Apple,
Oracle, Google, and Microsoft, along with a few well-
known hedge fund guys in a reserved section at the front.
George frequently watched CNBC while on the treadmill,
so he recognized some of the players. The gathering here
was like the Fortune 500 version of an Oscar party.

Attendees were being served refreshments by a flock of extremely tall and gorgeous young women in futuristic white uniforms.

On the dais at the front of the room were four stainless-steel-and-white-Ultrasuede modern club chairs. Expensive-looking, even from a distance, each one probably worth more than George's car. Directly behind the stage was an enormous LED screen with two other equally sized screens on either side, at forty-five-degree angles. Amalgamated Healthcare was spelled on each in bold black letters. The room itself also was mostly white, with row upon row of padded Ultrasuede seats with folded writing arms. Also white, of course. George was impressed, making him wonder if the presentation had been arranged by the same consultants who handled the iPhone and iPad product releases for Apple.

George took a seat in the very last row and waited. At exactly ten o'clock the room lights dimmed, and four people appeared on the speakers' platform: three men and one woman. At the same time, a choral group, reminding George of Celtic pop music, could be heard very faintly from hidden speakers, giving the event an ethereal atmosphere.

George's eyes were drawn to the woman. He recognized her immediately. Her name was Paula Stonebrenner, and it was because of her that he'd been invited to this presentation. Paula was dressed in a smart business suit, with just enough white ruffles around her neck to broadcast her femininity. She was attractive in a classic, Ivy League fashion.

Paula had been George's classmate at Columbia Medical School, and he had gotten to know her reasonably well back then. "Reasonably well," as in they hooked up once or twice. They had been attracted to each other in the first weeks of medical school and ended up going out for drinks with some other new friends, and one thing led to another. "Another" being the roof of Bard Hall, the medical school dorm at Columbia. George still considered it the most risqué sexual episode of his life.

After the initial sparks George's interest abruptly waned when he discovered another Columbia classmate, Pia Grazdani. Pia was dark, exotic, and an off-the-charts gorgeous mix of Italian and Albanian heritage. Her mere presence swept him off his feet. Her aloof manner captivated him. And her callousness stomped on his heart. She resisted any and all attempts at friendship, let alone romance. Throughout high school and college George had never had trouble getting women to go out with him. He had an outgoing personality and was a starter on all the right sports teams. He was used to being the one to call the shots. Not so with Pia.

Prior to Pia, George had been one to avoid commitment. He would rationalize his quick departure from relationships as his version of "compassion," likening his exit to a girl getting stung by a bee. It hurt briefly but was quickly forgotten. And it wasn't like he was being selfish—all through high school and college his desire to succeed, whether as a doctor or businessman, had taken precedence over social attachment, which for him had been more about entertainment than an opportunity for self-learning.

George understood all this now, even though he hadn't in the past. And again, it was all because of Kasey and her unique understanding of interpersonal relationships. She had a natural intuition about people that had drawn George to her like a hungry mouse to cheese. Kasey was the first woman who had become a best friend and confidante to George before becoming a lover. It had been a revelation for George, a kind of rebirth that made him understand what he had been missing.

Today George had to admit that Paula looked fantastic. He also had to admit that he really didn't know anything about her other than she was smart as a whip, fun to be with, and what he used to call a "live wire." After being essentially dumped for Pia, Paula had acted the part of spurned lover. She wouldn't even talk to George for the rest of that year. But by the second year, she didn't seem to care. They happened to live in adjacent dorm rooms and had a hard time ignoring each other anyway. By their final year they were friends, or at least friendly acquaintances.

For a moment George entertained the idea of walking down to the dais and saying hello to Paula, but then chickened out. Instead he watched with growing fascination as she interacted comfortably with the three men on the stage and with some of the financial VIPs in the reserved section at the front. She took a seat in one of the club chairs with two of the accompanying men. The third man stepped forward to speak. From George's perspective he was extremely impressive. He was meticulously dressed, standing ramrod straight with a commanding, almost military presence. His graying hair literally sparkled in the glare of the halogen spotlights. On the huge LED screen behind him appeared his name: Bradley Thorn, Amalgamated's president and CEO.

"Welcome!" Thorn boomed with a broad smile. Without a visible microphone, his voice filled the large room. George wasn't surprised. Everything was wireless these days.

Conversation hushed. People who had not yet found a place now rushed for a chair. George glanced back at Paula as well as the other two men seated beside her. With sudden shock George recognized one of them, and scrunched down in his seat, as if that would keep him from being seen. His pulse picked up.

"Oh, shit," he murmured.

3

Sitting on the stage was the internationally known radiologist Dr. Clayton Hanson. He was also the chair of the residency training program at L.A. University Medical Center, someone George happened to know quite well, better than any of the other professors and attendings. He was essentially George's boss, and George was currently playing hooky. The reason they knew each other well was because, besides being George's superior, Clayton considered himself to be a lothario (the man was not without ego), and he had hit on Kasey even when he knew she and George were an item, although that was before the engagement.

The year before George arrived on the scene, Clayton had divorced a fading actress after twelve years of a dysfunctional marriage and was intent on making up for lost time. George had heard rumors that Clayton's frequent transgressions had been a significant factor in his former wife's decision to seek the divorce.

As George was one of the few unmarried residents, Clayton had initially sought him out for hints on how to meet some of the young fillies (Clayton's word) that he assumed George would be privy to. That had never come to pass, but over time Clayton and George had established a friendship of sorts that for the most part had evolved into Clayton's trying to fix George up with the women so that he, Clayton, could meet their friends.

George's immediate problem was that before coming to the presentation he hadn't bothered to get permission to leave the hospital, so he was AWOL with one of the radiology bigwigs onstage in front of him. Even though it was his last day of an easy rotation, and he had covered himself, he felt uncomfortable. He considered getting up and walking out but decided doing so would call more attention to him than just remaining in his seat. Luckily he was a good distance from the dais, and Clayton showed no sign of having spotted his resident.

George took a deep, calming breath and directed his attention back to Paula. She certainly did look terrific and impressively "together." He found himself regretting that he hadn't followed up with her back in medical school and wondered if reviving an acquaintance with her would fulfill his promise to Kasey.

George's musings were interrupted by Thorn launching into a slick presentation of Amalgamated Healthcare's spectacular growth. He explained that the company was positioned to take full advantage of the Affordable Care Act, something most other insurance companies thought impossible, given the law's restrictions on profit, but he and his inordinately competent team had figured out a way and were leading the charge. All they needed was an infusion of more capital to continue their spectacular expansion.

"The politicians, whether they meant to or not, have put the health insurance industry in the driver's seat to manage what will more than likely balloon to nearly twenty percent of the United States' GDP," Thorn continued. "Most of us know deep down that they should have passed a kind of Medicare for everyone. But they didn't have the courage. Instead they have handed the keys to us on a silver platter. This is an unprecedented opportunity, particularly in view of what you're going to learn today. The world, not just the United States, is on the cusp of a paradigm shift in medical care as the profession is dragged kicking and screaming into the digital age. And we, Amalgamated, are going to be leading it."

George felt a jolt of electricity surge through his body. Thorn had hit a nerve. Over the last several years, George had become vaguely uneasy about what was happening in medicine in general and in the specialty of radiology in particular. There were somewhat fewer positions available and salaries were heading south. It wasn't an overwhelming change but nonetheless noticeable. Consequently Thorn's words were jarring, giving substance to a nebulous yet vexing fear that he was entering the medical profession after it had passed its zenith.

"Our country," Thorn continued, "is going to experience a democratization of medicine that is going to catch the medical profession by surprise, but not Amalgamated. Already the general public's main source of medical information is not doctors, as it's been for a number of centuries: It is the Internet and social media. To illustrate my point, compare the medical profession as you know it today to another industry, dominated by the iconic Eastman Kodak Company. Kodak thought it was in the film business rather than the image business." He paused. "We all know how well that went."

The audience laughed. Kodak had filed for bankruptcy in 2012.

"The medical profession thinks it's in the sickness business. It is not. It is in the health business. Preserving and maintaining health and preventing disease are the future of medicine, not treatment in the form of ever more drugs and procedures. And I'm not talking about prevention in a passive sense. I'm talking about prevention as an active process, but not wasteful, like yearly physicals and full-body CT scans. And when treatment *is* needed, it will be directed for the individual, not some imaginary person representing the statistical mean.

"This is important, because a third of the almost four hundred billion dollars the public pays the pharmaceutical industry is totally wasted. That's one hundred thirty billion dollars going down the drain. The drugs involved often have no positive effect on a specific individual. If a drug trial showed that it only helps five percent of patients, that means it doesn't help ninety-five percent, even though

CELL   29

side effects are pretty close to one hundred percent. Bad odds!

"We at Amalgamated don't want to waste money on useless drugs and dangerous procedures. We want to treat the individual, not a statistical construct. How will this come to pass? Through this app!" Thorn waved toward the LED screens behind him as if he were a conductor of a symphony orchestra. Coinciding with his gesture were the first thirty seconds of Beethoven's Fifth Symphony. Simultaneously the word *iDoc* flashed onto the screens in foot-high bold black letters.

After pausing for effect, Thorn turned back toward the audience: "A glowing example of the failure of current medicine is the fact that the shortage of primary-care physicians has never been solved. As a result, there are too many unnecessary and expensive visits to emergency rooms, too many specialists seeing patients who don't need to be seen by them, too many procedures on patients who don't need them, and too many patients being prescribed unneeded drugs. All of which means a massive number of unnecessary, wasteful *payouts*. Well, my friends, all that is going to change; there's a new doctor in town! The twenty-first century's primary-care physician is an FDA conditionally approved smartphone app, and its name is iDoc!"

Thorn again gestured toward the giant LED screens as the images of three smartphones made by the world's largest manufacturers—Apple, Samsung, and Nokia—flashed. The phones displayed a single app: a white square containing a red cross with *iDoc* spelled out along the horizontal arm. George caught his breath from another jolt. He'd seen the icon before.

"iDoc and its incorporation into the smartphone application platform is a result of our close working relationships with leading smartphone manufacturers and developers. The end result is a marvelous convergence of the Internet, mobile phone technology, quantum cloud computing with our state-of-the-art D-Wave quantum supercomputer, social networking, digital medical genomics, wireless biosensors, and advanced imaging. iDoc will be the doctor of tomorrow, and we have it today!

"We've licensed the distinctive symbol of the International Red Cross, as we felt it imperative to use a universally recognized icon. Amalgamated Healthcare will also be making an additional donation to the organization with each download of the iDoc app. And we're not stopping there. Amalgamated will mimic the Affordable Care Act in—what else?—affordability! Enrollees with incomes of up to four hundred percent above the poverty line will either have their smartphones subsidized or given out free. Regular phone plans will stay in effect for enrollees, but data plans will be converted to unlimited. Our subsidization of the data plans will again mimic that of the ACA. All data generated by the app will be stored on our cloud services, enabling an acceptable baseline phone configuration of three-G capability with a minimum of thirty-two GB of memory. Any current enrollees who now fall below those smartphone specifications will be upgraded at our expense."

Now George felt a chill descend his spine. He had the

distinct feeling he was witnessing history in the making. With the idea of a smartphone functioning as a primary-care physician, something he had thought about in the past, he was in shock. His mental association of the Amalgamated Healthcare presentation with one of Apple's product releases was magnified. This was a big deal. He was also amazed that Amalgamated would be able to absorb all these costs and still have a profitable business plan. What was he missing?

4

George glanced around the room at the other attendees. No one spoke. No one coughed. No one moved. The only sound was that of the faint Celtic choir in the background.

George redirected his gaze toward the dais. Thorn was still twisted around, staring up at images of the smartphones like a proud father. When he turned back the crowd burst into applause.

"Hold your excitement," Thorn said. "There's more. Shortly you are going to hear brief presentations from our three other speakers this morning. First will be Dr. Paula Stonebrenner." He gestured toward Paula, and George looked over at her. She stood briefly and nodded to the audience. If she was nervous, it didn't show. There was a smattering of applause.

Thorn continued. "Dr. Stonebrenner, I know, doesn't look old enough to be an MD, but I assure you that she is. She will be giving a very short overview of iDoc and its capabilities. She is the best person for this task, as she is the individual who gets the credit for the idea of a smart-phone functioning as a twenty-first-century primary-care physician. There have been multiple apps for smartphones configured to do various and sundry medical functions, but it was Dr. Stonebrenner who came up with the brilliant concept of putting them all together in a purposeful algo-rithm to create a true ersatz physician on duty twenty-four-seven for a particular individual, truly personalized medicine."

"Holy shit!" George whispered to himself. He felt a surge of color suffusing his face. He couldn't believe what he'd just heard and didn't know whether to be angry or flattered. Suddenly George realized why Paula had invited him to the presentation. They'd had a conversation about this years before. She hadn't come up with the concept. She'd gotten the idea for a smartphone primary-care phy-sician from him!

When George had first come out to L.A. for his resi-dency, he'd known that Paula was coming, too, not for a residency but rather for a job with Amalgamated Health-care. They'd talked about being in the same city before graduation. She'd been in the MD-MBA program during medical school, a fact that they'd argued about on occasion. It had been George's opinion that she shouldn't have taken a slot to become an MD if she had no intention of ever practicing medicine. There were too many people who really wanted to be doctors who couldn't get a spot in medical school, and that was leading to a shortage of primary-care doctors. Paula, of course, had seen the issue differently. It had been her contention that the business of medicine was so important there had to be people who understood all sides of it. Neither convinced the other.

When George arrived in L.A. he tried to contact Paula a few times, but she never returned his calls. He didn't have her home number or address, so he'd only left messages at Amalgamated's main number. He never knew if she got them or not. But then, after an emotionally draining trip back home for Thanksgiving 2011, he made a more determined effort to track her down. His mother, Harriet, had died unexpectedly while he was home and, coming back to L.A., he had never felt more alone. He hadn't been particularly close to his mother, but watching her die was one of the most painful episodes of his life.

George's father had died when he was three and his mother remarried when George was four, but George never got along with his stepfather. On top of that, his stepfather had a son three years older than George. Then his mother and his stepfather had a daughter, and George ended up the odd man out, spending his high school years living with his grandmother, with whom he had a close relationship. During medical school his stepfather died, and his mother developed a series of health issues from smoking and obesity, which turned out to be deadly just four days short of her sixty-seventh birthday.

The day had started out routinely, but by early afternoon Harriet began wheezing and then developed chest pain. When George suggested that they call her doctor, she said she didn't have one. Her primary-care physician had changed his practice to the concierge model, which Harriet had refused to join because she thought the yearly payment way too steep. When Harriet turned sixty-five, she tried but failed to find a doctor who would accept Medicare.

So on that fateful Thanksgiving Day there was no doctor to call or see. And she refused to go to the hospital. George pleaded with her to go but was accused of meddling. He tried to call a few of the local physicians that he could find online but wasn't able to get anyone on the phone. He needed someone either to see her or tell her to go to the hospital. While he was making the calls, his mother became short of breath and began to perspire. He called 911. The dispatcher said the local ambulances were all occupied but that one from a distant town would be there ASAP but couldn't give an ETA.

With growing consternation George watched his mother turn ashen. Realizing he couldn't wait any longer, he managed to get her into the backseat of her car despite her reluctance, and rushed her to the local hospital. When he pulled up to the ER, he discovered it had been closed. "Consolidation" was what the corporation that bought the facility had called it. George drove as fast as he could to the next closest hospital, which was owned by the same corporation. It was located a half hour away, and by the time George pulled in, jumped out of the car, and opened the back door, his mother was dead. The sheer frustration of it all nearly drove George mad. He had never cried much, even as a child, but on that cold, dreary day he sat in that car and wept.

5

George reached up with both hands and rubbed his eyes to get himself under control. It always bothered him to think about his mother's passing, and since Kasey's death the unwelcome remembrance of the episode had become more frequent. The two episodes shared a similarity: Both had occurred in his presence.

Blinking his eyes open, George looked back at the dais. Paula had sat down and Thorn was saying, "I am also pleased to introduce to you Dr. Clayton Hanson." Thorn pointed over to Clayton, who, like Paula, rose to his feet to acknowledge a bit of applause. From the standpoint of appearances, Clayton looked as good as Thorn, decked out in equally expensive gentlemen's finery. Where he surpassed Thorn was his overly tanned face, accentuated by his carefully coiffed silver hair. He was old enough to appear learned and young enough to attract women of any age.

"Dr. Hanson, vice chair of academic affairs for the L.A. University Medical Center's department of radiology, will be giving us an overview of iDoc's advanced imaging capabilities, but before Dr. Hanson, I would like you to hear from Lewis Langley. He'll be saying a few technical words about the unique character of the iDoc algorithm."

Langley nodded slowly at the mention of his name but didn't stand. He didn't look anything like the typical software guy and was miles away from the other two men with whom he was sharing the dais, wearing shit-kicker boots with black jeans that were topped off with a huge, silver-plated Texas longhorn belt buckle. To round out the outfit, he wore a black sport jacket over an open-collared black shirt.

For the next few minutes George found it hard to concentrate on Thorn's words. His unexpected trip down memory lane of that awful Thanksgiving Day and his mother's death had him freaked out. On the flight back to L.A. after the funeral, he had found himself agonizing over the way the lack of primary-care physicians had contributed to the nightmare.

As fate would have it, the airplane magazine had an article about a phone app that could anticipate heart attacks. That had been the stimulus that made him think about the phone as a primary-care doctor. There were already six billion cell phones in the world and the technology was there; it just needed to be channeled. Although he didn't do anything about this revelation—what could he do as a first-year resident—he did mention the idea to Paula when he finally did get in touch with her.

They had met for a drink, and after some small talk he told her his mom's sad story and his idea of a cell phone functioning as a full-blown primary-care physician. He was convinced a device like that would have been a god-send to his mother and probably would have saved her life.

Paula was immediately taken by the concept and told him the idea was perfect for Amalgamated, which alarmed George. It was his belief that if anybody did it, it should be the medical profession, not an insurance company, since the smartphone, in a very real way, would be practic-ing medicine. Paula's response was to laugh, pointing out that the medical profession would never get around to it, having dragged their collective feet at the idea of competi-tion of any sort as well as their disinclination to embrace the digital world.

In the end, George's effort in reconnecting with Paula didn't pan out. As busy as he was with his first year of residency, he didn't call her for months, and when he did, she declined the offer of getting together. The next time he had heard from her was just the previous week, when she texted him the invitation to the event out of the blue. The fact that the presentation was about the smartphone being a primary-care physician was a complete and total surprise.

George again considered getting up and walking out. She obviously latched on to his idea and ran with it without any attempt to connect with him even just to acknowledge his contribution. George squirmed in his seat, his mind racing to think of what to do about it. He shifted his weight to stand and leave. The man next to him even moved to let him by, but George didn't get up. Instead he relaxed back into his seat. What purpose would it serve to walk out? Just wanting to get away was a childish response.

It ended up being a good thing that he stayed, too. Thorn still had a few surprises. "Amalgamated Healthcare is proud and will be announcing to the media that we are near the end of a very successful beta test of the iDoc algorithm and app. For almost four months, twenty thousand people here in the Los Angeles metropolitan area, who had signed strict NDAs, or nondisclosure agreements, have been using the iDoc app with truly phenomenal success. As a primary-care physician, iDoc has proven itself to be utterly reliable, far better than a flesh-and-blood general practitioner under our current health care system. And this sentiment comes directly from our participant surveys. Enrollees love it!"

George swallowed with some difficulty. His mouth had gone dry. He'd seen the iDoc app on Kasey's phone but had not known what it was, and she hadn't told him. She had been part of Amalgamated's beta test! The news also gave him a queasy feeling in the pit of his stomach.

As Thorn went on to explain that iDoc would be immediately and immensely profitable, George shook his head with a mixture of disgust and admiration. iDoc was going to be performing an end run around the whole medical industry. It was about to become the doctor!

"Please!" Thorn called out after allowing the excited murmuring that had erupted to continue, obviously enjoying the moment. "Let me make one more point before I turn the floor over to Dr. Stonebrenner to provide technical details. With the success of iDoc's beta test, Amalgamated is about to launch the program nationally. Concurrently, we will also be looking to license the program internationally, particularly in Europe. To that end we've been in negotiations with multiple countries, particularly those with extensive, dependable wireless infrastructure. I can confidently report that negotiations are rapidly progressing. The need for iDoc is global. Of course, this underlines how very good an investment in Amalgamated Healthcare is. We are about to conclude deals with several hedge funds, but another round of funding will be required. Our market is global. Our market is massive. Now let me turn the floor over to Dr. Stonebrenner."

As Paula stepped forward, George did a rapid Internet search for the meaning of a beta test. He vaguely recalled hearing the term but wouldn't be able to define it if he was pressed. He quickly found out that it's a term for the second round of software testing in which it's used by a limited but sizable audience to ascertain user acceptance while at the same time seeking to identify and fix glitches or problems.

As Paula began speaking George wasn't sure how he felt about her taking over his idea without even getting in touch with him. At the same time he realized he hadn't exactly pursued her.

"Think of iDoc as the Swiss army knife of health care," she was saying. "Attachable sensors and independent probes that communicate wirelessly will make the phone a versatile mobile laboratory." As Paula spoke, a slick video presentation demoed the app's capabilities. "The property of capacitance is what enables smartphone touchscreens to sense our fingertips. But the screens also have the ability to detect and analyze much smaller things, like DNA or proteins to enable it to identify specific pathogens or particular disease markers. An Amalgamated client could simply place a saliva or blood sample directly onto the touchscreen for an analysis, and treatment would be based on the patient's past medical history and unique genomic makeup. Recent leaps forward in nanotechnology, wireless technology, and synthetic biology make iDoc possible. With our supercomputer we will constantly monitor, in real time, a host of physiological data on all iDoc users of all vital signs. The sky is the limit. iDoc can even extend into the psychological realm because iDoc has the ability to monitor the client-patient mood, particularly in relation to depression, anxiety, or hyper states, and then communicate with the patient accordingly for on-the-spot counseling or referral to a mental health specialist."

Paula then went on to describe how the app is able to monitor many of these functions, in particular those followed routinely only in an intensive-care unit, by the use of a bracelet, ring, or wristband with built-in sensors that communicate with the phone wirelessly. She demoed special eyeglasses that can be worn for additional monitoring of the real-time function of blood vessels and nerves in the retina of the eye, the only true window on the interior of the body. She explained that a continuous recording is made of the EKG and, if needed, the smartphone can function as an ultrasound device for studying cardiac function by merely having the patient press it against his chest.

Paula paused for a moment and stared out at the audience. From their stunned silence she knew she had their undivided attention. "Okay," she said soothingly, switching gears, "so the question then becomes, what will iDoc do with this enormous wealth of real-time data? I will tell you. It will do what any good doctor would do and do it better, much better. Thousands of times a second all the data will be correlated via its cloud service by the Amalgamated supercomputer with the client-patient's full medical history, the client-patient's known genomic information, and the totality of current medical knowledge that is being updated on a continuous basis."

Paula then gave a specific example and talked about the app's ability to diagnose a heart attack, not only when it is happening, but also well before, so that it would have the ability to alert the patient days before the attack was going to occur. Paula then touched on iDoc's ability to follow and treat chronic diseases like diabetes. With iDoc and an implanted reservoir of insulin, blood sugar could be tracked in real time and the correct amount of insulin could be released automatically to keep the patient's blood sugar continually normal. In a very real way, for a diabetic, iDoc is essentially curative.

George found himself nodding. It was apparent to him immediately that iDoc had handled Kasey's diabetes and why she didn't talk about it. Kasey's word was her bond, and she had obviously signed a nondisclosure agreement. He remembered how pleased she was at the time, being free of her usual burdensome monitoring. George even knew she had had some sort of implanted device. Now he knew what it had been. It had been a reservoir just as Paula was describing.

Paula concluded by saying that embedded reservoirs have been and would be used for various ailments, and not just for chronic diseases, noting that it would be the answer to the problem of poor compliance that a number of patients demonstrate when it comes to taking medications as instructed.

Despite his irritation at having been, in his words, ripped off on the concept, George became progressively impressed by what he was hearing. He could tell everyone else in the room felt the same. Paula was offering understandable specifics, and everyone was listening with rapt attention. George could easily see why iDoc would make a superb primary-care doctor, especially when the doctor was available 24/7 to answer a patient's questions without the inconvenience of having to make an appointment, travel to an office, and wait to be seen by someone who might be rushed, distracted, or not able to find the appropriate patient records, and, worse yet, might have forgotten half of what he or she learned in medical school.

"From the outset," Paula continued after another astutely planned pause, "we wanted to make iDoc extremely personable. The client-patient can choose the gender of his doctor avatar as well as his or her attitude in relation to being paternal or maternal in tone. So far there is also a choice between forty-four languages and several accents. There are also choices available regarding how the patient would like to be notified when his iDoc doctor wants to have a chat when stimulated by a change in the client-patient's constant physiological or mental monitoring.

"I want to emphasize that iDoc never has a memory lapse, never gets tired, never gets angry, is never on vacation, and never has a drink, pain reliever, or sedative. And lastly, client-patients can select a name for their avatar doctor, either made up or from a preset list. If they don't want to be bothered, a name will be selected for them with a choice of ethnicities. For privacy concerns, if a client-patient's speakerphone is activated, iDoc will ask patients if they are alone and if it's okay to have an open audio conversation. iDoc will strictly guard patient confidentiality, using the full gamut of biometric identifiers.

"What I have just given is a rapid, superficial overview of iDoc. It uses an extraordinarily versatile algorithm. As Mr. Thorn mentioned, the reception by our client-patients throughout the beta test has been exceptionally positive far beyond our expectations and hopes. People love iDoc and already are telling us they don't want to give it up at the conclusion of the test period and are eager to share their experience with family and friends, which they have been strictly forbidden to do. iDoc has already saved lives as well as time and inconvenience for the patients that have it, and it has saved money, too." Paula paused on that note, letting the audience absorb the information. When everyone realized she was done, applause erupted. Paula waited a few beats, acknowledging the audience's response, then said a quick thank-you.

George marveled at why other people had not come up with the iDoc idea. After Paula's presentation it seemed intuitive, given current technology. He watched Paula return to her seat as the third speaker approached the front of the stage. George hoped he might catch her eye, but she didn't look in his direction.

Lewis Langley addressed the audience for only a couple of minutes. Even from where George was sitting he could see his cowboy-style fitted shirt had snaps instead of buttons. With his hair that was cut long, giving Langley a rather wild, artsy look, George got the impression he was the right-brain, creative type in contrast to his left-brain colleagues.

"I'm not going to take much of your time," Langley said with a discordant New York accent. "There are only three things I want to convey above and beyond what you have already heard from Mr. Thorn and Dr. Stonebrenner. First off, and most important, the iDoc algorithm was written to be heuristic so that it would improve itself by learning on its own over the course of time. This has already proven to be the case to a marked degree during the beta test. As a backup to iDoc, Amalgamated has employed a large group of internists, surgeons, and other specialists who rotate through a twenty-four-seven state-of-the-art call center. At any given time there are at least fifty of them on hand.

"These doctors assist iDoc's automated decision making as a default mechanism whenever there is the slightest problem. At first, at the outset of the beta test, there were quite a few calls, maybe as often as twenty percent of the episodes. But that changed rapidly, and during the course of the three-month beta-test period, the number of calls coming into the center dropped by eleven percent, meaning the iDoc logarithm is indeed learning.

"The second issue I want to explain is that important subjective issues have been meticulously researched and included in the iDoc algorithm, such as pain and suffering associated with treatment options and possible outcomes, something traditional medicine has always had great difficulty considering. Cost was another issue taken into consideration in the iDoc algorithm. For example, generic drugs are prescribed, provided the efficacy between the generic and the brand-name drug is equal. If the brand-name drug is superior, it is prescribed.

"The third and last issue I want to mention is that it is my firm belief that iDoc will bring about a miraculous democratization of medicine, somewhat akin to what the Gutenberg Bible did for religion. iDoc will free the general public from the clutches of doctors and the medical profession just as the Bible freed the public from the clutches of priests and organized religion. iDoc will be making the paradigm of the practice of medicine personal, meaning that if a drug is prescribed, it will be prescribed because iDoc knows that it will benefit the specific patient rather than knowing it will benefit five percent of patients with the hope that the specific patient will be part of that five percent. Because of this democratization of medicine, I believe the introduction of iDoc will prove to be on par with or more important than other major technological milestones, such as the development of the computer, the Internet, the mobile phone, and DNA sequencing."

Dr. Clayton Hanson was the final speaker to address the audience. Despite acknowledging to himself that he was acting ridiculous, George flattened himself down in his chair throughout Hanson's brief talk. His remarks, in contrast to those of the other speakers, were pedestrian. He talked briefly about the medical imaging capabilities of iDoc, particularly ultrasound in conjunction with a wireless handheld transducer. He listed as an example the cardiac function tests that could be performed from the privacy of the patient's home. Until now these tests required multiple hospital visits and thousands of dollars. His point was that not only was iDoc a better primary-care physician than a flesh-and-blood individual, it was also going to save society a significant amount of money immediately and over the long haul.

Thorn stepped forward again as soon as Clayton finished and took his seat. "Thank you all for attending. And before I open the floor to questions, I want to remind you that we'll be having a reception and buffet lunch in the restaurant on the first floor of this tower immediately following our presentation, so we all have a chance to speak personally. Okay, who's first?" A number of hands shot up. The excitement in the room was palpable.

6

George took the elevator down to the first floor and walked toward the restaurant's entrance with a number of the other attendees. He was deep in thought, debating what to do next. He knew he should head back to the hospital but couldn't let the opportunity to confront Paula pass, even if he risked being seen by Clayton. He rationalized that he wouldn't be long, and he hadn't received any texts or calls from Claudine Boucher, so things were undoubtedly fine in the MRI unit. George wasn't surprised, since Claudine was one of the more accomplished residents on her last day on an MRI rotation; she knew the ropes in spades.

He walked into the restaurant, which was reserved for Amalgamated, leaned on the bar, and ordered a Diet

Coke. Again, the caffeine was a slight risk, considering he had already had coffee, but, hey, he was rolling the dice today. With his drink in hand he moved to a corner of the room, waiting for Paula to appear. He wanted to avoid any conversations with strangers, if possible. The truth was George couldn't shake the feeling of inferiority to these successful market warriors. They were a part of the real world, an arena outside the hospital in which he had limited experience.

He spotted her as she strolled in with the other speakers. There was a smattering of applause. It was apparent that the presentation had elicited a very positive reaction. Luckily for George, Clayton immediately veered off, zeroing in on an attractive female in an expensive business suit. George gathered up his courage and walked over toward Paula. Eyeing the situation, looking for an opportunity to present himself, he saw she looked even better up close and was obviously totally at ease in what was to George an alien environment. He wondered what might have happened between them during their first year of medical school if he hadn't been such an immature ass. Just then she looked up and caught sight of George and smiled broadly. Encouraged by her grin, he headed straight for her.

"George!" Paula exclaimed. "You made it!"

"Hello, Paula." George put out his hand to shake but she disarmed him by pulling him toward her and kissing him on the cheek. She seemed genuinely happy to see him.

She looked around, still holding on to his hand, and spotted Bradley Thorn shaking hands just behind her.

"Bradley, excuse me, this is a dear friend of mine from Columbia Medical School, George Wilson."

Thorn peered at George over his half glasses. He was holding one of Amalgamated's spreadsheets.

"George, this is Bradley Thorn, my boss. George is a radiology resident over at L.A. University Medical Center. Which makes him one of our new employees!"

"My pleasure," Thorn replied. "Excuse me." He turned from George, his sights set on a big-name CNBC host standing nearby.

Paula smiled at George and shrugged. "Sorry. He's in 'biz' mode." She aimed another beaming smile at George; she was obviously still on a high after the excitement of the presentation.

"Hey, no problem. I get it." George didn't want her to feel defensive.

"I really am glad you came," she said. "Thanks!"

"Me, too. It was lucky that I could get away," George said, feeling a bit nervous and less confrontational now that he was actually talking with Paula. "It's the last day of this month's rotation, so the resident I'm supervising is entirely comfortable working alone. Tomorrow will be a different story. July first. I'll be shepherding one or more first-year residents. You know what that means."

She gave him a blank look.

"July first. The first day of residency, nationwide, for freshly minted medical school grads?" He was trying to help her remember all the requirements to becoming a full-fledged specialist.

"Oh, right. Aka, the deadliest month of the year for

patients." She chuckled, although there was truth in the statement. Both knew that hospital deaths spiked in July, when thousands of new residents began attending patients.

"I'll be in the ER next month . . . well, tomorrow, actually," George said. "Supervising a few first-years there. It's my last year as a resident. Finally I will make some real money." He had meant to say it in jest, but it didn't come out that way. The look on Paula's face was confirmation.

Paula regarded him for a beat, sensing his nervousness. "Thanks again for coming, George. I really wanted you to be here. So . . . what do you think of iDoc?"

"I think the app is amazing. A real paradigm shifter, just as it's being billed. Wish I had thought of it." His eyes stayed close on her.

"And, of course, you did. Don't think I've forgotten. It's why I wanted you to be here for our announcement, so you would see it was becoming a reality, not just an idea no one acted upon. It's actually happening!"

George was taken aback. He had not expected such honesty.

"It was a huge amount of work," she continued. "Tens of thousands of man-hours. Millions upon millions of dollars. But we did it. And it works. It works better than we ever imagined. It's the answer, George. Better care. Lower costs. That's something the ACA will never do on its own."

George didn't quite know what to say. He had been so sure that he was going to have to argue to get the credit for giving her the idea.

"Do you have any free cash?" Paula inquired.

"Pardon me?" George was thrown by the question.

"Sorry. I didn't mean it like that. What I meant to say was that whatever you have, invest it in Amalgamated stock. It's going to go through the roof. And that's not insider trading advice. Maybe if I had told you yesterday, but not after today's presentation to the investor community at large. I'm leveraged to the hilt with stock options and—"

"I'm a medical resident, Paula," George replied in an even tone. "I make a bit less than fifty-five thousand dollars a year putting in eighty-hour workweeks and trying to pay down my med school debt while subsidizing my grandmother's assisted-living expenses. Stock options are not an *option* for me. I'm sure they are fine for you with what I'm sure is a significantly higher salary, but not for me."

Paula took a step back as if he had just thrown a splash of cold water in her face. "Hey, I'm just trying to be a friend, an appreciative one at that. I'm certainly not going to apologize for my compensation package, if that is what you are implying. I work hard for what I earn, and my work is valuable, as time is going to prove. Not just to my employers, but to the general public. Because of that, our company's stock will rise. Considerably." She paused. "We all make choices in life, George. I'm happy with mine. You should be with yours, too."

George didn't quite know how to respond. He had been feeling outclassed by Paula's success and then annoyed by her hubris, but her frank response disarmed him.

"Hey! Remember our old argument about how wasteful

you thought it was for me to be doing the combined MD-MBA program?" Paula asked. Her tone had changed again. It was now nostalgic and teasing.

"You've won that one, obviously," George conceded.

She laughed, visibly relaxing as she took him by the arm, leading him to a quiet corner of the room. "Listen, no more of this. We're friends. Why don't you come over to my house for a visit? We can catch up some—in a more personal environment."

"Well . . ." George stammered. She had him off balance again.

"Come on. I bought a house not too long ago and have barely had time to try out the pool."

"I'm not sure that we should—"

"What? Catch up on old times? Truth is, George, I don't have a lot of friends out here. Colleagues, yeah, I got plenty of those. But I have been working nonstop, twenty-four-seven—we both know what that's all about. I'm realizing I need people I can relax around, where there is no competition to get a particular project done. I don't have too many such friends here." She laughed again. "Actually, I don't have *any* at the moment. So, what do you say? No pressure."

George studied her face. As far as he could tell she was sincere, which was sad in one way. It sounded as if she didn't have much of a life. But he was in that same sad boat. "Sure," he replied. Her vulnerability was not only appealing, it was her saving grace.

"Great! I'll text you my address. It's in Santa Monica. How about Saturday? One o'clock okay?"

"Well . . . I *am* off Saturday," George conceded.

"Keep it in mind. A *friend* date. We've been down that other road, and it didn't work. And . . . there's one more caveat. You cannot mention Pia Grazdani. I do not want to even hear her name. Deal?" She smiled. A genuine warm smile.

"Deal," George said. Her warmth was infectious. It made George want to be around her.

"I can even pick you up if you want. The company has, in their infinite wisdom, bequeathed me a brand-sparkling-new Porsche Carrera to show their iDoc gratitude." She smiled again.

George shuffled his feet and changed the subject. "Is iDoc really that good? I mean, there were some pretty bold statements made in your presentation. Were you exaggerating a bit for the sake of the potential investors?"

"We were not exaggerating in the slightest. iDoc is truly fantastic. Maybe even better than we explained. To be perfectly honest, we actually held back to a degree."

"In what way?"

"Well, for instance . . . and how is it that you can turn me into a shameless blabbermouth?" She wasn't looking for an answer to her question, and George noticed that she had grasped his arm again. "Our beta-test group is using smartphones just like the one you have in your hand, Mr. Nomophobe."

"Nomophobe?" George questioned. "What the hell is that?"

"It's the fear of being out of mobile phone contact."

George did have his phone in his hand. He had the

ringer off but wanted to be sure to feel the vibration if Claudine texted him.

"What we could have added to the presentation was a solution that we have come up with during the iDoc beta test. The problem with the smartphone is . . . well, it's not a problem so much as an inconvenience that has the potential to become a problem . . . is the *battery*. iDoc runs constantly with its vast array of wireless sensors. Batteries run down, *fast*. Our beta testers need to recharge all the time. Three times a day plus charging it overnight while asleep. While that isn't a deal breaker, it is an inconvenience."

"So what's the solution to that?"

"Graphene," she whispered.

"Graphene?" George replied, matching her hushed tone. "Never heard of it."

"It's been around since the sixties. It's not like it's a secret, even though I'm trying to keep this between us because we're presenting iDoc to investors as it will run today, not tomorrow. Anyway, it's also not a secret that we've established close relationships with the world's major smartphone manufacturers. We became aware of graphene's potential by accident. UCLA discovered a process to make a nontoxic, highly efficient energy-storage medium out of pure carbon. Graphene. It's a ridiculously simple technology and Amalgamated helped fund their efforts in finding a way to mass-produce it with small embedded electrodes."

"You lost me."

"It's a supercapacitor. It charges much more rapidly

than a chemical battery. It's high density, in that it can hold a lot of electrons, and we can make it one atom thick. Long story short, the technology will have the capability to charge a smartphone from zero percent to one hundred percent in one second. Flat."

"Seriously?"

"Absolutely. Smartphone models with graphene-based batteries will begin rolling out this fall." She looked around; still, no one was within earshot. "Now, that *is* a secret of sorts. As co–patent holders in the technology, we've asked manufacturers to not release any information about it until we go wide with iDoc. We want to over-whelm the public's perception that iDoc is revolutionary. The new battery technology coinciding with iDoc's release will reinforce investors' assessment that a new paradigm has been entered. And it will also help serve to get any non-smartphone users into stores to buy new ones."

"And if you can't afford a new phone?"

"We'll subsidize it. Or, more accurately, Obamacare will subsidize it. That's another bit of holdback, too."

"How can—"

"Everyone in the beta test loves iDoc, George. It's better than a real doctor. For all the little things patients want to talk to their doctor about and can't because that doctor is unavailable. The acceptance of iDoc was imme-diate. It will change medicine. We're talking health care, not sick care, as Bradley alluded to during the presenta-tion. Let me give you a personal example of how this works. Recently I woke up with a sore throat. My first concern was strep, as a friend of mine had been diagnosed with it. I dropped a saliva sample onto the designated location of my phone's touchscreen and asked iDoc for an analysis. Within so many seconds, strep *was* detected in the flora of my mouth. iDoc e-mailed a script to my local pharmacy and the prescription was waiting for me when I arrived. I was subsequently contacted by iDoc at later intervals, unprompted, asking to monitor my saliva again. Might have forgotten, but iDoc did not."

"But what about this call center? Isn't that cheating? Because real doctors are the backup?"

"Not at all. iDoc has been learning. Learning *fast*. Just as Lewis Langley reported. iDoc is using the 'real doctor' backup at a significantly lower rate now than at the beginning of the beta-test period."

"Where is this call center located?"

"Upstairs on the seventh floor of the neighboring building, which houses Amalgamated's home office. Would you like to see it? I'd be happy to show it to you." She was enjoying this. Her tendency to show off was taking over.

"You can leave here?" George motioned to the crowd of investors.

"Yeah. The sad reality for me is that when it gets to crunch time, these hedge fund guys would rather talk to a man than a woman. They're more than happy to make small talk and hit on me, but serious investment talk is reserved for Bradley. I think they believe that I'm some sort of a PR front man."

George scrutinized her. If she resented the sexism, she

wasn't showing it. She just seemed to be acknowledging a fact.

"Okay. Why not? Let's check it out," George said.

George followed Paula into the Century Towers. The building was sleek, modern, high-tech, and oozed prestige. Paula reminded him that it also had an unfortunate nickname, the Death Star, a reference to *Star Wars* and the ultimate weapon in the Galactic Empire's arsenal. The name had nothing to do with Amalgamated. The building was bestowed the moniker because its lobby bore a striking resemblance to the interior of the film series' Death Star and because Hollywood's top talent agency, so secretive and powerful that it literally terrified everyone, including many of its clients, had taken up residence in the tower. Paula said that Thorn didn't mind the nickname. In fact he hoped its suggestive powers would cause employees and vendors to pledge their loyalty to him. A fantasy, of course, but Thorn liked to indulge in them from time to time.

Paula led George through the massive white marble lobby and over to a concierge desk, where she arranged visitor credentials for George. With the proper guest pass in hand, they approached the bank of elevators, where the IDs were scrutinized by two large and intimidating guards.

"They take security seriously here," George said under his breath as they entered an elevator.

"You don't know the half of it," Paula replied.

After they exited the elevator they had to show their

credentials to another couple of guards at the entrance to
the call center. Even though they obviously knew Paula,
they checked her ID and scanned it into a reader along
with George's. Paula and George walked into what looked
like a call center on steroids. It was a massive open space
divided into comfortable cubicles with six-feet-tall, thick
glass partitions serving as walls. Each office was occupied
by a single, carefully groomed, white-smocked man or
woman. Each cubicle also held a sleek glass table and
ergonomic chair. And that was it. Nothing else. There
were no computers, no monitors, no headphones, no
papers or pens visible. Nothing, save an occasional insulated coffee mug. What astounded George was that the
glass walls acted as computer monitors. The keyboards
were virtual impressions on the glass desktops. George
could see images of medical files flashing by. FaceTime-
style chats with patients were projected as well. The operators were zooming in on this or that by touching their
desktops. George noticed that a few doctors were using
some sort of 3D hologram while viewing MRI and X-ray
images of internal organs and bone structure. They could
manipulate and rotate these images as well. Some of the
pictures were going from one doctor to another with
texted voice-recognition messages. George was stunned.

Paula could tell George was impressed.

"What the . . . ?"

"Pretty sweet, huh? We combined cutting-edge technology with a couple of Hollywood set designers and . . .
voilà!"

"Tony Stark."

"Pardon me?"

"*Iron Man*. It reminds me of the movie." George felt as if he had been literally transported into the future.

"It's funny you say that, because, as I said, we actually did hire some Hollywood set designers to help with the design." She pointed to various features as she spoke. "Each cubicle is wired for sound so there's no need for headsets. Cameras are embedded in the glass walls for doctor-to-patient face-to-face chats. That's why they wear the smocks. Professionalism is key to our patients' having confidence in the system. We even have a hair and makeup room, and the doctors, they're all board certified and work only four-hour shifts to ensure that they remain fresh and on top of their game. Overhead air systems suppress the sound of the conversations so there's no background noise and privacy is protected. Medical records and current vital signs are displayed on the walls, as you can see. Whatever image or file a doctor cares to view is controlled by desktop touch controls. The doctors can also enlarge and highlight and make notes on any image they choose simply by touching their desktops. Three-D holographic technology enables the doctors to better view and evaluate a condition and then diagnose it."

George noticed a young man and woman in white futuristic outfits similar to those he had seen at the presentation carrying beverages into various cubicles. Paula followed his eyes.

"We want to make the doctors' experience as pleasant as possible, too," Paula said, "so, among other things, they can order drinks whenever they want. No food is allowed, though. For that, we have a dining hall. Wolf-gang Puck handles the food for us. It's quite good."

"I can imagine."

"The doctors can take breaks whenever needed. There's no punching the clock here. They earn, on average, twenty-three percent more income on a per-hour basis than that of a typical medical specialist. Their stress levels are much lower, too, because they don't have to worry about running an office."

George scanned the room. "You said these are all board-certified doctors?" He noticed that they did appear cheerful. The ones treating patients were doing so with a smile.

"Yep. They're mostly internists, along with some pedi-atricians and ob-gyns. We have a few general surgeons, orthopedists, ENTs, ophthalmologists, and dermatolo-gists, too. Questions from iDoc users are routed by spe-cialty after being handled first by a general internist."

George was upset. Even though the room was beyond impressive, it seemed as if doctors were being reduced to glorified call-center operators. "iDoc isn't going to work," George blurted before he even had time to process exactly why he said it.

"Why?" Paula asked, startled. The outburst came across like a dose of sour grapes.

George immediately regretted having said it, but he couldn't take it back. But now that it was out there . . . in for a penny, in for a pound. "There are two major problems as I see it," George said, thinking it through out loud. "First, there's the lack of human touch, which, in spite of this here"—he waved his arm around the room—"can't be replaced by what is essentially a robot that is acting as the first responder. Second, there's the issue of confidentiality, which is huge. People will be carrying around their complete medical histories, which could be hacked or compromised even in an unintended way."

"Human touch is not an issue," Paula said, shaking her head. "That's been proven by the reaction of twenty thousand people during the beta test. Hardly a small sample. iDoc's acceptance has been extraordinary. And it has cut down regular doctor appointments and emergency room visits by an astounding forty-five percent. No one in the beta-test group complained about the human-touch issue. They *did* say over and over again how much they appreciated the ease of use on a twenty-four-seven basis. Being able to talk with their iDoc doctor when it suited them and for as many times as they felt the need to trumped any other issue. Think about it, the average person gets less than an hour of face time with their primary-care physician in an entire year. You call that a human touch? I call that missing in action. Availability trumps all other issues. Doctors over the years have made themselves progressively harder and harder to reach. E-mail has helped, but not enough doctors have embraced it to make a difference."

George opened his mouth to respond but couldn't think of any rational comeback.

Paula sensed she won the point and pressed forward. "As for hacking, iDoc has the most advanced firewall technology available. And we don't see privacy as the issue it once was. In an era when one hundred percent of the population has health insurance available to them and preexisting conditions can no longer preclude getting insurance, privacy diminishes in importance. As to your last point about accidental access, the iDoc app is biometrically accessed. It will only open for access when the intended user presses his fingerprint on the app. Access closes after sixty seconds of nonuse. And that's just the first level. iDoc uses voice recognition in answering questions or divulging personal information. It also uses EyeVerify, which analyzes the blood vessels in a user's iris to verify authenticity. Its accuracy is on par with that of a fingerprint. Also, since iDoc monitors vital signs, it always knows where the user is in relation to the phone. Finally, iDoc is quantum cloud based. Very little actual personal medical information is stored on the phone itself. What data is stored we encrypt. So, if someone's phone is stolen, there's not much anyone can get off it. We can also wipe a phone clean remotely if a patient notifies us of a lost or stolen phone or in the event of death, when iDoc recognizes that vital signs have ceased."

George was silent. They seemed to have all the bases covered, and covered well. He still didn't want to believe it was all so nice and tidy, but there was little he could say that would sound reasonable.

"A doctor working here in the call center isn't all that different from a radiologist like yourself. You're both just interpreting data generated by technology."

George ignored the comment and moved to firmer ground. "You're blurring the line of what a doctor is by cutting the primary-care physician out of the equation and acting as one yourself. 'Yourself' being Amalgamated, an insurance company. When did their executives go to medical school?"

Paula stared at George with her lips pursed. "A blue-ribbon team of the nation's top doctors contributed their knowledge and experience to the development of our algorithm. iDoc also has all known and recorded medical knowledge at its disposal—textbooks, lab studies, journal articles. In short, it is the most knowledgeable doctor in the world, and it forgets nothing and is constantly updated. On top of that, it has the added benefit of continuous, real-time vital signs. It can compare that data against the patient's complete medical history in less than two-tenths of a second. It can take any new information, such as test results, and compare it to the patient's historical data and all known medical knowledge and make a diagnosis in less than half a second. I don't mean to offend you, George, but with a choice of being treated between you or iDoc, I choose iDoc."

"Well . . ." George said, clearing his throat. "I appreciate your candor. Point taken." He wasn't offended so much as surprised at her frankness. If iDoc was half as good as they claimed, she was right. He decided to ask how iDoc would affect him if he were sick, thinking of his stint in the ER beginning the next day. "How does it work when someone has to go to the emergency room?"

"It's simple. If the hospital is owned by Amalgamated Healthcare, which is a distinct possibility, since we've bought up a number of hospital chains, we'll soon have an

integrated and automatic wireless hookup. iDoc will know
when a client-patient enters one of our hospitals, and it will
alert the staff because iDoc will have sent the patient to
the hospital in the first place. Theoretically, client-patients
will not even have to approach anyone on staff; they can
just take a seat. The appropriate personnel will be alerted
to their presence and can locate them by both GPS and
facial recognition. Staff will know why that individual is
there, if not by iDoc vital sign readings and known medical
history, then by having been told why the patient asked to
go to the ER. iDoc will forward that information through
the appropriate channels. Basically, you will be triaged
immediately upon entering the facility. If it is not an Amalgamated hospital, the iDoc physician will consult directly
with the emergency room physician, explaining why the
patient needed emergency care, or the patient's medical
history and vital stats can be downloaded by a licensed
handheld device provided to the ER by Amalgamated. The
information can then be uploaded into the hospital's computer system and accessed by the ER staff. Handheld down-
loads are how our beta testers are operating now."

George tried to think of other reasons why he thought
iDoc wouldn't work as well as Paula believed, but he
couldn't come up with any. He wasn't sure exactly why
he hoped the system would fail, although he guessed it
had something to do with his viewing it as competition.
He changed the subject: "Are you really an iDoc user or
was that story you told about strep for effect?"

"I absolutely am an iDoc user, and I love it like everyone else."

"Let me see it?"

"Not concerned about HIPAA, huh?" Paula teased as she pulled out her phone and opened the app. She held the phone up a foot away with the screen facing her and asked: "How are my vital signs today?"

A crisp but caring woman's voice responded in a slight English accent. "Hello, Paula. Your phone is on speaker. May I proceed?"

"Yes. Speakerphone is fine." She glanced at George and turned the phone so that he could see the screen. On it was an animated image of an attractive woman in a white doctor's coat. Speaking to George, Paula whispered: "I always loved English accents. They seem so authoritative and reassuring."

"Excellent," Paula's iDoc doctor responded to Paula's giving permission to proceed. "Your vital signs are entirely normal, but about an hour earlier, there was the suggestion of anxiety, not enough to warn you about but enough to alert me that something out of the ordinary was happening. I also noticed that your sleep was interrupted last night. Your periods of deep sleep were shorter than usual. How are you feeling?"

"Much better. I was anxious about a big presentation I had to give this morning. I should have given you warning."

"I do appreciate as much information as possible in advance."

"Okay. Bye." Paula closed the app.

George grinned, impressed. The short interaction was uniquely personable. "Nice. *Much* better than I imagined."

"The program is heuristic, too, like you heard at the presentation. So much so that my iDoc avatar has been learning to relate to me in the manner I like to be talked to. I can't say that any of my primary-care doctors ever bothered to."

"You have a point there." George checked his watch. "I have to get back to the hospital."

"I'll go out with you. I have to get back to the potential investors."

She accompanied George to the elevator. After the doors closed Paula said softly, "I wish your mother had had iDoc."

The comment startled him. "Thanks! Me, too." George realized his mother might still be alive today if she had had such a device.

"During the development process, I included a test that I named 'Harriet.' For your mom."

George turned and studied Paula's face. He didn't know what to say in response, as it was truly a generous gesture. Paula was full of surprises today.

"Also, I insisted that an anti-addiction program be included for specific drugs, alcohol, and particularly cigarettes, such that iDoc knows immediately when any are ingested. iDoc will interrupt and initiate a conversation with the patient. Not like after one glass of wine or anything, but if certain levels are reached or heavy habits established, it will take action."

While George was touched by her thinking of his mother, he couldn't shake an underlying resistance to the app. "Won't that be just plain irritating? Sounds like it could be viewed as Big Brother."

"I'm sure it is irritating to some people, and they can decline the conversation. If they do that, it won't continue to hector them. But that is not what has happened in the beta test. In fact a number of our smokers have been able to quit. Immediate intervention with every episode seems to help a lot of people. Patients can't hide their habit from iDoc because it constantly searches for offending agents."

"I guess that might be helpful," he said, wondering if it might have gotten his mother to stop smoking, but he doubted it. She would have just turned the app off.

"Well, thanks for the tour," George said as they walked across the lobby. "And for inviting me to the presentation." He thought briefly about bringing up the fact that Kasey had been part of the iDoc beta study and had died possibly because her phone had been charging, but he couldn't do it. He didn't want to think about Kasey, much less talk about her with Paula.

"You okay? With all of this?" Paula sensed George was a little overwhelmed.

"Would it matter if I wasn't?"

"It would matter to me. As I admitted, our talk those few years ago was my initial inspiration to pursue it."

"Thanks. I appreciate that, but to be honest, I'm not sure how I feel. It's a lot to get my head around. You guys—an insurance company—are assuming a lot of responsibility." He put his hand out to shake. "It's been an interesting morning. Thanks."

"Thanks for coming. It meant a lot to me."

George smiled and turned to leave. Paula called after him.

"Why radiology?"

George turned back. "What?"

"Why radiology? I always meant to ask you. After all the grief you gave me in medical school about the MD-MBA program and taking up space in medical school while never intending to practice medicine on real human beings—and here you end up in a residency program that, for the most part, avoids patient contact. It's ironic. iDoc uses avatar doctors and you apparently prefer patient avatars in the image form of X-ray, MRI, and PET scans."

It was her second reference to his chosen specialty. Was she picking on him? Her tone didn't sound like it, but he wasn't sure. "There is definitely some truth in what you say."

"I always had you pegged for a GP or an internist. I never suspected radiology. What motivated you?"

"I don't think anything really happened," George said. Suddenly he could hear Kasey's voice in his head. She had helped him understand his career motivations, namely that he had gone into medicine in order to feel worthy of people's respect. The issue stemmed from a vain attempt to gain his stepfather's respect. He wasn't sure he was up to sharing that now with Paula.

"Well, it is a big difference from the way you talked in our second year."

"To be truthful, the farther along in medicine I went, the less tolerance I had for direct patient contact. It was a surprise. Actually, at first I wondered if I was really that shallow. Maybe it was because I got the feeling I was coming down with every disease I encountered."

"That happened to all of us, even if we didn't talk about it."

"It happened to you, too?"

"Absolutely. It's human. Your interest in radiology had to come from something else. When we were first introduced to it, I was intimidated," Paula said. "Were you?"

"I liked it from the word 'go'!" George said. "I was intrigued by its definitiveness. It could make a real diagnosis that could lead to definitive treatment, especially with radiology becoming more interventional."

"Well, there you go," Paula said. "That makes sense."

"To be completely honest, someone told me that I have too much empathy and that I needed a specialty that distanced me a little from my patients so I could be objective. Like, I don't know how people can become oncologists. All the more power to them. I couldn't do it. No way."

"That I can relate to as well, even more than the hypochondriasis. Thanks for being honest."

"You're welcome," George said. He checked his watch and winced. "Well, thanks again for inviting me to this presentation. Now I have to get back to the hospital for sure."

She gave him a brief hug good-bye before he headed for the door.

"Keep the idea open of your coming over to my house on Saturday, Dr. Honesty," she called after him.

7

Lewis Langley terminated the call and pocketed his phone. He was troubled. He scanned the room, looking for Bradley Thorn. He spotted him holding court with two hedge fund managers whose faces he recognized from their frequent appearances on financial shows. He knew Thorn would be pissed but Langley didn't want to waste any time. He pushed his way through the crowd until he reached the CEO's side. Thorn reluctantly turned to him, irritated at the interruption.

"I need a moment," Langley whispered in Thorn's ear.

"Now? In case you haven't noticed, I'm busy."

Langley just stared at him, raising a single eyebrow.

Thorn hesitated. The last thing he wanted to do was step away from the potential investors standing in front of him, but Langley looked upset. In private Thorn joked that his dealings with Langley were similar to Pope Julius II's dealings with Michelangelo. Langley was a genius but could be a pain in the ass.

"Excuse me, gentlemen, I'll be right back," Thorn said, following his tech manager.

"It better be good," Thorn said quietly. "They were eating out of my hand."

"I just became aware of something. I don't want to rain on our parade, but my IT head just reported that a bug seems to have appeared in the iDoc application. Reappeared, actually."

Thorn's face turned hostile. Langley could tell that this was the last thing his boss wanted to hear, especially in the present company. But Langley didn't care. Diplomacy was not his concern, nor was Thorn's reaction. But the success of iDoc was. "This newest incident happened at Santa Monica University Hospital, same place as the first. We thought it had been a fluke at the time but apparently not."

"What kind of a bug are we talking about?" Thorn asked, though he wasn't sure he wanted to hear. "Something serious?"

"I would qualify it as serious. Especially if the media or the FDA became aware of it. Two patients involved in the beta test have died."

Thorn swallowed hard. "How many people know about it?"

"Just the IT supervisor. Me. And now you."

"No, I don't know about it. Just you and your IT man do. This is your responsibility. Deal with it, and do it quietly and effectively! That's your job." Thorn looked around, making sure no one was within earshot. "And if we need to have a conversation this sensitive, *this* would not be the time or place for it. Don't be such a goddamn cowboy, even though you look the part. Furthermore, fix your errors, Langley! Or I'll get someone who can." He turned to head back to his guests.

"You don't understand," Langley snapped, grabbing Thorn's arm. Thorn stared at Langley's hand until it was dropped. "My take is that it's not an error. At least technically speaking. Rather, the program is working *too* well. We might not want to fix it. In fact, this kind of bug may appeal to certain parties we're currently negotiating with, namely Centers for Medicare and Medicaid Services. It might be just what will get CMS to take iDoc for all its beneficiaries."

"Explain yourself!"

"My sense is that the IPAB set up by the ACA might find this bug entirely to their liking. If they do, and force CMS's hand, that's eighty-seven million potential client-patients in the plus column." Langley had the habit of lapsing into geek-speak punctuated with acronyms, but it didn't trouble Thorn. He knew Langley was referring to the Independent Payment Advisory Board and the Affordable Care Act, but he was still confused. "All right! All right! You are going to have to explain in more detail. But not now, for Chrissake!" He straightened his tie and plastered a broad smile on his face before walking off to rejoin the waiting hedge fund managers.

8

Greg Tarkington entered the office of his oncologist, Dr. Peter White. Greg was nervous. He had noticed that the MRI technician had been reluctant to make eye contact at the conclusion of the procedure earlier that morning. The resident, Dr. Boucher, did the same. Greg sensed it meant bad news. After everything that Greg had been through, he knew the ground rules regarding ancillary personnel: Divulge nothing. But Dr. White couldn't hide behind that dictum, and finally he spilled the beans.

"I'm afraid the MRI showed several questionable lesions in your liver. We aren't sure they're cancer metastases, so we will have to biopsy them, and we want to do it sooner rather than later."

The doctor spoke calmly, as if discussing an ingrown toenail that needed treatment. At least that's how it sounded to Greg. He was tired of being patronized. He was tired of the whole experience since he had first noticed that the whites of his eyes had turned yellow. That had been the very first symptom that started the nightmare. Then came the tests, the surgery, and the chemotherapy, which had been a torture.

"So the pancreatic cancer is back?" Greg's voice was accusatory.

"Well . . ."

"Straight up, Doc! I don't have time for equivocation." Greg's worst fears were materializing. He wanted it all out. Now. No more false hopes.

Dr. White sighed. "As we have discussed, it's a very difficult cancer to treat. Its location and anatomy are . . . problematic. We have done the best we can. If the biopsy confirms that these new lesions are the same cancer, then we will have to be aggressive."

"Will that mean more chemo?"

"I'm afraid it does."

"But the chemo is killing me! It already compromised my kidneys. I'm still undergoing dialysis. On a less frequent basis than before but . . ."

"There are a lot of arrows left in our quiver, Greg. If more chemo is needed, we will choose agents that don't have kidney toxicity."

"Like what?" Greg wanted specifics. His goddamn life was on the line.

"I can't say exactly what that might be. Not yet. Let's wait and see what we are up against."

"How much time do I have?" Greg pressed.

"The biopsy has yet to be done—"

"How much time if the biopsy is positive?"

"I can't say."

"Guess!" he demanded. Dr. White was not going to get away with hemming and hawing. Not today.

"I've never been right when forced to give a guess in such a situation, but let's just say that it would be a good time to get your affairs in order. I'm sorry, Greg, but you are just going to have to buck up."

The comment hung in the air.

"Buck up?" Greg repeated mockingly. "After all I have been through and you're telling me to 'buck up.' Worse, you're being evasive. But it's okay. I'll contact iDoc when I get home and get what I need." Greg knew he was being confrontational, something he had not done up until that moment, but now he didn't care. He was sitting on the business end of a death sentence.

"I am not being evasive. The answers to your questions are unknowns," Dr. White replied. He was aware that Greg was part of the first cohort to use iDoc. He had been impressed with the app since the number of off-hour phone calls had dropped significantly. Emergency room visits and requests for office visits from others in the program had plummeted, too. "But let me remind you that iDoc hasn't gotten the results of the MRI yet. I received the preliminary report by calling the radiology resident. When iDoc does receive the results, please let me know if it offers any new perspective. As I understand it, its algorithm has significant resources of knowledge available. So in the event that I'm missing anything, I would welcome hearing about it."

He started making notes on a digital tablet. "But most important, we have to ascertain what these liver lesions are. We need to schedule a biopsy and a series of pre-biopsy clotting studies."

"iDoc can do the clotting studies the morning of the biopsy," Greg said.

"I'll give you the script anyway," Dr. White replied without looking up. He continued typing into his device.

Greg had never felt so helpless. Even in the last go-round of chemo he had always had hope. If hope was still alive anywhere inside him now, it was doing an excellent job of hiding. Greg's iDoc chimed in with a short selection of Bach's Cello Suite no. 1. The music normally had a calming effect on him, but not today. Recognizing that iDoc wanted to talk, Greg moved to a quiet corner of the hospital's hallway and clicked ANSWER on the app. His doctor immediately appeared.

"Hello, Greg. May we talk? You are on speakerphone."

"Yes."

"I've just been apprised of your last MRI study. I am sorry to have to tell you that there were several abnormalities seen as reported by one of the more senior radiology attendings. Would you like to talk about this now or later?"

"Now," Greg said without hesitation.

"Would you like me to be frank or just supportive?"

"Frank and supportive, if that is possible."

"It is possible. First I have to say that on a statistical basis these lesions are most likely metastatic cancer, hardly good news, considering all that you have been through. I am so sorry about this, but we must be proactive. A biopsy has already been scheduled, which will give us the definitive answer. Once we have that result we will consider our options.

"I also know you've just come from a meeting with your oncologist, Dr. White. Based upon the notes that he entered in your medical record, I know you're aware of your current situation. This is a stressful circumstance for you, Greg, as it would be for anyone, and your vitals reflect that. It would be best for you to go home. I'd like you to have a sedative, but I don't want to administer it until I know you will not be driving. Your pulse rate is up and you're perspiring more than—"

"Stop!" Greg said, impatient to get to the heart of the matter. "Just give me specifics about the biopsy. What are the chances that the liver lesions are in fact cancer?"

"Under the circumstances the chances are 94.36 percent. I'm terribly sorry to have to give you this information, but it is the most accurate that I can determine, considering thousands of similar previous cases."

Greg had wanted it cut-and-dried and that's how iDoc just gave it to him. Tears welled up in his eyes.

"Please go home and lie down!" iDoc said. "Your pulse is going up. You need to relax. Call me when you get home, and we will talk more. There are some new promising treatments available."

"You remember that my kidneys are still not functioning up to par."

"Of course I am taking that into consideration. Now please go home and try to relax."

Greg clicked off his iDoc. *Thank God for Dr. Williams*, he thought. Dan Williams was the name he had chosen for his iDoc physician. A Dan Williams had been his football coach in high school, a man he had worshipped.

9

George hustled toward the front of the hospital, still hoping that his unauthorized departure had gone unnoticed. As he approached the main door he spotted Greg Tarkington coming out. The man was clutching his smartphone. His face had an intense, strained expression. George slowed down, debating whether he wanted to say something to the patient. He decided he would rather not; his excuse was that he was already late getting back. But Tarkington saw him as they were about to pass each other.

"Hello, Dr. uh . . ." Tarkington stammered. He stopped.

"Wilson," George finished for him.

"Yeah. Sorry. A lot on my mind at the moment." He put away his phone and stood silent.

Here was an example of what he had just been talking about with Paula. He felt an overwhelming empathy for this man but was unable to think of anything to say.

"I just learned that the MRI wasn't good," Tarkington managed. "I mean it wasn't good news. Sorry for putting you on the spot earlier. Who wants to tell someone that?" He tried to smile.

George was taken aback. Tarkington felt empathy and compassion toward *him*, the doctor. George experienced a moment of profound guilt.

Tarkington shrugged and looked at the ground. "Life has its challenges," he said, raising his eyes to George's.

"It does." George was at a loss. "You seem to me like a person who meets the challenge," he finally added after a pause. He was awed by Tarkington's courage and wondered if he would have the same, were the situation reversed. He also wondered if it wouldn't have been better if the man hadn't had the MRI.

"Well, I'm not going to roll over without a fight. It's going to have to take me kicking and screaming."

George found himself thinking that under different circumstances he and Tarkington could have been friends. He admired the guy, even admitted to himself that he liked him. George also wondered if he really had what it took to be a good doctor. Seeing people confront their mortality was unsettling at a very deep level.

"I'm sure your doctor has a plan of action," George said. "There's more than one way to beat these things."

Tarkington nodded. "Well . . . thanks. I appreciate what you doctors do. But I need to get home and think this through." He gave George's arm a squeeze as he walked past. It was a melancholy sort of gesture reflecting a human need to connect.

As George watched the man walk away, he wondered if he could have offered more support. Then he turned and entered the hospital, thinking how much easier it was to spend time with Tarkington's MRI printout than with the man himself. It was so much less emotional, so much more scientific, and so much more an intellectual exercise. Yet ultimately it was about another human being, and in this situation it was like being responsible for the man getting a death sentence. George shuddered. That was the part he really didn't want to think about. Maybe even radiology wasn't safe enough for him. What if he had taken the same MD-MBA course that Paula had taken? If he had, he might be living in a Santa Monica house with a pool and driving a new Porsche Carrera without ever having to be touched, however obliquely, by something like pancreatic cancer.

George walked into the MRI control room, where Claudine and another technician, Mark Sands, were in the midst of a study. Mark was an African American with whom George had spent a lot of time. Of all the technicians, Mark understood the MRI best in all its technological subtleties. Under his guidance, images progressively wiped across the screen, generating anatomical slices of a human body in a fashion that never failed to astound George. Claudine glanced up and gave George a thumbs-up, which George interpreted to mean that things had gone well during his absence.

George raised his eyes and glanced through the observation window at the huge, doughnut-shaped magnet. He could see the feet and lower legs of a woman protruding from the MRI. He guessed from the woman's position that it was another abdominal study.

With the equipment on autopilot under the watchful eye of Mark, Claudine took a moment to quickly review what had transpired during George's absence. It was confirmed that there had not been any problems and no one had come looking for him, which eased George's residual anxiety. Soon he was feeling entirely relieved about having been out. Clearly he had not been missed.

Using a monitor, Claudine went through the images of a torn ACL, which had been the first case she'd done with Susan's assistance after George had left. Next she showed George a bothersome lower back done with Mark's help. In both cases the tests were diagnostic and well done.

"What's up with this current case?" George asked, nodding toward the patient in the adjacent room.

"Her name is Claire Wong. She's forty-three years old and has a history of lobular breast cancer. She's been treated with a mastectomy and chemotherapy combined with radiation. Although she's currently asymptomatic, her oncologist wanted the abdominal MRI, just to be certain there aren't any additional problems. So far it looks good."

George nodded again, feeling an uptick from the unease

the encounter with Tarkington had generated. The idea of another cancer case made him feel superstitiously uneasy. Moving over to Mark, he looked over the man's shoulder at the most recently formed image. To his chagrin he immediately noticed something that Claudine had missed. "Uh-oh! That doesn't look so good. It seems that there is some definite retroperitoneal thickening. Can you guys see it?"

"I think so, now that you've pointed it out," Claudine said. She took a laser pointer from her pocket and outlined what she thought George was referring to.

"That's it. Let's review some of the previous slices," George suggested.

Mark pulled them up. George studied them closely, then pointed at a portion of the small intestine. "There's thickening of the bowel wall as well." George used his finger to trace along the problem segment.

Again Claudine and the technician could see the condition after George pointed it out.

George shuddered inwardly. This case was as bad as Greg Tarkington's in terms of its implications for the patient, but George's thoughts were interrupted. Suddenly the door opened and Clayton Hanson poked his head in.

"Can I have a word, George?"

"Sure," George replied as he felt a quickening of his pulse. He could only guess that Clayton had seen him at the presentation after all. As George headed for the door he tried to think of a plausible excuse for having left the hospital without getting permission and without formally signing out. Nothing came to mind. He knew he was considered one of the best radiology residents. Clayton himself had said so. Was he ever going to grow up about facing authority figures? After all it had been a medically oriented event, he had covered his responsibilities, and Clayton had been there himself.

"I noticed you over at the Amalgamated event," the older doctor said sotto voce as George joined him in the hall. There were a number of passersby.

"Yeah. I saw you, too," George said. At least Clayton wasn't saying it in a confrontational manner. That was a surprise. And a relief.

"What did you think?"

"Well, it's quite a bit to digest." George searched his mind for a diplomatic response since he hadn't decided exactly what his feelings were. And he had no idea why Clayton would ask him such an open-ended question.

As George hesitated Clayton went on. "Well, let me tell you what I think. Amalgamated wouldn't be a bad stock for a young man to invest in, if that was why you were there."

Rather than respond, since Clayton knew full well that George had no money, George said, "What's your involvement?"

Clayton studied George a moment before answering. "I have a sizable investment position in Amalgamated. I was involved with an earlier generation of iDoc, helping them look at it from the imaging perspective."

"That got you onstage?" It was a bold question. Clayton could easily take offense. But the question was nagging at George.

Clayton paused before answering, as if measuring his

response. "Thorn and I have come to know each other well over the years. Actually, he's my brother-in-law. He's married to my younger sister. After all the family time spent together and the inevitable health-care-related discussions, he's come to trust my medical instincts." Clayton studied George's face for a reaction. George gave none. He wasn't going to intimate, even with his expression, that nepotism was the reason that Clayton had such a prestigious seat at the event. George was a realist. The guy could seriously impair George's radiology career if he chose to do so.

"What's your relationship with Paula Stonebrenner?" Clayton asked. He was looking at George with raised eyebrows. "It looked like she made a beeline for you at the reception. You banging her?"

George took a step back. Clayton was known for blunt, even vulgar, comments but they were usually unintentionally inappropriate. This one seemed deliberate. George assumed Clayton was taking a shot at him for forcing him to reveal the family connection to Thorn.

"We were at Columbia Medical School together."

"And . . . ?" Clayton wasn't letting up.

"We dated a little our first year," George admitted, feeling a little like Clayton was taking advantage of George's subordinate role. "We're just friends now. Maybe even that's too strong a word. We're acquaintances."

"Sorry, I shouldn't have asked," Clayton said, backing off. "It's none of my business." Clayton knew about George's fiancée's recent death and had been lately encouraging George to be more social. He had even invited

George to a couple of parties at his home, which George had respectfully declined. George imagined Clayton meant well, but he had always been put off by Clayton's treatment of women, as if their existence were solely for his enjoyment. Kasey had been harsher in her assessment. As a radiologist, George truly admired the man, but as a person, it was another story.

"Paula is an impressive woman," Clayton offered. "I've gotten to know her a bit while working on the iDoc project. Maybe you should think about sparking that fire again."

"She is impressive, I agree. But as far as dating again . . . I don't know."

"I know you're still trying to work things out . . . about Kasey. Things like that never really go away. You just find a way to live with it. Paula's attractive, considerate, incredibly bright, and on the fast track to professional stardom. That's something to think about."

George stared at the floor, nodding his head. What Clayton was saying about Paula was both accurate and kind. He was demonstrating his ability to flip from crass to considerate. That was his saving grace, from George's perspective.

"Just make sure you sign out properly next time," Clayton said as he turned to leave.

George was stunned. Clayton was switching directions again, this time from personal to professional.

"I had everything covered," George said, stumbling over an excuse.

"No matter," Clayton said. "I won't say anything to the chief of radiology, but from now on do us both a favor and follow protocol whenever you leave the hospital. I don't want you screwing up at this point in your career. You've been doing so well."

"I will," George assured Clayton. "And thanks, I appreciate it."

"No problem. And think about some Amalgamated stock. It's worth mortgaging an apartment to free up some cash if need be." He headed off down the hallway with a wave over his shoulder before George could respond.

George watched him disappear down the hall. Clayton had managed to get one last zing in before leaving. George had to hand it to him; the guy was way ahead of George in manipulating people. George wanted to yell out that in case Clayton had forgotten, he didn't have a pot to piss in or a window to throw it out of. He didn't own his apartment. He rented. And *that* was a struggle. With his salary, he'd have to go out as far as San Bernardino in order to find something affordable to buy, and the commute would kill him. Clayton knew all this. He just enjoyed screwing with George.

10

George drove his aging Jeep Cherokee up behind his apartment complex and parked. He was very much out of sorts, having been reminded by Clayton of his impecunious circumstances in the middle of a very expensive, money-worshipping city. Once inside his tiny apartment, he went into his closet and pulled down the cardboard box in which he stored Kasey's things. There wasn't much, since she had not finished moving in with him. Just a few clothes and personal items. For some time he had avoided looking in the box, but now he wanted to see something specific.

He rooted through the box and found Kasey's cell phone under a small stack of sweaters. Always cold, she was a firm believer in layering, and had sweaters handy at all times. One of George's fondest memories of her was her throwing one on and cuddling up against him on the couch to watch a movie. George pushed such thoughts out of his head and plugged her phone into his charger. Once it powered up, he punched in her passcode. He wanted to make sure she had had an iDoc app. She did. It was in the dock section for apps at the very bottom of the display face, so no matter which screen she was on, it was always available. He had seen it but had never asked her about it, and she had never offered an explanation. Now he knew why: the nondisclosure agreement she'd had to sign to become part of the iDoc beta test.

George pressed the icon, curious to see what might happen. It opened, but the screen was blank except for an icon similar to the one on the app. Apparently iDoc had been wiped clean, as Paula had mentioned. He wasn't surprised. It made sense to protect the privacy of her health information. He put the phone back and set the box on the closet shelf. Then he grabbed a beer from the fridge before retreating to his threadbare sofa, where he was enveloped by the black hole sensation of Kasey's loss. When he allowed himself to think about it, he marveled at just how much he missed her. At the same time he recognized that he had to pull himself out of the hole that fate had cast him into, as he had promised her.

The trouble was, knowing what he had to do and actually doing it were two entirely different things.

From his perspective, being in L.A. didn't help. Some people fantasized it was a hedonistic center, but that hadn't been George's experience. He had found L.A.

could be a cold city to outsiders, and with the busy schedule of a resident, he didn't have a lot of time to meet any
new people other than fellow medical center employees,
like nurses. Meeting Kasey in the hospital had been a total
but wonderful fluke.

A few weeks earlier, with his promise to Kasey in mind,
George had tried a couple of online dating sites, but they
turned out to be a bust. As far as he could tell, no one on
those sites told the truth about anything. Maybe he
should see Paula as a friend. She was a known quantity.
Seven years before, he had royally screwed up what could
have been a rewarding relationship, which might not bode
well, but at least now there was a new element. Apparently
a portion of her current success stemmed from her taking
his idea of using a smartphone as a primary-care doctor.
They had that in common. Maybe her invitation to visit
was something he should take seriously.

Out of desperation for human contact—any kind of
human contact—George took another beer and went
outside. He strolled over to the parking area behind his
apartment complex. Earlier, when he'd arrived, he'd seen
one of his neighbors, Sal DeAngelis, polishing his red
vintage Oldsmobile convertible. The guy was nuts about
the vehicle.

Sure enough Sal was still there, polishing away. He had
his earbuds in, and as George approached he could hear
the tinny jangle of doo-wop music leaking out of the tiny
speakers. Sal didn't see him right off so George hung back
and watched the man work. Sal lived next door and the
men became acquainted from proximity more than

anything else, sharing a common wall in their kitchens and living rooms. Sal was a friendly, outgoing, red-faced, stocky, retired plumber replete with a serious beer belly. He also was in the early stages of Alzheimer's, as well as a host of other medical problems, all of which he had been in the habit of discussing ad nauseam with George. Sal had never understood the fact that George was a radiology resident rather than a clinical doctor, so he constantly plied George with questions outside his specialty. Then a few months ago he had stopped. Although George had appreciated the respite from answering the same questions over and over, he was curious as to why they had suddenly stopped.

As George watched Sal work, he realized sadly that after his living in Los Angeles for three whole years, Sal might have been his closest friend. It was unfortunate, because there was little commonality and few shared interests.

As George observed his neighbor, he prepared himself to have a conversation about cars, and one car in particular. From previous interactions George was well aware that Sal's fire-engine red convertible was a 1957 Oldsmobile Golden Rocket 88 with a 371-cubic-inch displacement Rocket V8 with J2 Tri-Power carburation. He also knew that it produced 277 horsepower under the control of a Jetaway Hydramatic transmission. George didn't know the first thing about the engine or transmission in his own Jeep, but as for the vehicle in front of him, he knew everything and nothing. Finally, he reached forward and tapped Sal on the shoulder.

Sal's face lit up in a broad smile. He yanked out his earbuds.

"George! Check it out," he said, pulling George around to his side of the car. "Just today I found a pair of original, mint-condition floor mats." He opened the driver's door and pointed to two mats still wrapped in plastic. "They're primo! Primo!" Sal also had the habit of repeating phrases.

"Nice!" was all George could come up with. Floor mats were floor mats as far as he was concerned, but he didn't want to dampen Sal's enthusiasm. "Gonna take them out of the plastic?"

Sal hesitated. "I'd hate to mess them up," he said as he pulled George back to the front hood, which he was about to open. "Have I showed you my new carburetor yet—"

George had seen the carburetor. At least three times, and he was not looking forward to a fourth viewing. He took a risk and steered the conversation away from the car even if it might open the proverbial floodgate. "How's it been going with your urinary tract symptoms? Still get that burning?" Suddenly George's curiosity had gotten the best of him. He also felt sorry for Sal since everyone else in the apartment complex steered clear of him so as not to have to slog through the same health-related conversations day in and day out. George knew the man had two older sisters and had even met them once during his first year in L.A., but George hadn't seen them since, though Sal often talked about them longingly. The guy was pretty much alone in the world. All he had was the Oldsmobile. And George, for whatever that was worth.

Just then the sound of a horn made both men jump. George looked around for the offending automobile. But there wasn't any. The horn was the ringtone from Sal's phone. The man snapped it up from the car's front seat and switched on the speakerphone.

"Hello, Sal, it's Dr. Wilson. You're on speakerphone. Is it all right for me to talk?"

"Yeah, sure, it's okay. Sure," Sal responded.

"I've noticed two things over the last few minutes," the physician said in a rich baritone. "Your blood sugar has been falling lower than I would like and your heart rate is over one hundred. Take a moment and have something healthy to drink, like orange juice, and then rest for a spell. Is that possible?"

"Can I finish polishing my car?"

"I'd rather you did not. It would be much better if you got some sugar now, along with some rest. When your pulse rate stabilizes, I'll let you know. Then you can go back to polishing the car."

"Okay, okay." Sal turned off the phone and glanced guiltily at George.

"What doctor was that?" George knew that Sal's primary-care doctor had been Dr. Roland Schwarz, and that clearly was not him on the phone.

Sal glanced around to make sure no one else was within earshot. He shielded his face with his hand and spoke in a low voice. "I'm not supposed to tell anyone but you are a doctor, so it probably doesn't matter. My new doctor is something called iDoc. It's a—"

"I know what it is," George said. He was shocked. *iDoc again!* "When did you start using the app?"

"It's been a month or two now, I guess. Month or two. I can't remember exactly."

George was taken aback. After a presentation that day heralding a new paradigm for medicine based on digital technology, he found out his neighbor was part of the Amalgamated beta test. It was a shock, not as much as ascertaining his deceased fiancée was part of the program, but a shock nonetheless.

"Can I see your phone?" George asked.

"Sure. Sure." Sal handed it over, pleased that George was taking an interest.

George turned the phone over in his hand. The phone's protective case was a startling electric orange. "Quite a shocking color," George said.

"I picked that out myself. I was always misplacing the damn thing. Now it's hard to miss."

George turned the phone over to look at the screen. He stared at the iDoc icon on the screen, just like the one on Kasey's phone and just like the one on the huge LED screen at the Amalgamated presentation. "How long did you say you've had it?"

"Can't remember exactly. My mind isn't sharp as a marble anymore." He laughed at his own joke. "A couple of months or so, I guess."

George suddenly understood why Sal's medical questions had stopped. He had a 24/7 doctor in his pocket who didn't mind being asked the same questions over and over. "Do you like having a doctor to talk with whenever you want?"

"Love it. I use it all the time. Love it," Sal said. "I used to have trouble remembering to take my meds, but not now. iDoc tells me whenever I need to take something.

And it'll remind me if I forget. But most important, I don't have to think about the insulin anymore. It's automatic. Auto—"

"What about Dr. Schwarz?" George interrupted. "You used to see him quite a bit."

"Not anymore. Nope. Not anymore. He put the reservoir thing in, but that was the last time I saw him." Sal raised the waistband of his T-shirt to show George a thin, nearly invisible scar on his left lower abdomen.

George's reaction was complicated, adding to his general unease.

"But you're by far the best doctor I've ever met. The nicest, too," Sal said. He seemed to have sensed George's not-so-positive reaction.

"And the name, Dr. Wilson?" George asked. "Where did that come from?"

Sal blushed. "I hope you don't mind. I had to pick a name . . ." Sal didn't finish his sentence.

"It's okay. Really! Thanks, Sal. I'm flattered. But I gotta go. Make sure you follow iDoc's advice and rest up." George handed Sal back his phone. "Catch you later, buddy."

"Later, Doc. Later," Sal said, watching George walk off. He pocketed his phone and started to put away his polishing kit.

George headed back toward his apartment, going through the back gate. He took in the relative rundown condition of the complex, which didn't improve his mood. With a wry smile he imagined how it must compare to Paula's home. Although he'd never been to her house, he

knew Santa Monica had become a high-end neighborhood loaded with celebrities and studio executives living
in multimillion-dollar homes.

George's apartment complex, likely built in the sixties
from the look of it, was an eyesore. It was a poorly constructed U-shaped structure, just like a gazillion other
apartment buildings strewn across the greater Los Angeles area. Inside the U was a small, unappetizing pool
ringed by a few scraggly palm trees and other plantings
fighting for life. The building was two stories high with
mostly one-bedroom units, although there were a few
studios and two-bedroom apartments as well. The building manager lived in a ground-floor studio next to the
back gate. His contribution to the building was a bad
joke, as George had come to learn over the years. At
exactly 3:00 P.M. every day the guy began drinking. If he
made an on-site inspection of an apartment past 3:00 P.M.,
a drink was always in hand. And since he was hungover
every morning, he was MIA before noon.

The ground-floor units of the complex had small
fenced-in patios facing the pool. George estimated that
the rickety fences hadn't seen a coat of paint in at least ten
years. George occupied a one-bedroom unit, as did Sal.
Sal's apartment was just to the left of George's, and on the
other side a wannabe actor slash waiter. His name was Joe.
George didn't know the last name, and he didn't want to.

The actor's apartment, like Sal's, was the mirror image
of George's but, unfortunately for George, their bedrooms
shared a shoddily constructed common wall without insu-
lation. Consequently, George already knew quite a bit

about the actor, since he could hear the man's conversations as clearly as if he were in George's apartment. Joe worked at a nearby Beverly Hills restaurant and had lots of one-nighters that he picked up at the dive bars on Sunset over in West Hollywood. These sexual escapades often woke George up. A few times, desperate to get back to sleep, George pounded on the common wall, but it had never done any good. It was apparent that Joe's attitude toward women was not all that different from Clayton's.

Since George had so many nights that required him to stay in the hospital on call, he'd tolerated the Joe the Actor issue, but now that he was about to begin his final year of residency, which had no scheduled night call, he knew he was going to have to do something.

George skirted the pool, glancing over at two inked-up twenty-something girls floating on rafts. They lived in one of the upstairs units. They were drinking PBR beers from tallboy cans and didn't acknowledge George as he passed. He assumed his lack of body art combined with his somewhat combed hair was a factor.

Rounding a sad-looking palm tree, George started toward his door. Besides Sal, George was friendly with only one other tenant. His name was Zee, and George really didn't know him all that well. He wasn't even sure if Zee was his real name or not. He was in his mid-twenties and used to work for a computer gaming company. He had gotten laid off when a major new product bombed upon its release. According to Zee, he had nothing to do with that particular product, but since he was the low man on the totem pole, he was one of the employees who got their walking papers. Now he supported himself playing poker on the Internet, a career choice George never knew existed until Zee gave him the 411 on it.

George knew Zee to be incredibly computer savvy and capable of fixing anything and everything associated with hardware and software. That talent had come in handy on occasion. Zee had helped George with a number of iPad and iPhone issues. George was also aware that Zee was an accomplished hacker since he had regaled George with hacking stories while fixing whatever computer device wasn't working. It seemed to George that Zee hacked secure sites just for the fun of it. Zee bragged that he could hack into anything.

Slamming the door behind him as he entered his apartment, George was in a strange mood. iDoc had invaded his world without his even having been aware of it. And it was an idea he had supplied to one of its creators! He wasn't sure if he was depressed or just pissed off about the whole thing. The distinction probably didn't matter.

"Shit!" George shouted while glancing at the bare shelves in his refrigerator. He had forgotten to stop at Ralph's grocery on his way home. The empty fridge underscored how sad and devoid of pleasure his life was.

He looked around the room. He had no pictures on the walls and no photos. There had been a few of Kasey, but after she died he put them away. They were too painful to look at every day. His only addition to the furniture that had come with the apartment was the flat-screen TV and a bunch of radiology textbooks. Sad. Very sad indeed.

11

George entered the radiology main conference room, checking messages on his phone while balancing a cup of coffee on his iPad. For a small gaggle of first-year residents it was the first day of residency. He was still in a blue funk from the previous day and still couldn't decide how he felt about Paula and iDoc.

Feeling decidedly antisocial, George took a seat in the very last row. He liked a lot of his fellow residents and some of them were very accomplished, but he wasn't close to any of them. For the most part, they were married, some with kids and living a completely different life from George's. In truth he felt envious, and it made him miss Kasey that much more.

George sipped his coffee and tuned out the welcoming

speeches. He had heard them all, ranging from the warm to the threatening. George stifled a yawn as he eyed the first-year residents. There were more women than men this time around, and all appeared eager to go. They were scrubbed up in crisp, freshly laundered and pressed white coats. He had made it a point to look over the list of the first-year residents a few days before and noticed they were all married.

George's mind wandered as the meeting droned on. Over the last few months he was supposed to have been dreaming up some sort of research project for his fourth year, but he hadn't given it much serious thought. He wondered about the possibility of doing a year of subspecialty radiology as a way of putting off the decision about what he was going to do after he graduated from the program. After the previous day's presentation at Amalgamated, he wasn't as sanguine about his professional future as he had been prior to it. Would he end up working for Amalgamated or its equivalent? Unfortunately he thought the chances were depressingly possible.

At the conclusion of the department's welcoming conference there was a modest spread of doughnuts and coffee to encourage mingling. George watched it all from the periphery, feeling disassociated. Just then Clayton caught sight of him and sidled over before George could escape.

"The women are getting better looking every year," Clayton whispered.

"It's just that we're getting older," George replied. "Plus they're all married, so it doesn't matter."

Clayton glanced over at George. "Someone got up on

the glass-half-empty side of the bed this morning. What's your first rotation this year?"

"Supervising emergency imaging in the ER."

"Good!" Clayton said, pleased. "I had told scheduling to assign you there, but you never know. Can't count on anyone anymore. Listen: I heard through the grapevine that there's a knockout first-year ER resident from Stanford. Single, since that seems to be a prerequisite for you. Her name is Kelley something or other. Check her out. I'm always thinking about you, buddy."

"Okay," George said. He wasn't interested, but he didn't want to get into it with Clayton; better to let him think all was well with his clumsy efforts to fix George up. George definitely wanted to stay on the man's good side. George saw Carlos Sanchez, the first-year that he was scheduled to supervise. It was an excellent opportunity to ditch Clayton. "Excuse me, that's my newbie over there. Better go get him situated."

"Go to it." Clayton smacked George on the butt with his folder. He had once confided that carrying a folder around always made you appear busy, and even better, you could end any conversation instantly just by waving it and saying you had to go. The guy was a superb radiologist and a great teacher, George thought, but he had his fair share of idiosyncrasies.

George approached Carlos, a bright, eager Mexican American whose record George had perused when he'd gotten the assignment. Carlos had breezed through UCLA Medical School with stellar grades. With radiology being one of the more desirable specialties, all of the department's residents had done extremely well in medical school, George included. When George first met the young man a few days earlier he'd been impressed with his eagerness. He had already read several of the main texts written about emergency imaging, but reading textbooks about what to do was one thing, actually doing it was another.

"Hey, Carlos!" George said, offering his hand.

"Dr. Wilson," Carlos replied, grabbing George's hand and giving it an eager pump.

"Just George will be fine. I'm about to head out but wanted to let you know I'll see you over in the ER after the reception."

"I'll go with you," Carlos said, setting down his coffee.

"No! Stay and try to meet as many of the staff members as you can! It's important for you to get the lay of the land. See you in a few!" George headed for the exit, waving over his shoulder in a fair imitation of Clayton.

"Okay, boss," Carlos called after him.

12

George leaned back and stretched in his chair. Carlos did likewise in unconscious imitation. George glanced at him, making sure Carlos wasn't messing with him. Apparently not. They were in the ER's radiology reading room, where most of the light came from the viewing monitors. They had just finished going over all the X-rays taken the night before in preparation for their conference with the ER staff. George had found three X-ray cases that had been misread by the emergency medicine residents in the current batch.

"Would you like to present the details?" George asked.

"No!" Carlos replied, shocked. "It's my first day. I'd make a fool of myself."

"You would do fine. But I'll leave that up to you. If

you change your mind, let me know," George said, remembering his own reluctance to speak when he was a first-year resident.

The door opened and a shaft of daylight pierced the reading room.

"Dr. Wilson?" one of the ER secretaries called out. "Dr. Hanson is at the main ER desk and wants to see you."

George rolled his eyes and pushed himself out of his chair. "Start going through this morning's X-rays," he said to Carlos.

George stood outside the reading room, waiting for his eyes to adjust to the sunlight streaming through the floor-to-ceiling windows. The place was packed with patients who had not been deemed true emergencies, illustrating the chronic problem caused when the general public used the ER as primary care.

George spotted Clayton chatting up Debbie Waters, the charge nurse known for being a no-nonsense taskmaster and for her excellent work keeping the ER running smoothly. On seeing George, Clayton immediately broke off and walked over to him.

"Did you meet that first-year ER babe yet?" he asked, seemingly unconcerned about being overheard. "You know, the one I mentioned earlier, from Stanford."

"That's why you pulled me out of the reading room?" George's tone of mild admonishment had no effect on Clayton.

"Someone has to look out for you, my friend," Clayton said. "It's time you left the past behind you, where it belongs. Tell me! Have you at least laid eyes on her?"

"No, I don't believe I have. It was a busy night last night. Lots of films."

Extending a hand, Clayton motioned for George to be quiet and nodded toward a young woman who had just come out of one of the enclosed cubicles. She was fashion-model tall and seriously attractive in a healthy, vibrant way. Even in scrubs it was obvious to George that she had a rocking-hot body. She walked past them, tapping away on her tablet.

"Now you have," Clayton whispered. "What a sight. Agreed?"

George turned away from Clayton and rolled his eyes. Dutifully he watched the first-year ER resident approach the main desk to drop off paperwork before taking the next clipboard from the to-be-seen rack.

"They don't get much better than that," Clayton said.

"She's definitely attractive," George admitted, although at this point he was watching Clayton, not Kelley. The man was shameless.

Clayton watched as she stopped to go over a chart. "You better get busy before some surgical resident gets all up in that. But if it doesn't work out, I can put in a good word for you with Debbie Waters."

"The Queen of Mean?" George was shocked. He could feel his face redden as he briefly glanced over at Debbie.

"Hey, she said she was interested in getting together with you," Clayton protested. "And you need to get out more. I'm worried about you. You have to have some balance in your life. You work too hard. Seriously. Invite her to have a drink at the W Hotel! She likes it there. I happen to know."

George stole another glance at her. Luckily Waters's attention was directed elsewhere. He had always admired how well she kept the ER on an even keel even when all hell was breaking loose.

"She's a lot of fun, even though she can be a bit bossy," Clayton said. "She's very entertaining when she is taken out of her element here in the ER trenches. Believe me! Work is work. Fun is fun. She's a pistol. Don't judge a book by its cover!"

George knew everybody was intimidated by Debbie Waters. He had seen her give more than one tongue-lashing to unprepared surgeons all the way down to janitors. She didn't discriminate.

"Debbie would be perfect for you," Clayton persisted. "Hell, you don't have to marry her. Come on! I'll break the ice."

"No way. It's not that I don't find her attractive. It's just that she's so damn . . . domineering." He realized Clayton wasn't about to drop the subject. George added, "I'll talk to her when she isn't quite so busy."

Clayton shrugged. "It's your call." He glanced down at his watch. "I have to get back to work. I hope to hear you made some progress on one of these young fillies soon. You need to be entertained to pull you out of your funk."

George shook his head in disbelief as Clayton walked off. In a way it was touching that Clayton was concerned about him. He had also heard rumors that Clayton and Debbie had been more than good friends.

Despite his misgivings George was intrigued. If Debbie Waters really had said she'd like to get together, he'd be a fool to not follow up. When you worked in the ER it was best to have her in your corner.

Reaching the main desk, George pretended to look through the to-be-seen charts while watching Debbie out of the corner of his eye. As usual she was juggling about ten different tasks. As George waited to see if she would even acknowledge him, one of the orderlies dropped a sheaf of paperwork on the countertop in front of him.

"The patient in Trauma Room Six is dead on arrival," the orderly stated.

"And do you have a name, or are you going to make me weed through all of this to find out?" Debbie demanded. She aimed her pen toward the clipboard in front of her.

"Tarkington," the orderly replied.

George's head shot up.

"Thank you. That wasn't so hard, was it?" Debbie said dismissively as she crossed out a name on the master sheet in front of her.

George edged along the countertop, angling for a look at the paperwork, though he wasn't sure he wanted to know that his patient had died. He glimpsed the given name Gregory before Debbie snatched away the chart. As her eyes met his there wasn't an ounce of recognition.

So much for Clayton's good word, George thought. He turned and headed down to Trauma Room 6. The dead patient was lying on a gurney, his clothes torn open, revealing a bare chest. An ER doctor was off to the side typing on a tablet. A male nurse was busy detaching the EKG leads from the individual's chest. A crash cart with a defibrillator stood off to the side.

George looked at the dead man's face. He just wanted to be sure it was the Tarkington whose MRI George had supervised the day before.

"What was the cause of death?" George asked the ER doctor.

The resident glanced up and shrugged. "Don't know. If I had to guess, probably a heart attack. Whatever it was, he was long gone by the time he got here. He was as cold as an ice cube."

"Was there a resuscitation attempt?" George asked, looking over at the defibrillator.

"No. Like I said, the guy was already cold." He gave George a look of "what can you do" and left.

"Are you okay, Doctor?" one of the orderlies asked as he came in to retrieve the crash cart.

"Yeah, I'm fine. Thanks," George mumbled. Yesterday he had assumed Tarkington was in for a rough time, but he didn't think the man would be dead within twenty-four hours! George couldn't shake the feeling that the episode was directed at him to remind him yet again that life was fragile, unpredictable, and unfair, and that he better squeeze what he could out of it while he was able. Worse yet, he felt a strange and irrational complicity, as if he were somehow responsible. Had it not been for him, the lesions in the man's liver might have been overlooked, and had they been overlooked, the man might be alive, happy, and unsuspecting while enjoying life with his family.

George wondered again if medicine had been an appropriate career choice. Maybe he didn't have the emotional strength necessary.

Just then an orderly poked his head into the trauma room. "Excuse me? Are you Dr. Wilson?"

"Yes?"

"Dr. Sanchez asks that you return to the image-reading room to view a possible hip fracture."

"Okay, thanks," George said. He looked back at Tarkington's lifeless body, then began walking back to Carlos. Passing the central desk, he paused to take another look at Debbie Waters. She was still at it, barking out orders. It might be interesting to find out what made her tick. And he did need to get out of his rut.

13

S al DeAngelis glanced up at the clouds scudding across the sky. *What a great day*, he thought. He was dressed in a red T-shirt that had I LOVE MY OLDSMOBILE emblazoned across the front in white lettering. It was a gift from his oldest sister, Barbara, and happened to be his favorite piece of clothing. It was the same red as the exterior of his ride, and the off-white lettering matched the upholstery.

Sal carried a can of car wax in one hand and a toolbox in the other in case he came across something that needed repair. He had washed the car, and now it was time for a wax. He had only a vague sense of when it had last been waxed and couldn't pin the exact date down. The reality was it had been the day before and the day before that.

He started on the grillwork, intending to proceed to the hood and front fenders. But he would never make it that far. All of a sudden an unpleasant feeling spread through his body. It was a sensation he used to experience frequently before iDoc entered the picture, when he would forget to eat on a regular basis. Since iDoc, such episodes had been a thing of the past. But now the sensation was back, and back with a vengeance.

He put down the can of car wax, tossed the polishing rag onto the hood of the car, and made a beeline for his apartment. Inside he went directly to the refrigerator and grabbed the half-gallon container of orange juice he had just bought. With shaking hands, he filled a glass and gulped it down. He stood still, waiting for the dizziness to recede.

Unfortunately he didn't feel any better. With some difficulty he poured another glass of OJ. When that had no effect, he panicked, especially since he had begun to sweat profusely.

Dashing into the bathroom, he stared at his reflection. Perspiration was now literally drenching his face, and he could feel his pulse in his temples thumping rapidly. This was bad.

He dashed back out to the car, where he had foolishly left his phone. Even before he got to the car he heard his phone's honk. Relieved at having his doctor available, he held the phone in front of his face. His hands were so sweaty that iDoc couldn't make a biometric read of his fingerprints, so it automatically switched to visual verification. Finally, his iDoc doctor avatar appeared on-screen.

"Sal, we're on speakerphone again," Dr. Wilson said. "Can I speak openly?"

"Yes!" Sal shouted at the phone.

"I can tell you're very anxious. I suggest you lie down."

"Something's wrong! My blood sugar is out of whack."

"Nothing is wrong," Dr. Wilson answered in his calm, reassuring voice. "You're agitated. You need to lie down."

"I need sugar," Sal shouted back at the phone.

"Your sugar levels are normal," iDoc stated soothingly. "Please, Sal. Go inside, lie down, and close your eyes."

"Screw that!" Sal blurted. He knew he was getting worse, despite the orange juice. Dang it all, iDoc wasn't working right. Damn computer glitches! Maybe he even screwed it all up himself. He might have broken that thing they put in him when he was bending over waxing the car. Sal pulled his T-shirt up to inspect the small, narrow pink scar on the left side of his lower abdomen. His anxiety growing, he tossed his phone onto the front seat of the Oldsmobile and massaged the pink scar with his fingertips. He'd always been afraid to touch the area, but now he pinched it, feeling the square, waferlike object implanted under his skin.

With sudden resolve, he bent down and opened his toolbox, rifling through his collection and sending screwdrivers and wrenches clattering to the concrete floor of the carport. There it was! His utility knife. He extended the razor-sharp blade, then looked back down at the thin scar, evaluating it. Abruptly changing his mind, he turned and ran. *George!*

Sal pounded hard on George's front door, nearly shaking

it off its hinges. There was no response. Sal's anxiety level shot off the scale. He gasped for breath. On top of everything else, his COPD was acting up, causing him to wheeze.

"George! George! Open up, it's an emergency!" George's door didn't open but the door to the adjacent apartment did.

"What the fuck, dude!" An angry, sleepy Joe stood in his doorway, sporting a pair of paisley boxers and nothing else. He looked at Sal: wild-eyed and clutching an open utility knife. "Whoa!" Joe immediately took a step back into his apartment, pulling the door halfway closed. "I'm trying to sleep, you crazy old fart!"

Unlike George, Joe had never found Sal worthy of sympathy and, having been awakened after a night of wild sex, he regarded Sal with irritation and disgust.

A naked tattooed young woman had come up and was peeking over Joe's shoulder.

"What the hell are you doing disturbing everybody!" she yelled at Sal.

Sal didn't respond. Instead he sprinted away, tearing down the path to his Olds. He yanked open the driver's-side door. For a moment the world spun. He was forced to wait until the vertigo passed. As the sensation subsided, he climbed behind the steering wheel, still clutching the knife in his right hand. Securing the lap belt he'd retrofitted in the vintage vehicle didn't cross his mind. He turned the key and the engine roared to life. At least the Olds wasn't going to let him down. He was vaguely aware of the muffled voice of iDoc Dr. Wilson, still trying to get him to go into the house and relax.

Sal threw the car into reverse and backed up too fast, colliding with the trash cans lined up opposite his parking space. Unconcerned, he put the car in drive and careened down the street. His mental capacity was deteriorating quickly as he tried to get to the L.A. University Medical Center. They had an ER and would help him. George would be there, too. Without thinking about what he was doing, Sal hiked up his T-shirt and used the utility knife to try to cut open the scar on his left side. He had to get the damn device out!

Sal had been told what they were embedding in the fatty tissue just under the skin of his abdomen, but he didn't really understand. He was leery of all things high-tech but had trusted that the doctors knew what they were doing. Now something had gone wrong. What he sensed on an intuitive level was that the damn thing in his belly was killing him, and he wanted it out. He felt no pain as he cut into his tissue.

Irrational as it was, a part of his compromised brain was horrified by the narrow jets of blood spurting onto the Oldsmobile's white leather upholstery. But he had no choice. Gritting his teeth, Sal pushed the blade in as far as it would go and then drew it laterally. He could feel the tip scrape across plastic or metal.

Sal knew the route to the medical center by heart. He sped up. Suddenly there was a sickening sound of metal against metal, and he felt the shudder of his car as it rico-cheted off a vehicle parked along the street. *Jesus!* He used the back of his right hand to try to wipe the sweat from his eyes while still holding the utility knife. Suddenly he was bouncing along the sidewalk without knowing how he got there. He wrenched the steering wheel to the left, sending the Olds careening back onto the street, clipping the back end of a parked Mercedes. Now he was driving into oncoming traffic; horns blasted as Sal yanked the car back into his own lane.

Sal thrust his index finger inside the four-inch gaping wound, feeling for the implant. Just as the tip of his finger touched the edge of the object he glimpsed the red blur of a traffic light. Its message no longer registered in his brain, and he sailed through the light and onto Wilshire Boulevard. He was totally oblivious to the cacophony of metal slamming into metal.

"Hey! Watch out!"

The loud yell came from less than a foot away. Sal jerked his head up. He had arrived at the hospital. A man on crutches, crossing the street, whom he had almost hit, had just screamed at him. Sal slumped his weight to the right. At that point it was all he could manage to do, using his body weight to turn the wheel in that direction. The car swerved and jumped the curb, crashing through a privet hedge, still moving at over forty miles per hour.

Sal's foot no longer responded to the feeble messages sent from his brain and remained heavy on the accelerator. Shocked parking valets dived out of the way as the Oldsmobile plowed across a patch of grass on a direct path toward them. Their abandoned valet stand exploded into a mass of flying wooden shrapnel as the car-turned-ballistic-missile blasted through it on its way toward the floor-to-ceiling windows of the contemporary-designed ER.

The Olds knifed through the plate-glass wall and bounced across the ER's marbled foyer, barely missing the department's stunned concierge greeter, frozen in her tracks, digital tablet in hand. The car zipped by Debbie Waters's command post and smashed into a massive LED screen displaying a slide show of the medical center. The vehicle crashed into the screen's supporting concrete, its back end rearing up in the air before slamming back down onto the marble floor.

The old car was not equipped with an airbag. Sal was launched through the car's disintegrating windshield like a rocket-propelled grenade. Headfirst his body buried itself into the display board. He was killed instantly.

Sal's smartphone followed him through the windshield, deflecting off a shard of glass that sent it skidding across the sign-in desk and into the lap of a shocked Debbie Waters.

For a split second no one in the emergency department moved. Then, as if a television image had suddenly been unpaused, all hell broke loose.

BOOK
TWO

14

George felt and heard the tremendous crash. His first thought was *earthquake*. He'd felt a few temblors in his three years in Los Angeles, but this didn't seem to fit the bill. It was too localized. His mind raced through the other possibilities, arriving at the one option almost everyone considered these days: Was it a bomb? A terrorist act? All around him, people were leaping out of their seats and heading for the door.

Dust and smoke streamed through the shattered floor-to-ceiling windows. A trail of debris was strewn across the lobby, ending at the smoldering wreckage of an automobile at the base of what had been the ten-foot-high LED screen. Three staffers had surrounded the fuming hulk of the vehicle and were dousing it with fire extinguishers.

Patients who had been waiting to be seen were either
scrambling to get out the entry doors or were standing
immobile, staring vacantly at the scene with shock. Luckily, it appeared that no one, either patient or employee,
had been hurt in the crash.

George noticed Debbie Waters trying to get things
organized, pointing here and there with a cell phone in
her hand, as if it were a conductor's baton. George scanned
the room, coming to rest upon the wrecked vehicle. He
froze, recognizing the car immediately, even in its man-
gled state. Its vintage and rarity left few conclusions for
George to draw. His eyes moved past the large fragmented
windshield to where a number of orderlies and doctors
were extracting a mutilated body.

Rushing forward, George got a look, better than he
really wanted. It was Sal. His body was a mess, with major
head and torso damage. But George knew it was his friend,
and the familiar T-shirt clinched it, even if Sal's face was
unrecognizable. As they pulled the body free, it was placed
on a gurney and rushed down to one of the trauma rooms.

At that instant the Los Angeles Fire and Police
Departments invaded the ER. A number of firemen in
full gear came in through the missing windows. Senior
hospital officials arrived as the remaining patients were
escorted away from the debris.

George rushed down the main hallway, grabbed one
of the portable X-ray machines, and pushed his way into
the trauma room where they had taken Sal. By the time
he got there the doctors had decided that the patient was
beyond saving, mostly due to the massive head trauma.

"No ID. At the moment anyway," the head of the trauma team said to the ER nurse holding a tablet in her hand, entering notes. "List him as a John Doe—"

"His name is Sal," George interrupted. "Salvatore DeAngelis. He lives at 1762 South Bentley Avenue, apartment 1D."

The group turned to him with surprised, quizzical looks.

"He is my neighbor."

George walked off down the hall as Sal's body was covered by a white sheet. Another iDoc patient was dead!

S o, other than his Alzheimer's symptoms," the LAPD detective said to George, "were there indications of any other factors at play? Drugs, alcohol?" The detective was trying to be gentle, obviously picking up on the fact that George had an emotional attachment to the victim beyond being a neighbor.

"No. Nothing," George replied. He was at a table in the ER staff lounge, his head in his hands, still trying to digest what had happened. The detective, seated across from George, was typing notes into his smartphone.

"Had he been drinking much lately?" he asked. "I mean, did he drink during the day as far as you know?"

"No. Sal didn't drink alcohol, not even beer."

"Were you aware he had been diagnosed with depression and was taking medication to treat it?" the detective asked.

"No—I mean, he hadn't mentioned it. But I wouldn't

have expected him to, either. A lot of people, even someone as open as Sal was, don't talk about psychological
problems. He was a gentle, seemingly cheerful guy. I've
never known him to have ever done anything reckless or
illegal."

"I understand." The detective took some more notes.

George eyed the policeman's phone, noticing a thin
red bar across the top of the display face. Even though he
was reading upside down, he was pretty sure the word in
the bar was RECORDING.

"Are you taping this?" George asked, surprised.

"Yeah," the detective replied. "It makes things easier
later. People tend to forget details." He glanced up.

"Don't you have to ask my permission first?" George
asked. He was surprised and, needing something to take
his mind off the reality of Sal's death, found himself irritated that he was being recorded without his knowledge.

"No. It doesn't work that way," the detective responded
offhandedly. He returned to his line of questioning.
"Were you aware that Mr. DeAngelis had an appointment
here today?"

George ignored the question. "If you're recording the
conversation, why are you taking notes, too?"

The detective stopped typing and looked up. "I take
notes of my initial thoughts of questions that may not be
appropriate at the time. Or maybe my own reaction about
something that was said. I know how to do my job, Dr.
Wilson. As I assume you know how to do yours."

"I'm sorry," George said. "I'm upset."

"It's okay."

"Anyway, I was not."

The detective looked confused. "You were not what?"

"I was answering your question. You asked me if I was aware that Mr. DeAngelis had an appointment at the medical center today. I was not. I knew he had been coming here for tests recently, but he hadn't shared the details about them, and I didn't ask. We have HIPAA rules. A right to privacy. That extends beyond these walls." George had done his fair share of violating HIPAA rules, especially after Kasey had passed away, but without knowing why, he wanted to rub this guy's nose in it. "You probably shouldn't have even told me he was taking medication for depression when you get right down to it. I'm not his personal physician. His current doctor is a . . ." George motioned to the detective's cell phone. He trailed off, unsure of just what he meant to say.

"Is a what?"

"Nothing. It doesn't matter."

The detective stared at George in silence. "His family," he finally said, moving on to another topic.

"Estranged at some level. I'd met his two sisters once. Actually I had been thinking about trying to contact them this week."

"Why was that?"

"Because Sal's Alzheimer's was advancing. I was hoping to get them involved in his life."

The detective nodded. "Okay." He stood up. "I think I have the gist of it. Thanks for your help."

"Sure. What is the 'gist' that you got, anyway?"

"That the man got confused and overwhelmed while driving his vehicle. Likely due to his Alzheimer's. And a tragic accident resulted. We're lucky no one else was injured. Or killed. Remember that crash out at the Santa Monica farmers' market a few years back? A gentleman, in his mid-eighties, I think, plowed his car right through the market's produce stands, killing nine people, including a three-year-old girl. Another fifty-some people were injured. By comparison, we got off easy here today."

"Yeah. Easy," George mumbled.

"Thanks again for your time." George watched the officer turn off his phone and then leave.

George made his way back to the ER reading room and threw himself into a chair. Carlos was glad to see him, since a number of X-rays needed review. George thought keeping busy might be the best thing he could do to feel better. He delved into them but struggled to keep his mind focused. He had the paranoid feeling that death was mocking him. He knew such thoughts were irrational, but that didn't make them any less disturbing.

"There's one more," Carlos said, bringing up an X-ray of an arm fracture on the monitor. "I think it's a—"

"Excuse me," George said, cutting off Carlos as he abruptly stood. "I need to step out a moment."

Carlos looked at him surprised. "Yeah. Sure. Everything okay?"

George remained silent a moment. "Not really." He turned and left the room.

"Will you be back soon so we can finish?" Carlos called, but the door had already closed, and George apparently hadn't heard him.

15

Bradley Thorn's office was on the top floor of the tallest building in Century City. It was both extravagant and massive. His ego demanded it, as did his sense of inferiority, instilled in him at a young age by a domineering, sadistic father. Bradley heard "the hospital must have switched babies" routine too many times to count. It was mean and abusive on his father's part. But then his father's personality had enabled him to rise to the top of the health care game. The father had been ruthless, developing a computerized method of paying doctors as little as possible and delaying the payment for as long as possible, which had amassed him a fortune and ultimately the leadership of Amalgamated Healthcare.

Bradley inherited control of the company just two

short years earlier, after the senior Thorn suffered a massive stroke. It was a tragedy for the previously robust Robert Thorn. For his son, it had been a godsend.

Bradley was physically fit and in excellent health. He was confident women found him attractive, although he was never sure if that was enhanced by thoughts of his money or not.

At the moment, Thorn was meeting with Marvin Neumann, a celebrated hedge fund genius who was thinking of putting some $500 million into Amalgamated to take iDoc international. His money would also help with the acquisition of more hospitals. Thorn had told him that's where the big profits were, especially since Amalgamated would be paying itself for hospital services.

Neumann in turn told Thorn he had some demands to go with his money. He wanted a seat on the board of either Amalgamated or iDoc. Which one, he hadn't decided. Neumann also cited medicine's tendency to overemphasize the good and ignore the bad in their testing results. He wanted to be absolutely certain that iDoc's beta test had been as well received as Thorn had reported at the presentation.

"Absolutely!" Thorn protested. "If anything, we have been conservative in our appraisal. Please be assured that I'm not about to risk my reputation or the company's for a short-term gain."

"That's comforting to hear," Neumann said. What he didn't say, though he was pretty sure of it, was that Thorn would likely risk everything to be regarded as a hero. The guy was both pretentious and insecure, and everyone knew the stories of him and his father. But family and personal failings aside, the hedge fund guru felt Thorn had stumbled upon something big, and he wanted a piece of it. He just needed to have a position to be able to watch the company's progress and steer it away from trouble if need be. Health care in the United States was a notoriously politicized arena. That's why he would eventually insist upon seats on both boards. But in these preliminary negotiations he would suggest that one would suffice. He'd demand both board seats when Thorn was about to lay hands on the cash. It was a ploy Neumann had used to great effect in the past.

"The beta test has been a fantastic success far exceeding our most optimistic predictions," Thorn bragged. "As we said, the patients love it and it is going to truly solve the primary-care shortage worldwide. And lower costs. What more can you ask?" Thorn jabbed his finger at Neumann. "And iDoc is going to revolutionize addiction treatment. Whatever the addiction, iDoc will offer immediate, real-time feedback when a client-patient indulges—"

"Okay, okay, I get it," Neumann interrupted. He didn't need to hear a repeat of what had been said at the presentation.

"Well, I'll get back to you about a board seat," Thorn said. "It'll have to be brought up with the current board."

"Of course," Neumann said, standing.

"Thanks for coming in." Thorn stood as well and shook hands with Neumann, escorting him out of his office.

Neumann paused at the office door. "Say hello to your

father for me. We used to play tennis on occasion on our Sun Valley trips. I hope he's doing well."

"I will. I will," Thorn replied with a smile plastered on his face.

As Thorn waved his good-bye to Neumann he glimpsed Langley stretched out in a club chair in the anteroom, leafing through a magazine. Thorn shot a glance at his secretary.

She gave him a shrug, mouthing the words: "He just showed up."

Irritated, Thorn beckoned Langley into his office. Thorn had a built-in distaste for creative types like Langley.

Thorn pointed to a chair and walked around behind his desk.

Once seated, Langley cleared his throat. "We've investigated this supposed glitch that I told you about yesterday. At first I thought it was a regression of the bug we'd seen during the first few weeks of the beta test. But it's not. Nor is it actually a glitch in a literal sense, even though we can call it that. The application just made determinations from a different set of criteria and learning points than we would have suspected."

Thorn was irritated. It seemed to him that Langley was deliberately trying to confuse him. "I'm not following you. What the hell do you mean by a 'literal sense'?"

"The algorithm is weighting variables differently from how we thought it would. That's the core of the problem, if it is a problem."

Thorn threw up his hands, exasperated. "You know

the key to running a large business like Amalgamated? You delegate. You hire good people and get out of their way. Now you want to drag me into the weeds? Have you considered the fact that if I am consumed with the details of your job, it might hinder my ability to act effectively for the company as a whole? My fund-raising is essential to securing future contracts for Amalgamated. Are you following me?"

"This is not a routine programming problem. And it is spreading."

"What do you mean 'spreading'?"

"Exactly what the word means. It started at Santa Monica University Hospital but now has appeared at Harbor University and even at the L.A. University Medical Center."

"Shit!" Thorn exclaimed, running a hand nervously through his hair. "What kind of numbers are we talking about?"

"Not many yet. Besides the two cases at Santa Monica University Hospital, there have been two cases at Harbor University Hospital and two at L.A. University Medical Center."

"Have these all occurred since we spoke yesterday?"

"Not the ones at Santa Monica, but the other four, yes."

"And they all resulted in death?"

"Unfortunately, yes!"

"Are we going to see a surge in this problem or is this going to remain an isolated phenomenon?"

"I can't say for certain; I can only guess."

"Okay, guess!"

"I don't think we will see a surge. But nor do I think the issue is going to go away. In fact I am sure it is not."

"All right, you win. I need you to explain to me what is going on, but not in your usual tech-speak."

Langley leaned forward. "These deaths are a direct outgrowth of the heuristic nature of the algorithm—"

Thorn put his hand up. "What do you mean by 'heuristic'? You've bantered this term around without really explaining it to me."

"As I said yesterday and have told you before, the application is capable of learning. We have all seen that iDoc learns. It progressively makes its own decisions, decisions that were not programmed into it per se, but that are based on past outcomes."

"That means the iDoc algorithm is getting better because of its heuristic nature. Isn't that what you are saying?"

"Exactly. It is learning and getting better faster than we predicted."

"But still there have been these six deaths."

"Correct. But remember the algorithm is not aware that it's doing anything *unwanted*. In fact, it is doing what it thinks is best for everyone, the victims included."

"So how many deaths do you think there will be?"

"As I said, there is not going to be an avalanche. Right now we are seeing an incidence of just over three hundredths of one percent. I don't see it ever going over four hundredths. And as I said, the Independent Payment Advisory Board set up to control costs for Medicare and

Medicaid is intrigued by what is happening and is looking more favorably on iDoc as a result."

"How did they learn about this glitch?"

"As part of their due diligence in evaluating iDoc for Medicare and Medicaid beneficiaries, we allowed them access to our servers. They became aware of the deaths at the same time as we did. They are intrigued."

"So they don't want us to stop the glitch."

"Their only concern, and a big one, is that it remain undiscoverable, for obvious reasons. If the media were to get hold of the story, it would be an unmitigated disaster."

Thorn nodded that he couldn't agree more. "Okay! All this is highly classified; no one gets wind of it. Make a few inquiries; see what ripples resulted from it so far. You said there were a couple of cases at University Medical. Clayton's over there, have him sniff around to make sure no one is suspicious. Tell him I asked for his services specifically. But do not give him the details, just the basics. Again, how many are in the loop as of now?"

"At Amalgamated? The same as before: three. Me, you, and my IT head, Bob Franklin. And Franklin's a team player, so no worries there."

"Okay. Besides Clayton, no one else here at Amalgamated should know about this. No one! What about at IPAB?"

"I don't know for sure. Two, maybe three folks. They're a secretive bunch and don't share much because they are not politicos, but rather power brokers who have been appointed without having had to go through congressional confirmation hearings. Their task is to reduce the deficit by reducing Medicare and Medicaid spending. It's all about power. And power is knowledge that no one else has."

"Well said. At least there is no worry there. And I assume there should be no trouble at the medical examiner's office."

"Right! No problem there, considering the medical histories of the cases."

"Good. Thank the Lord for small favors."

Langley stood up. "All right! I'll get in touch with Clayton and have him make sure there are no problems over at L.A. University. As the premier academic institution in the area, if there is no problem there, it should be smooth sailing elsewhere."

"I agree. Later, come back here. I want a more complete explanation of what is happening. I presume you know, since the algorithm is your baby."

"No problem. It will be my pleasure!"

16

George was still upset about Sal's horrific death and was glad he didn't have a noon radiology conference to sit through, as it had been canceled for the first day of the new academic year. Such conferences always required a certain amount of socializing, which at the moment George didn't think himself capable of. Passing the time in the ER's isolated radiology viewing room was much less demanding and considerably less stressful.

As he sat staring into the middle distance, he wondered what on earth could have gotten into Sal to make him act so bizarrely. Sal had been a pretty calm individual. Could it have been the Alzheimer's?

While George stayed hidden in the viewing room, he let Carlos do the running around that went with the territory of being a radiology resident assigned to the ER. George was happy to remain secluded, because the ER was still as chaotic as he had ever seen it, with construction workers cleaning up the debris and seeing to the broken windows despite the usual onslaught of patients. Some of the ER's exam rooms could still be used, but the ones close to ground zero were out of commission, so the ER had temporarily taken over a portion of the nearby outpatient clinic building. The trauma rooms had not been damaged, and were still in use. But it wasn't easy. With all of the construction people around, it was difficult to get the major trauma patients out of the arriving ambulances and into the proper rooms. Nevertheless, to her credit, Debbie Waters was making it happen.

Some time later Carlos breezed into the room, saying, "There's a bunch of images that have to be read." He dropped into the chair next to George and booted up the monitor.

"How is the ER shaping up?" George asked.

"They got rid of the wrecked car already. Most of the debris, too. And they have covered the broken windows with plywood. The scuttlebutt in the media is that the driver of the vehicle was trying to commit suicide."

George looked at Carlos, shocked.

"They're just speculating," Carlos said, catching George's expression. "You know the tabloids. Gotta juice everything up."

George shook his head.

"One of the ER residents told me that they suspected some of the driver's abdominal wounds looked self-inflicted,"

Carlos added as he entered the first patient's hospital number into the computer. "They found a utility knife in the car with blood on it. Can you imagine? The guy must have been nuts."

George shook his head again. He had trouble believing Sal would do such a thing. And how could they tell what was self-inflicted and what wasn't, considering that Sal's body had gone through the windshield before smashing into the LED screen? Suddenly George asked, "How do they know the blood didn't get on the knife as a result of the crash, considering all the gore. The victim had exsanguinated. Blood was over everything."

"No clue." Carlos shrugged as he pulled up the first image.

George didn't like the thought of Sal being remembered as a crazy weirdo on a suicide mission, possibly trying to take innocent people to their graves with him. George decided to check things out for himself once he finished up with Carlos.

An hour later George emerged from the peacefulness of the reading room. He was impressed that the ER was pretty much back to normal except for all the plywood and the large hole in what had been the wall-size LED screen. After asking around a little with the orderlies he learned that Sal's body had been sent down to the hospital morgue. With all the questions he had, he decided to pay a visit. It was a place he had never before had the occasion or the inclination to visit.

George rode an elevator down to the sub-basement. The doors opened onto a desolate hallway. It was eerily quiet in contrast to the rest of the hospital. Lines on the concrete floor of various colors gave directions to different destinations: power plant, refuse, recycling, storage for this or that. George followed the black line leading to the morgue. After a couple of twists and turns he found the place. But no one was home. An empty desk sat in the anteroom, where George expected to find one of the attendants.

Opening an inner door, George wandered in to look for someone. It was a lonely place, looking more like a set for a horror movie than a modern medical center. The place smelled weird, too. And was quiet. He promised himself he would view Sal's body as quickly as possible, then get the hell out.

The surroundings also reminded him of Pia's visit to the morgue back at Columbia Medical School when she was intent on investigating the death of her research mentor. That had been a very unpleasant experience that had almost gotten him kicked out of medical school.

Suddenly a diminutive man dressed in a long, soiled white coat stepped out of a refrigerated room. Both were startled at their near collision. The man took a step back and momentarily raised his arms as if to defend himself. Apparently he didn't encounter too many live people.

"Can I help you?" The guy's tone wasn't all that friendly, either.

"I'm looking for a body. The deceased's name is Salvatore DeAngelis."

"You family?" The guy still sounded annoyed. George

thought the diener would have been happy to see a living human being.

"No. I'm—we were friends. Neighbors, actually."

"Then you can't see him. We don't allow 'friend' visits. Just family members and approved personnel with direct business—"

"I work at the medical center," George said, pointing to his white coat and name tag. "I'm a radiology resident."

The man was clearly not impressed. "I have strict orders. No unauthorized visitors view the deceased. HIPAA rules. You should know all this. With all the celebrities in town, we have to be very strict, especially since the debacles over Michael Jackson and Farrah Fawcett. People take photos and sell them to the tabloids." He looked down at George's hands as if he might have a camera ready to start snapping away. "If I just let whoever in here to see any body they wanted—"

"I don't want to see any body," George interrupted. He couldn't believe the guy. "Mr. DeAngelis was a close friend, and I'm a doctor on the staff." George's voice rose more than he intended. He took a deep breath and spoke in a more even tone. "The patient was involved in the auto accident in the ER upstairs this afternoon. I'm sure you heard about it. Well, I was there when he crashed. I helped identify him."

"Of course I heard of the crash." He waved as if shooing away a fly. "And that is another reason not to let you see the body. It might be a medical examiner's case, being an accident and all."

George threw his hands up in disgust. "Okay. Fine. I'm out of here." It was a lost cause, and he didn't want to hear the guy babble anymore. "Thanks anyway," he added sarcastically.

George made his way back to the elevator and punched the call button. *What a jackass*, he silently voiced. When the elevator arrived he boarded, irritably pressing the first-floor button.

Just as the doors were about to close, he noticed the doors of the elevator across the way opening. He got a fleeting glance at the passenger stepping off.

Was that Clayton?

George hit the OPEN button on his car just in time. The doors retracted back, and George leaned out. It was Clayton! And he was hurrying in the direction of the morgue. What the hell was Clayton doing?

Making a snap decision, George stepped out of the elevator and hurried after the radiology chair. Maybe he was going someplace other than the morgue. But what else was in the sub-basement that might interest him? George had no idea.

George hustled down the hallway and rounded a corner, briefly catching sight of Clayton farther ahead and immediately disappearing as the corridor turned again. He was definitely moving fast, George thought. Was he carrying a package of sterile gloves? That's what it had seemed like from the brief look George got before the elevator doors had closed.

George rounded the final corner in time to glimpse Clayton arrive at the morgue and enter.

George slowed down. His intuition was telling him to leave. But his curiosity propelled him forward.

He approached the morgue's double entry doors and peered through one of the small windows. George noticed that the diener seemed much more accommodating with Clayton. George watched him nod as Clayton spoke to him and then lead the way into the morgue proper while Clayton followed, donning his gloves.

What the hell?

George debated what to do. His intuition was still telling him to get the hell out before Clayton reappeared. This time George listened.

17

George opened the door to his apartment and slumped in. He was exhausted. His afternoon at the ER had been extremely busy, with multiple major trauma cases pouring in, requiring all sorts of X-rays and CT scans. A few MRIs had been needed as well to diagnose strokes. It had been even more chaotic after three when Debbie Waters's shift was over. Her replacement was not nearly as adept.

George found some leftover Chinese take-out in his refrigerator and popped it in the microwave. He scoffed it down while standing in the kitchen. To call it a meal would be kind.

Without turning on a light George threw himself onto the couch. With his hands behind his head he eyed the darkening ceiling. The sun had set, and he faced another long, lonely night. Tired as he was, he could not sleep, thinking about Amalgamated. There was no doubt in his mind that the combination of the federal health care reform empowering the insurance industry and Amalgamated introducing iDoc would turn medical care on its head. And what had Clayton been doing down in the morgue? George still thought it was odd.

George was roused from his musings by a knock on the door, a rare occurrence that was fast becoming rarer still with Sal gone.

It was Zee. A pair of sunglasses and a frown covered his still acne-prone face. The fact that there was no sun was apparently immaterial.

"What the hell happened, dude?"

"You mean in the ER?" George knew Zee was one of the few people in the complex who spoke to Sal.

"Yeah." Zee walked in uninvited and collapsed on George's couch. "Man, it is wicked dark in here."

George turned on a lamp and sat down. He considered suggesting to Zee that he remove the sunglasses, but thought better of it.

"That crash was on my Twitter stream all day. Everyone thought he was a suicide bomber at first." Zee looked around the room, taking in George's sparse furnishings. "You need a decorator or something. This place is depressing."

George frowned. He knew Zee was right, of course, but it bugged him being called out on it by someone whose own apartment was also nothing to write home about.

Zee shifted back to Sal. "He totally trashed Westwood on his way to the hospital. It's like he OD'd on Grand Theft Auto or something." He gazed up at George's ceiling and sighed. "I liked Sal. He was always cool with me." Then he squinted at George. "So . . . you were there, right? You saw it?"

"Yes. I watched them pull him out of the wreckage."

"No shit." Zee whistled. He was oddly impressed. "What did he look like? Cut to shit, I bet."

"It wasn't pretty," George agreed. "He exited his vehicle through his windshield. No airbag. Didn't use his seat belt. I really don't know much beyond that." George felt odd talking about it, as if doing so were disrespectful of Sal.

Zee sensed George's reluctance to talk about the crash. "Sorry, dude. I know you were tight with him. Guess that's why I stopped by." Zee paused, looking like he wanted to say something else. After a minute he continued.

"A lot of people are now saying suicide."

"I heard that, too," said George. "But I don't think so, Zee. I think he was having a health emergency and was just trying to get to the ER."

Zee nodded. "Weird, though. I would have called an ambulance or gotten someone to drive me."

"Who knows what he was thinking?" George shrugged.

"Does he have any family? Someone to notify?"

"Two sisters. I met them once back when I first moved in three years ago."

"A suit on the five o'clock news was saying he had no known family."

Now that George thought about it he was surprised the police hadn't asked more questions about the sisters when he mentioned them. Zee suddenly launched himself off the couch.

"Gotta roll, dude. It's a damn shame about Sal." He headed out the door. "Catch you later, I got an online session scheduled. I'm up eight hundred for the week."

"Later," George said as he got up. "Thanks for stopping by." George knew Zee was referring to his new career as an online gambler. It supposedly subsidized his living expenses. He had to be doing rather well, considering his rent was $1,500 a month and his unemployment insurance couldn't have been much more.

George sat back down. Someone should make an effort to contact Sal's sisters. George thought he would do it if he had their phone numbers. But he didn't even know what state they lived in, or their names. Were they married? Did they use their maiden name? He had no idea.

Since Sal had listed George as the person to contact in case of emergency, he thought there was a good chance no one had spoken to them. Believing it was the least thing he could do for Sal, George went down to see the building superintendent.

George knocked on the super's door. He could hear the television on inside. It sounded like a baseball game. He knocked again, this time on the narrow window next to the door. The blinds parted and a pair of red eyes peered out.

"Whadda ya want?" The tone wasn't unfriendly; in fact

it was the opposite, it was hopeful. But the man was clearly inebriated.

"I just . . . never mind. Sorry to bother you." George waved him off and took a step back. From past experience George knew that when the guy was this far gone, he talked endless gibberish. George did not want to subject himself to that. He'd find another way.

The blinds snapped shut and George could hear the guy moving for the door.

"I'll come back!" George shouted through the closed door. "I gotta run." The door flew open before he could get any farther.

"Come on in, buddy," the super said as he dusted the remnants of what looked like Doritos off his wrinkled T-shirt. "Got some brewskies in the fridge and the Dodgers are playing the Giants."

"Tempting, thanks. But I'm on call," George lied. "I have an issue with my sink, but it can wait."

Those were the magic words to get the super to go back inside. He stumbled back a step. "Yeah, best if I take a look at that kinda thing in the daylight anyway." Clearly, the last thing he wanted to do was handle a job. "But stop by anytime to shoot the shit, whatever . . ." The guy was weaving on his feet in an effort to keep his balance.

"Okay. I will, for sure. But not now. Thanks. Gotta run."

George headed back to his apartment but slowed down as he passed Sal's door. Thinking, *Just in case,* George walked over and tried the knob. No luck. It was locked. George continued on to his own apartment, fretting.

Once, when he'd lost his own keys, he had climbed the fence and jumped the lock on his sliding door. It would be pretty easy to do the same thing for Sal's apartment. And it would give him something to do rather than sit and stew. It was the least he could do. It wasn't like the man was going to care if he broke in.

George headed out of his apartment. He looked around to make sure he was alone. The coast was clear. He stepped past the anemic shrubs that ringed the outside of the fence and put his hands on top of the wooden structure. It was a little loose, like everything else around the complex, but it seemed sturdy enough to hold him. He hoisted himself up and swung his legs over. Unfortunately it was dark on the other side, and he landed on a potted plant, tipping it over on its side. In the process he lost his balance and fell, hitting the side of the fence hard, tilting it outward at an odd angle. He scrambled to his feet, shaken by the fall, perspiring in the heat of the night while trying to catch his breath.

Damn! Didn't see that coming!

He peered over the now-leaning fence and scanned the courtyard area. There was still no sign of anyone about. He was fairly sure the noise had gone undetected. He looked down at the pot fragments and clumps of dirt that had spilled out of it. In the dark it was hard to tell for sure, but it looked like Sal had been growing tomatoes in it. Not anymore. He pushed the fragments into the patio corner with his foot and then tried to pull the fence to its original position. No luck. And pulling it made a lot of noise. He'd try to deal with it later from the opposite side.

George tried the glass sliding door. It was locked, but it was an older model, so all he had to do was lift the sliding panel up to disengage the latch.

A moment later George was inside the apartment, waiting for his eyes to adjust to the dark. He didn't feel at all comfortable turning on the lights. He felt like a burglar. A thud from above made him freeze, then he realized it was just the tenants in the apartment upstairs moving around. He had a flashlight app on his phone. Until now he had only used it to read menus in dark restaurants, but now he flipped it on. It threw a strong but concentrated beam of pure white light through the phone's camera flash feature.

He panned the light across the room, wondering where Sal would have kept his personal phone book. He moved into the kitchen, searching the counter below the wall-mounted landline. Nothing. He methodically worked his way through the kitchen, pulling out drawers and digging through them. They were filled with papers, but there was no particular order. Sal must have saved every piece of paper he ever received. George found an address book and was encouraged, only to see that it was brand-new, with no entries at all.

He returned to the living room, checking the coffee and end tables. No luck there, either. All that was left were the small bedroom and tiny bathroom. In the bedroom he found a number of magazines, old newspapers, and letters. He groaned but, having come this far, steeled himself to go through it all, hoping he might find a letter from one of the sisters. For one who was so meticulous about his car, Sal didn't seem to mind that his apartment was a haphazard mess.

George carried all the material over to the bed. Holding the phone with the flashlight in his left hand, he began rapidly shuffling through it. Nothing. His eyes shifted to the nightstand. There was a television remote, the latest issue of *Car World*, a book about the Civil War, and . . . aha! A worn address book!

The sound of a dog barking outside startled George. He sat still and listened. He heard it again and relaxed, recognizing it as coming from out on the street, not from the courtyard. He reached for the address book, but stopped his hand in midair. He heard another, more disturbing noise. It sounded as if the door to the apartment was opening slowly. A chill ran down George's spine.

With his heart pounding, George started to stand up when a blinding light hit him in the face. A second later another bright light hit him from outside the window.

"Freeze!" The command came from a disembodied male voice.

George froze, not from the command but from sheer terror. In the next instant the bedroom's overhead light flipped on, flooding the room.

"Hold it right there!" ordered a uniformed LAPD policeman standing in the doorway, his firearm pointed at George, who had dropped the phone. "Hands in the air!"

With great effort, as if his muscles were refusing to function, George raised his hands. They were visibly trembling.

"I got him!" the policeman yelled to his partner in the courtyard. "Get your ass in here on the double!"

The officer in the bedroom advanced toward George. "Drop to the ground, facedown! Spread your arms and legs! Now!"

George obeyed and immediately felt a sharp pain in his back as the officer's knee pressed into it. A moment later the second officer charged into the room. He grabbed George's wrists, cuffed them behind his back, and quickly patted him down. "He's clean!" The two officers roughly hauled George to his feet.

George stood by the police cruiser at the rear of his apartment complex. The uniformed officer who had apprehended George was looking down at his smartphone, taking notes while he interviewed George. He had George's driver's license along with his hospital ID tucked between the two of his fingers holding the phone.

"And how long did you say you lived here?" the policeman inquired.

"A bit more than three years," George answered. His voice was tremulous from the adrenaline still coursing through his system and his cognition was not what it should have been, but otherwise he had recovered for the most part. He was now feeling indignant about how he was being treated.

A small group of bystanders, many in sleepwear, were watching the proceedings. George looked vainly for Zee but didn't see him. Instead he recognized an older woman in pajamas among the group who lived up on the second floor.

"Mrs. Bernstein!" George called out to her. She frowned and looked away. George turned his attention back to the cop. "You don't want to tape this, too?"

The policeman looked up. "Pardon me?"

"Just wondering why you're not taping this. I was recently told by an officer that details can be forgotten if you're not careful." George angled his face down to try and read the cop's phone. "At least I don't think you're taping this."

The cop stared at him. George knew he was coming off as a smart-ass, which wasn't his intention, but it was hard to stop. The whole episode felt surreal.

"Sorry. It's just that one of your colleagues was interviewing me earlier today and he . . ." George trailed off, realizing that he was digging himself into a deeper hole.

"You were interviewed by another police officer earlier today?"

George backpedaled, getting nervous. "Yes. But not because I did anything wrong. It was right after Sal's car crash, which I'm certain you have heard about. Sal's the neighbor whose apartment you found me in." George nodded down toward the IDs that the officer had between his fingers. "I'm a radiology resident at L.A. University Medical Center and your colleague was trying to put together a picture of what had happened."

"What *did* happen?"

"Sal—Mr. DeAngelis—apparently got confused and crashed his car and killed himself. I guess. I mean, that's what appears to have happened. He had Alzheimer's and multiple problems. Anyway, I wanted to try to help by getting in touch with the two sisters whom I had met some time ago, to let them know what had happened. I was looking for their contacts."

"So you broke into a neighbor's apartment at night to get in touch with a dead man's sisters?" The policeman smiled sarcastically.

George opened his mouth to respond, then stopped.

"Look, I just wanted to call Mr. DeAngelis's siblings and let them know he died today. Is that a crime?" George said.

"The way you went about it is. You couldn't have asked the building manager to let you in?"

"Ha! I tried enlisting the super's help but . . . The man has a drinking problem, in case you hadn't noticed."

George and the officer looked across the way to where the second officer was interviewing the super. The man was still having trouble standing. He kept leaning against the building before pulling himself up straight and crossing his arms in front of him in an attempt to appear sober.

"And I leave for work early in the morning before he gets up," George continued. "Look, I didn't think it would be all that big a deal. I have the exact same apartment, and I've gotten into mine through the sliders a number of times when I forgot my keys. I thought I'd just go in, grab the phone numbers, make the call, and that would be it."

"And you didn't trust the proper authorities to make those calls?"

"Listen!" George said, his voice progressively rising.

"The fact of the matter is that I don't think anyone was told about the sisters. I had mentioned it earlier today to the detective who talked to me, but I had heard through a friend that during the evening news it was stated the victim had no family. And I was told earlier that I was listed as the patient's contact person in case of emergency. Just me! Tonight I realized someone had to try to get a hold of the sisters. I was only trying to help." By the time George finished, he was practically yelling.

The second police officer stopped talking with the super and looked over at George. The small crowd of neighbors and passersby went quiet, too.

"Sorry," George said to the cop. "It's been an emotional day."

With a look of exasperation, the officer turned George around. Without saying anything further, he unlocked the handcuffs, setting George free.

Trudging back to his apartment, George realized that he had narrowly succeeded in talking his way out of being arrested. The super being so obviously drunk had helped. Still, George was furious with himself. What the hell had he been thinking? Back inside his apartment, he again threw himself onto his sofa, thinking that he had to get a grip.

18

It was a busy morning for George in the ER. The department was jammed with patients and the construction crew. The heat wave just made things worse. Patients suffering from heatstroke and heat exhaustion were streaming in, and there had also been an uptick in heart attacks and respiratory problems. The high temperatures also brought out the infamous L.A. road rage. A couple of fender benders had resulted in a shoot-out and a knife fight. Victims of both were currently being treated in the trauma rooms. The result was that George and Carlos were overwhelmed with radiology studies. Of the six possible stroke cases, they had determined that five were in fact positive, requiring immediate medical intervention. The sixth case turned out to be an ophthalmic migraine masquerading as a stroke. There had also been two head traumas. On one, the CT scan showed a subdural hematoma, requiring immediate surgery. The only good news was that George was so busy, he didn't have time to think about Sal's death, Tarkington's passing, or his own near arrest. He'd been holed up in the imaging room since seven thirty, working nonstop.

Just before eleven, Carlos returned from a quick coffee break to find George surveying a new batch of radiological studies.

The first was a chest film of a driver in a recent accident whose airbag did not deploy.

"What do you see?" George asked Carlos.

"A fracture of the clavicle . . . and several ribs." Carlos pointed to the fractures in turn.

"Anything else?"

"There's a small amount of fluid in the lungs."

George was impressed. Carlos was picking up the nuances quickly. "Good. Let's go on to the next case."

"I saw Dr. Hanson out there in the ER," Carlos said as he brought up the next image. It was a pelvis.

"Really! What was he up to?" George asked. As Clayton was head of the teaching program in radiology, the residents generally liked to know when he was around, since they knew they were being evaluated on a month-to-month basis. They would alert each other when he was lurking nearby, usually by tweet or text. But George was more sensitized than usual, since Clayton had showed up in the ER only the day before.

"It seemed like he came in to talk with Debbie Waters.

He just ignored me and asked Debbie if he could have a private word with her, even though she was obviously busy."

"Is he still out there?" George asked, unsure if he should be concerned or not. Under the circumstances, his talking in private with Debbie was a tad worrisome.

Carlos shrugged. "He was when I came in here."

George stood up, cracked the door, and looked outside. Sure enough, Clayton was leaning against the main desk, folder in hand, having a prolonged tête-à-tête with Debbie. Now, that was particularly unusual behavior in the middle of the day, especially with the level of confusion swirling around them. Vaguely, George wondered if they might be resurrecting their own rumored relationship. But if that was the case, it was even more unusual that they would do so in plain sight. The one good thing was that he couldn't imagine that they could be talking about him for so long.

At that instant both Clayton's and Debbie's heads swung around and seemed to stare in George's direction. George pulled back, alarmed that they might be able to see him spying on them. He quickly let the door close and went back to where he had been sitting.

"This is a seventy-eight-year-old woman who fell in the shower," Carlos said, beginning where he had left off, but then changed the subject. "Hey, what's this about Clayton Hanson liking the ladies? Is it true? It's been tweeted around us first-year residents, particularly to warn the women."

George laughed. He noticed it was the first time Carlos left off the "Dr." in referring to Clayton. He was already loosening up. "I think I'll take the Fifth on that issue," said George, directing their attention back to the film. "Let's get back to work. What's your take here?"

At that moment Clayton opened the door and stepped in. Although he had appeared relaxed at the ER's central desk when George had looked out at him, now he seemed anxious and rushed, as if whatever he had been discussing with Debbie had gotten him fired up.

"Can I have a quick word, George?"

Carlos immediately stood up. "Excuse me. I need a bathroom break anyway." He quickly left the room.

George felt his pulse quicken. He had no idea what was coming but feared that Clayton might have learned of his near arrest. The administration did not take kindly to residents having run-ins with the law.

But Clayton just lowered his voice and asked, "Did you have time to chat up Kelley?" He took Carlos's seat and leaned forward.

"No," George said, bewildered. Why was that even remotely important enough to come in and interrupt a reading session?

"A little slow on the draw, are we?" Clayton teased, with eyebrows raised.

"I have to wait for the right moment, and with the crash and all it probably won't happen today either. I actually haven't even seen her. A lot of the routine ER visits are being seen over in the clinic building with the construction going on." George would have liked to tell Clayton to ease up on his efforts to perk up George's nonexistent social life, but he didn't have the courage.

"If you don't jump on this, you'll be losing out possibly, I've heard, to a couple of hot-ticket first-year orthopedic residents from Harvard." Clayton laughed as he gave George a light jab to the shoulder. The laugh sounded false, like it was forced.

George didn't answer, restraining himself from asking Clayton what he had been doing in the morgue.

"Have you at least followed up with Debbie Waters? The more I've thought about it, you would really have some fun with her."

"Debbie's not interested in me. My sense is that she's after bigger game than a resident."

"Not true! She's just being professional. She doesn't want any more hospital gossip. She got her fill of that when we dated a few years back. I was just talking with her, and she confessed that she'd been eyeing you for months. She's been hoping you would show a little interest."

George laughed. "Yesterday I tried to get her attention, but she pretty much just ignored me."

"That is not true. She thinks you're quite handsome."

George rolled his eyes.

"Hey, give it a shot," Clayton persisted. "As a personal favor to me. I mean, after I talked you up and everything."

"Does she know about Kasey?"

"Of course. She has a lot of respect for you being serious with someone with problematic medical issues."

"Is that it? She feels sorry for me?"

"Hell no. It's respect, not sympathy. Jesus, lighten up. She'd like to be your friend."

"Are you bullshitting me? If you are, I have to tell you that I'm a bit vulnerable right now."

"Swear to God. I'll go out there right this minute and bring her back here to the radiology reading room so she can tell you herself."

George was horrified. "No! I'll figure out my own way to talk with her."

"Okay. All right. I'm going to count on it, so don't be shy. It's not healthy to be isolated like you are. Even considering the, you know, the tragedy and all. Like I said, it's not like you have to marry Debbie, for Chrissake. Just get out. Pretend you're normal."

"I appreciate the concern, but my ego has taken a few hits lately."

"I wish I was back in my twenties." Clayton got to his feet and opened the door to the ER. "No grass would be growing under my feet. I can tell you that."

Carlos, who had been waiting outside, strolled back in, passing Clayton with a nod and suck-up smile. Clayton ignored him.

"What was that all about?" Carlos inquired, nodding toward the door that was settling into its jamb.

"You wouldn't believe it if I told you. Let's get these films read."

Carlos revived the monitor. It had gone to sleep.

As the image of the X-ray came up, George found himself marveling over the absurdity of the head of the radiology resident program worrying about George's social life. But be that as it may, he began to wonder how he might approach Debbie, having now essentially promised Clayton that he would.

"Do you remember this case?" Carlos asked.

"I think so. A seventy-eight-year-old woman who fell in the shower, injuring her right hip. So what do you see?"

"I see a fracture," Carlos said.

"That's a start," George teased. "Give me a full description!"

A half hour later they were caught up. Done for the morning, Carlos was ready to grab lunch before the noon radiology conference. "I'm heading over to the cafeteria. Want to join me?" he asked.

"No, thanks. I'm not hungry," George lied. He was hungry, but he had made a decision to speak to Debbie Waters. He felt some anxiety kicking in, but better now than never. Prepared as he was ever going to be, he stood up and wandered out into the ER proper.

It took some time for his eyes to adjust to the glare from the bright light in the ER with the L.A. midday sun streaming in through the windows, including the new ones that had just been installed. Debbie was at the main desk as usual. George could hear her snappy commands from where he was standing. He wandered over to the in-box and pretended to be leafing through the various cases. It was what he had instructed Carlos to do whenever there was some free time, in order to be familiar with the clinical status of the patients before looking at their films.

"Nothing to do?" Debbie demanded sharply. George panicked for a second, then realized she was lambasting a couple of LPNs. "Trauma Room Eight needs to be cleaned up," Debbie barked.

"That's not our job," one of the LPNs objected.

Debbie was ready for them. "The fuck it isn't. You'll be out the door if you two don't pull your weight. We're swamped, in case you haven't noticed."

The LPN who initially objected opened her mouth again but then thought better of it and huffed off with her coworker. Debbie's language, while crass, got the job done.

"Damn bitches," Debbie cursed under her breath, but was loud enough for George to hear. He stole another glance in her direction. Her eyes strafed across his face before going back down to a bunch of ER charts in front of her. She glanced up a second later and recognized George. She even smiled.

"Can I help you?" she asked with a trace of solicitation in her voice.

"Uh. Maybe," George said, screwing up his courage. "I was just speaking with Dr. Hanson . . ."

"Don't tell me he went ahead and told you that I wanted to . . . Never mind. Now I'm embarrassed." But she didn't look it.

George cleared his throat. "There's a . . . there's no reason to be embarrassed. I've been admiring the way you're able to run the department and keep order. Even with all of the unexpected . . ." George nodded toward the construction crew working on the LED display board.

She smiled at the compliment and leaned forward and lowered her voice. "Thank you."

"You're welcome." He glanced around. Serendipitously he seemed to have her attention without anyone else noticing. That is, if he didn't count a young boy of about ten sitting a few feet away. The boy was holding an ice pack over a knot on his forehead while his mother was texting someone. The kid smiled knowingly. He might be young, but he was picking up the signals. George winked, then turned back to Debbie.

"I was wondering . . . if maybe you would like to meet for a drink one night. I mean, I know you are busy and all—"

"How about tonight?" she interrupted. "I get off at four, and I could meet you at six."

George paused with his mouth open, surprised. "Okay. Great!" Damn, that turned out to be a lot easier than he thought! "Six it is."

She smiled. "How about the Whiskey Blue over at the W? It's close enough to walk, but they have valet parking if you prefer."

"Perfect," George said. "See you this evening."

"I'll look forward to it."

George waved bye to her as he headed back to the reading room. He was feeling better than he had in months. He'd have to remember to thank Clayton for prodding him out of his doldrums.

19

George followed Carlos into the tiered conference room carrying the remains of a vending machine lunch.

"That shit'll kill you," Carlos said.

"That's what I hear. You know where I can find a good doctor?" George joked. After his little chat with Debbie, George's appetite had returned, but he realized he didn't have enough time to wait in line at the cafeteria. He wondered if Kasey would approve of his going out with her. He guessed she certainly wouldn't think Debbie was his type of girl. Nor did he. There was an in-your-face toughness about Debbie that conflicted with what George had found so appealing about Kasey's warmth and generosity. But at least he wouldn't have to wonder what to say. Debbie wasn't one to allow lulls in the conversation.

George took a seat near the back of the conference room near Carlos, who introduced George to some of his fellow first-year friends. They plied George with questions about the daily meeting schedule, and George explained that generally there were three a day: seven A.M., noon, and four thirty P.M., and they should consider them mandatory. If they didn't show up, they had better have a good excuse. He added that every other Thursday, the noon conference would be a didactic lecture in physics that was a particularly must-attend event.

As he finished talking, Claudine walked into the room and made her way over. Carlos noticed her and tapped George on the knee to get his attention.

"Hey, Claudine!" George grinned. "Take a seat. Have you met everybody?" George waved toward the bevy of first-year residents.

She didn't smile back. "Did you hear about the two patients we saw on Monday?"

"What two?" George asked.

"Greg Tarkington and Claire Wong."

"I know about Tarkington. I was in the ER when he was brought in DOA."

"The same thing happened to Claire Wong this morning."

George was shocked. "You mean she died?"

Claudine nodded her head solemnly. "She was brought in and declared dead on arrival."

"I was in the ER all morning and didn't hear anything about it." George shook his head. Tarkington had been a shock. Tarkington and Wong was more than a shock.

It seemed like a statistical improbability. What the hell was going on?

"It spooked me," Claudine said. "We MRI'd both two days ago. It just feels so odd. I mean, I suspected that they were both terminal, but having them die within forty-eight hours . . ."

"Both had bad diseases," George replied, as if such a comment could explain the two unexpected deaths.

"It makes me feel responsible somehow," Claudine said, "even though I know that's not rational. Still. They seemed so normal and healthy and probably would still be if we hadn't done the studies. I'm afraid we opened up a can of worms."

George, aware of the first-years watching and listening, said reassuringly, "You have to remember, the diseases in both cases were remarkably aggressive, Claudine. Their deaths are surprising, but not unexpected."

"Okay. Just wanted to tell you." Claudine nodded absently and walked off to find a seat.

George felt momentarily addled. First, about openly dismissing the oddness of the two deaths coming so close together. Second, because those deaths were temporally and most likely causally related to the MRIs they did. His reflex motivation was to make Claudine feel better, even though he should have let her feelings initiate a dialogue so that they could all share their feelings. The trouble was that this new bit of news struck directly into his own sensitivities, reawakening his paranoia that death was stalking him; that he was personally responsible, not the MRIs.

"That was weird," Carlos whispered to George. "I

can't believe she really thinks that MRIs could have caused two deaths."

"Well, both MRIs suggested cancer recurrence," George said. "The patients had probably heard the results from their oncologists. With all that they had been through, that had to be devastating news."

"Yeah, but . . ."

"Listen, I don't want to talk about it anymore at the moment. Do you mind?"

"Of course not. Sorry."

"You don't have to be sorry," George assured him.

George didn't want to dwell on these thoughts. Instead he forced himself to think that at six P.M. he was going to be at the Whiskey Blue Bar like a normal person, chatting with a very confident and attractive woman.

At that moment Clayton descended the central aisle. As he walked, his eyes darted around the room. For a brief second his eyes locked on to George's, and he shot him a thumbs-up.

George smiled and nodded out of courtesy but was confused as to what Clayton meant by it. The only thing he could think of was that somehow Clayton had already learned that he and Debbie were planning to meet over at the W Hotel bar that evening. *My God!* George thought. *There are truly no secrets in the hospital.*

20

George had a better time with Debbie at the Whiskey Blue than he had anticipated. He couldn't believe three and a half hours had passed since they arrived. She was the perfect distraction, even if a bit rough around the edges. She had a smoker's voice, but it fit like a glove with her colorful, sailor trash talk, and she had an opinion, a strong opinion, about almost everything. They met a number of her friends, including several of the bartenders, who greeted her by name. It was apparent she was a regular customer. It was all very social and L.A. A few B-list celebs came in, too, and Debbie even knew a couple of them. There was nonstop chatter about all sorts of superficial subjects and nothing about medicine or, most important, death.

Along with the lively conversation there were a lot of drinks, all on Debbie's tab, which she insisted on under no uncertain terms, and she did the ordering. George wasn't about to make an issue of it. The only problem was that George had such a good time, he didn't keep track of how much liquor he was throwing back, and ended up quite drunk.

Debbie on the other hand just sipped and was quite sober. George hadn't noticed. He was having a ball, and the only thing he had had to eat was some salted nuts and dried wasabi peas.

During the course of the evening, Debbie related that she had completed her nurse's training at the University of Colorado, but had come to L.A. as soon as she had her degree and had worked at the University Medical Center ever since. "I started out in the ER, and I'm still there," she said with obvious pride.

When George asked about her personal life, she was happy to fill him in. She told George she'd never been married, had dated a few of the staff doctors, including Clayton for a time, but she didn't want to talk about them, adding that she preferred to date people outside of the medical profession. George agreed with her on that issue, but said he hoped to see her again.

Finally Debbie looked at her watch. It was after nine thirty. "This place is getting so damn crowded. And this girl has to get up in the morning."

Even through the fog of booze, George realized she wanted to leave. "Time to go home?"

"Yes. Where do you live? Close by?"

George gulped. Damn, she was direct. "Uh . . . yeah. A few blocks . . ."

"Let's go back to your place and decompress. All these people . . . I need a little quiet time."

George felt a spark of panic. He knew he wasn't ready to sleep with anyone, and he didn't want her to see his crummy apartment. Groping for a reply, he said, "Well . . . my housekeeper canceled today and—"

"Oh, come on. I don't care about that. And, besides, I don't want you driving tonight. Is your car here?"

George had to think. "Left it with the valet." He produced his parking ticket.

Debbie snatched it away. "I'll get this thing validated and drive you home, then catch a cab from there."

George realized that she had a point about driving, particularly when he stood up. He could tell he'd drunk way more than he should have. Her concern bumped his regard for her up a couple of notches. "Okay. Good idea. Thanks."

The ride to George's apartment wasn't more than five minutes, and Debbie spent the time quizzing George about his friends outside of the hospital. The relative lack of which was embarrassing to admit, but he did. What he didn't say was that the friends he had had been Kasey's.

"A smart, handsome man like you should have loads of friends. I mean, I know about your fiancée, but it is time that you let the past be the past."

George didn't want to discuss Kasey, mainly because he himself was trying not to think about her. And then, before he knew what he was doing, he found himself talking about Pia Grazdani and his ridiculous infatuation with her in medical school. He couldn't stop himself. In that vein, he even launched into what his Pia infatuation did to his relationship with Paula. It was as if all the alcohol had been a kind of truth serum.

To her credit, Debbie seemed both interested and sympathetic. "Don't give yourself a lot of shit about that. Hell, I've experienced the same kind of self-destructive relationship myself."

"Really?" George asked, but he still wished he had kept his mouth shut.

They arrived at his apartment, and George got out his cell phone with some difficulty. "I'll call you a cab. Is there some company you prefer?"

"Hold off on the cab. I said I wanted to relax for a few minutes. Let's go inside." Before George could respond, she was out of the car, hand on her hip, waiting for George.

George launched into another face-saving apartment-apology campaign as they were about to cross the threshold of his front door. "I've been meaning to do something with the place, but a residency is so time-consuming—"

"Sweetie, I don't mind a bit. Please quit worrying," Debbie said, pausing to look around after entering. "You're right. It's a piece of shit. But whatever, I don't care." She spotted George's iPod dock, fished her own phone out, and put on some music, cranking up the volume. George sat on the couch and watched as she took a joint from the bag.

"Wanna get high?" She didn't wait for a response and immediately lit up. "I so need this. After all the crazy shit in the ER this week." She took a hit from the joint and passed it to George. George hesitated. The last time he smoked weed was when he was an undergrad, but he didn't want to risk putting her off. *What the hell*, he thought, and took a drag, inhaling deeply. He started coughing immediately.

"You okay, sweetie?"

"Yeah. Wrong pipe."

A loud thumping boomed through George's apartment wall. It was the wall common with Joe's apartment. George realized who it was and burst out laughing. Joe the Actor was pissed at the noise! In light of all the times George had been disturbed by Joe's wild orgies, it made George's evening.

"Why are you laughing?" Debbie said, laughing, too. The weed was kicking in for both of them.

"Because," George giggled, "he keeps me up all the freaking time with an endless stream of hookups."

They continued laughing until Debbie said she wanted something to drink. Something alcoholic.

"I have some Jack Daniel's. Will that work?"

"Absolutely." Debbie reached over and turned up the volume on the iPod speakers while George went into his kitchen to retrieve the liquor and some glasses. "No ice! No ice!" Debbie called after him. "Straight and neat!"

George wasn't really up for more booze but poured a couple of drinks anyway and brought them back to the living room.

Debbie was dancing to the music. George stopped and

gawked. She caught him looking and smiled, putting her hand out for the drink.

Debbie sipped her bourbon. She was suddenly serious despite the pot and the alcohol. "Okay, so what's the deal with this neighbor of yours who crashed into the ER?"

"He was just a friend." George didn't want to discuss Sal any more than he wanted to discuss Kasey.

"Ironic, huh? That he died right next to you and you were friends with him."

"We were more acquaintances than friends," George hedged. "The guy was lonely. I felt sorry for him." George felt guilty distancing himself from Sal.

Debbie kept prodding for details about Sal's wild ride to the hospital, then began asking questions about what George thought about iDoc and Amalgamated Healthcare. She confided that Clayton advised her to put money into Amalgamated and wondered what George thought.

George's mind was reeling from the alcohol and pot. With some difficulty he told Debbie that Clayton advised him to do the same, but it didn't matter, because he didn't have enough money to invest in anything. George then tried to change the subject, but Debbie was persistent. She kept bringing the conversation back to Sal's story and what George thought about iDoc.

Suddenly all the alcohol and marijuana caught up to George. The giggles had been replaced by pervading sleepiness. Debbie hardly seemed to notice and switched to what George thought about iDoc's helping Sal by taking the burden of insulin out of his hands.

George made a huge effort to marshal his thoughts and answer. He made it a point to sit up straight and take a deep breath: "iDoc undoubtedly helped the guy, not only with his diabetes but with all his medical problems. iDoc was *someone* whom Sal could talk to whenever he wanted, which was pretty damn often because of his Alzheimer's. Prior to iDoc, Sal used to bombard me with medical questions every time he saw me. That stopped with iDoc."

"Let me ask you this: Do you think iDoc added to Sal's problems in any way?"

George thought about that one before answering. "As far as I'm concerned, iDoc was a big plus for Sal." Despite his best intentions he couldn't suppress a mighty yawn. "I'm sorry!" he added. And he was.

Debbie could see that George was having trouble keeping his eyes open. Still she continued. "Is there anything about the situation that bothers you?"

"Well, yes!" George said, trying desperately to think. "One is that Sal's sisters haven't been told of his death as far as I know, and two is all this talk that Sal crashed into the ER to commit suicide. He liked life, and his car, as silly as that might sound, too much to commit suicide."

"I heard he had been taking medication for depression."

George grimaced. "People get prescribed all kinds of things they don't need. You know that. Anyway, I never saw him act depressed."

"The advancing Alzheimer's. Losing his faculties. That could have made him contemplate suicide. I heard he had self-inflicted wounds, apparently done while driving."

"I heard about those wounds. It confused me enough to go down to the morgue to check them out for myself."

Debbie looked surprised that he had made that effort. "I've never been down there."

"Most people haven't. I don't advise it."

"What did you find out?"

"Nothing. I wasn't allowed to see the body, supposedly because of HIPAA rules. That seemed weird, because I am a resident. Strangely, though, I saw Clayton down there."

"What was he doing?" She set her drink down and eyed him closely.

George didn't respond, losing his battle trying to stay awake. In slow motion he sagged back and his head flopped to the side.

Debbie was not to be denied. She gave George's shoulder a shake. He revived with some difficulty. His eyes were glassy.

"You didn't answer," Debbie said. "What was Clayton doing in the morgue?"

George licked his lips. His eyelids were fluttering in an attempt to keep them open. With effort, he forced himself to sit up straight. "I have no idea. I did find it rather strange at the time."

"So you didn't see Sal's body?"

"No. But let me ask you a question: Do you know which ER doctor was in charge of Sal's case?"

"Why do you want to know?"

"I wanted . . ." He stopped and his eyes closed for a couple of seconds. "I wanted to ask why they thought some wounds were self-inflicted."

"What's your opinion about what iDoc will do for your career?"

"Huh?" George was having trouble organizing his thoughts about such an oddball question coming out of the blue. Debbie was staring at him expectantly.

"I guess I'm worried that I might end up working for a health insurance company. I worry—"

"But you think iDoc is perfect for people like Sal," Debbie interrupted. "With all his medical problems and then with prostate cancer added to the list."

"Sal didn't have prostate cancer."

"Yes, he did. It was stage-three, small cell."

"I never heard that," George said, reviving to a degree. He was surprised. Sal had never mentioned it when he'd told him about all his other health issues.

"It was only discovered recently," Debbie said. "I can tell you from my perspective that iDoc is going to be a godsend. It's going to keep a lot of people out of the ER who shouldn't be there."

George started to tell her that he was not going to be able to stay awake for another minute, but he didn't have to. She checked the time and jumped up.

"Damn it all," she blurted. "Do you know what time it is? And it's a school night. This girl has to get home and into bed ASAP."

George felt a wave of relief as she used her cell to call a taxi. After that, she got her stuff together while George watched.

"Thank you for the great evening," she said. "You don't have to get up. I can see myself out."

He stood up anyway with the intention of at least walking her to the door, but had to lean on the arm of the couch for support.

"Stay where you are," she ordered. "You need to get to bed right away yourself."

"I agree." He put his hand out for a shake. She smiled and gave it a pump along with an air kiss to the cheek. A moment later she was gone.

George stumbled into his bedroom. He decided he'd just lie down for a few minutes before taking off his clothes . . .

21

The next day George arrived at the medical center with a raging hangover. He couldn't remember all the details of the previous evening, but he hoped he hadn't made an ass of himself. Coffee was what he needed. He filled a fresh cup and sat down with Carlos to go over the films taken the previous night. There were a lot, but despite a big thumper of a headache, George was determined to be thorough and accurate.

Halfway through, they came across a film of a wrist that had been definitely misread as being normal. The patient had been released untreated despite there being a fracture of the navicular bone. George pointed it out to Carlos and explained that it was easy for doctors not trained in radiology to miss it. George passed the information on to the head of the ER so that the patient could be tracked down and asked to return to the hospital for a cast.

After finishing going over everything, including CT scans, Carlos left to find out what was "cooking" in the ER, while George sat with his head down on the desk and nursed his hangover. He downed a couple more ibuprofen tablets, happy to have had some quiet time.

Feeling reasonably together, he walked into the ER and approached the central desk, where Debbie as usual was ordering the staff around. Obviously there was no hangover holding her down. He tried to catch her eye, but it was difficult. Lots of things were going on with some major trauma on its way in by ambulance. The sirens already could be heard approaching.

George went around the back of the main desk, where he wasn't more than five or six feet away from Debbie. He stood and waited. And waited. Just when he thought she might be intentionally ignoring him, she glanced over and nodded at him before going back to her work. She *had* been ignoring him. The nod wasn't what he had expected. He didn't know what to expect, but it was more than he got.

Oh, well, George thought. He tried to attribute the rebuff to her preoccupation running the ER. But nonetheless the snub nagged at him. Had he done or said anything that had upset her? He had certainly been drunk. He could easily imagine how he might have offended her considering the state he was in.

Suddenly, she jumped up and rushed past him. *What*

the hell? Then he realized that she was responding to a
call from the orderlies down in the major trauma rooms
waiting to receive the incoming severely injured patients.
He was about to walk off when he looked down at the
papers Debbie had spread out on her desk. A familiar item
pushed into one of the cubbyholes caught his eye. It was
a broken smartphone in an electric-orange case. George
could see that the phone's display screen was riddled with
cracks. It was Sal's phone! The sight of it felt like a little
beacon calling to him from his much-maligned friend.
He picked it up and tried to turn it on: nothing. It needed
to be charged or it was broken. Most likely it was both.

George glanced around. No one was paying him any
attention. He made a sudden decision and pocketed the
phone. It would probably end up in the trash anyway. With
his prize tucked away in his pocket, he retreated back to
the protective environment of the imaging room. He was
reaching in his pocket for the phone when Carlos burst in.

"We got a slew of major trauma cases on their way in,"
he shouted.

"Okay, ease up," George said. "It'll sort itself out.
There's nothing we can do to be more prepared than we
already are. Did you alert the technicians?"

"Yes, and they have both portable machines outside
the trauma rooms."

"Perfect. We're ready to rumble."

"But there is a pregnant woman who just came in with
severe abdominal distress—acute pain with vomiting and
diarrhea. Waters told me to organize an ultrasound stat."

"We'll have to wait until after the major trauma is under

control," George said. "Which ER physician is handling the woman?"

"A newbie. Her name is Kelley."

George nodded. At least he'd be able to say that he talked to the woman if Clayton asked, but he wasn't sure what he was going to say about Debbie if Clayton asked, as George assumed he would. Friendly last night, Ice Queen today—that is, *if* he was reading her right.

Two minutes later the trauma cases came rolling in: nine victims from a four-car, one-motorcycle wreck on the I-405 Freeway. There was a flurry of activity to deal with them all, including one case of major thoracic trauma requiring tracheal intubation and a chest tube. The portable X-ray machines, all the X-ray rooms, and even the CT room were needed. Despite the commotion there were several occasions when Debbie could have spoken with George, but she didn't. George couldn't figure out if this was intentional or if she was just preoccupied.

Eventually, when the excitement died down, George and Carlos took the opportunity to catch their breath in the suddenly quiet imaging room. For a while it had been like a train station, with ER residents and surgeons being apprised of the radiological findings. Suddenly a shaft of light intruded on their peace.

"What the hell now!" George demanded, the light exacerbating his headache, which had not quite disappeared. He turned to look at the newcomer and saw the silhouette of a tall, slim woman in scrubs.

"I'm sorry. I don't mean to interrupt. When you have a moment, I'd like to discuss a patient with you."

George saw it was Kelley Babcock. "No! Wait," he said, rising out of his chair. "I'm sorry. That sounded rude. We just finished a full slate of trauma imaging and . . . well, you know. Anyway, how can we help you?"

We have a patient six or seven months pregnant with severe abdominal distress," Kelley said, leading George and Carlos down the ER hallway. George noticed that she had precise, handwritten notes clipped to the patient's file, which she had downloaded and printed out. She had done her homework. In addition, she herself looked organized and meticulous with her hair in a ponytail. In contrast to all the other ER residents, some of whom seemed to revel in looking as if they had been through a war, with blood-soaked scrubs, Kelley kept hers clean and fresh, changing them whenever the need arose.

She was acting as the patient's emergency room physician, although a more senior resident was supervising. She told George that there had already been a surgical consult, which had ruled out an acute abdomen that would have required emergency surgery. With that off the table, the working diagnosis was viral enteritis.

"The patient is currently being hydrated," Kelley continued, all business. "Before she's discharged, we think her pregnancy should be evaluated, since she had been lost to follow-up. She hasn't been seen in the OB clinic since her initial visit four months ago."

George glanced over the file as they walked. Kelley's

description of the case and what should be done seemed spot-on. George was impressed.

"An OB consult has been called," Kelley continued, "but all the OB residents are tied up with deliveries. According to their recommendation, an ultrasound needs to be done in the interim, which is why I stopped by to see you."

Suddenly George realized he was reading a familiar medical history. He glanced up at the patient's name at the top of the file: Laney Chesney. He recognized it immediately. He had had a past association with the patient and the memory tugged at his heartstrings. She was a juvenile diabetic, just as Kasey had been. But Laney had had a tough life, suffering a traumatic childhood with a drug-addicted single mother. She had run away from home a number of times, ultimately living on the street. George suspected she had supported herself by prostitution and had developed chronic liver disease and a cardiomyopathy.

"I know this patient," George said, holding up the file and coming to a halt. They were still a good distance from the patient's room. Kelley and Carlos stopped alongside him. Flipping through the chart to the radiological studies, he continued, "As I remember, Laney is a particularly endearing girl with huge, sad eyes. She looks about twelve."

"I think that is a fair description," Kelley said. "How do you know her?"

"I did a number of interventional radiology studies to determine the status of her heart," George said. "I remember the outlook wasn't rosy, to say the least."

"Your memory serves you well," Kelley said. "I read over her entire case. Eight months previously she was put on the waiting list for a heart transplant, but because of her liver disease and poorly controlled diabetes, she has a low priority."

"Jesus," George said, glancing back at the echocardiology studies. He remembered feeling very sorry for her. "And on top of it all, she gets herself pregnant. Holy shit!"

"Seems that she's made all the wrong choices," Kelley said, "but it is hard to fault her, considering her social history."

"I suppose there is no need to ask if she is married or has any kind of social support."

"Not married," Kelley responded. "She doesn't even know who the father is. When she was initially seen for her pregnancy she was advised to abort because of her cardiac status, but she categorically refused."

"Maybe it's the only thing that has given meaning to her life," George said.

Kelley nodded. "It's a tragedy for sure. I hope we can help her. As I said earlier, she hasn't been in to see anyone on follow-up for almost four months now. It took the severe abdominal complaints to get her in here."

"That doesn't sound like her. When I was involved, she was always careful about keeping her appointments, particularly because of her diabetes. Do you know why she hasn't been back in?"

"No idea, but maybe the questions about aborting spooked her."

"Didn't you even ask?" George shot back. Losing a

patient like Laney with progressive and demanding medical problems was anathema in an academic care center. The group started walking again.

"No. I haven't asked," Kelley replied. "Good question, though. I should have."

George studied Kelley's face. She didn't seem thin-skinned or defensive, which she could have been, considering his tone. She had confidence: another good trait.

They arrived at Laney's room. She had been moved to one of the back rooms as far away from the rest of the ER as possible, since she would have to wait a significant time before being seen by one of the OB residents. The hope was that she could get some much-needed rest. The ultrasound machine, along with a technician, Shirley Adams, was already on hand. An IV was running into Laney's left arm.

"Laney, this is Dr. Wilson and Dr. Sanchez," Kelley announced. "They will be helping Miss Adams do the ultrasound."

Laney looked up at her visitors, her face brightening.

"We know—" George started.

"—each other already," Laney finished.

George managed a smile. Laney was genuinely relieved to see a familiar face. She was a petite girl with Irish-pale, milky-white skin. The huge belly protruding from such a tiny frame made her appear further along in her pregnancy than six or seven months.

"Promise me that you won't let them take my baby," she said to George straight off. "Promise me!"

"I promise." George was taken aback by her intensity. It was obvious she was terrified, much more scared than when he had done her echocardiogram. "The ultrasound will not hurt the baby, and it's needed for his or her benefit." He explained the procedure, making sure that Carlos heard, as this was his first ultrasound. George then asked why she hadn't followed up with her medical appointments.

"Because I have my own doctor now. He sent me here to the emergency room because he couldn't figure out exactly what was causing my stomach problems."

"What's the doctor's name?"

"I'm not supposed to say."

"Why is that?" George questioned gently.

"I don't know actually."

"I think you should tell us so we can get in touch."

Laney looked from George to Carlos.

"It is important," George persisted. He could not imagine why she didn't want to say.

Laney cleared her throat. "It's called iDoc. I wasn't supposed to tell anyone, but you are doctors, so I guess it is all right."

George rocked back. iDoc? The freaking thing was everywhere. "You're a part of the iDoc beta test?" he asked incredulously.

"I am." She motioned to her shoulder bag on the bedside table. "It's in there. My diabetes is not an issue anymore. And you know how out of whack that was."

"I remember. But I'm amazed that you have iDoc."

"I got it through Medicaid," Laney explained. "I was told that I was lucky; that not many people on Medicaid got it, at least not yet. I like it a lot."

"What exactly are you two talking about?" Kelley asked. "What is iDoc?"

George gave her a very quick description of the iDoc app.

"That's impressive," Kelley said. She sounded sincere but made a somewhat skeptical face to George, out of Laney's line of vision. "Listen! I need to run. I have a full plate out there. Laney, you obviously know that you're in good hands," she said, motioning to George and the others. "I'll be back to check up on you in a bit." Kelley gave Laney's arm a reassuring pat as she left.

"I'll fill you in later," George called after her. Then he turned back to Laney. "This won't be hard for you or your baby." He turned to Shirley and Carlos. "Let's get this done!"

Carlos pulled George aside while the technician got the ultrasound machine up and running next to Laney's bed. "What should I be doing here? I feel like the odd man out."

"Once Shirley starts the study, I want you to handle the probe yourself so you'll have a better feel for how the study is done. Actually doing it will help your interpretation immensely. Just be patient! I felt the same way you did back when I was starting out."

22

Clayton strode into the ER looking for George. When he didn't see him, he went directly into the radiology imaging room. There he cornered another radiology resident who happened to be using the ER imaging room even though he wasn't officially assigned to the ER.

"You know where George Wilson is?"

"I think so. I believe he's performing an ultrasound in the back. Can I help you—"

Clayton walked off without a reply, clearly preoccupied. He went back out to the main desk and got Debbie's attention.

"Could I have a moment to talk with you in private, Miss Waters?" Clayton asked. Although there was a comparative lull, the ER was still busy. The main desk was a beehive of activity.

"Of course, Dr. Hanson," she said, and told one of the other nurses to take over. Debbie led Clayton back into a windowless storeroom and closed the door.

"Well, how was it?" Clayton asked, abandoning any pretense of formality. "As bad as you expected?"

"Pretty much. He's boring. He drinks too much and can't handle his liquor. It was like going out with a frat boy. I'm done with those days, Clayton."

"It couldn't have been all bad."

"Actually, he seems like a nice enough guy. How's that?"

"Better. How much do I owe you for the drinks?"

"Nearly a hundred."

"One hundred! Christ!" Clayton handed over the cash. "You must have drunk up a storm."

"I didn't. He did. And I had to do all the talking."

"He's still grieving," Clayton said impatiently. "His fiancée just died, for God's sake. As far as I know, this was the first time he's gone out. Be a little more sympathetic! More important, what were you able to learn?"

Debbie frowned.

"Okay, I'm sorry," Clayton apologized. "I appreciate your making the effort. Just getting him out was a big positive. Thank you."

"I did it for you. Just remember that."

"I do, but what did you learn? What was his response to DeAngelis's death? Is he taking it in stride or not?"

"The jury's still out. One thing that I did learn was

that he saw you going into the morgue. He was trying to get a look at the body, but he was turned away."

"Shit! That's inconvenient, him seeing me. I didn't see him."

"What were you down there for?" Debbie asked.

"It's not important," Clayton replied. "Administrative stuff."

Debbie shrugged. "There is more. A couple of things are bothering George about his neighbor's death. The first is that he's worried that the dead guy's sisters haven't been notified."

"I'll make sure that happens." Clayton hadn't been aware that DeAngelis had relatives. "What else?"

"The other thing is the gossip about suicide from the 'self-inflicted' wounds."

"Well, that's not so good."

"He also said something about wanting to know which of the ER residents was in charge of DeAngelis's case."

"Did he say why?"

"He said he wanted to inquire about the self-inflicted wounds."

"Did you tell him which ER resident was involved?"

"No, and I don't think he is going to remember about last night. He was three sheets to the wind. Why do you care what he thinks, anyway? I didn't get the impression that he and his neighbor were really friends. They had nothing in common."

"In terms of what you know, less is better, Deb, trust me. Did you guys talk about iDoc?"

"A little. I think everything is okay in that department. He said he thought iDoc was a big plus for DeAngelis."

"Well, that's good," Clayton said. "Listen, I really appreciate your help in this. I want you to continue seeing George socially, to keep track of what he's thinking and doing about DeAngelis's death."

Debbie's eyes narrowed. She wasn't happy. "I thought that this was going to be a onetime mission."

"I need to continue to monitor his mind-set. It's not like I'm asking you to do anything onerous, and I'll pay the tab."

"You promised me *we* would get together! You and me!"

"We will. We will. What about this weekend? It's the Fourth of July holiday. That might work."

She looked at him askance, as if she didn't trust him.

"Just let me look at my schedule, and I'll get back to you. But . . . it is important that you keep tabs on George for me. I want to know if he is going to keep stirring the pot about his neighbor's death."

"All right!" she grumbled, though she wasn't thrilled. At the same time she knew she would do just about anything to win Clayton back. She had been devastated when he had moved on from their short but intense affair.

23

The ultrasound test on Laney progressed smoothly. Carlos was a bit tentative at first but quickly gained confidence. On the monitor they could see the clear image of a baby boy. George made sure that Laney could see everything, too, since the child meant so much to her.

All of a sudden George and the technician saw something that made them both start. George immediately rotated the monitor so that it was out of Laney's line of sight. Both Laney and Carlos sensed the change in atmosphere.

"Is there anything wrong?" Laney asked anxiously.

"No, everything is fine," George mumbled as he motioned to Carlos to hand over the probe. Surprised but happy to oblige, Carlos gave it to him and stepped aside.

George moved the probe's tip to Laney's left side while staring at the monitor to guide him. He pressed in firmly, moving the tip in small arcs, and kept it up for almost five minutes. "Okay," George said finally, lifting the probe off Laney's abdomen. "All done. We have what we need, Laney. Now, just try and relax! There will be a wait for the OB consult because of so many deliveries. They're knee-deep in newborns up there," he added, smiling weakly.

The metaphor fell flat. Laney was in no joking mood. She watched George closely as he handed the probe to the technician. "Take advantage of the quiet and get some sleep if you can," George added. He knew the medication they had given her to alleviate her stomach pains would have a sedative effect.

Turning to Carlos, George said, "Help Shirley clean up, then meet me in the imaging room." He gave Laney a quick smile and a reassuring squeeze of her arm, and then left.

George retreated to the imaging room to be alone for a few minutes. He was stunned at Laney's bad luck. It seemed unfair that she had to endure such horrific medical problems.

A few minutes later Carlos joined him. "So what's up? I saw your reaction. What did you see?"

"Grab a seat," George said as he pulled up the study on the monitor. He zeroed in on the fetus's head. At first Carlos couldn't see the problem. "Look at how much the fetus's head is distorted," George said, using a pen as a pointer. "Look how it slants back right above the orbits. Do you know what that means?"

"Not really," Carlos responded.

"It's a condition called anencephaly, meaning essentially no brain and probably no spinal cord. There's no hope. It's tragic, especially with Laney's reluctance to have an abortion, but this changes everything. Her life is too much at risk to give birth to a child who will either be stillborn or die within days of birth."

Carlos nodded in understanding as he stared at the image on the monitor, digesting the terrible implications.

George got up and went to look for Kelley. He found her busy suturing up a laceration. At his insistence she stepped out into the hall, keeping her gloved hands clasped to her sterile gown as George explained the bad news.

Kelley was stunned and dismayed. "The poor woman. Can you go back and tell her?"

"Sorry, but I don't think that would be appropriate. That's the purview of the doctors taking care of her, meaning you or your resident. Actually, the diagnosis is not official until it is read by an attending. I'm sorry. Of course you could wait for the OB consult to tell her. It's your call. You and your resident."

"I have several more lacerations after this one." It was clear she wanted help.

"Talk to your resident when you're finished. I hope you understand; information like this is not for the radiologist to give to the patient."

"Okay, I understand," she said reluctantly. "I'll let my resident know. My guess is that he'll want to wait for the OB consult."

"Whatever! But it's important for the OB resident to know the results of the ultrasound before seeing Laney."

"Of course," she said.

"I could handle that part for you if you want."

"That would be great. Thanks." She tried to smile but her lips twitched.

"What I'll do is get a radiology attending to review the case immediately so that it will be part of the record. That way, when the OB resident comes down, it will be available. But I'd still like to talk to whomever it is first."

"Got it," Kelley said, then added, "In some respects this could be a blessing in disguise. With the condition of Laney's heart, I doubt if she would live through giving birth. Do you think the OB people will now be able to convince her to have an abortion?"

"We can hope."

"God! What a tragedy. As a woman, I can really relate."

"I can well imagine. I'll get the final read on the ultrasound and we'll go from there."

"I appreciate your taking the time to come and tell me. Thank you."

"You're welcome. My pleasure. By the way, I happen to think you are doing a bang-up job after being here only two and a half days."

"Thank you again."

"I mean it," George said. "Now, get back to your suturing. We'll talk later."

George poked his head into the imaging room and got Carlos's attention. "Everything hunky-dory?"

"No problems, boss," Carlos reported cheerfully.

"I'm going to get an attending to sign off on the ultrasound. Text me if there are any problems."

Carlos gave a thumbs-up.

Back in the ER proper, George saw Debbie carrying on as usual at the main desk. As he passed, he caught her eye, and to his surprise she actually smiled back. Maybe he hadn't done anything to upset her last night, after all.

There were a number of radiology attendings who could sign off on Laney's ultrasound, but Clayton, an authority on ob-gyn imaging, was probably the best. For George it represented a degree of irony, considering the man's womanizing. He made a beeline for Clayton's secretary. "I need to see Dr. Hanson."

"He's finishing a cardiac catheterization. I can tell him—"

"That's okay. I'll find him. Thanks!" George knew the cath room Clayton preferred. Just as George approached, he was snapping off his sterile gloves.

"George!" Clayton said. "What brings you to this neighborhood?"

"I was hoping you had a moment to look at an ultrasound on a gravid young woman in the ER. I'd like to get it into the record before she has an OB consult."

"Sure. I have a moment right now." He waved for George to follow. "How many months pregnant?"

"Around seven," George said. He then gave an encapsulated version of Laney's case, including what he thought the ultrasound showed.

"Geez," Clayton commented. "Poor thing!"

They went into an empty reading room. George sat

down at one of the terminals and began entering Laney's hospital number.

"I ran into Debbie Waters earlier," Clayton said. "She said she had a really good time, which I was pleased to hear."

George was skeptical. "Did she actually tell you that?"

"Of course. She had a good time and looks forward to doing it again. You are in luck, as I happen to know she is in between boyfriends."

George was frankly disbelieving. "She barely gave me a sideways glance this morning. I admit I had more to drink than I should have. I was worried that I had offended her."

"She didn't mention anything other than she had a good time." Clayton pulled over a chair and sat down to watch as the video of Laney's ultrasound began. He watched it several times, freezing the frame at key points. Finally he said, "Unfortunately I totally agree with your impression. Definitely anencephaly. For sure the fetus is doomed. I'll sign off now." As he did so he added, "They've got to get her to abort. No sense risking the mother's life." When he was finished he turned to George. "Done. Anything else?"

George shrugged. "That's it. I appreciate your time. Thanks."

"Glad to be of help." Clayton smiled and stood up. "But don't let Debbie Waters's workday persona put you off. I'm telling you, she had a great time last night. And tell me the truth: Did you enjoy yourself or what?"

"I did. She is very personable outside of the ER."

"There you go," Clayton said. "You follow up on her. She has talents you wouldn't believe." Clayton clapped George on the back. "Always looking out for you, buddy."

George beat a hasty retreat back to the ER. After what Clayton had told him about Debbie, George wanted to catch her before her lunch break. He was in luck. There was a relative calm in the ER activity.

"Hey there," Debbie said, grinning as she saw him approach. "Where have you been this morning?"

"I've been here," George said. "You didn't see me?"

"No, but I'm not surprised. It's been hectic. I wish this heat wave would let up." She cupped her hands around her mouth and leaned toward George over the countertop. "How do you feel?"

"A little worse for wear," George admitted. "Sorry I drank so much last night. I hope I didn't say anything inappropriate."

"You were a perfect gentleman. We have to do it again. You game?"

"Yes, but with a lot less booze."

"Now, what can I do for you, or are you just saying hello?"

"There is something specific. I think it would be a good idea for the OB consult on Laney Chesney to come see me first. The fetus has anencephaly."

"Ouch," Debbie said in dismay as she wrote down the request on a sticky pad. She glanced around to see if anyone was watching them. No one was, so she added: "I really did enjoy our evening together. You were gracious to all my friends, which I appreciated. I do hope we can do it again soon."

"Me, too," George said, though in reality he wasn't entirely sure he was up for a repeat.

He headed back to the imaging room, where Carlos was going over a new batch of films to review. As there were no surprises, at least according to Carlos, George suggested they put them off until after the radiology conference.

24

George walked back into the emergency room. He wanted to find Kelley and check Laney's condition. The ER was really busy, not quite as bad as it had been early that morning, but with the heat wave still going strong it was busier than usual for the time of day. Kelley and all the other ER doctors were just trying to keep their heads above water. It took George a few minutes to locate her and ask if the OB consult had seen Laney. He had expected to have been paged if the consult had shown up, but it hadn't happened.

"They are still busy upstairs, so not yet, but the resident slotted to do the consult called about fifteen minutes ago and said that she would be down within the hour. They're wrapping up a couple of final deliveries."

"Did you tell Laney . . . about the ultrasound result?" George asked.

"My senior resident did. I just couldn't handle it. But he did a good job, and it was a good learning experience for me. She took it better than I feared."

"I hope you don't feel that I copped out."

"Not at all. I understand. Actually at one point I thought about going into radiology to avoid such situations. We're doctors, but we're human, too. But in the end, the drama of ER medicine was too much to pass up. I felt that after all those years of schooling I wasn't about to shortchange myself." She stopped and glanced up at George. He had stiffened up on that last comment. "I'm sorry. I didn't mean it like that."

George put up his hands. "Don't apologize. I'm not offended." But in truth he was, a little. He took a step away but then turned back, remembering something else. "One more thing. Do you know offhand which of the ER residents was in charge of DeAngelis's case?"

"I don't know, but I can find out."

"Please do. I want to ask about the self-inflicted wounds."

"I'll find out the name for you."

"Thanks. Hope you guys catch up before the evening commute."

Kelley nodded before heading back into the fray.

George returned to the imaging room and went over the latest films with Carlos. About forty minutes later Kelley walked in with a tall, African American woman. George got to his feet as Kelley introduced her as Dr. Christine Williams, one of the senior OB residents.

George said he wanted to make sure she knew the results of the ultrasound before she saw the patient and offered to go over it with her if she wanted.

"Actually I already saw the ultrasound report," Christine said. "How did you get it in the record so quickly?"

"I put a rush on it so that it would be there for you. We knew how important it was going to be in determining how the case should be handled. I assume you will be trying to convince her to abort?"

"I can already give you some feedback on the patient," Kelley offered. "After my senior resident gave Laney the results of the ultrasound, Laney said she would still not abort, no matter what."

They were silent for a moment.

"Well, let me examine the patient and talk to her," Christine finally said. "With her cardiac status and the fact that the fetus is not viable, it would be tragic to let her try to deliver."

George felt terrible about the case. Once again a study he was involved with had changed someone's life, and not necessarily for the better, although in this case the imaging might save the patient's life. And to think that he believed radiology was going to be a shield from such things.

"Thanks for offering to go over the ultrasound with me," Christine said. "But it's not necessary. Instead I'd like to see the patient."

"If it is all right with you, I'd like to come," George said. "Laney and I go back a ways. Maybe I can offer her a bit of support. She doesn't have any friends that I know of."

"Be my guest," Christine said graciously.

They made their way down the long hallway. As they walked, Kelley caught George's eye and gave him a thumbs-up sign in recognition that he was doing something a bit more than the usual radiologist might.

The door to Laney's room was closed. "We've let her sleep," Kelley explained. "She was exhausted." Kelley knocked on the door gently so as not to frighten the young woman. When she didn't hear any response, she knocked harder and called out Laney's name. Still there was no sound from within. A shadow of concern crossed Kelley's face. She opened the door and all three doctors stepped into the windowless room. The lights had been dimmed.

Laney appeared to be asleep. Kelley called out to her again as she approached the side of the bed. George and Christine went to the opposite side. Kelley gave Laney's arm a gentle shake. "Laney?" There was no response. She tried again. "Laney? Are you all right?" Still no response.

Concern ratcheted up in the room.

"Laney?" George yelled as he reached to check her pulse. He couldn't find one. "There's no pulse!"

Kelley quickly opened each of Laney's eyes between her thumb and index finger and shined in a penlight. The pupils were dilated and nonreactive. "She's not breathing!" Kelley cried.

"My God," George blurted as he yanked the pillow from beneath Laney's head. He leaped up onto the bed to begin CPR, noticing Laney was loosely holding her phone in her right hand. Christine grabbed an ambu bag from the top of an oxygen cylinder while Kelley used the intercom to call a code.

Within two minutes an entire resuscitative team headed by a senior resident swept into the room and went to work on the patient. Having gotten wind of what was going on, even Carlos appeared just as it was announced that Laney had flatlined, meaning there was no cardiac activity whatsoever. A moment later someone called out that Laney's temperature had fallen below ninety degrees Fahrenheit. Regardless of the negative signs, they feverishly continued their attempt to resuscitate her.

With nothing to do, George turned on Laney's phone. He pressed the iDoc app icon just as he had with Kasey's. He saw that, as with Kasey's, the iDoc app had been shut down and wiped clean more than an hour previously. Knowing what he did, he guessed it meant that Laney had not had a heartbeat for all that time.

"I think she's been dead an hour," George announced. He held up the phone. "According to iDoc, anyway."

"An hour!" The leader of the resuscitation team motioned to the man doing the chest compressions to stop. "Now we know why we haven't been able to get any cardiac activity. An hour? Christ! This patient is long dead! That's it. Let's pack it up, guys! Even if we managed to get a heartbeat, the brain would be gone."

The team began gathering up their gear. George, Kelley, Carlos, and Christine appeared transfixed by the situation.

On his way out of the room, the head of the resuscitation team approached George, who he knew was a senior resident. "Dead an hour? That doesn't look good for our ER. How long was the patient left alone?"

"Almost two hours," Kelley said, answering for George. "I'm the junior resident assigned to the patient."

"What is this, your third day?" the team leader questioned. He let out a long, slow whistle. "They'll have fun with this one at the morbidity and mortality conference. Let's hope the media doesn't find out about it. But I suppose we shouldn't be surprised. It is July!" He snickered as he herded his team out the door.

It was a devastating parting shot to the first-year resident. Everybody in the room knew what he meant by "July."

For a moment George couldn't speak. Laney's death had brought back the horror he had felt waking up next to Kasey's corpse. She, too, had been dead long enough to be cold. Again the question came back: Why was death stalking him? Or was it rather that he was somehow the culprit, bringing death to everyone around him, starting with his own mother?

"Oh, my God!" Kelley said, forcing back tears. "What a disaster. I feel so bad. I should have checked on her."

One of the ER nurses put her arm around Kelley's shoulders. "It wasn't your fault. Don't listen to that resident. Nurses and orderlies should have checked on her, too. If it was anybody's fault, it was everybody's."

"What that resident said was completely uncalled-for and mean," Carlos said, waiting for George as the most senior resident to speak.

"If it was anybody's fault, it was ours," Christine said.

"OB shouldn't have made her wait. Sometimes the system just doesn't work. We should probably have one resident in charge of ER consults rather than just relying on who happens to be free."

George remained silent, staring at Laney's lifeless face. He wandered out of the room, ignoring the others. He couldn't shake the sense that something was wrong in his world. Very wrong.

25

Carlos brought up a chest X-ray on the monitor and gave the pertinent history of the patient to George, sitting next to him. Carlos was still chafing at George for not standing up for Kelley. Like everybody else, Carlos knew that Laney's death was a system error, meaning there were a number of people who could be faulted. The senior medical resident's picking on a first-year resident amounted to bullying.

"What's your take on this film?" Carlos asked, his voice reflecting his disappointment at George's reaction to the incident. "Do you think there's a secondary finding?" The X-ray had been taken to evaluate probable rib fractures, but Carlos had spotted a possible secondary finding. He wasn't sure whether or not there was hilar lymphadenopathy, or swollen lymph nodes, at the portion of the lung that carried all the blood vessels to and from the lung as well as the bronchial tubes. Carlos knew that lymphadenopathy was a finding common with a number of infectious diseases but could also signify lung cancer. Although detecting it obviously carried a great significance, it wasn't a black-and-white call.

George was staring blankly at the monitor and didn't respond.

"Are you okay?" Carlos asked. His disgruntlement was changing to concern.

George broke from his trance. "Sorry. I'm a little pre-occupied, I guess." He stood up. "Excuse me. We'll finish up with this current batch of films later."

George left the imaging room, aware that Carlos was most likely mystified by his behavior and wondering when George was going to snap out of his reaction to Laney Chesney's death. He imagined that Carlos would have believed that George, as a fourth-year resident, should be inured to such incidents.

George was on a mission. He knew he was supposed to be at the radiology conference at four, which didn't leave much time, but he decided he needed to talk to Kelley Babcock. As bad as he felt about Laney, he was sure she felt worse. He found her sitting alone in the doctors' lounge, hunched over a cup of coffee.

"Kelley?"

She looked up. George could see her eyes were red.

"You mind?" He nodded to the empty chair next to her.

"I don't own it."

Not the most welcoming of invitations to join some-one, but he took it anyway.

"Dr. Warren Knox," Kelley said unbidden.

"Pardon?"

"You asked me who the ER resident in charge of the DeAngelis case was. It was Dr. Knox. But he has the day off."

"Thanks. I'll talk to him the next time he's on duty. But that's not why I'm here." He cleared his throat and began. "I recently had two people on whom I'd done MRIs pass away." He paused, thinking of the best way to phrase what he wanted to say. "I take it personally when a patient dies, too. Maybe I should have learned better how to compartmentalize, put it in a box—I mean, it's not like I don't put it in a box. I do. But I only pretend the box is shut tight, and things leak out."

Kelley looked up at him, curious.

"I guess what I'm trying to say is that I'm sorry. I was upset and . . . I should have stood up for you with that medical resident. He was definitely out of line when—"

"Thanks. But it's not just me or my guilt I'm upset about. I mean, I should have gone back to check on her, I accept that lapse. But it is also something else. It's just . . . the unfairness of who gets dealt a bad hand. Why have I been so lucky? She was so young." Kelley stirred her coffee absently. "When my father died I thought my life was over. I was home alone with him . . ." She paused. "I was just a dumb thirteen-year-old teenager, and there I was with my father having a heart attack right in front of me." She shook her head at the memory. "I wanted so badly to be able to help." She looked up at George. "It's probably why I went into medicine, and emergency medicine in particular. But now that I'm here, my great fear is about somebody coming in that ER door needing and expecting Superwoman and getting a very ordinary, scared little girl from Kansas who can make mistakes."

George watched Kelley as she went back to stirring her coffee. He thought she was possibly more beautiful on the inside than on the outside. Now, that was something.

"I don't know what you think about my opinion," George said. "But I am one hundred percent sure you are going to be a super ER doctor. I mean it."

"Thank you. That's a real compliment coming from someone in his fourth year."

"Despite what that medical resident said, don't beat yourself up about Laney Chesney. Like the nurse said, we all have to take some blame. Hell, even me. I told her to get some sleep, and I'm the one who wanted the OB consult to come see me before going to her. That was an added delay."

"You're just trying to make me feel better."

George sat quietly a moment, then looked up. "You're right. But I'm beginning to think it wouldn't have mattered even if she had been checked on by you or anyone else."

Kelley looked at him, puzzled.

George looked around to make sure no one was listening in. Suddenly, in response to her honesty, he had the urge to be totally open with her. "I know this is going to sound a bit off the wall, but people are dropping like flies around me. I mean, I'm seriously beginning to think I'm the Grim Reaper."

"What do you mean?"

"They're all very sick to begin with, don't get me wrong. But they're still dying before they should be."

"I'm not following you."

George counted on his fingers, "Kasey Lynch, Greg Tarkington, Claire Wong, Sal DeAngelis, and now Laney Chesney. Five people. My fiancée, my next-door neighbor, and three patients. My fiancée was three months ago, then the other four in the past three days." He absentmindedly took Sal's cell phone from his jacket pocket and set it on the table.

"Fiancée?" Kelley appeared dumbfounded. "Your fiancée died?"

"Unfortunately, yes. But I don't mean to drop that on you." He looked her in the eye. "As bad as that was, and believe me it was bad, it's like these deaths are accelerating." He paused, worried that he was coming off as a crazy. "I feel as if death has been following me around, and I should be doing something about it."

"What can you possibly do?"

He shrugged. "It's just a feeling I have." He suddenly felt embarrassed, wondering what could have made him open up with someone he hardly knew but would like to get to know. "Sorry. Forget I said all that. The point I'm trying to make is that I might have had more to do with Laney's death than anyone."

Kelley looked at George skeptically. "Are you being serious?"

"I don't know, to tell the truth. Anyway, don't be too hard on yourself about Laney. I don't think it was your fault in the slightest."

Kelley looked at the smashed-up phone that he was twirling absently on the table. "Cracked your screen, I see. Did the same with mine, but not nearly that bad."

George looked down. "No, this isn't mine." Earlier, with the help of a charging wire, he'd managed to get the screen to come on.

"I see it has the iDoc app."

"Yeah, it does. Well, it did, anyway."

"You seemed to know a lot about iDoc when we talked earlier."

"I've been learning quite a bit. A crash course, you could say. For better or worse it's going to play a big part of medical care in the near future. Medicine as we know it is going to change dramatically."

"Really?" Kelley said. She straightened up in her chair. "I'd love to hear more about it."

George gave her a five-minute summary of what he knew about iDoc. She seemed intrigued. Her eyes never left his face.

Just then the door to the lounge opened and a nurse stuck her head in. "Dr. Babcock, your presence is required in the emergency room."

26

Clayton took the time to head back to the ER yet again, hoping he wasn't calling too much attention to himself. Once more he was on a mission for Amalgamated, at the behest of Langley and secondarily Thorn. First it had been to try to locate the drug reservoir that had been implanted in Sal DeAngelis, which was a bust. Then it had been to gauge the general reaction to DeAngelis's spectacular death, particularly from his neighbor who, by chance, happened to be Dr. George Wilson, which was ongoing. Now it was another death of an iDoc beta-test user, someone who was a Medicaid beneficiary, by the name of Laney Chesney. Clayton had recognized the name immediately, and unfortunately George Wilson was involved again.

The news of any problem with iDoc had bothered Clayton considerably. He had all his assets, including his entire IRA, tied up in the company. Inadvertent deaths with iDoc were the last thing he wanted to hear about. "Have you alerted the FDA about this problem?" Clayton had asked Thorn. Either yes or no had potentially bad implications, but Thorn had failed to answer.

Clayton reached the ER, which was as busy as he'd ever seen it. Holiday eve traffic had resulted in the expected mayhem. Six ambulances were lined up at the receiving dock, several still unloading their patients. Clayton made a beeline for the reading room, hoping to see George about the Chesney girl. He hadn't decided exactly what he was going to say, but there was no George anyway.

Checking his watch, Clayton understood why and lambasted himself for not remembering the Thursday compulsory physics lecture for all the residents. So much for confronting George. Instead he went to the main desk to see Debbie. He knew she was officially off at three, but she was so conscientious, she was always around for another hour at least. Sure enough he found her sitting at the desk with the charge nurse on duty for the three-to-eleven shift. They were still going over the patients whose cases were pending.

Clayton interrupted the conversation and took Debbie aside. She was surprised and wary to see him. Clayton didn't waste words: "I heard a young pregnant woman passed away here in the ER. I'm sorry, I know that's tough on you and everybody else."

"Bad news travels fast," Debbie said, eyeing Clayton suspiciously.

"How did it happen?"

"Cardiac," Debbie said. "The patient had a long history of progressive cardiomyopathy."

"You okay?"

"Yeah, I'm okay. But it's my own damn fault. I dropped the ball. I should have been sending people down there to continuously monitor her when I realized that the OB resident couldn't show up for several hours. But a lot of folks around here should have checked in with her without having to be told by me or by anybody. It's standard freaking procedure, for God's sake."

Debbie paused and looked up at Clayton. "What's this sudden sympathy? It's not like you to come down here in the middle of the day, worried about my mental status."

"Well, there is an ulterior motive. My understanding is that unfortunately George Wilson was again involved. I'm worried about his response, because the patient, like DeAngelis, was part of the iDoc beta test."

"What the hell are you worried about? I don't understand. Do you think he's dangerous in some way?"

"Let's just say that we don't want any adverse publicity at this stage of the iDoc testing. He's a smart guy. We need to know what he's thinking in case some intervention is called for."

"So you want me to sound him out about both Laney Chesney and Sal DeAngelis? Make sure he won't make any waves? Is that what I'm hearing?"

"Always right on the money," Clayton said. "Sharp as a tack! I knew I could count on you."

"Wait a second. One condition. You and me. We start going out again."

"Absolutely. I would want that even if you weren't helping me with George Wilson," Clayton lied. "You know that. I like you. It's just that my ex-wife was giving me such problems, I had to back off for a bit. It's better now. I know I mentioned this weekend. How about dinner at Spago Saturday night? Does that work for you?"

Debbie beamed. "Actually, it sounds wonderful. Okay, I'll do it."

Clayton gave her a wink and a light swat on the butt with his file folder as he walked off. He was pleased, even if he'd had to agree to a Saturday-night dinner. Well, maybe he could get out of it. He checked his watch. He headed over to the hospital's parking garage. The valet raced off to retrieve his red Ferrari, which they always parked near the checkout desk. An hour earlier he had gotten a call that asked him to come to an emergency meeting with Thorn and Langley over in Century City. He loved moving among the business elites. If he had to get his shoes muddy once in a while for the privilege, so be it. The mud made him indispensable.

Clayton, Thorn, and Langley were gathered around a small table in Thorn's expansive corner office. The massive windows in the room looked south and west, offering a stunning view of Santa Monica Bay and the Pacific Ocean, not that Thorn noticed it anymore.

Their discussion was about what they were now officially calling "the glitch." Langley brought the others up to date on all the latest aspects, including specific details on the position taken by CMS and the Independent Payment Advisory Board. While Langley spoke he kept puffing on an e-cigarette, which irritated the hell out of Thorn. He was convinced that whatever Langley was blowing around the room was going to get trapped there and he'd be smelling it later. When things were not going smoothly, which they clearly weren't, Thorn was less tolerant of people's foibles.

"As I have said, my major fear is word getting out," the tech genius was saying. "The media—"

"Will blow it all out of proportion," Thorn finished. "We are all on the same page in this regard. No disagreement whatsoever."

"Then why not disable it?" Clayton asked. "Is that still a possibility?"

"We tried once when it first appeared," Langley said, "before CMS was in the picture. But getting rid of it is not as easy as it sounds. The basic program learns almost too quickly. To totally get rid of it would require rewriting huge sections of the code, a time-consuming endeavor, to say the very least."

"What's the current situation in the trenches?" Thorn asked impatiently, looking at Clayton. By "trenches" he meant the people dealing directly with patients: doctors and nurses and the like.

"As far as I can tell there is no suspicion at the facilities where the events originated," Clayton said. "Santa Monica and Harbor, no problem whatsoever. It has also been okay at the L.A. University Medical Center, except for some mild concern about a resident radiologist under my supervision, as I have informed Langley."

Langley nodded.

"But other than that, nothing," Clayton continued. "Also, I'm happy to report no problems coming from the medical examiner's office, either, which I have been monitoring. There's not been a blip on the the radar screen. No one has requested an autopsy on a deceased iDoc beta participant. The beauty of it is that everyone *expects* these people to die, given their medical histories. Of course it helps that the medical examiner's resources are stretched as thin as they are, so their forensic examiners are encouraged to sign off on terminal cases with few questions asked."

"Back up a minute. Who is this radiologist?" Thorn asked.

"His name is George Wilson," Clayton said. "It's an unfortunate convergence of events. He was engaged to one victim, friend to another, and did radiological studies on three others, one of whom he had a bit of a bond with. She died this morning. At this point he's only aware that three of the five are iDoc users, including the one today. But still, even three . . . I mean, what are the odds?"

"Odds aren't worth shit when it comes to reality," Thorn retorted. "We can't make even one mistake. Our whole game plan could be undermined." He paused and looked directly at the others to be sure they were taking this in. "And our careers." He turned to Langley. "These clustered episodes show that the algorithm will have to be tweaked. If iDoc identifies a termination case in the future, before it takes action, have it spit out the name and case number. Then have it look at the proximity of other terminations and factor in the relationships of the health care professionals who are involved. LinkedIn, Facebook, Instagram, Tumblr—you can use those sites and others to find the connections. Once we have them, we'll develop protocols for the number of connections and how frequent they are to be acceptable within a set period of time. Are you following me?"

"Yes, I am." Langley smiled. "I know exactly what you're looking for and I will have my team deliver."

Clayton felt a little dizzy after Thorn's impassioned monologue. He didn't understand a word.

"Good," Thorn said, clapping his hands together. "Now, moving on to the situation at hand . . . what do we do, if anything, about this resident radiologist?"

"Well," Clayton said, "I don't think we should do anything yet. But I have arranged to keep him on a short leash and monitor him closely. I've engaged an attractive and effective fifth column, if you will, who has already informed me that although he is impressed with iDoc, he's not buying the generally accepted theory that his neighbor was suicidal, which in his mind is iDoc case number two. I'm afraid he might be compelled to look into the case a bit more. What we don't want to do is anything that arouses his suspicions that iDoc has anything to do with the deaths. Unfortunately something did happen that made him more suspicious, and that's that he saw me down in the morgue when I went and tried to retrieve that reservoir for Mr. Langley." Clayton leveled an accusatory gaze on the techie.

"We were hoping for a material confirmation of what actually happened," Langley said in his defense. "Obtaining the reservoir would have been helpful to ascertain that the insulin was the determining factor in the death."

"I can't believe that! You already knew," Clayton shot back. He was angry that his going down to the morgue had put him and the program at potential risk at a time when he hadn't been made fully aware of the situation and its seriousness.

"Enough!" Thorn interrupted. "We're all on the same page. I want to know more about this George Wilson fellow."

"Actually, you've met him," Clayton said.

"How? Where, for Christ's sake?"

"At the investor presentation at the Century Plaza Hotel. He's a friend of Paula Stonebrenner's. I saw her introduce you to him."

Thorn was shocked. "Seriously? Jesus, it's a small world sometimes. Okay, continue."

Clayton gave them some background on George, including his having been involved to a degree in exposing a conspiracy at Columbia Medical School while he was a student there. On hearing this, Thorn's face darkened. Clayton also described George as one of his best residents, conscientious to a fault, a hard worker and bright.

"How are you going to monitor him?" Thorn asked.

"As I've said, I've arranged for a friend to keep George under surveillance over the next few days, which I feel are critical. If he calms down, then we're good. If he doesn't, I'll let you know. I imagine you can best handle it at that point."

Thorn nodded, deciding if push came to shove to turn the situation over to his security department as a code-red emergency. The security department's entire hierarchy was composed of former mercenaries. He was confident they could handle doing whatever was necessary.

"You know, it's a good thing this is happening," Langley said, interrupting.

Thorn and Clayton looked at him, puzzled.

"We didn't plan on this 'glitch,' but all the same that is what a beta test is for, to identify and resolve this kind of unexpected phenomenon. It's a lot better than finding out about it after we go national. In a way, this situation in and of itself is a mini beta test."

"I wish I could feel as optimistic as you," Thorn said. "I don't like threats that could possibly derail our program."

"Well, I like looking on the bright side," Langley said. "We might learn some really important lessons from this radiology resident, depending on how his involvement unfolds. And with Clayton keeping tabs on him, we can intervene if need be, which lowers the risk to an acceptable level. I think this situation is a blessing in disguise. It has created a nice controlled environment to get some potentially helpful data about security for iDoc in the future."

27

George had been moping since he'd gotten home. Compared to Kasey's, Sal's, Tarkington's, Wong's, and now Laney's, George's life was a walk in the park, since he was still alive. But he was unable to shake a sense of complicity in all their deaths. Talking with Kelley earlier made him feel better by getting it out in the open, but not for long.

He was sitting on his couch in the dark, mindlessly TV channel surfing, when his doorbell rang. He ignored it, hoping whoever it was would go away. But it rang again. Then again. Reluctantly George got up and opened the door, thinking it could only be either Zee or his drunk-ass building superintendent. It was neither. He stood dumb-struck staring at Debbie Waters.

"Aren't you going to invite me in?" she said. "If you're entertaining, though, I can come back another time."

George found his voice. "No! No! Let me get a light."

Debbie came in and looked for a place to sit as George turned on a floor lamp and turned off the TV. She had to make a conscious effort not to comment on the state of George's apartment.

"I was driving by and thought of you," she said, deciding the best place to sit was in a vinyl club chair. She wanted to avoid the couch so as not to give mixed signals. "I hope you don't mind my stopping by, but I needed to talk with someone. I'm still weirded out about the Chesney girl dying during my watch."

"I can understand," George said. "Her death bothered everyone. She was a sweet girl who hadn't had a lot of chances in life. Before you came I was just sitting in here in the dark, trying to make sense of her passing."

"How exactly does it bother you?" Debbie asked. She wanted to get this mission for Clayton over with as fast as possible. "It certainly wasn't your fault."

George started to reply, then paused. It was a bit of an odd question, since the answer was so intuitive. "I don't think it was anyone's fault, Debbie, if that's what you're worried about. I think it was more of a confluence of errors and oversights. What bothers me is the fact that she was dealt such a bad hand throughout her short life. I don't know if you are aware of the details, but suffice it to say she had multiple major health issues, some of which I helped to define. Add in her train wreck of a childhood, and it's just tragic, at all levels."

"That's it?" Debbie asked.

George regarded her closely. He suddenly had the sense that she was interrogating him rather than having a real discussion. He was glad he hadn't shared his thoughts about his own sense of responsibility. He sensed he should hold his cards close to his chest. His subconscious picked up something a bit off about Debbie. And until he could identify what that something was, he'd play it safe.

"So you're okay?" Debbie asked, studying his face. "I thought maybe this episode on top of DeAngelis and then of course your fiancée . . . I don't know . . . I was worried about you."

"How do you know about my fiancée?" George asked.

"Clayton filled me in," Debbie said without blinking an eye. "That's why I'm worried about you."

"Thanks. I appreciate it." And he did. Other than Kasey, he hadn't had a woman in Los Angeles express much concern about his well-being. As a consequence, his guard dropped a little. Maybe he had misjudged her.

"You look troubled," she said. "What are you thinking about?"

"Well, I did—do—have this crazy idea about death stalking me. I know that sounds paranoid. I mean, these patients all had serious illnesses, particularly considering what you told me about Sal."

"Pardon?" She looked confused.

"The prostate cancer."

"Oh. I forgot I had mentioned it."

"How did you know?"

"I'm not sure."

"Really?" George asked, his guard back up.

"Oh, I remember now. His accident was so freaky. When the crash happened, his phone rocketed out of the car and literally landed in my lap."

George felt a twinge of guilt for having essentially swiped the phone from her desk. Of course he thought it was going to be thrown in the trash.

"Even though it looked worse for wear, I hooked it up to one of the handhelds that Amalgamated gave us for their iDoc clients. It can retrieve their medical histories and recent vital signs data to help us make an initial diagnosis. His phone was jammed from the impact of the accident, but I was able to get some of the latest data downloaded into the reader before it completely crashed. And that included the results of a recent prostate biopsy. It was the last entry in his medical history."

"That's fascinating," George said with obvious interest. "Do you think he knew? Is that information still in the hospital computer?"

"It never got that far," Debbie said. "And he probably didn't know about the diagnosis." George's sudden eagerness scared her a little. She was certain that getting him riled up was not what Clayton had in mind. He just asked her to gauge George's state of mind about the deaths, hoping he had put them behind him, and here she was aggravating the situation. "It was obvious pretty quickly that the guy was dead, so there was no need for further medical history. I just read it off the handheld. I never uploaded it."

"Interesting," George commented as all the disparate

facts swirled around in his brain. If Sal didn't know about the prostate diagnosis, then there was an interesting parallel with Kasey. Suddenly he blurted out: "I wonder if Greg Tarkington and Claire Wong were iDoc users? If they were, that would be an odd coincidence."

"Who are Greg Tarkington and Claire Wong?" Debbie's warning bell was dinging. Clayton was not going to be happy.

"They are two patients I did MRIs on who have also recently shown up as DOAs in your ER." George moved to the edge of the couch. "I have a favor to ask. Would you see if you can find out if they were part of the iDoc beta test?"

Debbie was about to beg off, but George didn't give her a chance. "Sorry," he said. "I'm just thinking out loud, but there is something else." He could see her stiffen up, but he went on anyway. "There is the issue about an implanted reservoir. My fiancée had one to control her diabetes. Sal had one, too—or at least he thought he had one. He showed me a scar on his abdomen. Laney? I don't know if she had one, but it stands to reason that she did since she had diabetes, too. I suppose I should have noticed when the ultrasound was done, but I was distracted by showing Carlos the ropes. I can find out about Sal to be one hundred percent certain, since I know the name of his former primary-care doctor. Sal had me call him a couple of times. I'll see if he has a record of it. Sal had said that he had put it in. Sal and Laney must have had one because, like Kasey, iDoc was controlling their diabetes. The only way for that to happen was for them to have implanted reservoirs."

"What are you talking about?" Debbie demanded. She was becoming progressively alarmed. "Implanted reservoirs?" He had completely lost her, and his sudden enthusiasm was scary. She had a feeling that she had somehow made things worse for Clayton.

George stared at Debbie. "What about it?" he asked. "Can you get this kind of information about Tarkington and Wong for me from the ER records?"

"Absolutely not!" Debbie stated categorically. "None of these people were my patients. I'm the charge nurse. One thing that the hospital admin has driven home to us is the sanctity of individual health records. My accessing patient records would be a clear violation of HIPAA, which I remind you is taken very seriously at the medical center. You know that. Anytime someone tries to access a medical record who is not directly involved in the patient's care on an ongoing basis, a red flag goes up in the medical records department."

"You're right," George said. He had been severely reprimanded after he had accessed Kasey's records without authorization, even though he was engaged to her. At the time he'd been surprised at how quickly he'd been caught.

"Listen," Debbie said, trying to do some damage control. "This thought you have that death is stalking you is ridiculous. I'm sorry, but it is crazy. As your friend I must tell you that you have to just let it go. You have been a victim of coincidence. Believe me, if you persist, you're risking getting yourself in trouble." She thought about saying it was a certainty but didn't dare, thinking he'd smell a rat.

"Thanks for your advice," George said, but his mind was churning. He had another idea. Suddenly he thought Paula might be able to answer his questions. Amalgamated had to have a master list of iDoc beta-test participants. Then he thought of something else: "I remember the names of Tarkington's and Wong's oncologists. I wonder if I call them, if they might be willing to tell me if the two patients were with iDoc. It wouldn't be divulging their medical histories per se."

"I don't know. I doubt it. Listen! I'm going to say it again. You have to let this drop. You are letting your imagination run away with itself, and you are going to get yourself in deep shit if you're not careful." Debbie stood up. Suddenly she wanted to get out of there as quickly as possible. Clayton was not going to like it. She didn't know exactly why she felt that way, but she did. "I gotta run," she said as she headed for the door.

George was snapped out of his reverie. He appreciated Debbie's unexpected visit, as it had focused his thinking. "Are you sure you have to go? I really appreciate your dropping by. I can get out the Jack Daniel's again."

"No. Thanks. I really have to go. I feel better having spoken with you. Thanks, George."

"Sure. Anytime. Should we call a taxi?"

"No, I drove."

"Then I'll walk you out to your car."

"It's not necessary. I'm a big girl!"

"I insist," George said. "I really do appreciate your coming by."

He walked her out to her car in front of his apartment building. He gave it one last shot to get her to stay or even go out to a local bar, but she was intent on leaving. He waved as she pulled out into the traffic.

He headed back into his apartment complex, perplexed by her hot-and-cold behavior. The light was on in Sal's apartment. Good. It must be the sisters. He debated whether or not to say hello and extend his sympathies, but he wasn't sure they would even remember him.

He got to his front door and changed his mind. He decided he should make the effort to say hello and find out if there were any plans for a service. As he approached the apartment he could see into Sal's living area. There weren't two older women inside, but two men. Thirtyish, in dark suits and ties! They seemed pretty damn busy, too, whatever they were doing.

George glanced at the super's door, thinking about inquiring exactly who was in Sal's apartment. But imagining that the man was drunk as usual, he decided to just see what he could learn on his own. He went out to the rear of the building to check out Sal's parking place. In it he saw a large, late-model black SUV with dark tinted windows. He doubted it was another tenant's. More confused than ever, he returned to Sal's patio fence.

George hunched down to avoid being seen from inside Sal's apartment. At the same time he glanced around the complex hoping no one was watching him. He didn't want to risk another run-in with the police, which must have been precipitated by someone seeing him climbing over Sal's fence.

Through the sliding glass door he could see all of the living area and the kitchen. The men in the suits were seemingly searching the apartment, as he had done. One was actually vacuuming Sal's faux oriental carpet with a handheld DustBuster. Weird! George wondered what, if anything, he should do.

For lack of an alternative plan, he decided to check in with the super, drunk or not. With some reservation, he rang the bell. When the super opened the door, George saw that, as expected, the man was plastered. Having come as far as he had, George plowed ahead. "I thought you might want to know that there are two men in DeAngelis's unit searching the place."

"I know. I gave them a key."

"Who are they?"

"Police. Or something or other," the super replied, scratching his head. He looked as if he hadn't shaved for a week. He was holding on to the door frame for support and still wobbling.

"They don't look like police."

"They had badges. And a paper that was some kind of warrant."

"What are they looking for?"

"No idea."

George was confused. "You didn't ask?"

The super, whose name was Clarence, had to think that one over. "I might have. Can't remember."

George realized this was hopeless and turned to leave. "Okay, thanks."

"Sal's sisters are in town," Clarence yelled, as if he just remembered it. "There's a memorial service they got planned for tomorrow. Hang on." He reached to a table just inside his door and grabbed a piece of paper. He held it as far away from himself as he could while attempting to read it. "Carter's Funeral Home. Two o'clock. If you want to go. Said they wanted to bury him as quick as can be and skedaddle out of town."

"Thanks, Clarence." George walked off. He was amazed that the service was scheduled to take place on the Fourth of July, not that he imagined too many people would want to show up.

George headed back to his apartment, still curious as to who exactly was searching Sal's. If they were government agents of some sort, as Clarence thought, he'd have to guess they were FBI. But why in thunder would the FBI be searching Sal's apartment?

28

With a nervous smile Debbie Waters rang Clayton's doorbell and surveyed the home and surrounding manicured grounds, noticing an extra car in the driveway. This was the life she wanted. She was in her mid-thirties now and the clock was ticking. She knew she had a smoking-hot body, at least according to some male friends. But how long was that going to last? What she didn't want to do was end up living an ordinary, middle-class life. Every day in L.A. she saw both extremes: the haves and the have-nots. She deserved to be a have, and Clayton was her ticket.

His home was near the top of a winding road in Bel Air. It was too big for the lot it sat on, but wasn't anywhere near as large as some of his neighbors'. Still, his place was impressive. Especially to an ER charge nurse earning $89,000 a year. A nice salary, yes, but not for this zip code.

Clayton glanced at a security monitor in his kitchen while on the way to his front door. It was Debbie ringing the bell. He wasn't surprised, as she'd called ahead. He had told her not to come over to the house because he had guests, but she insisted. In actuality, he had only one guest and he was not about to let her meet Debbie. Knowing Debbie as he did, that would be a disaster.

Clayton had parted with half of his net worth in his divorce and was stretched to the bone trying to pay the mortgage, taxes, and upkeep on his house. The idea that he even had a mortgage at his age was frightening. He needed those Amalgamated stock options to come through for him, so inconveniences like this were . . . well, he had to put up with them.

He had no qualms about using Debbie as a spy, but having her show up at his house uninvited was not acceptable. He knew he was considered a catch in some circles, and those circles included Debbie Waters. But the feelings were not mutual. She was certainly attractive physically, but among the social coterie he preferred, her mouth and manners of a truck driver didn't mesh. Yet he needed her to think otherwise, at least long enough to get her to continue to help with George Wilson.

He opened the front door and for a moment the former lovers regarded each other across the threshold.

Clayton broke the silence. "This isn't good," he hissed.

"If that's the way you want to be, you're on your own," Debbie said. She turned and headed for her car. "I have some new information about George Wilson I thought you'd want to hear, but fine," she called over her shoulder.

"Jesus!" Clayton groaned, recognizing that Debbie was manipulating him. He should just let her leave. The last thing he wanted was for her to be there with the young, would-be actress waiting in his library, but he needed to hear what she had to say. He darted after her. She was already in the car, closing her door, when he caught up with her. He grabbed the handle.

"Okay, what did you learn?"

"No. You were just rude to me. If you want to know, you'll have to come to my place." She started the car engine and put it in gear. "Let go of my door!"

"Wait! Damn it!"

She didn't, and he had to jog along beside her to keep up as she descended his driveway. He still had a hold of her car door.

"Okay! Okay! I'll come over to your place. Just give me some time to get rid of my guest. I'll tell him I have to run back to the hospital." Damn, he hated her for doing this to him. "I'll be over in an hour."

"*Him?* Right," she scoffed, not buying that it was a man visiting with Clayton. She loved that she had interrupted his evening and was making him come running to her. "Okay, one hour! Or I don't tell you what I learned."

Clayton stood at the base of his driveway and watched her drive off. He promised himself he would make her pay when this was over. Maybe he could get her transferred to their newly acquired affiliated hospital down in Long Beach. That would teach her.

29

George was feeling a lot better. Debbie's surprise visit had pulled him out of his depression. After a quick shower and a bit of food in his belly, his mind started to kick back into gear. What he had realized was that, immediately prior to their deaths, all of the patients in what he now referred to as his "coincidental cohort" had had a history of serious medical problems compounded by the discovery of a new, life-threatening medical issue.

What he was most interested in knowing was whether or not Tarkington and Wong were part of the iDoc beta test. He knew Debbie was right that it was against HIPAA rules to try to access anyone's health records. But there was Paula Stonebrenner and maybe she could help. With her high-level connections at Amalgamated there was a good chance she could find out if they had been part of the iDoc test or not. One way or the other it would be good for her to know that there was a slight but real chance that something might not be completely copacetic with the iDoc algorithm. Especially when it came to people with serious illnesses. Either that or someone might be intentionally causing trouble. He remembered reading an article in the previous six months or so that Internet hackers could access medical devices that depended on wireless technology. Certainly iDoc fit into that category in a big way. Someone might be interfering with iDoc either merely for the challenge or in a deliberate effort to sabotage Amalgamated for some perceived slight (a lot of people had reasons to hate insurance companies) or for financial gain.

George wondered about the best way to approach Paula. She could easily take offense, but he wanted to try anyway. He decided to text her.

Sitting on his couch now with the lights on and the TV off, he sent her a short "Hello." He didn't have long to wait. She responded in minutes. Soon they were bantering back and forth about how impressed he had been with iDoc from the presentation and what a good job she had done. George could tell she was pleased with the compliments. Next they switched to the idea of possibly getting together. Once he felt she was relaxed, he returned the conversation back to iDoc.

Hey, I was just wondering. Were there any glitches with iDoc during the beta test?

No. Why do you ask?

I remember an article about hackers hacking into wireless medical devices.

Absolutely nothing like that with us. Flawless. ☺

George realized he needed to up the ante.

Something has come to my attention at the medical center.

He got a period of silence after that. Finally:

What's that?

We should talk.

Okay. Call me.

I'd rather talk in person. You up for that?

When?

How about now?

Not possible. It's late. But you can call me if you want.

George sighed. Okay, he'd call. He would have much preferred talking with her directly to gauge her reactions, but he'd take what he could get. She picked up on the first ring.

"Okay, what's up?"

George cleared his throat. He sensed she was already on the defensive. "I imagine this might be a sensitive subject, but I can't ignore what I'm seeing."

"This is about iDoc?"

"Yes . . . well, no! It's more than that. I know of three iDoc users that have died. They all had significant medical issues but they all died abruptly and prematurely, immediately after a diagnosis of yet another serious medical issue or a worsening of their original illness." He didn't want to say that all of these deceased had a personal connection. He didn't want this to appear personal.

"I have also done MRIs on two other patients who died abruptly. I'm wondering if they were part of the iDoc beta test as well." George paused, waiting for a response. Paula was silent. "Did you hear—"

"Yes. I heard you." Her tone was all business. "You don't know if the MRI patients were a part of the beta test?"

"No. I don't. That's partly why I'm calling. I was hoping that you could tell me. If you have a pen handy, their names are Greg Tarkington and Claire—"

Paula interrupted. "I wouldn't be able to tell you whether they were part of the test or not. Do you remember our conversation regarding the level of security for iDoc? It is taken very seriously. As part of our preliminary approval, we certified that we would respect HIPAA. Even if I were in a position to find out, which I couldn't, I wouldn't be able to tell you."

Paula's comments were interrupted by a sudden chorus of "YES! YES! YES!" coming through the wall from Joe's apartment. His neighbor had apparently come home early. George dashed into his bedroom and closed the door.

"What was that noise?" Paula asked. Apparently it had been loud enough for her to hear.

"A neighbor. Probably a TV."

"Your walls must be paper-thin."

"It's not the best construction," George admitted. He winced. Now she had a hint of how decrepit his apartment was. Since sounds could still be heard from Joe's apartment he went into his bathroom and closed the door. He sat on the lowered toilet seat. At least it was quiet.

"I didn't hear your last response," he said. "Could you repeat?"

"I said I couldn't tell you what you asked even if I could find out."

"Just so you know, this isn't about me wanting iDoc to fail."

"I hope not, George. At the same time I could understand if you are a little pissed that I took your suggestion and ran with it without at least letting you know. I was specifically told not to for security reasons. iDoc is a huge investment. But please don't make a fool of yourself over this. Wild public accusations about iDoc will reflect badly on you. I promise you, if there are any problems with iDoc, I will let you know. So far there have been no problems. None!"

He knew she was going to say that. "My motivation has nothing to do with spite."

"I hope not. I am more certain than ever that iDoc is the future of medicine in the digitalized world. Doctors had their chance to continue to lead medicine, but they didn't take it."

"I can see iDoc's potential, believe me. It truly is amazing. But I can't ignore what I believe is a very real glitch or something."

"And how would iDoc be responsible for these premature deaths?"

"You tell me."

Paula sighed, purposely wanting George to hear her reaction. "The beta test is huge, George. Twenty thousand client-patients. There are bound to be some inexplicable medical events and deaths. I am sure that all deaths of beta-test participants are being looked at very carefully. And I'll bet that iDoc has probably prevented many deaths, as it would have saved your mother. People with serious illnesses are the ones whom iDoc will actually help the most."

"Why do you believe that?"

"It's simple. iDoc is able to titrate lifesaving medication according to real-time physiological values rather than trying to treat symptoms, which is the old 'sick' care medical paradigm. iDoc is the perfect primary-care doctor since it is based on an algorithm that is capable of learning and will be continuously upgraded as new medical information is incorporated."

"I'm concerned it can't handle what's on its plate now."

"You know what a Luddite doctor is, George? I run across them all the time. MDs who have been dragging their feet in the acceptance of digitalized medicine, even something as intuitive as electronic records. Come on! This is a no-brainer!"

"You have a point. A strong one. But that isn't my issue. I'm concerned about iDoc not operating as you intended. Listen, I appreciate everything you've said. I just hope you can allay my concerns."

"Okay. I'll look into it. Promise."

"Can we still get together?"

She laughed. "Of course we can still get together. It was my idea, remember?"

"I think I can explain better in person. Believe me, I am not motivated in the slightest by spite, or pique for that matter."

"Okay." She laughed.

"Well, I'm free for the holiday weekend. For the first time in three years!"

"Unfortunately, since I didn't hear from you about Saturday I have made other plans. I'm scheduled to go to Hawaii in the morning. I'll be back Monday night. Let's talk then."

"Okay. Sounds good," George replied, hiding his disappointment. "Have fun! Bye."

"Bye." She hung up.

George went back out to his living room and sat on his threadbare couch listening through the wall to the sex session still going on. The difference in lifestyle between him and Paula sunk in heavily. The idea of going to Hawaii for the weekend was beyond his comprehension. It reminded him of what his grandmother had told him more than once:

We live and die by our choices in life. They make us who we are.

30

Debbie enjoyed tormenting Clayton. Why he was so worried about George anyway was beyond her. But since he was, and since he had come to her for help, she was going to use it to her advantage.

Once Clayton showed up at her place, Debbie made him pay. For forcing her to spend time with George, for one. And for entertaining someone other than herself, for another. She knew it was a woman and took great delight in having made Clayton rush away from whatever they had been up to. Whoever the broad was, she had to be steaming mad, even though Clayton had probably used the excuse he had to go back to the hospital.

Eventually, after making him grovel sufficiently, Debbie got around to telling Clayton about George's progressive interest in the five sudden deaths, at least three of whom were iDoc test subjects.

"He actually asked me to look in the ER records to tell him whether the other two patients were part of your iDoc study."

"And what did you say?" Clayton demanded. Finally he had gotten her talking.

"I told him no. I'm not going to risk a HIPAA violation. Listen, Clayton, the fact that he even thought he could ask me such a thing is your fault. You have me asking him out. You know he's not my type. He lives in a fucking shithole."

Oh, the irony, Clayton thought. If only he could tell her exactly what caliber of man she deserved. Self-awareness was not Debbie's strong suit. Whatever did he see in her before? Well, he knew the answer to that. Now he had to keep reminding himself that this was work. *Just think of the stock options*, he kept telling himself.

"George is also interested in knowing if Salvatore DeAngelis had a reservoir inserted by iDoc. He thinks he did, but he wants to be certain."

An alarm bell went off in Clayton's brain. He could feel his face redden.

"What is he talking about?" Debbie questioned. "What is a reservoir? How does it relate to your iDoc?"

"It's something technical. But I'm interested he talked about it. Just tell me everything that he said."

Debbie gave him the whole story as she remembered it. Clayton listened closely, asking questions and making her repeat things to make sure she was remembering them correctly. When he was satisfied he'd gotten everything he could from her, he stood up, ready to leave.

Debbie was horrified. "Where are you going? Don't leave now!" She jumped up, grabbing his favorite single-malt scotch, which she kept on a sideboard.

"I have to go. Sorry. It's not even an option to stay." He didn't want to leave any doubt in her mind that he was leaving. Five more minutes in her faux-everything living room was more than he could bear, even though he could remember a few wild scenes in the past when the decor wasn't an issue.

"Why do you care what George thinks?" She was pouting now.

Clayton brushed her off. "He's under my charge. It's part of my job."

"What is it about these deaths? What are they to you?"

Clayton paused. "It all relates to George Wilson's state of mind. That's all I can really say about it at this point."

She looked hurt.

Clayton knew he might very well need her help again, so he swallowed his pride and buttered her up. "Thank you for your efforts. Really! You've been a tremendous help, but now I have to run. Sorry! I'd love nothing more than to stay and have a drink and then . . . have a little fun. And we will do that soon. I promise. In fact, Saturday at Spago Beverly Hills. It will be a great evening. But for now I want you to continue to monitor George closely. Just for the next few days. And you let me know right away if he decides to act on his concerns. Okay?"

Debbie was not happy with having to go on seeing

George, and even less so about the possibility of Clayton putting her off. "Despite what you might think," she said, "I have some plans myself in the near future. I'm not just sitting around waiting for you to call."

He put his arm around her waist. "This is important." He bent down and kissed her. God, he resented Thorn for putting him through this.

"I'll think about it," she said. "And you better not cancel on me for Saturday night!"

"Not a chance. I promise. I'm looking forward to it." Clayton gave her a wink as he opened the door. "No worries. It'll be a wonderful evening." Once outside, he literally ran to his car. He had brought his Lexus SUV since he didn't like to leave his Ferrari parked on city streets. Starting the car, he hoped to hell his date was still waiting for him. As he accelerated away from the curb, he wondered when he should tell Thorn the bad news about George's interest in iDoc reservoirs.

31

George was off from work for the Fourth of July for the first time since coming to Los Angeles, but he had no desire to spend it at the beach. Instead, he wanted to use the day digging into Kasey's, Sal's, and Laney's deaths. The first thing he planned to do was get in touch with Sal's primary-care physician, Dr. Roland Schwarz. George had had the opportunity to talk with him briefly six months previously on Sal's behalf. Sal had been confused about the doctor's orders, and George stepped in to clear them up. He remembered that Schwarz, although somewhat curt, had been cooperative and reasonably knowledgeable.

George dialed Schwarz's office number with the

intention of leaving a message. He was caught off guard when Schwarz himself answered the phone.

"This is Dr. Schwarz, how may I help you?" Schwarz bellowed brusquely.

"Hello, Dr. Schwarz," George stammered, not prepared to talk to the man himself. "This is Dr. George Wilson calling. I'm at L.A. University Medical Center. We spoke on the phone a few months back regarding a patient by the name of Salvatore DeAngelis. I'm calling now with a few additional questions."

"I'm seeing patients today," Schwarz snapped. "If you academic types want to talk, you can come by the office." With that he hung up.

George was so amazed that the man was seeing patients on the Fourth of July that he hardly even registered the guy's rudeness. If the man wanted him to come to his office, George would oblige.

D r. Schwarz's practice was in Westwood Village, on a quaint, tree-lined street normally populated with throngs of UCLA students. But as it was a summer holiday, the streets were quiet; anyone who wasn't on break was down at the beach for the day. It was, after all, Southern California.

The medical center where George worked was within walking distance from Schwarz's office, so George was able to use the hospital garage for his car and make his usual breakfast run. He finished his bagel walking down Braxton Avenue, looking for the doctor's building. He found Schwarz's name on a faded shingle bolted onto an old Mission-style ediface.

George stepped inside and surveyed the room, noting that there wasn't a receptionist, a secretary, or even a nurse present, just a half dozen patients waiting to be seen. They all looked up, evaluating George as he walked in. He gave them a quick grin and took an empty seat, not wanting to risk looking as if he were going to cut the line. Once he settled into a seat everyone relaxed.

George waited while several people who had arrived before him were seen. Schwarz would poke his head out of the adjacent room and call a name off a clipboard, then usher in the patient. Glimpsing the interior, George could see that the entire office consisted of just two rooms: the waiting room and a combination exam room/office. George understood that his name wasn't on the clipboard and that if he didn't get up and nab Schwarz he'd be sitting there until closing time.

The next time Schwarz popped his head out George made his move. The man whose name had been called stood up at the same time, creating a moment of confusion. George apologized, saying that he was a doctor and was only there to have a quick word with Schwarz.

Schwarz watched the exchange over the top of a pair of bifocals. George turned to him expectantly but was unceremoniously told to take a seat. Chastened, George did as told while watching Schwarz usher his patient inside.

George scanned the room. Everyone was staring at him as if he were an intruder bent on making their wait longer. Finally, Schwarz reappeared.

"Doctor?" Schwarz called to George.

George jumped up and hustled into the exam room. What immediately caught his attention was the computer monitor on Schwarz's desk. It was one of those massive old-school cathode ray tubes that took up the entire desk-top. George hadn't seen one in years. By appearances, Schwarz was as old-school as it got. He had a full gray beard with a balding pate and a set of bifocals that dangled by a string around his neck. To his credit, he wore a clean, crisp white coat and a well-knotted if out-of-style tie. One thing he had going for him, at least, was that he projected an aura of knowledge and trust. But he wasn't friendly. He was cantankerous and curt toward George, just as he had been on the phone. He didn't invite George to sit down. Instead he said, "I don't have a lot of time, so get to the point."

"I appreciate your seeing me," George began, "and I'm amazed that you're seeing patients on the Fourth of July."

"I have no choice but to see patients on holidays. I'm being squeezed by insurance companies and their reimbursement rules. Just to make ends meet, I practically have to work twenty-four-seven."

"I can imagine how difficult it is."

"No, you academic doctors have no idea," Schwarz replied, shaking his head. "What type of doctor are you anyway? A specialist?"

"Yes," George admitted, almost as if apologizing. He felt reluctant to say he was just a resident.

"I assumed as much. Why are you here, then? Be quick! I need to get back to seeing patients."

"It's regarding Mr. Sal DeAngelis."

Schwarz ambled over to an old-fashioned file cabinet and fingered through a batch of folders, locating the one with Sal's name on it. He opened the file and looked up at George. "Okay. What?"

"First, did you notice any suicidal ideation in the patient?"

"For Chrissake," Schwarz complained with a grimace. "Are you a psychiatrist?"

"No. I'm a radiologist."

"I have no idea if DeAngelis had suicidal ideation." He glanced through Sal's chart. "I never wrote that, but the man was a pain in the ass." Schwarz ticked off Sal's indiscretions. "He couldn't remember anything I told him, he never took his medicines as ordered, and he was always losing track of his blood sugar. What else do you want to know?"

"Did you treat him at all for depression? Was he taking any antidepressants?"

"Not diagnosed nor prescribed by me."

George nodded. That must have been iDoc. "How about prostate cancer?"

Schwarz glanced at Sal's chart. "Well, it seems that he did have prostate cancer. Here's a positive biopsy report that was recently sent to me, but I didn't order it and I never saw him for it." Schwarz held up the paper. "The damn thing was just sent to me from your medical center, since I am the GP of record. The fact of the matter is that

I hadn't seen the patient for the last couple of months since he became part of the iDoc beta test. The last time I saw him was to put in a reservoir for iDoc. Amalgamated Healthcare paid me a whopping forty bucks."

"So Mr. DeAngelis definitely had an implanted reservoir."

"As I said, I put it in myself. It was mostly for his diabetes, as I recall."

George nodded. "How long was the reservoir supposed to last?"

"In Mr. DeAngelis's case, at a minimum two years." Schwarz stared down at Sal's file. "God! I hate health insurance companies. They never want to pay, and make you jump through hoops to get reimbursed. I've put in a bunch of those reservoirs for Amalgamated. They gave me a short course on how to do the procedure—they want them all in at the same spot on the lower left abdomen off to the side in the belly fat—but once I did the implant, like with DeAngelis, I lost the patients. As I said, once DeAngelis had the reservoir, I never saw him again. The good news was that he also didn't call me anymore. That was a relief, to tell you the goddamn truth. I put in hours talking on the phone to my patients and do you know how much I get paid for my time? Nothing! I hate talking on the phone. Amalgamated is a bitch of a company. They actually offered me a job, but I told them where to stick it. Goddamn leeches."

"How deep did you embed DeAngelis's reservoir?" George asked cautiously. "Was it just under the skin or deeper?"

The man was getting agitated. "Are you taking care of DeAngelis now? You aren't from Amalgamated, are you?" he said accusingly.

"No way," George exclaimed. "I'm at L.A. University Medical Center."

Schwarz eyed him, eyes narrowing. "Why all these questions?"

"I'm interested in the case."

"Interested?" Schwarz asked, raising his voice. "'Interested' does not denote a doctor-patient relationship. Are you treating him or not?"

"I'm actually a resident radiologist at the medical center and—"

"Are you family?" Schwarz said, his voice rising.

"No, I'm an acquaintance. We were neighbors. As I said, I'm a radiologist and—"

Schwarz's face went dark. He slammed Sal's folder shut. "You deceived me in order to obtain confidential patient information. That's a violation of HIPAA!"

"The man is dead!" George said. "I'm trying—"

"That doesn't make things any better, young man! Your chief of radiology is going to hear about this! Now you have to leave!" He pointed toward the door.

George knew he'd hit a brick wall and raised his hands up in surrender. "Okay, okay. I'm out of here. Thank you for your time."

He exited through the waiting room, avoiding the open stares and stunned expressions of the seated patients. It was apparent they had overheard the exchange.

32

George headed for the back entrance to the emergency department, stopping in the laundry to pick up a white coat. He was fretting over Schwarz's threat to call the chief of radiology. With George's previous HIPAA violation involving Kasey's records, he knew that such a call could cause serious trouble. The possibility of getting Schwarz riled up had never even occurred to him. He tried to put the thought out of his mind but couldn't. Instead he tried to think of ways to lessen the impact if the chief approached him, but nothing promising came to mind. Luckily he had other things to think about, and reasoned that nothing was going to happen until after the Fourth of July weekend no matter what. He was determined to reassure himself that Kasey's, Sal's,

and Laney's deaths—as well as Tarkington's and Wong's—
were coincidences and not the result of some sort of conspiracy or wireless hacking.

George heard the uproar in the ER even before he
entered the public reception area. As he expected, the
place was packed. With the heat wave still gripping the
city, he anticipated it would be busy, especially with holiday traffic and injuries associated with celebrating the
Fourth, such as burns and eye injuries from fireworks.

He spotted Debbie Waters and made a beeline for her.
She was again holding court at the front desk, but this
time she caught sight of him immediately.

"What the hell are you doing here?" she said in her
commander-in-chief persona. "You're not on call, are you?
You should be at the goddamn beach."

"Maybe later," George said. "Got some errands to get
out of the way."

"Like what?" Debbie demanded. "I hope to hell you
aren't still agonizing over the deaths you were upset about."

"Well, they are still on my mind. But the reason I'm
here is to talk with Warren Knox. Is he in today?"

"He is, but he is acting senior resident. Why do you
want to see him? The man is very, very busy."

"I won't need much of his time. I just have a couple of
questions about the DeAngelis case."

"What kind of questions?"

George leaned over the counter so he could not be
overheard. There were a lot of people about and he did
not want anyone listening in. "I want to ask him about
those so-called self-inflicted wounds. I have a theory

about them, which doesn't have anything to do with suicidal ideation, that is if the wounds are where I suspect they might be."

Debbie frowned. "You've got to get off this band-wagon, I'm telling you!"

"I can't. I'm convinced that DeAngelis was not sui-cidal." George looked around the area. "So where can I find Knox?"

"Trauma Room Eight." Her response was flat. She went back to barking out orders to several orderlies who had arrived with gurneys, acting as if they didn't know what to do.

"Okay, thanks," George replied. She didn't look at him, much less acknowledge his thank-you. George shrugged. It was as if she were irritated.

George made his way down to Trauma Room 8, where he found an ER team just finishing preparations to send a bicyclist up to the OR. He had been hit by a bus and sustained massive trauma.

It wasn't hard to figure out who Knox was because he was in charge. Like most of the residents, the man was dressed in blood-spattered scrubs. He looked weary and in sore need of a shave, as if he had been up all night. George waited to speak with him while he finished up with the ER paperwork.

When George explained why he wanted to talk, Knox waved for George to follow him. He said he had to hustle to the next case but that George could tag along. He led George toward Trauma Room 6, where a homeless man who had been hit by a train was going to lose both legs just below the knee. The patient needed to be stabilized before he, too, would be sent up to surgery.

"It's about Sal DeAngelis," George said. "You remember him, right?"

"I'll be remembering him for a long time. What's your question?"

"I heard about the self-inflicted wounds. Were they on the wrists like most suicides or what? And why did you feel they were self-inflicted, since the man had lacerations all over his body?"

"They were on the abdomen. Lower left." Knox indicated the area on his own body as he spoke. "They were surgical in appearance and not at all like the other lacerations on his body from the trauma he sustained. We also found a utility knife in the vehicle with blood on the blade. That helped ID the source of the cuts. There's no doubt the man was trying to injure himself. And it's obvious that he succeeded." Knox paused at the door to Trauma Room 6. "I need to get in here," he said. "If you have any more questions, maybe we can talk later." He then pushed open the door and disappeared into the room.

George stood for a moment in the corridor, thinking about what Sal had been doing. According to Knox there was apparently not much doubt that he had been cutting himself with a utility knife. Maybe Sal was after the reservoir. The surgical-style cuts were in the lower abdomen, where Schwarz had reportedly embedded the reservoir. Maybe in his panic Sal had decided that the reservoir was the source of his troubles, and he wanted to take it out.

The thought didn't make George feel any better. In fact it made him feel worse. Sal might have been right.

George made his way over to the emergency radiology viewing room, ducking into its peacefulness, glad to leave the chaos of the ER behind.

Carlos was working there and was surprised but glad to see George. "What the hell are you doing in here? I figured you'd be kicking back on a beach in Santa Monica right about now, which is where I'd be."

"I wish. Maybe later."

"Well, since you're here, would you mind looking at some films with me? I'm not sure about a few of them. It will save me from having to take them over to radiology to find someone to check them out."

George was glad to look at them. It would help take his mind off Kasey, Sal, and Laney.

When he and Carlos were done, George went to a free monitor and pulled up the radiological studies on Tarkington and Wong, which he had the right to do, since he had done their MRIs. What George wanted was abdominal flat plates, if they were available. They were, for both patients. And both gave full evidence of what he was looking for. Tarkington and Wong had embedded reservoirs, just as Sal, Kasey, and Chesney did. The presence of reservoirs suggested that they were part of the iDoc beta test, but were not proof. George wanted to be certain.

George glanced over his shoulder at the other people working in the room to make sure they were not paying him any attention. When he was sure no one was watching, he used his resident password to try to access both patients' histories. Each time he tried, the computer refused him access, stating that his request violated hospital rules and that his attempts had been reported to the center's records department. George winced. He knew this was not going to look good, especially if Schwarz followed up on his threat.

Changing tactics, George looked up Tarkington's and Wong's MRIs and wrote down the contact numbers of their referring oncologists. He put in a call to both, leaving his cell number. He knew that in doing so he might cause future waves for himself, but he was at a loss for what other avenue to take. If they were part of the iDoc beta test, it would further advance his theory that iDoc was either malfunctioning or being hacked. If they weren't, then it would confirm that his paranoia was getting out of hand.

While mulling this over he decided to try the medical examiner's office. He phoned, and after identifying himself as a doctor, was transferred to one of the forensic investigators on call.

"I was hoping for some general information on some recent deaths," George said. "Actually, one was a few months ago, but the others are very recent. Do you think you would be able to help me?"

"That depends," the investigator said. "Who am I speaking with?"

"I'm Dr. George Wilson, a resident in radiology at the L.A. University Medical Center," George said. "I've noticed that on a number of recent terminal cases, the patients had implanted drug reservoirs. Has your office had any experience with such devices? If you have, can you tell me if they are removed in the course of an autopsy?"

"I'm afraid I don't know anything about that, Doctor," the forensic investigator replied. "But if you want to give me their last names, I can see if there is anything in the records."

George was pleasantly surprised to be making headway. He imagined it was because it was a holiday, and he didn't have to go through the ME's public relations office. "The family names were Lynch, DeAngelis, Tarkington, Wong, and Chesney," George said.

There was a silence on the line. All George could hear was the clicking of a computer keyboard. Finally, the investigator's voice came back on the line.

"None of those patients needed to be autopsied."

George was surprised. "Why is that?"

"They had terminal illnesses that were confirmed by their doctors, so the forensic autopsy was waived. It means the cause and manner of death were known for their death certificates. Pretty cut-and-dried stuff for what we're used to."

"Okay. Thank you." George hung up, discouraged. Then another idea hit him. He was going to pay another visit to the morgue.

George rode the elevator down to the lower basement. He was alone in the car again and, indulging in a bit of morbid humor, he guessed that not too many people needed to visit the dead on the Fourth of July.

As he neared the morgue he was struck by the disagreeable odor emanating from the place. It seemed worse than on his previous visit. It made him wonder how someone could work there day in and day out.

On this occasion, the diener was at his desk, but it was a different man. George introduced himself and said, "I'm here to talk about drug reservoirs embedded in patients. Are they routinely removed?"

The diener's face was a complete blank. He had no idea what George was talking about.

George probed the man on the subject of drug reservoirs from various angles, but it was apparent that the morgue as a general rule took no notice of them. In fact, George learned that the dieners were instructed not to remove or handle any medical devices whatsoever, particularly on those cases slated for the medical examiner's office. "We don't remove anything," the diener said. "And that includes endotracheal tubes, IVs, nasogastric tubes, embedded catheters."

George cut the man off. It was obvious he was getting nowhere fast. George thanked the diener and beat it out of there. So much for that idea.

George returned to the emergency radiology viewing room and took one of the chairs off to the side. As he was mulling over his options his cell phone rang, jarring him from his thoughts.

"Hello."

"This is Dr. White. Is this Dr. George Wilson?"

"Yes," George replied, straightening up in his chair. This call just might mean progress. "Thank you for returning my call. I'm a resident radiologist at L.A. University Medical Center, and I have a question about a former patient of yours. Greg Tarkington."

"You're a resident in radiology?" Dr. White asked. His voice reflected a mixture of disbelief and irritation. "I'm a busy man and this is a holiday. Why—?"

"I performed the last MRI on Mr. Tarkington."

The oncologist seemed to calm down a degree. "Okay. What's your question?"

"Was Mr. Tarkington taking part in the iDoc beta test? I'm helping Amalgamated with their testing. I've agreed to submit a couple of standardized forms whenever a beta-test subject dies. I thought I remembered Mr. Tarkington saying that he was, but I can't locate any documentation. I thought you might be able to help me." George lowered his voice in the hope of conveying an us-versus-them bond. "It's easier to talk doctor to doctor than to try calling Amalgamated, especially on a holiday." George held his breath. It was a fairly weak explanation for the call, but he hoped it might just get him the information he wanted.

"Tarkington was part of the study," Dr. White said without hesitation, his attitude changing for the better. "And you can tell Amalgamated that iDoc made his life much easier and mine too by fielding many of his questions. I wish more of my patients had it."

"Did you know that he had a drug-releasing implant?"

"Of course, although it wasn't for any of the drugs I prescribed. The implant was for his diabetes. He mentioned more than once that it handled his blood sugar levels better than he had been able to. It was one less issue for him to deal with in a very trying time."

"Thanks for your time. I appreciate your calling back."

"Glad to be of help. Keep up the good work!"

George ended the call and wondered if Dr. White, while advocating iDoc for his patients, had any idea of the extent to which medicine was about to change. But be that as it may, George was appreciative of the man's cooperativeness. George now knew for sure that Tarkington, like Kasey, Sal, and Laney, had been part of the iDoc beta test: four known iDoc users with drug implants . . .

George's phone rang again almost immediately. It was a call back from Wong's oncologist, a Dr. Susan Jefferson! George was surprised and pleased that both doctors had gotten back to him so quickly, especially on a holiday. He was also impressed, guessing that both doctors were conscientious about their professional responsibilities in a very emotionally demanding specialty.

George gave her the same story he'd given Dr. White. Dr. Jefferson was equally forthcoming, and confirmed that Wong was part of the iDoc beta test as well. So now George had confirmation that all five deaths in his cohort used iDoc and had implanted drug reservoirs.

George's suspicions ratcheted upward. While he was still inclined to believe that a glitch was responsible, or that a malicious hacker was involved, a new possibility occurred to him: What if iDoc was intentionally serving as a "death panel"? It would certainly help Amalgamated's bottom line, either as a company policy, which was an extreme thought, or more likely as the work of a rogue programmer sitting on a lot of Amalgamated stock options. But almost as soon as the idea occurred to George, he dismissed it out of hand. He couldn't imagine anyone doing such a thing during the beta test. If someone were thinking of such an awful thing, he'd certainly wait for iDoc to go national before unleashing it.

As George was thinking in this vein, he remembered a few high-profile cases recently in which doctors or nurses had taken it upon themselves to relieve patients of what they thought were to be their final months of painful treatment. Maybe these health care professionals were motivated by nothing other than compassion. On the other side of the coin were those bean-counter professionals who thought about resource allocation, which meant freeing up beds for patients who would be returning to society to lead productive lives rather than having them occupied by people who were terminal. George remembered a case in which a Brazilian doctor had been responsible for the deaths of over three hundred patients.

All these thoughts gave George an unpleasant shiver. It was a scary side to the concept of digitalized medicine and an awful distortion of the idea of the smartphone becoming an ersatz physician. iDoc was undoubtedly going to prove itself a fantastic idea and the wave of the future, and to have it hijacked for whatever reason would be a colossal tragedy. This realization brought George back to the importance of the embedded reservoir in the execution of any kind of death panel. As Sal had apparently sensed, if iDoc was killing people, it had to be done with the help of the reservoir. George felt he needed to focus on that.

Suddenly an idea struck him. It was a crazy idea, but possibly a good one. He remembered that Sal's funeral service was set for that afternoon. If he could only remember where.

George pulled out his cell and Googled local funeral homes. He only got to the Cs before hitting upon Carter's Funeral Home. As soon as he saw the name, he remembered it was the one Clarence had mentioned. While he may not have been able to examine Sal's body in the morgue, he just might be able to do so at the funeral home. Or at least talk to the embalmer. He didn't know how they might react, but it would be worth a try. Worst case, he would get a chance to pay his respects to Sal.

With sudden resolve, George leaped out of his seat and bolted for the exit, startling two ER residents.

He dashed out into the ER proper, pulling off his white coat as he ran. His first stop was an empty exam room, where he grabbed a pair of surgical gloves just in case. Then he headed for the parking garage.

"George! Hey! Over here!"

George pulled himself to a halt. To his astonishment, Debbie was waving him back.

"I meant to ask you earlier," she said, "are you up for Whiskey Blue again tonight? I'm thinking of heading over. I'm going to need a break after today. It's a circus here."

"I don't know," he said, a little out of breath. Her constant switch from hot to cold bewildered him. The last thing he wanted to do was go back to the bar. At the same time he didn't want to burn any bridges. "I'll text you when I get home."

"Where the hell are you going in such a hurry?"

"Believe it or not, I'm heading off to a local funeral home."

"A funeral home? What on earth for?"

"Sal DeAngelis's service is today." He leaned close to Debbie and whispered, "To be honest, since I can't imagine many people are going to show up, I'm hoping I'll have the opportunity to inspect the body. I have a new theory about his self-inflicted abdominal wounds. I think there is a good chance that he was trying to remove his drug reservoir. What I'd like to do is find out if he had been successful."

Debbie eyed him as if she thought he was going off the deep end. "You're crazy! You have to stop this shit!"

"I know, it sounds ridiculous, but I'm committed. Let me put it this way: I'm beginning to think that 'something is rotten in the state of Denmark' when it comes to Amalgamated Healthcare."

"I have no idea what you are talking about," Debbie said irritably.

"Amalgamated Healthcare, or at least somebody in the company, might not be as ethical as the Amalgamated front office wants us to believe."

"Isn't it a little cliché to blame the health insurance

company?" She glanced down, seeing what he had in his hands. "What are you doing with surgical gloves?"

"Just in case." He waved them at her as he headed for the main entrance.

"In case of what?" she called after him.

"I'll text you later about tonight," he said, ignoring the question. A moment later he was in the connector, half power walking, half jogging on the way to the garage.

33

Clayton was lounging by his pool, enjoying lunch at a table under a yellow-and-white-striped umbrella. He was in the company of a bikini-clad young woman who was twenty-five years of age, while a mister system puffed out sprays of cool vapor to combat the heat. He'd had her over the night before, and although she left in a huff while he was off on his command visit to Debbie Waters's apartment, Clayton had managed to patch things up that morning.

Just then Clayton's cell phone rang. He leaned over and stared at its display. He wasn't on call and couldn't imagine who would be phoning. It was Debbie. He frowned, debating whether to answer.

"Excuse me," Clayton said, deciding he had little choice

but to talk with her. "I need to take this." He moved away from the table to talk privately. "What?" he demanded, a little harsher than he had planned.

"Is that any way to say hello? Especially to someone who's going out of her way to help you?"

"I'm sorry. I'm just in the middle of something."

"I hope you're having a wonderful time," Debbie said sarcastically. "I'm slogging it out here in the ER."

"Did you have something to tell me? If so, out with it. I told you I was busy."

"I can only imagine. But you better be nice to me or I won't share the important information I just learned, smart-ass."

"I am being nice. I answered, didn't I?"

"Are we still on for Spago on Saturday night?"

"Of course we are! I'm looking forward to it." Clayton rolled his eyes.

"I just had a word with your favorite resident. Seems he is on a fucking crusade."

Clayton winced. "You'd better explain."

"He is still focused on those deaths because, as he said, 'something is rotten in Denmark,' whatever the hell that means."

"It's a quote from Shakespeare, which is pretty damn famous."

"Careful, buddy. You're on thin ice with me."

Ignoring the comment he said, "Do you have any idea what he was referring to?"

"Amalgamated Healthcare, most definitely. He's bent out of shape about something called a reservoir. He left the hospital with a package of surgical gloves, going to DeAngelis's funeral."

"Shit," Clayton mumbled. He could feel his stomach start to suds up. This George problem was going from bad to worse. "Okay, Debbie, thanks," Clayton said as amiably as possible. "I appreciate the info, but I gotta run now. Talk soon, and see you Saturday night."

Clayton hung up without waiting for Debbie to say good-bye and speed-dialed Thorn. The executive's voice mail picked up, and Clayton could only leave a message asking Thorn to call him back ASAP. It was important.

Clayton went back to the pool, smiling at his young lady friend, and tried to refocus his attention on her. But he couldn't. There was way too much at stake to relax. Something had to be done, and done quickly.

34

George had the suspicion that Carter's Funeral Home had been something else in its former life. Incongruously it had a steep gabled roof with windows climbing up to the apex. Maybe it had been a restaurant, he guessed, inappropriate as that was. He surveyed the U-shaped parking lot. There were only a half dozen cars, mostly toward the rear. If employee vehicles were subtracted, then that didn't leave much in the way of mourners. From George's perspective that was auspicious. He was counting on few, if any, visitors coming to view Sal's body.

George went inside. As he had hoped, the place seemed empty, without a soul in evidence. Low-level, mournful organ music from hidden speakers pervaded the place. On a pedestal was a guest book. He looked at the open page. There was only one scheduled service, and that was for Salvatore DeAngelis at 2:00 P.M. He checked his watch. He would have to hurry.

The front room on the right was a reception area with overstuffed upholstered seating. On the left was a room with various caskets on display. George walked down a central corridor, which ran parallel to the long axis of the building. He came to a room with open double doors. On a pedestal in front of a makeshift altar was a closed casket. A dozen or so folding chairs had been set up. No one was in the room. He checked his watch again, unsure what to do: fourteen minutes until the service was scheduled to begin. He couldn't tell whether or not he was looking at Sal's casket, but, considering that the man had rocketed through a windshield and impaled himself on an LED display, a closed-casket service sounded like an appropriate idea.

Wanting to get a better lay of the land, he continued down the main hallway. Through a partially opened door on the left he spotted two women with their backs to him talking in subdued tones with a man in a dark suit and a forlorn expression. *Sal's sisters?* he wondered. From the style of their clothes and hats, they looked like stereotypical old maids. A quick glance at the name on the door confirmed that it was the office of the funeral director, Myron Carter.

"May I help you?" a man whispered in George's ear. George nearly jumped out of his skin. He spun around, confronting the chest of a hulking man in a conservative suit similar to the funeral director's.

"Hopefully you can," George replied in a hushed tone. "I'm here to pay my respects to Salvatore DeAngelis."

"Back this way." The giant gestured back down the hall in the direction George had just come.

The man silently accompanied George back to the room with the closed casket and after a bow thankfully disappeared. Unfortunately there were now two people in the room. One was an African American woman, probably in her sixties, wearing a purple dress, the other a short Caucasian man about the same age. They were not sitting together. The woman had a snippet of a veil covering the top of her face, so it was hard to make out her features, but George didn't think he had ever met her. He knew he had never seen the man.

George decided to take a seat and figure out his best course of action. It would also give him a few moments to bow his head and say good-bye to Sal—and ask for his forgiveness for what he was about to do if he had the courage to follow through, which he doubted, what with mourners in the room.

He was convinced that if something had gone wrong with Sal's embedded reservoir, the evidence would soon be buried with him. But if George could get hold of the reservoir, he might be able to match the dosages still in it with the approximate date Schwarz had inserted the device.

As if answering his prayers, the two other people in the room suddenly stood up and walked out. George was alone with Sal's corpse. Checking his watch, he saw there were now only six minutes till two o'clock. If he was going to do anything, this was the time. Besides the canned music in the background, the only sound was the ticking of a grandfather's clock out in the hallway.

With sudden resolve, George stood up. His pulse was hammering. He felt as if he were about to rob a bank. It was now or never. After looking around to make sure he was still alone in the room, he tried to lift the lid of the casket. It cracked open with ease. He was relieved it wasn't secured.

After one more glance back toward the hallway, George raised the lid all the way and looked down.

Sal was dressed in a dark blue suit. There had been some attempt to put his face back together, but the result was grotesque. Again asking for Sal's forgiveness for disturbing him, George donned his gloves before unbuttoning Sal's jacket and opening his dress shirt to expose his marble-white lower abdomen. George paused for a moment to catch his breath when he caught sight of the wound where the large embalming trocar had been inserted to suck out the blood and intestinal contents and infuse embalming fluid. People assumed doctors were immune to such sights, but they were wrong.

Swallowing hard, George switched his attention to Sal's left lower abdomen. In addition to a number of abrasions, there were a few shallow, surgical-like cuts in the skin and a deep one that could very well have been made with a utility knife. George inserted a gloved index finger in the deep one and felt around inside the stiff, lifeless tissue. Nothing! There was no reservoir! George felt again to be sure.

Either Sal had succeeded in getting the reservoir out or someone else had. Maybe that was the reason Clayton had been down in the morgue the day George had seen him? Or perhaps more likely, could it have been the reservoir that the suits had been searching for in Sal's apartment the night before.

After putting Sal's clothes back in a semblance to the way they had been, George was starting to close the coffin when there was a piercing scream. In a panic he dropped the lid and spun to the voice. The scream had come from one of the women he'd seen in the funeral director's office. She was standing in the doorway with a hand clasped to her mouth in horror. The horror quickly turned to outrage.

"What in the hell do you think you're doing!" she demanded.

The other sister and the funeral director appeared right behind her.

"He opened the casket!" the first sister yelled, pointing a bony gloved finger in George's direction.

"This is a closed-casket ceremony, sir!" the funeral director bellowed.

"I . . . I know," George stammered. "I'm sorry. I just wanted to see if—"

"Look at his gloves!"

A gasp escaped the second sister. "Pervert!"

"No! I'm sorry! It's not . . ." It's not what? He didn't know where to begin. Then the hulking giant appeared behind the three.

In a panic, George scanned his options. The double

doors through which he'd entered were blocked by the four outraged but stunned people, but there was a second door that thankfully wasn't locked. George bolted for it and found himself in a second, empty viewing room. Through that room he returned to the main corridor, only deeper into the funeral home and farther from the front entrance.

Running the length of the hallway and passing the funeral director's office, he burst through one of the doors labeled STAFF ONLY. He skidded to a stop. He was in a tiled embalming room, which contained several metal worktables, one of which was occupied by another marble-colored naked corpse being worked on by a startled man in a large apron. The man was holding an embalming trocar, and in the corner a suction machine was loudly chugging away. George looked about wildly for an exit. He spotted one and bolted for it.

Outside, George could hear yelling as he sprinted around the building toward his car.

A moment later George was in his car, getting the engine going as the elderly women and funeral director piled out the front door, yelling for him to stop. George eyed them in his rearview mirror as he quickly backed up. He was just about to pull away into traffic when a massive hand slapped the driver's-side window. It was the hulk. Where the hell did he come from? The man leaned down and stuck his angry, red face up against the window, screaming at George to get out of the car.

George stepped on the gas, swerving his Jeep into an opening in the lane of traffic. In the rearview mirror he caught a glimpse of the hulk shaking his fist at him.

After a few blocks George slowed down, blending into the holiday traffic. That was close! As his breathing returned to normal, he started to think about the reservoir. He was more convinced than ever it was the key.

With sudden resolve, George pulled out his phone and located the nearest Los Angeles police station. It was the West L.A. Community Police Station on Butler Avenue. George turned at the next corner and headed in that direction.

As George wiped the sweat from his brow, a couple of police cruisers with their sirens blaring sped by him, luckily heading in the opposite direction. He wondered if they were on their way to Carter's Funeral Home. What if surveillance cameras had caught his face or, worse, recorded George's violation of the corpse. Was what he had done considered a crime? He didn't know. What he did know was that regardless of whether it was a crime or not, if his actions became public knowledge, it wasn't going to make him any friends at the medical center, especially with the conservative hierarchy of the radiology department.

35

Clayton pulled up to the gate blocking Thorn's drive-way. Envy crept over him every time he visited his sister and Thorn at their home. Clayton needed his own security gate to keep the likes of Debbie Waters from coming to his front door uninvited. Besides, he deserved to have a security gate. In L.A. it was a must-have status symbol.

The doctor pressed the intercom button and announced himself to a member of Thorn's staff. The gate glided back, and Clayton drove up the tree-lined drive. Thorn had finally returned Clayton's call, but when Clayton started to talk about George Wilson, Thorn had cut him off, telling him that he would prefer to speak in person rather than over Clayton's cell phone. Clayton agreed to drive the short distance from Bel Air to Beverly Hills.

Thorn's massive house was a Spanish Mediterranean revival, a style currently the vogue in Southern California.

Clayton was escorted to the pool, where Thorn was waiting with drinks. As soon as the staff withdrew, Clayton laid it on the line: "I'm afraid Dr. George Wilson is threatening to become a big problem."

"That's not good. Have you spoken with him directly?"

"No, but it came from a good source. She says he is convinced something serious is wrong with iDoc and supposedly is on a mission to prove it."

"That's worse than not good. That's fucking terrible." Thorn pulled himself out of his chair and began to pace.

Clayton watched him. He could tell Thorn was mulling over options. Clayton waited.

Suddenly Thorn sat back down. "Any idea what this resident plans to do?"

"He's not letting sleeping dogs lie, that's for sure. He is not buying the suicide story. Unfortunately he's become fixated on the implanted drug reservoir, and if I had to guess, I think he either suspects now that Amalgamated Healthcare via iDoc is culpable in DeAngelis's death, or he will shortly. My source said he was off to DeAngelis's funeral service with a pair of surgical gloves."

"But you are sure he is not going to find anything?"

"Positive. The reservoir was not in DeAngelis's body. I checked myself, at Langley's request."

"At least we have that going for us," Thorn said. He

nodded thoughtfully. "All right," he added, obviously upset at Clayton's news. "I was hoping that it wasn't going to come to this, but it is time to hand the situation over to the professionals."

"What do you mean by 'professionals'?"

"In-house professionals. I'll turn the situation over to Amalgamated's security department. I've been paying Thorton Gauthier and his people a king's ransom for their experience and expertise. Here's the opportunity for them to earn it."

Thorn had hired "Butch" Gauthier two years previously when he took over the company from his father. The nickname Butch came from Gauthier's hairstyle, a buzzed flat-top that was close-cropped along the sides. Thorn had heard about Gauthier through a golfing buddy who bragged about the ex–special ops, ex-mercenary turned corporate protector and how he got the job done no matter what. Thorn loved that Gauthier ran Amalgamated's security like a paramilitary group. It was the kind of raw-power, show-of-force mentality that made Thorn sleep better, knowing that just about any eventuality could be handled.

"What do you think Butch might do?" Clayton was growing concerned. He knew Gauthier's reputation. Clayton began to worry about what he had unleashed upon poor George Wilson. Then he remembered his stock options. Good radiology residents weren't hard to find. It was all a matter of priorities.

"That is totally up to Wilson," Thorn replied cryptically. "At this stage I think it best if none of us knows what might happen. I am confident everything will turn out just fine. The important thing is that George Wilson will not be allowed to destroy Amalgamated's plans for the future."

Well, Clayton thought, *at least he has his priorities in order.*

Fifteen minutes later Clayton was back in his car, heading home, hoping that he would now be able to concentrate on his original plans for the holiday. He tried to put George Wilson out of his mind, but it wasn't easy. The problem was, he liked George and thought of him as one of the best residents he'd ever had.

"It's a shame," Clayton whispered as he turned into his driveway.

36

The trip to the Valley had been uneventful. One never knew what to expect on the 405, regardless of the hour. A person could just as easily get stuck in a huge traffic jam at five in the morning as at five in the afternoon. But not today. Traffic flowed unimpeded. He guessed the heat wave had sent everyone to the beach.

George exited the 405 at Sherman Way and drove east a couple of miles. The signs on the one-story businesses strung along the seemingly endless boulevard changed progressively from English to Spanish. He missed the tow yard on his first pass and had to double back. Now he was there.

George had first inquired about Sal's car and asked where it had been taken. He was told one of two junkyards in Van Nuys. The first one, Rust-a-Car Yard, denied having received a red 1957 Oldsmobile. The people were not all that friendly, but George decided that he had to take them at their word and called United Salvage Yard. They confirmed that they had the vehicle.

The yard was surrounded by a boarded-over fence with coiled razor wire running along the top to discourage thieves. Basically it looked like any junkyard-cum-tow-yard. There was a small parking lot in front of a trailer that housed the front office. Two other vehicles were in the lot; one was a taxicab that was just pulling out.

George walked up to the trailer and pulled on the door. It was locked. He looked through the narrow glass window and saw a man inside behind a counter talking with customers. George was about to knock when he noticed the bell and a security camera pointed down at him. George rang. A moment later the door buzzed open, and George stepped inside.

The reception room was small and sparsely furnished. The counter was fronted by a thick glass wall of the type George was accustomed to seeing in banks and twenty-four-hour convenience stores. The man behind it was packing a sidearm and arguing with a young couple standing on George's side of the glass. They were dressed in casual beach attire and sporting lots of tattoos. They appeared to have been drinking.

"This is bullshit!" the guy yelled.

"It's a freaking scam!" the girl chimed in.

"We have a contract with the city," the attendant said with a bored voice. "These are the standard rates." The attendant looked like a Harley-Davidson biker, overweight with a graying ponytail and a ragged five-o'clock shadow.

"It's not just the rates. Where I was parked wasn't marked as a tow zone!"

"This is. Out! Of! Freaking! Control!" the girl huffed as she furiously typed a text message on her cell phone. "We're gonna be so late to the party," she added. She punched her companion in the arm in frustration. "Your boy better be at the door to get our asses in, I'm telling you right now."

"Ow! Relax a minute, okay!" he said, rubbing his pumped-up arm.

The guy behind the counter was unfazed. He'd been called names before. He slid a piece of paper through the slot at the bottom of the glass. "These are the published rates. If you got a beef with the street sign postings you can take it up with the city. They have a petition process."

"But I still have to pay it first?"

"Correct. It's two hundred twenty-two dollars for the tow, because the vehicle is an SUV. There's a fifty-dollar-per-day storage fee—which would be for just one day—that fee is subject to a ten percent tax. And there's a one-hundred-fifteen-dollar release fee. It adds up to three hundred ninety-two dollars. We take cash, debit cards, credit cards, certified checks, traveler's checks, and money orders."

"What a scam!" the guy said as he pulled out his wallet and produced a credit card. He glanced over at George. "Get ready to be raped, my man."

The man behind the counter fished the card out of the

window slot and slid it through his processor. His eyes flicked over to George, probably wondering if he was going to have a repeat performance when it was his turn.

George offered him a tight smile. Whatever hopes he had of getting access to Sal's car had diminished in the last two minutes, watching the attendant handle the couple. For one, George probably didn't have near enough cash on him.

The tow guy grabbed a walkie-talkie. "Joey. We got someone coming back for the black Escalade you just brought in." He pointed to the guy, then a door in the corner. "Sir, through here, please. Miss, you can wait out front. The gates will open when the vehicle pulls out."

She spun on her heels, heading out. "Asshole."

The attendant looked up at George. "How can I help you, sir?"

He escorted George across the yard to the back corner of the lot. Two large German shepherds growled at George as they passed.

"Fucking shame," the attendant said when they reached Sal's car. "It was a nice ride. I knew when I first saw it that the operator didn't live through the crash."

"Unfortunately no airbags in the classics," George replied, agreeably. He wanted the tow guy to feel like they were buddies.

George had gone for broke back in the office. He had opened his wallet in front of the attendant and took out all the cash in it—$317.00—and slapped it next to the window slot. He told the attendant this was everything he had and it was all for him—*if* he would let him take a look inside the totaled car of his dead friend. He described the vehicle, saying that the police station said it had been brought here. He even went so far as to tell the tow guy he was looking for a microchip. He thought that if the attendant believed he was looking for something of street value, like some kind of jewelry, then he might want to take a look for himself instead of accepting George's cash. But the guy had looked at the cash and simply said, "Sure."

The Oldsmobile looked as dead as Sal. Its front end was folded up on itself to less than a third of its previous length. The convertible top was down, which was how Sal had it ninety percent of the time. The engine block was pushed back into the front seat. George groaned. This was going to be harder than he envisioned. He approached the vehicle, looking for a place to start as the attendant's walkie-talkie crackled to life. "Danno? You got someone at the front gate."

"Copy that. I'm on my way." Danno turned to George. "I gotta go back to the office." He motioned to the car. "Knock yourself out, but be careful. And no walking around the lot. You stay right here."

"Okay. Got it," George said, offering a thumbs-up.

"You hurt yourself, I'm gonna throw you over the fence and pretend I never saw you. Understand?"

"Yes. I do."

"Good. I'll be back in fifteen minutes, so hurry up. You finish before that, come knock on the back door to the office."

"What about the dogs?"

"Like I said, stay in the middle of this open lane. Do not veer off."

"Got it again," George said.

Danno nodded and rushed off. George turned back to the Oldsmobile. He peered down into the wrecked convertible. The entire interior was littered with broken glass. The engine block took up most of what was the passenger's front seat. There was a little more room on the driver's side. George pulled out his cell phone, turned on its flashlight, and focused the beam under the engine and under the front seats for a quick look. Broken glass was piled up under there, too. He realized this was going to be a near impossible task—a microchip would be just slightly larger than a postage stamp and a couple of millimeters thick at best. That's if the reservoir microchip was in the vehicle at all. George took a deep breath. It was better to quit thinking and just get on with it. He bent over the driver's door and started sorting through the shards of glass with a broken windshield wiper blade.

A half hour had passed and George hadn't found a thing. He was covered in dirt, grease, and soaked in sweat. Frustration was giving way to anger. This little field trip had seemed like it was going to be a lot easier in the abstract. At least the attendant hadn't come back yet. He debated stopping.

George was in the vehicle's backseat now, lying on his stomach, shining light up under the front seat. At this point he was picking up each piece of glass and after examining it, throwing it out of the car. A sweep of the flashlight revealed that there were a lot more pieces left to go. He shifted his weight to get a better reach under the seat—

"Hey, buddy? Time's up." Danno had returned.

"Okay!" George replied cheerfully, without getting up. "Almost done." Now that he was being forced to quit, he didn't want to. He kept at it, moving faster, but stopped throwing the discarded pieces of debris out of the car. He was now merely pushing them aside. In the rush, he was cutting his fingers on the fragments.

The attendant shuffled around the dusty ground with his feet, waiting. He was obviously ready for George to leave pronto. "Now means now! Don't make me go get one of the dogs."

"Okay," floated up from under the seat. George sorted faster, becoming frantic. All this for nothing!

Danno's patience was at an end. "I'm about to reach over and grab you by the belt and haul you out of there."

"I'm coming." But he wasn't.

"Okay . . . On three. One . . ."

George kept sifting, sweat burning his eyes.

"Two . . ."

"Okay!"

"Three!"

George felt a hand grab his belt. His arms flailed as he was propelled backward out of the car and began staggering around, trying to regain his balance, when Danno let go of his belt. The man might have been overweight, but he was powerful.

"I gave you way more time than we agreed to. It's time to go."

"Damn it!" George screamed at the guy. "I know what I came for is in there! You have to let me keep looking!"

"I don't have to do anything. You want to keep looking? Come back in a couple of months when the LAPD releases the vehicle. You pay the tow and storage fees, and she's yours. We'll even tow it to your house. Although that'll be extra."

"Just five more minutes," George pleaded.

"No!" The tow guy trained a hard gaze on George, then glanced down as the sunlight caught a reflection on the front of George's dirty shirt. In addition to a few glass fragments, there was a thin, flat, gold-colored rectangular object. Danno plucked it off of George's shirt.

"Is that what you were looking for?"

George had his mouth open to argue some more but stopped and looked down at what the guy was holding in his hand. It was a microchip.

"I'll be damned," George murmured.

George sat in his car in the corner of the salvage yard's parking lot with the engine on and the air conditioner cranked up. He was overheated, but he was also elated. This just might be the Rosetta Stone to break the code. He had a magnifying glass app on his phone open that operated through its camera lens, which was focused on the small gold object in his hand. He could see a series of haphazard linear gouges on the surface, probably from the utility knife that had been found at the crash site. Apparently Sal had actually managed to cut the damn thing out himself! The poor guy must have intuited what was happening. That was George's current theory. And it made more sense than anything else he could think of. Way more sense than suicide.

George gave up trying to examine the chip with the magnifying app on his phone. He needed something more powerful to try to view the individual chambers that held the medication. To do that, he needed to go back to the medical center. He couldn't believe that he had actually gotten his hands on the damn thing!

Rap, rap, rap! George's head shot up and spun around to the noise. The attendant was knocking on the window with a short billy club.

"You can't stay here in the lot," he yelled through the glass, giving an unmistakable signal that George was seriously trying his patience. "Move it."

George waved okay and put the car in gear.

George scanned the rows of individual reservoirs on the chip. Each was the size of a pinprick, and there were thousands of them. George had researched the way the chip worked. Each individual reservoir had been assigned its own radio frequency, which, when received, signaled a thin layer of gold nanoparticles encapsulating a drug dosage to dissolve. The freed medication was then transported across the biological membranes, where it entered the bloodstream and spread throughout the entire body.

George was back at the medical center in the pathology lab, where he had commandeered a dissecting microscope to study the microchip. With the powerful magnification he could see that its myriad small containers were in fact empty! All of them. There was no way that could be considered normal for a two-month-old reservoir that had been intended to last at least two years. The chip also noted the type of drug it held: Humalog. George recognized the name as a brand of fast-acting insulin.

For George, it was now a question of whether or not the reservoir emptied pre-mortem or postmortem. Pre-mortem, meaning that the dosages were dumped en masse while Sal was alive. The implication of that was murder, whether by hacking or deliberate intent on behalf of the application's designers. Postmortem meant that after Sal had died and the reservoir had gone through the trauma of being gouged out of Sal's body, it had somehow released its contents. Then there was always the issue of it sitting for a few days under the broiling L.A. heat wave sun in a wrecked car. Maybe that, too, could have done it.

Of all the possibilities, George thought pre-mortem was the most realistic option, but he needed more proof, and he had an idea of how to get it. It was possible that Sal's broken smartphone combined with the microchip might be all he needed, provided he could get someone to help him. The first person that came to mind was Zee.

George switched off the light of the dissecting

microscope and left the pathology lab after thanking the technician who had helped him. He was pleased with what he had accomplished, but recognized something important: He needed to be careful. Lots of people, including Clayton and possibly the men searching Sal's apartment and surely Amalgamated, would be wanting Sal's microchip. It was, if he was right, a smoking gun.

George drove home, his mind going a mile a minute. He knew that he had stumbled onto something serious. The first person he should call was Paula. She had to know that her "baby" had been hijacked. He just hoped that she wouldn't blame the messenger, because he knew she would be both horrified and devastated. He wondered if he should call her while she was still in Hawaii, and then wondered why he was wondering. Of course he should call her as soon as he was certain. This wasn't something that could wait. People were literally dying.

37

A black SUV and a black van, both with dark tinted windows, pulled up and parked behind George's apartment complex. A bank of electronic listening equipment lined the interior of the van. Four men dressed in SoCal Edison uniforms alighted from the vehicles, leaving two men in suits behind in the SUV and two technicians in coveralls sitting in the back of the van.

The four men in uniform strapped on an array of impressive electrical tool belts. One went to a nearby pole and climbed up to tap the phone line. The other three went to the building's electrical panel and opened it, as if they were reading the meter. They then split up: Two men went through the complex and the other man walked around the side of the building.

All three quickly closed in on George's apartment, one in back and two in the front. There was no conversation or hesitation. They were professionals. It was all planned. Nothing was left to chance.

The two inside the complex rang George's doorbell. There was no answer, which they fully expected. Earlier, having checked his cell phone with GPS, they knew that George was in the San Fernando Valley. Yet they wanted to be sure his apartment was empty. One of the men quickly and effortlessly picked George's cheap lock.

Without so much as one word, the taller of the two disappeared inside the apartment while the other stood guard just inside the entrance. He peered out of a window. The pool area of the complex was empty. No one was about; it being the Fourth of July, most people with a car were at either the beach or a barbecue.

The other man in George's apartment worked quickly, hiding several small listening devices and cameras, linking them up wirelessly with a battery-powered amplifier hidden by his colleague on the back side of the apartment behind a downspout. The amplifier would catch the wireless signals from the devices inside the apartment and then relay them to the recording equipment in the van. All told, the whole operation took less than seven minutes.

Once safely back inside the vehicles, the four technicians waited to be picked up by a third vehicle. The car appeared moments later, stopping just long enough for the four men to scurry aboard. The men in coveralls were left behind in the van and the two suits were settled into the SUV, removing their sidearms and generally making themselves more comfortable. They knew it would most likely be a long night. But they were accustomed to it. Their jobs required long hours of boredom punctuated by sudden violence.

The man sitting behind the wheel dialed a number on his mobile phone and left a simple message: "We're good."

38

George turned into the street behind his apartment. He was exhausted and had a near accident while driving back from the valley. It seemed like rush hour even though it was a holiday. Pulling into his slot, he didn't notice the black SUV at the curb in the street. Or the black van that was parked half a block farther down the road. Such vehicles were more common than palm trees in the neighborhood, especially black SUVs.

George parked and grabbed his gear, carefully making sure the tiny drug reservoir was safely in his pocket, and raced to his apartment. He put everything except the microchip on the dining room table, and then located Sal's broken smartphone as well as Kasey's. With these in his other pocket, he ran outside and up the stairs to pound on Zee's door.

"Jesus! Hang on. I'm coming!" Zee yelled. A second later he yanked the door open and took in George's expression and appearance. "What the fuck, dude?" he said. "We have a fire in the building or what?"

"I need your help. Right now."

"Slow down, dude. I'm here," Zee said, trying to calm his clearly distraught neighbor.

George took a deep breath. "Okay," he said, realizing that he had to get himself under control. He knew that what he was asking Zee to do was going to take a long time, *if* he could do it at all. And that was assuming Zee was even willing. That was another big *if,* given that what George wanted Zee to do was very much against the law.

"I need you to do a job," George said, trying to maintain an even tone. "I'll pay you. A lot. I have almost ten thousand dollars in cash and credit."

"Whoa, dude! Cool it! You gotta start at the beginning."

"It's just . . . I know you haven't been working and money is an issue—"

"Money is an issue for me even when I *am* working. But let's hear what you got."

"I need you to do a little hacking for me."

Zee's antennae went up. "No hack job is little. Some are easy, some aren't. But none are little. Not to the hackee. Just explain exactly what it is you'd like me to do. And relax. You want a beer?"

George took a seat on the couch and said, "Yeah. A beer would be great."

Zee got the beers and George launched into giving Zee enough background on Amalgamated and iDoc to intrigue him. Luckily Zee found the idea of smartphones taking the place of primary-care doctors mind-blowing. He wanted to sign up for iDoc himself, explaining if he got the clap, he could get treatment without having to explain everything to a real person, case closed. "You know," Zee continued, "sometimes going to the doctor can be a little embarrassing. But you know something? I know a way for this iDoc to be even better."

"Zee, I'd like to keep this conversation on point," George interrupted.

"No! Hear me out," Zee responded. "When you go to the pharmacy to fill a prescription, you shouldn't have to deal with the pharmacist! That can be as bad as talking to the doctor. You know what I'm saying? All you should have to do is flash your phone or press your fingerprints onto a touch pad, and, bingo, you get your prescription immediately."

"That's a great idea, Zee, but we're getting off track."

"Sorry. Continue!" Zee said, holding his beer up to George in a mock toast.

"The iDoc concept is fantastic and it is the future of medicine. But I think there is a problem. Either by design or by accident it's gone beyond its mandate. I think it's been acting as a kind of death panel."

Zee just stared at George with a blank expression. Finally, he said, "Explain!"

George did. He told Zee that Kasey, whom Zee had known somewhat from time spent around the complex, had been a part of the iDoc beta-test group, as well as Sal. He then told Zee about Laney Chesney, Greg Tarkington, and Claire Wong, also members of the iDoc study who had serious illnesses on top of diabetes. "All five relied upon iDoc to medicate them in a truly futuristic fashion, functioning like a real pancreas, using an implanted reservoir of insulin and constant, real-time monitoring of their sugar levels in the bloodstream."

"I get it," Zee replied. "What's the rub?"

"I have reason to believe that iDoc killed all five by dumping the contents of their reservoirs into their systems all at once."

Zee looked askance at George. "If you are saying that the reservoir fucked up, I'm with you. Shit happens. But if you think it was intentional, I think you are crazy. I know a lot of those guys—"

"Proof!" George said, interrupting and getting the reservoir he found in Sal's car out of his pocket and setting it on the table. "Proof that the phenomenon I just described is real. Whether it is intentional or a glitch is why I'm talking to you. And to be honest, I'm thinking intentional."

Zee carefully picked up the reservoir and examined it.

"It can't be fully appreciated without magnification," George offered. "The surface of the reservoir contains thousands of tiny encapsulated doses of insulin. Each is individually programmed to be released upon reception of a particular radio frequency."

"I understand the concept. But why have you jumped to the conclusion that iDoc is killing patients?"

"The reservoir you're holding was implanted under Sal's skin about two months ago. It was supposed to last two or three years, depending upon Sal's blood sugar levels. That reservoir in your hand is completely empty. I believe iDoc sent a message to do a massive, total dump."

Zee set the chip down on his coffee table, revolted by the thought of where it had been and what it might have done. "How do you know that the reservoir dumped all its insulin just before Sal's death? Maybe it happened after it was removed from the corpse."

"Good question. And I don't know for sure," George admitted. "That's one of the reasons I need your help."

"And why do you think it was intentional?"

"In all five cases, the insulin dump occurred soon after a serious likely terminal diagnosis had been entered into their electronic medical records. That's a very odd coincidence."

Zee sat silent, staring at the reservoir on his coffee table. "Exactly what do you want me to do?"

George let out a sigh of relief with the sense Zee was softening up. "Several things." He pulled out a smartphone. "This was Kasey's." He turned it on and showed Zee the iDoc icon, then demonstrated how it didn't open. "I think Amalgamated wipes it clean after the patient dies, which makes a lot of sense. It guards the confidentiality of the patient's medical history."

George then produced the second phone and handed it over to Zee. "This was Sal's. It followed his body out through the windshield of the Oldsmobile when he crashed. It was obviously damaged. But it apparently functioned for a short time because an ER nurse was able to extract some medical information from it before it died, and I got it to turn on briefly."

Zee examined Sal's phone, turning it over in his hands. "Poor guy."

"Now, it's only an idea, but I think that perhaps in this case the app wasn't wiped clean. I want you to see if you can get anything out of the phone. Maybe a dump command or something like that."

Zee nodded, staring at the phone's shattered display face. "I might be able to do a kind of forensic autopsy. There should be some data still in its storage unit, if not in its processor." He looked up at George. "You're willing to pay me ten thousand dollars to do this?" Zee asked incredulously.

"I'd want a little more than that for ten thousand."

"Figured. What?" Zee frowned.

"I want you to hack into Amalgamated's central iDoc servers. If we can get Sal's whole record we can compare it to whatever you find on his phone. If it's intentional, like I suspect, I want to be able to prove it. Only then can we be one hundred percent certain of what is going on and if it's outside hackers or commands from inside Amalgamated that are responsible for the deaths."

"You're asking for a lot—"

"If I'm right, they killed my fiancée. You knew her. If I'm right, they killed Sal. You knew him. I'm aware of five deaths. How many others will die before they should when iDoc goes national and then international?"

"I don't know, man," Zee mumbled. He looked at the two phones. "This is serious shit, hacking into health records. It's on par with hacking into the Pentagon, for Chrissake."

"It is serious," George agreed. "So is killing people."

Zee nodded. George had him on that point.

"Amalgamated must have contingency plans to handle anyone with questions or suspicions. I want to be open with you. Doing this might put you and me in physical jeopardy, knowing what kind of money is involved. Billions are at stake, if not trillions. And that's no exaggeration."

From the grave look on Zee's face, George recognized he wasn't helping his case, bringing up the downside. Still, he felt he had to be honest. "Listen, Zee," George continued, trying to tone down the urgency in his voice. "I have to play this out whether you help me or not, but I need proof of what is going on in order to go to the media, which is my idea of what I will do if my worst fears are realized. And the only proof I can imagine getting is what I'm hoping you can provide me."

Zee softened a bit. "Are you serious about the ten grand?"

"I am. And if I'm right, I'm betting there will be a lot of job offers for the guy who helped expose it all."

Zee nodded, a little embarrassed. "It's just that I've had some recent online poker losses and, well, I have rent and bills and all."

"Help me and the money is yours."

"Okay, I'll do it," Zee said. "But with a couple of conditions. I use your computer when I try and access

Amalgamated's servers. And I only use your modem. When the shit hits, I prefer it hit there."

"No problem," George agreed immediately. "When can you start?"

"Give me an hour. I need to shower and grab a bite to eat to be fresh for this. It ain't going to be easy. I imagine they have created some serious firewall shit."

George felt a huge relief wash over him. "Okay, great! How can I help?"

"By paying me. Knowing that I can pay my past due rent will let me give you my undivided attention."

"Consider it done."

39

True to his word, Zee appeared at George's front door an hour later, freshly showered and wearing a pair of baggy sweats. He was holding a coffeepot filled with fresh brew. In his other hand, he was balancing a carton of Red Bull and a carton of Marlboro cigarettes on top of a fishing tackle box filled with tools, computer CDs, and other paraphernalia. In response to George's comment that he had a lot of stuff, Zee said he was loaded for bear.

George eyed the cigarettes. "I'd rather you don't smoke."

"Sorry, dude, but ciggies are a must if I'm gonna have any luck. It's the cigs or nothing."

"Okay, fine," George relented, recognizing that there were people who couldn't concentrate unless they had their smoking ritual, which was sometimes more important than the nicotine. He pointed toward his dining room table, where he had his laptop set up and ready to go next to Sal's smartphone. He'd put Kasey's back in the box in the closet.

"Where's your modem?" Zee said, scanning the room.

George pointed it out next to his TV. Zee went about inspecting it.

"It works well," George said. "The cable people said it was a good one."

"It's a piece of shit, but it'll do."

George realized that everyone who ever commented on his apartment either referred to it or what was in it as "shit." When all this was over, he'd have to address the issue. Assuming he was still around when it was over. He was painfully aware that what he was doing could very well impact his career.

Zee plugged in his coffeepot and stowed his Red Bull in the refrigerator, then settled down at the table and opened his toolbox. The time for small talk was over. He went to work on Sal's smartphone first, removing it from its orange case and opening its back. He put on a pair of binocular loupes and closely examined its inner contents.

George watched him for a while but became bored. He went to his refrigerator and scanned its contents. "Care for something to eat?" he called out to Zee.

Zee didn't even respond, which was a good thing, because there wasn't much of anything to offer. George took what was there and made a sloppy sandwich, eating it while standing over the sink. He again thought about calling Paula in Hawaii but decided to wait until he had some more proof that her beloved iDoc was in trouble. He imagined she was going to resist belief in a big way. He wondered what effect it might have on their friendship. Probably not good.

40

There was a prearranged knock on the back of the van. Steven, the shorter of the two technicians, reached out and unlocked the door. Andor Nagy, a handsome, powerfully built man, climbed in. He wasn't wearing his suit jacket and his tie was loosened.

"What's up?" Andor said with a slight Hungarian accent. He took a seat on a small bench along the side of the van.

Steven, manning the visual leads, pointed out Zee sitting hunched over a dismantled smartphone. "Your guess is as good as mine. We have what we believe to be a neighbor working on a smartphone, which we guess belongs to the mark."

"Any idea why?"

"None whatsoever. The neighbor came in more than an hour ago, but there has been almost no conversation."

"Where's Wilson?"

Steven pointed to another, darker screen showing the inside of George's bedroom. George could barely be seen lounging on his bed, watching TV with the sound turned way down.

Andor called up to Lee, who was manning the headphones a little farther forward in the van, to confirm that the two men in George's apartment had been silent.

"That's right. No chatter," Lee replied.

"What's he looking at online?" The laptop on the dining room table was angled so the screen wasn't visible to any of their cameras.

"Nothing. So far," Steven said. "He's just been messing with the cell phone."

Andor shrugged. "We'll just have to be patient, then. Has Wilson made any phone calls or sent any texts?"

"Nope."

"Let me know if and when anything changes," Andor said, rising to leave.

"You will be the first to know," Steven assured him.

41

George was roused from a deep sleep when Zee rudely shook his shoulder. George had fallen asleep in his clothes while watching television. The TV was still on.

Zee was in a dither. "I'm done, and I'm out of here." He looked like a madman. His eyes were red and his face drawn and pale. The combination of the night's activities plus all the coffee, cigarettes, and Red Bull had given him a visible tremor in his hands, and his voice was raspy.

"What do you mean you're out of here?" George asked.

"It means I'm out of here!" Zee disappeared out into the living room.

George leaped off the bed and ran after him while trying to get into his shoes.

Zee was throwing his tools and junk into the tackle box while muttering to himself, "Shit, shit, shit."

"Where are you going?"

"I'm dropping off the grid until this blows over."

"Until what blows over?" George said, bewildered.

"Everything," Zee replied cryptically.

"What did you find out?"

"Too much." Zee snapped his toolbox shut. "Way too much."

George couldn't believe what was happening. "What exactly do you mean by 'dropping off the grid'?"

"It means exactly what it sounds like. I'm heading for the hills until things blow over. I have some friends up north near San Fran. They got a cabin someplace in the High Sierras. That sounds about perfect at the moment."

George couldn't believe that Zee was leaving. "Why the rush? What did you find?"

"If you really want to know, you better get your ass up to my apartment while I get a few things together."

George wondered if he was dreaming. "You're planning on leaving right away? Now?"

"As soon as I can get my shit together." Zee moved to the door, then stopped. "The money you promised?"

"I have to go to the bank for that kind of money. I was planning to do so at nine o'clock Monday morning. If you can just wait—"

"How much do you have on you?"

George shrugged. "A couple hundred bucks." He'd stopped at an ATM after leaving the salvage yard, having been cleaned out by the tow guy.

"I'll take it. I'll get the rest later."

George handed over the money. "What about what I was paying you for?"

"Upstairs." With that Zee was out the door.

Mystified, George followed Zee up into his apartment. Zee ducked into his bedroom. George tagged along.

"Wait a second," George said, thinking he could reason with Zee. "Take a deep breath and calm down. What did you learn?"

Zee started throwing clothes into a couple of duffel bags. "You were right," he admitted. "Something weird is going on with iDoc. I was able to hack into Amalgamated's servers. I checked the records for all of them: Kasey, Sal, Tarkington, Wong, and Chesney. At first everything looked normal. In fact, I was about to give up. Then I noticed something odd. An artifact is the best way to describe it. It was hardly noticeable, but they're all the same. So, in each of the five patient records I backtracked and discovered this artifact that appears exactly seventeen minutes before the physiological data went nuts, signifying the beginning of the death event. Seventeen minutes on the dot for all five patient records. Pretty suspicious.

"I tried to figure out exactly what this artifact was—its reason for being, you know what I mean?" Zee didn't pause for an answer. "And while I was working through the possibilities, it hit me! Bam! I realized what it reminded me of: Stuxnet."

George shook his head. He had no idea what Zee was talking about.

Zee explained. "Remember when the U.S. and Israel

'supposedly' hacked into the Iranian computers that were running their nuclear centrifuges?"

"No. Can't say I do," George said.

"Well, the hack left an artifact behind. That's how it was discovered. The hackers wanted to show the Iranians manufactured one set of data while hiding the real data showing what was really happening. It's called a man-in-the-middle attack. The artifacts I found in the iDoc records are very similar, meaning someone hacked into the iDoc servers and did an overwrite of whatever was on those five records prior to the hack."

"I'm lost."

"The way I see it," Zee said while continuing to throw things haphazardly into his bags, "is that someone was trying to cover the tracks of either the application's dumping of its reservoirs or a hacker initiating the dump. Now that I think about it, it must have been a quick fix, because they intercepted each record at the exact same time prior to the patient's death. They should have varied that to hide it better, but when you're in a rush . . . Anyway—app dump or hacker dump—the records have been overwritten." Zee stopped packing and counted off the reasons on his fingers. "To hide the dump signal, to hide wherever the dump signal originated from, and to hide the subsequent physiological-signs data that showed the patients' reactions to the dump up to and including their deaths. The reason I'm confident of this is that Sal's cell phone definitely received an 'all-dump' message. I was able to retrieve his unaltered data records, so I'm absolutely sure in that particular case. Again, whether it originated as a function of the iDoc algorithm or as an outside hack, I do not know."

"You said they tried to hide it, but do you have any idea where the overwrite came from? Could you trace it to its source?"

Zee zipped up his bags. "It wasn't easy, but that's what I was doing just an hour ago. I found traces of a couple of high-anonymity proxy servers—they're called that because they try to hide their IP addresses, which a regular old proxy server does, too, but these things even try to hide the fact that they are proxy servers to begin with. They're very stealthy. Anyway, there are some tricks I know of to unmask them and get a read on who they're fronting for."

"And who is that?"

"That's why I'm out of here. That's what's most disturbing of all." He headed into his bathroom, emptying the contents of his medicine cabinet into a plastic garbage bag.

"One of the server banks they're fronting for is close by. If I had to guess, I'd say it's somewhere up in the Hollywood Hills. Weird location, huh?"

"That's making you run?"

"No, there's another location involved, either contributing to the overwrite or just monitoring it, someplace in Maryland."

George was surprised, knowing that Amalgamated was still not well represented on the East Coast.

"That one is not part of Amalgamated," Zee said, as if reading George's mind.

"How do you know?" George asked.

e I know it is . . . the federal government."

George sank down to sit on the edge of Zee's bed, shocked. This made absolutely no sense to him. "What?"

"As best I could determine, it's an agency that I couldn't even find a reference to on the Internet. It's called URI, Universal Resource Initiative."

"If you can't find a reference to it, how do you know it's the federal government?"

"I got in their system, dude! Stay with me here." Zee's nerves were completely fried, which obviously contributed to his outburst. He paused and tried to calm himself. "Sorry. URI is tied in with another agency called the Independent Payment Advisory Board. Now, that one does have references. A lot of them. It's well-known, and it's fairly new. It was set up by the Affordable Care Act— Obamacare—supposedly to advise on ways for cost control of Medicare and Medicaid. 'To bring spending back to target levels' is how I think they word their mission."

Zee moved into his kitchen, loading groceries and dry goods into more garbage bags. George followed. "I stumbled into a hornets' nest! And one thing I am absolutely sure of is that they are mighty pissed that I hacked into their setup. That, my friend, is why I am heading for the woods. Because they are going to be coming here. To this apartment—actually to your apartment, now that I think about it. And I intend to be as far away as possible. I advise you to do the same. You do not want to be here when they arrive. It's you and your computer that they'll be coming after at first. But there's no doubt that they'll trace it to me, with my history of hacking. It won't take them long to put it all together and realize that you don't know jack shit about hacking into computer systems. Even if you don't tell them about me, it won't take long. And that's not going to happen: You will talk. They'll do things to you to make you talk. Believe me."

"This sounds extreme, Zee," George protested. He tried to speak slowly in contrast to Zee's rapid pressure of speech.

"Hell it is!" Zee shot back. "Do you remember the case of Aaron Swartz last year? The Reddit dude? He was hacking into MIT, and that was just to get academic journal articles free of charge to give to students. Look at what happened to him."

"What happened to him?" George had never heard of the man.

"He's dead! They claim he hanged himself. They were going to throw the book at him and what he did was child's play in relation to what we just did. Think about it. They can't let you walk around knowing what you know."

Zee collected his duffel and garbage bags and started for the door.

"I just can't believe you're actually running."

"That's the only option. Run! And don't look back!"

"I can't leave. I have a residency position . . ." George trailed off, wondering just what his options were.

"You can't treat patients from jail. Or from a grave."

"You're overreacting, Zee! Look, you're all hyped up on caffeine and nicotine and—"

"What I'm hyped up on is survival! On breathing! Yes, call me crazy, but I'd like to be able to continue doing that!"

George followed Zee out of the apartment and down the stairs, trying to get him to give the situation more thought. But Zee was convinced he had given the situation all the thought it deserved.

In the carport Zee slung his bags into the trunk of his old Toyota and went around to climb into the driver's seat. He rolled down the window.

"Listen, George, grab some clothes and come with me. This is serious. Let it play out from far away. Get word out from where they can't find you. Then come back."

"No." George shook his head. "No way. I'll handle it from here."

"It's your life," Zee said. He shrugged. "All I can do is warn you."

George leaned down to the open window. "Listen, Zee. I'm sorry for getting you involved."

Zee shook his head. "You didn't force me to do anything. A hacker should always be prepared to take off. It's part of the gig."

"Thanks, Zee. I'm going to get this handled. Check in with me somehow, you'll see. But the thing is, all I have proof of is that iDoc apparently sent out a dump command to Sal's reservoir."

"The proof of that is on your dining room table. And it's pretty clear to me that the others got the same message."

"But who did it?" George demanded. "Who initiated the command? I don't have a bad guy! I need a bad guy, don't you understand? You can't leave me until you give me some more information!"

"I'm out of here while I can go. I did what I could."

"But I don't have the proof I need to go to the media!" George yelled in frustration. Considering the past ballyhoo about "death panels" when it was merely suggested by the government that it might be prudent to include talking with seniors about end-of-life treatment alternatives in the Affordable Care Act, he was sure that an exposé of the iDoc killings would ignite a firestorm.

Zee fired up his Toyota, its engine noisy in the stillness of the early morning.

"Do you have any ideas about what I could do to try to find the origin of the dump commands?" George pleaded.

Zee jammed his aged transmission into gear with a grinding noise. "I don't think much more can be learned from hacking. Probably the only chance you would have is if you can get someone on the inside who has broad computer access at Amalgamated." Zee held up his closed fist for George to bump. "Good luck, man."

George stared at the closed fist a moment, then tapped it with his own. "Same to you."

Zee pulled out, hitting a dip in the pavement at the entrance to the street, igniting a cascade of sparks from his loose tailpipe.

George watched the dilapidated car until it reached the corner and disappeared out of sight. He realized that Zee was probably right about the limited options. George immediately zeroed in on Paula. She had to have extensive computer access at Amalgamated. The only problem was whether he could convince her to help him.

George turned and headed back to his apartment. He didn't notice the black SUV as it pulled away from the curb and followed Zee.

42

"There he is," Michael Donnelly said, pointing to Zee's car making its way up the entrance to the northbound 405 Freeway. Michael was riding shotgun.

"I see it," Andor said. He backed off to put more room between the Cadillac Escalade and Zee's car so that Zee wouldn't suspect he was being followed. Then they, too, headed up the entrance ramp and accelerated onto the highway. Both men relaxed to a degree. Despite the early hour there was considerable traffic on the road to use as cover.

When they had first started out on the relatively empty city streets, it had been more difficult. Andor had to stay way back to avoid giving himself away. Whenever Zee's Toyota disappeared from view, Andor was forced to race ahead until Zee's vehicle was back in sight. Andor was experienced. He was careful to keep at least one car in between so as not to be too obvious.

Zee's earlier panic was mirrored by the occupants of the SUV. When things started happening in Wilson's apartment after a long, quiet night, they were caught off guard by the explosive activity. Overnight the home office had done a lot of research and they discovered that Zee Beauregard was a savvy computer programmer who had once been prosecuted for hacking. If Zee was helping George, he would probably need to be watched as well.

The technicians had listened to what conversation there had been that morning and assumed that something specific had ignited Zee's panic. The problem was that they could not figure out what it was, since conversation in George's apartment had been limited. When they told Andor and Michael, they had also been at a loss as to what to make of it. Andor and Michael had originally been tasked to follow George Wilson and handle him if need be, depending on developments, but now there was the issue of the neighbor who they assumed also needed to be watched.

While Andor and Michael had been hopefully waiting for more information from the technicians to understand what was going on, Andor had called Butch Gauthier, who was not excited about being awakened so early on a Saturday. His temper cooled as the reasons for the call unfolded. When he heard about Zee Beauregard's involvement, he told Andor that his instincts were entirely correct and to keep Zee under surveillance as well as George.

Andor had hung up with a twinge of relief, but the relief had been short-lived when Zee had come out and thrown his bags into his car. When Andor had called Butch again, the chief of security told him to follow Zee and that he would have another team sent to cover George Wilson in the interim.

Suddenly Zee's car shot ahead, zooming up a line of semi rigs, catching Andor by surprise.

"What the hell!" Andor griped. He sped up as Zee's car disappeared in front of the line of large trucks. When Andor passed them there was no sign of Zee. "Shit!" Andor said. "Where the hell is he?"

Michael twisted in his seat, looking back the way they had come. He was as confused as Andor. "He just vanished. I don't get it."

The road straightened out but there was still no sign of Zee. They sped up and passed another line of trucks. Still no Zee.

Suddenly Michael twisted around again and looked back. "Holy shit! How the fuck did he get behind us?"

"The bastard must have dropped back on the other side of that line of trucks we passed."

The next minute Zee was riding alongside them, obviously trying to peer in through the tinted windows.

"I think he's on to us," Michael said, stating the obvious.

Zee's Toyota sprung ahead, defying its age. Andor and Michael looked at each other.

"We don't have any choice," Andor said.

"I agree," Michael said. "I'll call Butch just to be sure."

Andor sped up, intending to keep the Toyota in sight while Michael hit speed-dial on his phone.

43

George decided to call Paula. He knew that there was a three-hour time difference between Los Angeles and Hawaii and had actually made himself wait for a time before calling. But the wait had been excruciating, and he couldn't hold off any longer. From the moment Zee had left, he'd thought about his course of action, and his conclusion was that Zee was correct. He had to call her. There simply was no other alternative, especially since he would probably become the focus of a criminal investigation due to the hacking that Zee had carried out.

He dialed Paula's mobile phone. As he waited for the call to go through he wondered how long it might take the authorities to come knocking at his door. With what he knew about government bureaucracy he sincerely doubted that Zee's panic was justified, at least not for a few weeks, at a minimum. By then George fully intended to have some verifiable answers about iDoc or at least an explanation of why the hacking had to be done. His knowledge of five deaths made George wonder how many deaths there had been in total out of the twenty thousand people in the iDoc beta test. There had to be more. Maybe a lot more.

As George listened to Paula's phone ring, his thoughts strayed. He had wanted to talk with Paula about his suspicions from day one, certainly not for "sour grapes," as she had intimated, but because he cared about her hard work being distorted by some unethical person or persons.

There still was no answer on the fourth ring. George progressively became convinced that he would have to be content to deal with voice mail and began to wonder if he should leave a message or just call back later or maybe text. After all, five A.M. Hawaii time is pretty damn early, especially for someone on vacation. He wondered if she was alone or sleeping with some guy. Then he wondered why such a thought even occurred to him.

Then to his shock the phone was answered.

"Hey, George! Good morning!" Paula said. Her voice didn't sound sleepy or gravelly. In fact, she sounded a bit out of breath.

"I'm sorry for calling so early and waking you up. I realize that it's only five o'clock in Hawaii."

"It's all right. No problem. I wasn't asleep. I was on the exercise bike getting in a little workout before breakfast. And I'm not in Hawaii. I'm home in Santa Monica. I changed my mind about the trip."

"You're here! That's great!"

"What's up? I'm surprised to hear from you this early."

"We need to meet ASAP! I'm afraid I've discovered something rather momentous. You'll want to hear this."

"Then tell me now." Her voice had become wary.

"I don't want to talk about it on the phone. Someone's having iDoc do something you didn't ever intend. I'll come to your house. I'd just as soon get out of my apartment anyway. I may be in trouble for some illegal computer hacking."

"What computers did you hack, George?" Suddenly she was dead serious.

"None. I'm not capable of it. It was someone I hired."

"And what did you learn?"

"In person," George said.

There was silence for a moment. "I would prefer to meet someplace public."

"Wherever you want."

"There's a place called Caffe Luxxe on Montana Avenue in Santa Monica."

"I'll find it. What time? Sooner the better."

"Ten."

"I'll be there."

44

George took a quick shower. After sleeping in his clothes, getting clean felt particularly good. He dressed rapidly. With more than enough time before he had to leave to make it to the Santa Monica coffee shop well before ten, there was something he wanted to do. He took down the cardboard box that contained Kasey's personal effects.

After smoothing out his bedspread, he spent a few minutes carefully taking Kasey's items out of the box and arranging them on the bed. It was his way of communicating with her, wondering what life would have been like dealing with her illness—the one that neither of them knew she had. How would they have coped? Would the illness and treatment have drawn them closer? Would she have wanted to go through with the marriage? Many questions popped into his head. But few answers. There was one thing for sure. He felt a deep, abiding anger. With what he knew now, there was a chance that someone had denied him the chance to say good-bye to her, to tell her how special she was, and how she had changed his life for the better.

The sudden crash of his front door splintering made George's heart leap in his chest. In a second he was on his feet, aware of a commotion in his living room. A second later George was confronted by a horde of people in ski masks charging into his bedroom, most in black uniforms but others in brown, all carrying weapons, serious weapons. And all the guns were pointed directly at him.

There were shouts: "Hands in the air! Now down on the floor! Now! Now! Down! Spread your arms! Spread those legs!"

Dazed and terrified, George did as he was ordered. More uniformed people swarmed in. He could feel bodies on top of him, pressing him to the floor. He was roughly searched by a dozen strong hands. Then his arms were yanked back painfully and his wrists snapped into handcuffs. It was like what had happened in Sal's apartment, only worse, much worse. In the next instant he was hauled to his feet, wincing at the pain in his shoulders.

Then the shouts from the various personnel that had swarmed him went completely quiet, like the sudden calm after a summer storm.

George warily looked at the faces of the people

surrounding him. Some had removed their black balaclavas but not all. Their affiliations were emblazoned on their bulletproof vests: FBI, Secret Service, and LAPD SWAT. The guns had been lowered, but not put away.

Then a man in a black suit walked into George's bedroom. Members of the combined task force silently gave way as he entered. The man's expression was neutral and calm. He held out a badge for George to read.

"I'm FBI Special Agent Carl Saunders," he said. "You're under arrest for fifteen counts of computer and wire fraud." He held an official document close to George's nose. "This is a warrant for your arrest." He then quickly changed documents, bringing one out from behind the other. "And this is a warrant to search your apartment." He glanced at a subordinate, saying: "Read him his Miranda rights."

When George was led out of his bedroom, he saw several CSI people packing up his computer and the disassembled mobile phone from the dining room table.

At first George was tempted to blurt out what he had discovered. But, having been read his Miranda rights, he decided that it might be best to just say nothing. None of these people were friendly and they treated him as if he were a dangerous, hardened criminal. He remained silent as he was frog-marched out of his apartment.

A number of his fellow tenants had gathered outside, having been roused by the law-enforcement invasion that had arrived in a fleet of vehicles, including an armored personnel carrier. No one spoke as George was forced into a paddy wagon.

Special Agent Saunders got in with him and they sped off.

George rode in silence, staring out the vehicle's tiny window as it sliced through L.A. traffic with its siren going. He looked over and studied his captor's profile. "You people don't waste a lot of time."

"You're in deep shit, my friend," Agent Saunders replied, glancing at him. "You're looking at twenty-five to thirty years in prison as well as a multimillion-dollar fine. Do you have anything you want to say about the charges?"

"I watched enough police procedurals to know it's probably best to wait until I've talked with a lawyer."

Agent Saunders looked at him with a mocking expression. "TV shows? You're something of a smart-ass for a doctor."

"How did you know I was a doctor?"

"We know a lot about you. We've even been in contact with your superiors at the medical center. It appears they intend to press charges on you in addition to the federal government's charges. You're in deep shit, my friend. On top of everything else, the hospital wants to prosecute you for HIPAA violations. As you might imagine, you are officially on administrative leave from your residency."

Oh, my God! George thought. What had he done to himself? Overnight he had become a total pariah and was on his way to jail. He glumly looked back out the window, wondering what would happen if he was wrong and his suspicions about iDoc somehow proved to be only circumstantial.

45

It had been a terrible day for George. Maybe the worst of his life, outside of the day Kasey had died. He was taken into custody and processed. Zee's concern about some sort of government involvement in a possible death panel conspiracy terrified him, now that he was in the hands of the authorities. As the day progressed he felt the urge to blurt out what he believed he had learned, and to explain why he was involved in hacking Amalgamated. But he held himself in check, afraid that if he talked he might get himself in even worse trouble, if such a thing was possible. He had the very real fear that his life as he knew it was over, having heard that he already had essentially been fired since that is what "administrative leave" meant. On top of that was the knowledge that if he was convicted as a felon, as the FBI agent confidently predicted, he would never be able to get a DEA license to prescribe controlled substances, making the practice of medicine, most any kind of medicine, difficult if not impossible.

Throughout the whole process, which had taken the entire day, George felt that he was already being treated like a dangerous criminal. Everyone he came into contact with was either curt or rude, or both. The entire booking process was humiliating: the mug shot, handing over all his belongings, being fingerprinted, enduring a full body search, a warrant search for possible pending charges, a health screening, including blood tests for sexually transmitted diseases. The whole rigmarole made him think that he was perceived as guilty until proven innocent rather than the other way around.

At last, at nine P.M., George was ushered into a small fifteen-by-fifteen-foot cell that smelled of urine and disinfectant, where he was finally allowed to call an attorney. An old-fashioned punch dial phone hung on the cell's wall. George picked up the receiver and wondered whom he would call. The trouble was, he didn't know any criminal attorneys. Hell, he didn't know any attorneys. And this was a holiday weekend! The thought went through his head that he very well might be held in this black hole of Calcutta for the rest of the weekend!

With mounting horror, George hung up the phone and eyed his three cellmates. One was passed out on the floor in a pool of vomit. Another was obviously an addict, his fingers heavily stained with the black tar of heroin. The third was a massive biker with tattoos running down

each arm and a mass of ink climbing up his chest. He was
watching George with a bored look.

George gave him a tentative smile and quickly turned
away.

"Hey!"

George felt a flash of panic. He was pretty sure the
biker was talking to him. Having no real choice, George
turned to the man. They stared at each other for a good
ten seconds. George wasn't sure if he was expected to talk
or what. Finally, the biker reached over and hiked up one
of his orange shirt sleeves.

George slowly shook his head in confusion. "I don't—"

The biker reached down and tapped his finger on a
tattoo on the inside of his massive, hairy forearm.

George took a tentative step toward the man. He had
no idea what the guy had in mind: Was he showing off the
quality of his 'inkmanship'? Or luring George closer to
grab him? George carefully leaned closer for a better look,
ready to raise holy hell if necessary. But it wasn't. He realized that the guy was pointing to a phone number tattooed
on his arm.

"He's a lawyer, and he's good."

How's your bank account?"

George held the holding cell's reeking phone away
from his face to avoid whatever germs were on it. He
hoped to take away nothing more than horrendous memories from this hellhole. The lawyer's name on the other
end of the line was Mario Bonifacio, and after he had

quizzed George about the particulars of the case and how George had gotten his number, he had gotten right to the point: He asked George about his financial resources.

"It's . . . I don't really have a whole lot of money."

"Credit cards?"

"Yes. Visa."

"The credit line?"

"Pretty high, I think. About ten grand."

"Okay. I'll take a credit card. My fee will be twelve hundred dollars. That's for my work today and tomorrow. I can't get you out of there tonight, so you'll have to cool it until morning. And smile, you're getting a discount on my fee because you're a referral from a trusted client."

George glanced at the biker, whose name also turned out to be George. He could overhear the conversation since George was holding the phone receiver away from his ear. The biker grinned upon hearing of the discount and gave George a thumbs-up sign.

"Will that be a problem?" Bonifacio inquired.

"No. That seems fair."

"It is fair. Now bail, that will be the big hit. A bondsman will want ten percent of the amount set by the judge. That is their fee, which you will not get back. Understand?"

"Yes."

"I don't suppose you know any bail bondsmen?"

"I don't."

"No problem, I'll take care of it. One thing I have to warn you about up front: Your charges are serious felonies, so they will come at you with a big number. But I know the filing deputy and can maybe get it reduced. You have no priors, so that's a plus."

"When will my arraignment take place?"

"In the morning. I'll be making calls to the jail after we hang up. You're going to need to pay me and the bail bondsman prior to the hearing. I assume you have a Visa card with you?"

"They have it with my personal effects."

"That's fine. No problem. Okay. Try and relax. I'll speak to you in the morning." Bonifacio ended the call abruptly, leaving George with a dial tone.

George hung up the phone and thanked the biker for the referral.

The biker nodded back and turned his attention to his fingernails.

George scanned the room for a place to sit. It hit him that he was stuck here for the whole night! Abandoned, how would he manage? He located the cleanest-looking spot he could find on the floor at the front of the cell and eased down onto it. He closed his eyes and shuddered. He was squarely in the center of society's garbage can. He had officially reached a new low in life, wondering what additional disaster the morning would bring.

BOOK
THREE

46

George was ushered into the courtroom along with three other men. A cramped seating area with a thick glass partition running up to the ceiling separated him from the courtroom proper. A narrow opening ran the length of the glass at face level so that the imprisoned men could be heard by the judge and attorneys.

George had met with Bonifacio and a bail bondsman early that morning in an interview room to take care of the necessary financial transactions after the lawyer had secured George's credit card. George thought both men had been sent from central casting. They were tall, overweight, and practiced marginal personal hygiene.

George was more exhausted than he could ever remember being in his life, which was saying something after slogging through four years of medical school and three of residency. During the night he had been joined by a number of other cellmates, and their activities squashed any hopes of getting even the briefest spell of shut-eye. One man had tried to "cuddle up" to George. The biker, apparently not concerned with politically correct attitudes toward gay men, had put an end to that in a terrifying flash of homophobic violence.

The topper for George had been when stomach cramps necessitated his use of the toilet. It was so filthy, he refused to sit down and tried to suspend himself in midair. As if he hadn't been self-conscious enough, his antics made his cellmates burst out laughing, taunting him as a "fucking aristocrat." Even the experience of obtaining toilet paper had been humiliating. The jailors literally made him beg for it.

George was a physical mess. He hadn't showered or brushed his teeth. Neither had the three men standing next to him. Their stench was nauseating, and he imagined he might not be much better.

Bonifacio, as big and beefy a man as the fellow who had recommended him, made his way over to George. The one thing he had going for him was that he was obviously very familiar with the goings-on.

"Doing okay still?"

George nodded.

"Good. I talked with the prosecutor. The deputy DA has assigned your case to a guy I know. He can be a dick, but the judge isn't so bad, so we might be okay. With your credit card limit, anything under seventy-five grand is good."

"What's the likelihood of that?"

Bonifacio shrugged. "Like I said, they got a lot of counts against you. We could be talking as much as a couple hundred Gs plus. But don't despair, I'm pretty well connected around here." The man smiled. From the looks of his teeth, George understood why he had such bad breath.

In keeping with his luck of late, George had to wait while the other three men were called before him. George's nervousness mounted as none of them made bail, which suggested that the judge was not in the best of moods. When George's name was finally called, Bonifacio and the deputy district attorney assigned to the case stood and announced their credentials. Then Bonifacio waived a prolonged reading of the charges and told the judge that his client pleaded not guilty on all counts and wanted a speedy trial to prove it.

The judge looked up, obviously surprised, and stared at George. "You don't wish to waive your right to a preliminary hearing within ten days?"

All three of the previous prisoners had waived their right to a speedy trial in the hope that by extending the process to the maximum, the DA might reduce the charges to get the case off the books. Bonifacio had explained to George that by insisting on his right it sent a psychological message to the judge that he was innocent, a ploy that enhanced his chances of being offered bail at a lower rate. Bonifacio insisted it was a strategy he had used to great effect. George hoped he was right. Getting released on bail was George's number one goal. His only chance to

defend himself from the charges against him was to sub-
stantiate that iDoc was being sabotaged, which wouldn't
happen if he was sitting in jail. There was no plan B.

"Your Honor, my client is absolutely not guilty. We
believe these charges will not survive a preliminary hearing, and we want to move quickly. We do not waive."

The judge looked down and studied his calendar, looking for the appropriate date, while George watched, his
mind spinning. His eyes anxiously scanned the room as
the seconds ticked by. Then by chance, he noticed a copy
of the *L.A. Times* sitting on the corner of the attorney's
table. Under a headline George couldn't make out was a
headshot of Zee. *What the hell?*

George pressed his head into the slot to get a better
look. It *was* Zee! And from this angle George could deci-
pher the headline, too: "Unemployed Gamer Killed in
High-Speed Crash." The subtitle read: "Yet Another
Runaway Accelerator Suspected." George's body went
numb with fear. Could Zee's death be just an awful coincidence? He sincerely doubted it. Remorse at possibly
involving Zee in something that led to his death overwhelmed him almost as much as his fear.

"George? George, you paying attention?" It was Bonifacio. He was looking at George with concern.

"Sorry," he managed. "What?"

"Your court date is set for July eighteenth," Bonifacio
whispered. "Pay attention or you are going to irritate you
know who. Jesus . . ."

The deputy DA was standing now and addressing the
judge. "Due to the seriousness of the charges, the people

urge the court to set bail in the amount of five hundred thousand dollars."

George's mouth dropped. Such an amount was far beyond his credit. On top of his fear and remorse was a sense of near-incapacitating anxiety that spread through him like wildfire. Was he doomed to stay in jail? How would he ever survive it? After the experience of the previous night, he didn't know. And after what had apparently happened to Zee, George felt as a matter of survival a need to get away from the clutches of the authorities.

The judge looked up at the deputy DA. "That seems excessive, Counselor. Why so high?"

"Because of the seriousness of the charges, we believe the defendant to be a flight risk."

Bonifacio cleared his throat. "Your Honor, Dr. Wilson is a fourth-year resident doctor at L.A. University Medical Center. He's always been an upstanding member of the community and has never been charged with any crime, not even a speeding ticket."

"What kind of bail were you seeking?" the judge asked Bonifacio.

"Sir, considering my client's blemish-free record, twenty-five thousand dollars would be more than enough."

"This was an assault on both corporate and federal government entities involving health care records, sir," the deputy DA countered.

The judge looked at George, evaluating him, and then began scribbling on the court documents in front of him. He looked up. "Bail is set at fifty thousand dollars."

George's knees buckled in relief.

Bonifacio turned to him and winked. "I'll have you out of here in an hour."

George was released and given back all his clothing and personal items, including his cell phone. He stepped out into the bright, hot sunshine. Oh, God! What relief! But then his mind returned to Zee.

George hustled down to the street corner and found a newsstand. He bought a copy of the *L.A. Times* and sat on the curb to read the article. Zee's car had apparently been going over a hundred miles per hour when it veered off the road and struck the concrete abutment of an overpass. The reporter believed it was another Toyota accelerator crash. George finished the article and sat staring into the gutter, his hands still trembling. It was definitely too much of a coincidence for the crash to have been an accident. There had been a number of such accelerator incidents in the past, sure, but what were the odds of it happening now? And if it wasn't an accident, it was murder. George had never been a conspiracy theorist, but this was turning him into one.

As he sat on the curb, George's mind went into high gear. He didn't see the traffic going by or the pedestrians who eyed him as they passed. He had started thinking something else. What if Zee had been killed not by the government, an idea that had been fostered in his mind by Zee's government paranoia, but rather by the individual or group of individuals behind the iDoc death panel conspiracy. In many respects this made more sense. After all, iDoc and Amalgamated were private entities.

George breathed out forcibly, unaware he had been holding his breath as his mind pondered this new concern. In many respects it was even scarier than worrying about the government, especially since the idea suggested he might have been safer in jail than out on the street.

Scrambling to his feet, George nervously looked around. He felt a bit of relief seeing that no one was paying him the slightest bit of attention now that he was standing. But this new line of thought evoked another worry: Maybe he shouldn't go back to his apartment, or at least not stay there. If the authorities knew he had been involved in hacking into the iDoc servers, then there was reason to fear that the person or persons responsible for the iDoc subversion knew as well.

Dusting himself off, he hailed a cab, giving the driver his address. He decided he wasn't going to stay there but needed some things, and reasoned that being there for a short time would be safe. After riding for a few minutes and allowing himself to calm down, he dialed Paula's cell. If he was to learn anything more about iDoc, he needed her help. Would she? He didn't know, but she was his only recourse.

As if expecting his call, she picked up on the first ring. "What the hell! You stood me up! I sat at that coffee shop for an hour texting you."

"I'm sorry, I'm sorry. My day didn't go as planned." Understatement of the year.

"You'd better explain, and it better be good." She was all business.

"I was arrested."

Silence. George gave her a minute for his comment to sink in.

"You're joking."

"I wish I was. The last twenty-four hours have been the worst I have ever spent. I knew you were waiting, but I couldn't call. I couldn't text. And, on top of being arrested, I've been placed on administrative leave from my residency, which is the equivalent of being fired, unless I'm acquitted, which probably won't happen, since I'm guilty as charged."

"What in the world are you talking about?" she said.

"I was arrested for hacking into iDoc," George said. "They grabbed me minutes after we spoke yesterday. I ended up spending the night in jail and just got out."

"Where exactly are you, George?" she said gently.

"In a taxi. I'm heading back to my apartment."

"What exactly are you accused of doing?"

"As I said yesterday morning, it wasn't I who actually hacked Amalgamated. It was someone I paid to do it. A professional gamer named Zee Beauregard. You can read about him on the front page of the local section of today's *L.A. Times*." George fought back tears from a flood of emotion. He paused for a moment before continuing. "Zee said he was able to access iDoc records on the Amalgamated servers."

"Really? You got through our firewall?"

"I didn't. Zee did."

Paula let out a mirthless laugh. "No wonder you were arrested! Why in heaven's name did you do it? And why is it a story?"

George didn't want to explain any more over the phone. "Let's do this in person. I'm more afraid than ever that iDoc has been compromised. And I'm not referring to the hacking. I'm afraid your baby has been subverted and is now killing people."

"George, do you know how that sounds?"

"Yes, I know. But meet with me. I'll explain it all. It's even more complicated than that. The federal government is also involved somehow on some level. Otherwise I wouldn't have been arrested quite so quickly. Look, it's truly complicated. After you hear me out, you decide if you buy any of it. But, please, let me explain it."

"I can't get my head around any of this, George. But for the sake of our friendship I'm willing to listen. Now, don't take this wrong, but remember back in medical school that you had a tendency to subscribe to conspiracy theories. One time you even argued that there was no way Oswald had acted alone."

"That was Pia's take. I was just mouthing it for her benefit."

"Well, regardless. When you said iDoc was in direct competition with the medical profession, I could understand why you were so negative. I mean, you come up with this great idea and instead of it being embraced by the medical profession, it gets stolen by the insurance industry. I can see where resentment might build up. That's all I'm saying. But if you're able to offer me some proof that iDoc has been subverted, then I'll give you the benefit of the doubt. But I need to know exactly what you think you've discovered right now, before you go spouting off to anyone else."

"I'll tell you everything. But only in person. I'm going to need your help, too, to be one hundred percent certain."

She sighed and paused a moment, thinking. "Okay, let's meet."

"Great! How about now?"

"Okay."

"I'm in a cab heading to my apartment, but actually I'm afraid to stay there."

"What about your friend? Why is he in the paper?"

"Because he died." George struggled to continue as emotion bubbled up. "He was driving on the freeway. The article says that his accelerator got stuck. It was an old Toyota. But that seems a little coincidental in light of the hack, don't you think? When he left me he was terrified the government was coming after him."

"Come directly to my house," she replied with an urgency that hadn't been there a moment ago. "Now! You can stay in my guest suite. Tell the driver to drop you at Four twenty-eight Sixteenth Street. It's north of Montana Avenue in Santa Monica. I'm not saying I'm buying all of what you're saying, but I don't want you to take any risk. So come now. Okay?"

"I need to get my car and a few things from home first.

I'll be careful, trust me. And I'll make sure no one follows me to your place."

"Okay. If you insist. But be quick!"

When George reached his apartment he asked the cabdriver to drive around the block while he looked the place over. Everything seemed quiet as usual for a Sunday morning, so he told the driver to let him out.

George warily entered the complex, nervously scanning the area as he went. All was quiet. Once inside his apartment, he grabbed the baseball bat he kept in the umbrella stand and made a quick tour of the other rooms. Then he double-checked that all the doors and windows were locked. He even checked the closets and under the bed. He knew it was paranoid, but he couldn't help himself.

Once George was satisfied he was alone, he first put Kasey's things, which were still spread around on his bed, back in the cardboard box and placed the box in the closet. He had been handling the mementos when the SWAT team had invaded. Then he went into the bathroom, locked the door, and took a quick, needed shower. Feeling a slight bit more like a normal human, he got out a small travel bag and rapidly tossed in some of his things. He then quickly picked up the baseball bat, despite knowing full well the security it afforded was purely psychological. After less than fifteen minutes he was ready.

47

George headed out, the duffel bag in one hand, the baseball bat in the other. He skirted the pool occupied by a single young woman whom George had never seen before, supine on a float, eyes closed, baking in the sun. She didn't stir. It was hot. Sweat was already building on George's brow as he went through the back gate out to the carport.

Before climbing into his car he gave the neighborhood a once-over by going out to the gutter to scan the street up and down, looking for anything out of the ordinary. He had never felt as apprehensive and distrustful as he did at that very moment. As much as he hoped no one was watching him, another part of him wanted to detect a suggestion of surveillance as he would then know for sure that his fears were justified.

A couple of people on the block were washing their cars, others walking their dogs as on any normal Sunday early afternoon. One of the dog walkers seemed to take issue with George staring at him and stared back for a beat. There were a couple of black SUVs with dark tinted windows parked along the street, but that was always the case, as popular as such vehicles were in L.A. But still . . . he wondered.

George watched for a time, but no one seemed to take note of his presence. Even the dog walker had moved on, replaced by a couple of kids with skateboards. Birds squawked and chirped, a dog barked, a sprinkler ticked its steady beat, and nothing happened. Finally he gave up and went back to his car.

George tossed his small travel bag in the Jeep's backseat, along with his bat, and climbed into the driver's seat. He turned the ignition, half expecting the car to blow up in a spectacular fireball as he'd seen in a dozen movies. Instead it turned over and coughed its way into its normal purr. He put the Cherokee in gear, backed out into the street, and drove off, carefully checking in his rearview mirror. He wanted to make sure that he wasn't followed, particularly after what had happened to Zee. He did not want to put Paula in any more danger than he had by just talking to her on his cell.

As George drove and thought about his current situation, he admitted to being a rank amateur in the intrigue arena. In reality, he had no idea what he was doing or what someone with means and know-how was capable of doing with regard to keeping a close watch on him. If such a person or organization were interested in his actions and whereabouts, they would know how to stay out of sight—and with the federal government having access to FBI and CIA tactics, anything was possible. With that thought, he started to scan the skies out of his sunroof for drone activity. As far-fetched as that seemed, he couldn't help himself; his paranoia had taken full and total control. He certainly didn't want to end up like Zee.

Amateur or not, George thought being careful was prudent, and settled on a simple ruse. He detoured to the medical center and entered its multistory garage. Inside, he found a place where he could observe the entrance he'd used and watched the vehicles that came in after him. After a quarter of an hour, when he didn't see anything at all suspicious, he exited the garage onto a street different from the one by which he had entered. As he picked up speed, he was confident he was not being followed.

George stayed on local streets to Santa Monica, purposely avoiding high-speed freeways. As he got closer, he even relaxed a bit. He was looking forward to seeing Paula and hopefully enlisting her help.

When her house came into view, he pulled to the curb and stared at it. It was a gorgeous, fairly new Mediterranean-style two-story home with a tile roof and Spanish architectural details. Worth at least three million, George thought, according to what he knew about L.A. real estate. In contrast to the run-down condition of his own apartment, he considered Paula's home a clear illustration of the relative values of an MD and MD-MBA degree. He knew he was being irrational and a tad envious, but still the difference was remarkable.

There was no driveway out front, which indicated there must be an alley around back. A moment later Paula came out the front door, appearing far too young to be the proprietor of such a house. With her hands she motioned for him to loop around back, proving he was right about an alley.

George dutifully drove to the next cross street, turned right, and then right again, into an alleyway, where he saw her standing ahead in the shade of an open garage door. She waved for him to pull his car in. He did as he was told, stopping alongside what looked to be a brand-new black Porsche 911 Carrera GT. He cut his engine and got out.

"Under the circumstances, I think it's better that your car not be seen from the street," she explained.

"I couldn't agree more," George said, grabbing his bag but leaving the bat in the car.

She came directly up to him and grabbed his arms, staring up into his face. "Are you okay?" She was clearly worried about him. "You're trembling."

George decided honesty was the best policy. "I'm not sure if I'm okay or not."

"You do look exhausted."

"That's about how I feel. I think the current term is 'fried.'"

"Well, come on in the house! Let's get you relaxed. Are you hungry? Thirsty?" She let go of one of his arms but solicitously maintained a hold on the other as she lowered the garage door.

George was encouraged at his reception. He hadn't known what to expect, being the bearer of disturbing news. He followed her into the backyard, taking in the extent of the residence. There was a pool, an attached Jacuzzi, a large terrace, and extensive manicured landscaping. Inside the house, he admired the elegant furnishings.

"This place is gorgeous," he said, standing in the middle of a combination family room and kitchen. The pool could be seen through French doors.

"Thanks," she said, smiling. "I'm glad you like it. I bought it furnished, so I can't take any credit for the decorating." She led him through the kitchen area and into a large, well-appointed guest wing with its own sitting room and bathroom. "This is where you'll be staying. And I imagine you could probably use a good nap, so . . ."

"I would rather talk first," he interrupted. "I'm too wired to sleep."

"Okay. We can do that," she said. "I understand. Why don't you drop your bag, and I'll show you around the rest of the house to get you oriented. It has its uniqueness. Then we can talk."

"I'd like that," George said. For the first time since his arrest he felt safe.

Paula gave George a quick tour, which he did find entertaining and even calming, giving him a chance to organize his thoughts.

The house had one feature he didn't expect: The previous owner of the house, a Middle Eastern businessman, had built a safe room in the basement that could be accessed rapidly from the second-floor master bedroom by a slide somewhat akin to a laundry chute. The access point started from behind a hidden wall panel and ended up in the basement just opposite the door to the safe room. Paula explained that the safe room was supposed to be able to withstand a major explosion and fire. The real estate agent had thought it was a selling point, but Paula regarded it merely as a curiosity.

"Want to try the slide?" Paula asked.

George looked into the maw of the concave, angled slide that disappeared into darkness. "I think I'll pass," he said.

"Come on," Paula urged. "Let your hair down!"

On a sudden whim, George went for it. He hadn't been on a slide since the third grade. He found it exhilarating. He even found himself capable of laughing when he and Paula ended up sprawled in a tangle of arms and legs on a mat in the darkness until Paula got a light on.

"Exactly what kind of business was the former owner in?" George asked as they glanced past a vault-like door into the safe room.

"I asked the same thing, but no one was able to tell me for certain. The rumor was that he was in the arms business and was murdered on a business trip last year."

Paula led George back up to the kitchen. She got out some sandwiches she had made earlier and a pitcher of iced tea. They ended up sitting on the terrace under a broad awning. As soon as they were settled, Paula wanted to hear about Zee.

George told her the little he knew, which was what he had read in the *L.A. Times*. She pulled the story up on her iPad, and they went over the article together. "This is all very . . ." Paula hesitated, struggling for the right word.

"Scary," George said.

Paula nodded. "To say the least." She then asked about George's night in jail.

"It was probably the worst twenty-four hours of my life," George admitted with a shudder. He went on to describe in detail the whole experience, including the shady lawyer who finally bailed him out and his biker buddy who had the attorney's phone number tattooed on his arm.

"What a horrid experience this whole thing has been," Paula remarked. "But the worst part is the death of your friend. And I agree, the stuck accelerator suggested in the newspaper article seems too coincidental."

"And too convenient," George added.

"No doubt," Paula agreed. She poured both of them more iced tea. "Okay, now let's talk about iDoc. What is it you believe is going on?"

George took a deep breath and started from the beginning with Kasey, although he didn't mention that he was engaged to the woman. He just described her as a close acquaintance and didn't say he had awakened in bed with her corpse. Paula didn't stop him to question the nature of the relationship, and he didn't say. He wanted to tell her but not just yet.

George went on to explain the other unexpected deaths: Tarkington, Wong, DeAngelis, and Chesney. He told her about his connection to them and about his need to violate HIPAA rules in his investigations. "The long and short of it is that all of these people were part of the iDoc beta test and all had been recently diagnosed, whether they knew it or not, with serious and most likely terminal illnesses."

Paula understood the implication immediately. "You're worried that iDoc has morphed into a kind of death panel?"

"Exactly!" George admitted. "I mean, there is a very low statistical possibility all this is circumstantial, but I sincerely doubt it could be. I believe iDoc is killing people it believes are destined to be expensive to treat and who have limited life spans even with the costly treatment they require."

Paula flushed. "Let me tell you! There was never even the thought of such a thing during the creation of iDoc. Never!"

"I believe you," George said.

"Then how could you jump to such a conclusion?"

"I didn't jump! It was forced on me!"

She looked at him skeptically. "It seems to me that is a rather big leap."

"Okay. Let me back up," George said. First he told her about the medical journal article he had read in the past about the concern that people might, in the future, hack into wireless medical devices, which were proliferating. He said that warning had stayed in the back of his mind, only to come to the fore when the deaths he had described began to take place.

"Have you any proof whatsoever?" Paula asked.

"Absolutely," George said. He then described the lengths he had had to go to, to obtain Sal DeAngelis's reservoir, which had been embedded under Sal's abdominal skin.

Paula was aghast as George described going to the funeral parlor and rifling through the dead man's clothes with the embalmed corpse lying in the coffin. "You really were motivated," Paula said. "I can't believe your nerve. I wouldn't have been able to do it."

"I wanted that reservoir," George said with emphasis. "I thought it would be key. I had to make the effort to check the body in the hospital morgue, but I'd been turned away."

"But you ended up getting it?"

"I did." George then described the ordeal at the salvage yard and how he finally got hold of the chip after what seemed like a futile search.

"So this reservoir is your proof?"

"Not by itself." George went on to describe how he had been able to get Sal's phone as well as having Kasey's. He explained that although Kasey's iDoc had been wiped clean, Sal's phone hadn't been because it had been damaged in the crash and still retained some information. That was how George learned, with Zee's help, that Sal's phone had received a global-dump command.

"Did that jibe with what you already knew?"

"Absolutely. When I had examined the reservoir, I could see that it was completely empty. And this was a reservoir that was supposed to last for two years or more, according to the doctor who had implanted it. Sal's had been under his skin for only a couple of months!"

"So this is what made you hire Zee?"

"Precisely," George said. He went on to tell Paula that when Zee hacked into Amalgamated's servers, he found no evidence that a dump command had been issued. Yet Sal's smartphone itself showed exactly the opposite. Nor did Zee find a dump command in any of the other records from the other patients. "But when Zee looked more carefully he saw it!"

"Saw what?" Paula asked.

"What he called the artifacts! Some minuscule evidence of an overwrite on the records. Zee sensed that the record in each case had been overwritten to delete the dump command and the recorded vital signs showing the effects of a dump command. He saw the same artifact at the same critical juncture in all five of the records seventeen minutes prior to death. It was his feeling that there had been a cover-up of the dump command coming from outside the server."

Paula was astonished, angered, disbelieving, and intrigued all at the same time. "Okay, what does all this mean?"

"With what proof I have, which is limited to DeAngelis's phone data, I believe that the dump command was probably a hack job, which was then covered up by another hack job by someone else."

"That's too complicated," Paula said, shaking her head. "In medicine, when you have confusing symptoms, the diagnosis is usually a single disease."

"I admit, I can't be certain, but Zee discovered something else. When he tried to trace the hacker it led him to two 'high-anonymity proxy servers.' He said on the other end of these proxy servers were very likely the sources of the hacks. One, he thought, was here in Los Angeles, possibly up in the Hollywood Hills, and the other was in Maryland."

"Maryland?"

"The server in Maryland was the one that spooked Zee. He told me the server was part of an obscure government agency called URI, standing for Universal Resource Initiative. The only thing he could learn about the organization was that it was loosely associated with the Independent Payment Advisory Board, which, if you don't know, was set up by the Affordable Care Act to advise Medicare and Medicaid on cost control."

Paula appeared crestfallen. "You think this is all some kind of ill-conceived cost-saving plan engineered by the feds?"

George shrugged. "I don't know. But that was one of the things that occurred to me. Either by the feds or Amalgamated."

Paula leaned forward, head in hands, quietly saying no over and over again. Then, suddenly, pulling herself together, she sat back up, looking directly at George. Anger had trumped dejection. "If you are right about all this, it is a terrible, terrible subversion of probably the biggest innovation in medicine to date. iDoc is going to save people, not kill them! It's going to revolutionize medicine, democratize it, taking it from essentially 'sick' care to true 'health' care, giving everyone their own twenty-four-seven doctor who intimately knows them and has access to the latest diagnostics and treatments available."

George didn't respond. Paula had flushed again with a wild look in her eyes. Enraged at the thought that iDoc might have been subverted, she had launched back into her sales presentation. He did not attempt to interrupt her. He understood that she was as shocked about it as he had been. He let her vent.

"You know as well as I," she snapped, "iDoc is going to reduce unnecessary medical procedures and break the stranglehold of medical specialists!" She stared back at George challengingly.

"I agree," George said, trying to calm her. "I agree with everything you've said. But there is a problem—these five suspicious deaths. It's a situation that has to be looked into and either confirmed and exposed or proven to be somehow circumstantial, if that is even possible with what is known."

"Okay, okay!" Paula said, struggling to get herself under control. "How can we look into it?"

George trod lightly; this step was crucial. "Your access makes you the only one who can confirm or deny the problem. How many people are there on the iDoc programming team?"

"I don't know . . . Two hundred, I guess."

"Is there anyone in that two hundred that you trust completely? Someone who would have full access and can definitively determine if the program has been compromised?"

She shook her head. "I'm not close to any of the programmers. Thanks to Langley, none of them have been made available to me. And to be honest, the only person among the key players I don't trust completely *is* Langley."

"Why?"

"Langley has implied on several occasions that I have been getting too much credit for iDoc. I wonder if he could be involved in some twisted scenario to discredit the first iteration, then rescue it."

"Your intuition notwithstanding, Langley probably has too much to lose to be involved in discrediting iDoc. It doesn't comport, at least in my mind. Let me ask you this: Who, if anyone, do you totally trust at Amalgamated?"

"Thorn. He is the only person I completely trust. And I think you are right about Langley having too much to lose, but I still wouldn't want to approach him with this. I think we should go to Thorn and tell him about what you've learned and what we suspect."

George grimaced and shook his head. "I don't know about that, Paula. And for the similar reasons I would hesitate before going to Langley. The money, power, and celebrity involved with iDoc is so off the charts that it would be difficult for the businessman in Thorn to be able to be objective."

"You don't know Thorn like I do. The man has character."

George shook his head again. "When I watch Thorn, I see the quintessential businessman, more interested in the bottom line than anything else," George said.

"I've known him for almost four years now, and he

has been like a father to me. He's a businessman for sure, but with integrity. I trust him implicitly."

"Maybe I should forget my paranoia about the government, and we should go directly to the FBI and have the agency either confirm my fears or lay them to rest?"

She shook her head. "As you suggested, the government might be involved somehow. Going to Thorn would be far better. He would know how we should proceed. I'm sure that Thorn will be as furious as I am if some group is subverting iDoc."

George remained hesitant. He admitted he didn't know Thorn like Paula did, but something was telling him not to go to Thorn and for the reasons he'd given. "I can't help but worry that Thorn will be influenced by what iDoc can do for Amalgamated's bottom line more than anything else."

"Look," Paula said, a little put out, "we all know what iDoc will do for Amalgamated's bottom line, but that is not the issue. Thorn above all else is a very ethical person." A thought hit her. "I wonder if the AMA could be the guilty party. Organized medicine is going to see iDoc as competition, no question. Maybe this is all an elaborate way of discrediting it from the get-go."

George was astonished at that suggestion. The idea hadn't occurred to him, but he knew it wasn't *completely* improbable. After all, in the late forties, it was organized medicine that thwarted Truman's attempt to create a national health care system in the United States. Still, the idea seemed like a total shot in the dark.

"Or it could be any one of a number of other

stakeholders feeding from the medical trough," Paula
continued. "Like big pharma or the American Hospital
Association, both of which will stand to lose money when
iDoc becomes fully operational and takes medicine from
sick care to preventative care."

George nodded. Having become relaxed and feeling
safe made staying awake progressively more difficult; he
was on the verge of collapsing from exhaustion.

"You need to sleep," Paula said, noticing George was
struggling to keep his eyes open. She reached out a hand.
"Come on. Time to take a nap! We can talk more later
over dinner. If you are okay with it, I'll make us a meal
so we can just stay in."

"A nap might be good," George admitted. He took
her hand and stood, feeling momentarily dizzy. "Just for
an hour or so. But I would like to reach a decision about
how to proceed with this iDoc situation. If it is intentional
killing, it has to stop. And I have a trial I have to prepare
for."

"When is your trial scheduled?"

"Soon. July sometime. I forget the exact date, but it is
not that far away."

"I think we should approach Thorn. The more I think
about it, the more I'm certain that he is the right person."
She was firmly set on the idea. "I'm sure he will at least
offer you legal help."

George's eyes fluttered, but he was too tired to reply.
He swayed, and Paula reached out to steady him.

"Come on!" she said. "You're about to fall over."

Paula led him back into the house via the French doors

into the great room. George didn't protest. After the heat outside, the air-conditioning felt heaven sent.

Once inside the guest bedroom, Paula closed the Bermuda shutters and pulled back the covers on the canopied king-size bed. From behind the bathroom door, she brought in a white Turkish towel robe and draped it over the foot of the bed.

"I don't think I've ever seen a person need sleep quite as much as you do," she said. "You've pushed yourself to your limit."

George opened his mouth, but she put her fingers on his lips.

"*Shhh.* Sleep. We'll talk in a bit." She backed toward the door.

George sank down onto the bed. He made one last effort at conversation. "If we confirm my fears about iDoc, we'll have to go to the media, no matter what Thorn says."

"Enough!" Paula called from the door with exaggerated authority. "We'll talk more after you have slept!" She flashed him a smile, then shut the door quickly to keep George from responding.

In the room's cool, dim silence George removed his clothes. It was with extreme pleasure that he slipped in between the clean, ironed sheets. The experience was such an extraordinary difference from what he had experienced the night before that it was as if he had been magically transported to a different planet.

Just before he fell into a deep sleep, he thought how utterly stupid he had been in medical school when he failed to follow up with Paula. What was he thinking? He was finding himself more and more impressed by Paula, and for the first time since Kasey's death he felt a kind of closeness with her that he was unsure he would ever feel again. He didn't know if he was ready just yet for romance, nor did he know if Paula would be receptive, considering their history and his current status. As a potential felon and an unemployed resident, his career prospects were far from rosy, but he didn't dwell on the thought. Sleep washed over him like a virtual tsunami.

48

George woke with a start. At first he didn't know where he was, as he had slept so soundly. Then he remembered, and the whole nightmare flooded back. *My God!* he thought. He was facing a trial that might send him to prison for years! After the experience of one night in the holding cell, he questioned if he could live through being incarcerated for an extended period. Then there was the issue of essentially having been fired from his residency. Could it be that his radiology career and maybe even his medical career were over? His only solace was that at least for the moment he was safely hidden away in Paula Stonebrenner's house.

Looking at the golden hue of the light coming through the Bermuda shutters, George sensed it was nearing sunset. Surprised, he grabbed his phone to see the time. He was amazed! It was almost eight o'clock in the evening. He imagined he'd been asleep for only an hour, which had been his plan. Certainly not over five hours!

George got up, wondering where Paula was and why she hadn't awakened him for the dinner she had talked about. He was eager to find her, but instead took advantage of the beautiful and convenient shower. He had rinsed off in his own apartment, but this experience was far better.

A few minutes later he was refreshingly clean, reasonably rested, and enveloped in the oversize Turkish towel robe Paula had put out for him. He left the guest suite and found Paula in the great room overlooking the pool, using her iPad. Delicious, savory smells were coming from the kitchen area.

When Paula spotted him she broke into a wide smile. "Back from the dead, I see. I hope you're hungry!"

"Very hungry. I'm sorry I slept so long. Why didn't you wake me?"

"You obviously needed to sleep."

"I hope I haven't kept you from your dinner."

"I've been happy to wait for you. I'm about to throw some steaks on the barbie by the pool! Sound good?"

"Sounds heavenly." He noticed that she had opened a bottle of wine. He picked it up and looked at the label. He didn't recognize it, but it looked expensive. "May I?"

"Please do. For both of us. I was letting it breathe a little."

George poured them both a glass, thinking how strange it was to savor the anticipation of what promised to be a pleasant dinner in the midst of all the tumult of the previous day and a half. There was a remarkable unreality to it all.

George watched as Paula continued her preparations for dinner, putting dressing on a salad she'd already made. Once that was done, Paula grabbed the platter with the steaks and motioned George to follow her out to the grill. He carried both glasses of wine. While she was checking the temperature of the grill she said, "You do know that Amalgamated has been in direct negotiation with CMS to use iDoc for Medicare and Medicaid?"

"I do," George responded.

"Maybe that's why Zee found that a federal agency was connected to the Amalgamated servers."

"Could be," George said. "It would be a relief if that were the case."

Paula put the steaks on the grill, asking George how he liked his.

"Medium rare," George said. "Can I help?"

"I think I have it under control." She set a couple of ears of corn on the upper level of the grill, and for a while they watched the steaks sizzle and contentedly sipped their wine. When the meat was done, Paula put it back on the platter with the now-grilled ears of corn. Carrying everything between them, they went back into the house.

"I'm more and more certain that I should talk with Thorn," Paula stated as they sat down. "Either with or without you. That's your call."

"With me," George said. Even though he still had reservations about Thorn, he was happy to have a plan of action.

She smiled. "Good. Because Thorn will certainly have

a lot of questions that I won't be able to answer." She then changed the subject. "What's this about your being placed on administrative leave?"

"It is exactly what you think. I haven't been technically fired, but it is as if I have been, at least in the short run."

"What will that do to your residency, now that you're in the last year, if you don't get reinstated?"

"It ends it unless some other program would be willing to pick me up. Whether that might happen, I have no idea. But if I can't finish my residency, I can't sit for radiology boards. Simple as that."

"And that means what for your future?"

George shrugged. He was at a loss. "Maybe I'll have to become a vitamin salesman? Truthfully, I have no idea. I'll have to talk with Clayton. I'm hoping he'd be my savior since he, and not the chief, is actually in charge of the residency program."

"Thorn might be able to help as well since he and Clayton are brothers-in-law. Thorn is married to Clayton's younger sister."

"I once asked Clayton how he became so deeply involved with Amalgamated, and he told me. That explains a lot."

For a few minutes they ate in silence, then suddenly Paula piped up: "Hey! I have an idea! Let's try to let the whole problem with iDoc, Zee's untimely death, and your radiology future slide for a few hours and just relax and enjoy ourselves. What do you say? We can't do anything about all this mess tonight."

George shrugged. "I'm willing to give it a try. And

the wine might help. Actually, I'm surprised I am eating as well as I am. And, Paula, everything is delicious."

"Thank you for saying so. And about the wine, I'm happy to say we have plenty." She refilled both their glasses. Suddenly her face lit up. "David Spitz and Rachel Simmons! Remember them?"

George certainly did. They were former friends and classmates at Columbia Medical and had dated off and on. George liked them both a lot, but they were always at each other's throats. "Of course I remember them: the Bickersons!"

Paula laughed. "Yes! Well, guess what? They're married!"

"No way!"

"Yes! I went to their wedding in San Mateo two months ago."

He whistled. "Will wonders never cease? I never saw that one coming."

"I don't think anyone did. Even they didn't."

They chuckled and continued talking about their common experiences with friends and professors and rotations while attending Columbia Medical School. Mostly in retrospect, they had enjoyed the four years of hard but rewarding work.

"You know," George said, "there is something I never told you but thought about a lot, even though I gave you some grief on the subject. I always admired the way you were able to deal with both medical school and B-school at the same time. For me, the demands of medical school were more than enough."

"Yeah, well, you worked at the blood bank and all the other jobs you held down. I didn't have to do that. My parents supported me financially."

"It was still impressive," George said. He didn't want to discuss his financial struggles, which hadn't improved as much as he had hoped.

As the evening progressed, they both surprised themselves by relaxing, something neither expected under the circumstances. It was helped by the second bottle of wine, the food, and the environment. As they continued chatting they both were able to let go of the past and even laugh about it. Paula thought that perhaps she was a bit too forward in pursuing George. He countered that he couldn't even explain to himself what he had seen in Pia Grazdani!

"It is embarrassing when I think about it," he confessed. "She clearly wasn't interested in me and, in retrospect, probably not capable of any kind of normal relationship with anyone."

George explained that Pia had disappeared in London, and even her father, high up in the NYC Albanian Mafia, had difficulty finding out what had happened to her.

"You mean no one has heard from her since then?"

"Not a word," George said. "Although her father called a couple of months ago, saying that he had finally come across some encouraging information and said he'd get back to me when something concrete happened, he never did. I've not heard anything since. I hope for her sake that he is ultimately successful in locating her."

There was a pause as each eyed the other, wondering

exactly what the other was thinking. It was Paula who broke the spell. "Maybe it's time to clean up the dishes."

"Good idea," George said. They carried their dishes to the kitchen counter. For a few minutes they worked in contented silence.

"You know, I'm amazed that I feel as relaxed as I do," George admitted.

"You've been a trouper, considering what you went through," Paula said. "But you definitely need more sleep, whether you know it or not."

"Oh, I know it," George agreed. "I'll be able to nod off with no problem, especially in that bed. It's amazing! Have you ever slept in it?"

"No, not yet." She smiled. "You know I'd been planning to go to Hawaii for a long weekend. I'm not expected back at work until Thursday. We have plenty of time to hash out our game plan. Feel free to stay here as long as you want."

"I appreciate that," George said sincerely. "Thank you. I don't know where I would have gone otherwise, because I surely would not have felt comfortable staying in my apartment."

"I'm glad I could help. Now it's time for bed. I'm exhausted, even though I didn't spend last night in jail." She smiled. "If you need it, I have some Ambien."

He shook his head. "I think I'll be fine."

She gave him a hug. After a moment he hugged her back. Hard. Finally, they let each other go. Paula quickly turned to the kitchen cupboards. "Okay, then! For breakfast!"

George watched while Paula pointed out where the fixings were in case he got up earlier than she did. They stood in the kitchen, awkward and quiet; both were tired but neither wanted the evening to end.

"Okay, then, good night." She gave George's hand a squeeze. George squeezed back.

"Good night." George watched as she mounted the stairs to the second floor and the master bedroom. Then he headed toward the guest suite.

49

George was still exhausted, but after sleeping for five hours that afternoon he found he couldn't fall asleep after all. He had turned off the light and gotten into bed, but as soon as he lay down, all his fears about his future returned. Although he'd been able to let his mind rest for a few hours about iDoc, Zee, his legal worries, and the fact that he was on a forced leave of absence from his residency program, in bed it was another matter. Try as he might, he couldn't stop thinking even though he had no answers, and, as Paula said, there wasn't any way anything was going to be solved that night.

After an hour or so of tossing and turning, he switched the light back on. He got up, pulled on the bathrobe against the air-conditioned chill, and padded over to a built-in bookcase. Paula had stocked it with a collection of novels and nonfiction. He scanned the titles for something to read. He was not choosy, he just needed to keep his mind occupied. He pulled out a worn copy of Barbara Tuchman's *The Guns of August*. He propped himself up in bed and began to read, hoping to fall asleep. But he soon realized that the book was too well written and too interesting. After several chapters he knew he needed to find something else. He was about to get up to find something else when he thought he heard a faint knocking. He listened and thought he heard it again.

Opening the door connecting to the main part of the house, he was surprised to see Paula standing there, also in a bathrobe, arm raised, about to knock again. She, too, was surprised by the sudden opening of the door. They both laughed, mildly embarrassed.

"Sorry to disturb you, but from my bedroom I can see the window to the guest room, and noticed your light was on. I didn't know if you were asleep or not and didn't want to wake you if you were, but since I was having trouble dropping off, I thought I'd come down and see if you were having trouble, too. If you are, I can keep you company for a bit."

"Great! Come in!" He chuckled. "I can't believe myself, I'm inviting you into your own guest suite!"

She followed him over to the sitting area. "You know, despite the circumstances that brought us together, I enjoyed the evening."

"I feel the same," he agreed.

She settled into the sofa, tucking her legs under herself.

"My mind wouldn't stop. And not just because of the iDoc situation. Tonight . . . Well, I wasn't as up front as I should have been."

George raised his eyebrows. "Go on!"

"When we were talking about our relationship in medical school, I wasn't completely truthful about how angry you had made me." She stared at her hands folded in her lap. "At the time it was a self-esteem issue for sure. I decided that I would never have anything to do with you socially again."

"Paula, I'm so sorry about what happened. In retrospect, as I said, I don't understand my own behavior. Truly."

"I recovered to a degree over the next three years, but not completely. When you called me during the summer of your first year of residency and my first year out here, saying that we should get together, I was tempted to tell you how angry and hurt I had been and not see you. But I decided on the spur of the moment to give it a go anyway. Can you remember what we talked about?"

George thought he remembered; he had babbled on about Pia.

"For the entire evening, all you talked about was how Pia was not returning your phone calls, texts, or e-mails and how worried you were about her, blah, blah, blah."

George grimaced. "Did I really do that?" He knew he did.

"You did. You carried on all evening, which brought up all the hurt from our freshman year."

"I'm sorry, I was such an ass. But I've grown up a bit."

What he didn't explain was that he had grown up because of Kasey.

The conversation went on for a while longer, with Paula finally taking the opportunity to express herself as she could not before. George was contrite and apologetic, asking Paula to understand that his behavior had stemmed somewhat from his being an addict of sorts, and the more Pia rejected him, the harder he tried to make the relationship work. Since honesty was on the table for the night, George decided to open up about Kasey.

"I never mentioned that Kasey Lynch, the first victim of the iDoc problem, was actually my fiancée," he said softly. "She was part of the iDoc beta test when she was diagnosed with advanced, stage-three ovarian cancer." What he still didn't include was that he had awakened with her dead in his bed.

Paula's mouth dropped open. "George, I'm so sorry! Here I am talking about my hurt feelings seven years ago, and you just lost your fiancée, possibly because of something I helped create!" She let out a sigh. "When did she die?"

"A few months ago."

"Are you still grieving? Of course you are. It's only been a few months."

"I'll probably always grieve. But I've reconciled myself to her loss, except to why it happened so precipitously. Her death is one of the reasons I have to find out exactly what is going on. Can we do that together?"

"Yes, George." She took his hand and squeezed it tightly.

George reached out and hugged her. It was obvious to

him that this time neither of them felt self-conscious about the hug. It lasted and lasted and led to a tentative kiss. The kiss led to another, and to both their surprise, the sense of attraction they had for each other since they had first met surmounted any reservations they held or the circumstances that had now brought them together.

With a certain desperation the two old friends hesitantly clung to each other, then abandoned restraint. They tore off their robes. Sinking into the canopied bed, they devoured each other, making mad, passionate love. For a few paradisiacal moments they allowed their minds and bodies to be completely absorbed in the giving and receiving of pleasure. Some time later, locked in an embrace as if afraid their coupling had been a dream and that the other was going to disappear, they fell into an exhausted, sublime sleep.

50

A muffled explosion sent a shock wave through the house, rattling the windows and waking George and Paula from their sleep. Both were momentarily stunned, particularly George, who, for the moment, as after his earlier nap, didn't even know where he was.

An alarm sounded, with a loud, intermittent, obnoxious, grating noise throughout the house. They looked to each other, wondering if it had been an earthquake. It was almost completely dark. What little light there was came from the pool, filtering in through the Bermuda shutters.

Paula was the first to act. She leaped from the bed, her silk nightgown billowing behind her, and rushed over to a small LED security screen mounted in the wall. She quickly typed in a code.

George scrambled out of bed and joined her.

The LED screen came to life, providing the first real light in the room, and began flashing a schematic of the house. It showed a blinking light at the front door.

"The front door has been breached," Paula croaked. She couldn't believe this was happening.

Now actual images of the property flashed on the screen, one after another, coming from security cameras throughout the property. Paula tapped out a command and the image shifted to the front door. It had been blown wide open. Through a cloud of smoke they could make out an armed figure dressed from head to toe in black, seemingly standing guard at the entrance.

"My God!" Paula voiced. She tapped out another command. The image switched to the main stairs and then the upper hallway. Three more figures in black could be seen dashing through the hall toward the master bedroom.

The phone rang.

Paula snapped it up. "Confirmed! Break-in in progress!"

George could hear a voice on the other end saying, "Ten-four! Police on their way!"

Paula dropped the phone and turned to George. "We have to get to the safe room! Now!"

"How can we get to it?" George blurted as he scrambled to pull on a pair of pants. Being naked made him feel even more vulnerable, if that was at all possible.

Paula turned back to the security pad, and they watched as the intruders flew back out of the master bedroom and paused, as if confused about what to do next.

"They're searching for me," she whispered over the sound of the alarm. "Who the hell are they?"

"Lord knows! They can't be FBI or SWAT." He remembered that the team of men who had invaded his apartment all had their affiliations clearly blazoned on their uniforms. These people did not.

They watched as one of the men made a call on what they guessed was a cell phone.

"Follow me," Paula said quietly. "There are back stairs to the second floor just outside the guest suite."

"Is that the best idea? The safe room is in the basement?"

Paula nodded toward the screen. "They already checked the master bedroom. We should go there and use the hidden slide."

George nodded his understanding.

They slipped out of the guest suite, Paula pulling George behind her as they ducked into the back stairway behind what looked like a closet door. Once there, they began creeping up the dark wooden steps. At the top, Paula came to an abrupt halt and ducked down, causing George to bump into her, nearly tripping over her crouched figure. She pointed ahead, down the second-floor hallway to a dark figure standing at the head of the main stairway, blocking their route. With no other option, they cowered in the darkness at the head of the back stairs and waited. The raucous noise of the alarm stopped as suddenly as it had started.

A whistle came from below, and the man silently sprinted down the steps in response.

"Now!" Paula whispered. She scrambled forward, urging George to follow. She hurried down the hall toward the master bedroom.

Hearing footsteps, the man who had just descended the stairs looked up, spotting them dashing past in the half light. "Stop!" he yelled.

They ignored him and kept running for the bedroom.

The man leaped up the stairs two at a time, yelling over his shoulder to his colleagues. "I have them! Master bedroom!"

George and Paula burst into the master bedroom, slamming the door shut as the man chasing them ran into it. George braced himself against the door while Paula flicked the lock.

The intruder threw his full body weight at the locked door, but it was lined with steel: another level of protection ordered by the former owner, for which George and Paula were now thankful. The man out in the hall repeatedly lunged at it, crashing into it presumably with his shoulder. It rattled but held.

The master bedroom was almost pitch-dark, with just an inkling of light coming in through the curtains covering the sliding glass doors that led to a balcony overlooking the pool area. They made their way over to the wood panel that covered the chute, with George holding on to Paula's nightgown. Locating the handhold ingeniously camouflaged in the panel's trim, Paula yanked open the panel to the chute. A whiff of comparatively stale, humid air wafted up from the chute in stark contrast to the highly air-conditioned air of the bedroom.

Paula grabbed George's arm and pulled him toward the yawning maw. George hesitated. Throwing himself down a black hole willy-nilly was a scary proposition, even though he had already done it earlier. But then it wasn't dark in the room.

"Go!" Paula commanded in a harsh voice. The man in the hall continued to pound away at the door. Boom! But now they could hear the sound of wood splintering. George realized that while the door itself might not give way, its frame was about to.

Sensing he could not hesitate another second, George launched himself feetfirst down the chute. The walls were of polished metal, and only an instant later he hit the cushioned floor of the basement. In the utter blackness he groped for a landmark. As he started to stand, Paula collided with him, knocking him forward onto his hands and knees.

"Sorry," she managed.

"It's okay." He scrambled to his feet again and then began inching forward with his hands outstretched, swinging them in a tight arc in the direction of the safe room in the hope of connecting with something to orient him.

He felt Paula place her hand on the small of his back, urging him forward toward the safe room's door. Then, for the second time that night, they were stunned. On this occasion, it was even more frightening than when the front door was blown open.

51

George and Paula were frozen in place, blinking against a blinding bright light shining directly at them. They were immediately set upon by several of the intruders, who grabbed them and bound their hands behind their backs with plastic ties. Whoever these people were, they were in a hurry. Not a word was spoken.

"Who are you and what do you want?" Paula demanded. With the anxiety of the actual chase over, her terror had morphed into rage.

The men ignored her and placed black hoods over George's and Paula's heads. Rapidly, they half dragged and half carried their two captives to the stairs, where they were unceremoniously hauled up to the main floor. Then, just as quickly, they were propelled out the back door, wincing in pain as their bare feet trod across the stone walkway to the alley.

Paula started to yell out but was immediately thumped on her back with a club. "You'll lose all your teeth if you do that again," a captor sneered.

George overheard the threat and remained silent. The next thing they knew, they were being forced into a van, pushed down to the metal floor, and covered with what felt like a heavy blanket. A moment later the door to the van was slammed shut, and they could feel the vehicle begin to move, slowly at first, along the alley. A few seconds later it lurched forward as it accelerated in the open street. Both George and Paula repositioned themselves to make breathing easier.

Their movements brought rapid retaliation. They could feel their captors above them pushing down with their boots to keep them from moving. They heard a police siren in the distance, but the blaring sound faded as the van raced in the opposite direction.

So much for the police, George thought, discouraged. They would find nothing but an empty house.

After several minutes George risked a whisper: "I'm sorry. I'm afraid I brought this on you. I tried to make sure I had not been followed."

"They must have tracked your car with GPS," Paula answered back just as quietly.

"Maybe so," George said. He'd never given a thought to having been tracked wirelessly.

"Regardless, it's not your fault. I'm sorry, too," she added.

"Quiet!" one of the men above them snapped. The boots pressed down harder.

George was aware they were moving quickly through the city streets, which he knew had little traffic at that hour. Despite the earlier warning, George moved to try to get more comfortable, forcing Paula to do the same.

"Stay still!" one of the captors warned.

As they rode in silence George tried not to think about what was going to happen to them or why they were being abducted. Their captors seemed professional and highly trained from the way they functioned with such efficiency, without the need to talk. He wondered if they were government agents because of their lack of identity, but that didn't make any sense, since he'd already been arrested. In fact, the only government agency that would act in this manner was the CIA. He couldn't believe that anyone thought he and Paula were terrorists, needing rendition to some place like Guantánamo.

After what George estimated was about forty-five minutes driving on what felt like flat Los Angeles streets, they started going uphill. It was steep enough for him to feel the pull of gravity. George suspected they were traveling up one of the numerous canyons of Los Angeles. He heard no conversation between the abductors, which suggested there was no confusion as to where they were going.

Suddenly the van slowed and seemed to pull off the main road. George guessed they had left pavement as he could hear gravel crackling under the tires. Then the van stopped and George heard a muffled creaking noise that sounded like a gate being opened. He strained to listen for other sounds that might give him a better sense of where they were. The van started to move again, still on gravel. After a minute or two it stopped again. This time the engine was turned off and a few moments later the doors opened, including the ones in the back.

Immediately George sensed dry air coming into the van. It was also decidedly cooler here than at Paula's house in Santa Monica. Putting together all the clues of drive time, uphill travel, and the change in temperature and humidity, he surmised that they could be somewhere up in the Hollywood Hills. Maybe the location to which Zee had traced one of the high-anonymity proxy servers that had something to do with overwriting the iDoc dump commands.

The blanket that had covered them was pulled away, and they were again half carried and half dragged out of the van. Outside of the vehicle, they shivered in the night air until blankets were draped over their shoulders. That act alone made them both feel more optimistic. If their abductors cared enough about their well-being, then the situation might be hopeful. They were pushed forward across the gravel drive on their tender bare feet until they eventually reached the relief of a paved sidewalk.

As he walked George could glimpse a section of the walkway through a small open space at the bottom of the hood covering his head. He could tell that a string of lights ran along the walk. He heard the howl of a coyote in the distance as they entered a lighted building and were pulled to a stop. To their surprise, their hoods were pulled off, and they were shocked to see all five of their abductors standing before them with their faces fully exposed.

Their captors were all large, powerful-appearing, racially diverse men with short haircuts that made George think of the Special Forces. All were armed with holstered sidearms. The fact that the men were allowing themselves to be seen sent a chill down George's spine. He knew that kidnappers never showed their faces *if* there was a chance that the victims would be released once ransom demands were made. Since their abductors had shown themselves, George worried that there were no plans for them to be released. His mind raced through all other options and came up blank, and a bolt of terror rippled through him again.

Paula, obviously panicked, nonetheless immediately launched into a vociferous tirade. "What the hell is going on here! Who are you? Why have we been brought here? You people can't go around kidnapping whomever the hell you damn want!"

George cringed. He was worried that she was inviting the beating that had been threatened earlier.

The men in black didn't respond. It became apparent that they were waiting. *Waiting for what?* George wondered. He looked around, noting that they were in a large reception or waiting room area. The place had a definite institutional feel. Everything was white, tan, or gray. The furniture was nondescript and definitely not new, maybe from the fifties or sixties. The floor was some sort of composite material, like old-fashioned linoleum. There were a scattering of dated magazines on side tables. For illumination, there were banks of harsh, recessed fluorescent lights.

All at once a door opened and three men and three women appeared. All were middle-aged and dressed in pressed white pants and shirts. There was no talk and certainly no smiles. The ethnically diverse group comprised a couple of African Americans, a Caucasian, two Latinos, and an Asian. What that suggested, if anything, George had no idea. They shared a common trait: All were large and muscular and appeared capable of handling an unruly person, if need be.

It was immediately apparent to both George and Paula that they had been expected. There was no conversation. The men in black merely nodded to the newly arrived attendants, then disappeared back out into the night. Their mission was apparently over.

For a moment Paula watched the men leave and, recovering from the shock, she turned to the attendants and directed a slightly modified repeat of the furious attack she had unleashed on the abductors. "Where are we? Why have we been brought here? This is crazy! We've been kidnapped."

The attendants were unfazed. The women pulled Paula back toward the door from which they had come.

Paula screamed, "Let go of me! I'm not going in here! What kind of freaking place is this?"

"Ma'am," one of the women calmly responded, "you are in a private mental health rehabilitation center."

"What! Why?" Paula demanded. She sounded more infuriated than scared. She tried to refuse to move.

The attendants were apparently accustomed to Paula's attitude. One of the attendants took a syringe out of her pocket.

Paula's eyes opened wide, and she quieted down. She did not want to be injected. "Okay, okay! I'll go." She hesitantly allowed herself to be moved forward into the facility.

"It'll be okay, Paula!" George called after her. "Just do as they say for now!" His mind was going a mile a minute, trying desperately to figure out what was happening. Then two of the male attendants grabbed George's arms and urged him to follow Paula.

George heard the heavy door close behind them with a concussive sound, advertising just how impenetrable it was. A resounding click indicated it was locked up tight.

Paula heard it, too, and was suddenly in a near hysteria. She tried to stop and free herself from the grasp of the attendants. "You don't understand!" she yelled. "We're here against our will! We've truly been kidnapped by those apes that brought us here! We need to call the police!"

The attendants said nothing, strengthened their grip on her arms, and nudged her forward.

She stared at their maddeningly calm faces in disbelief. "I said we've been kidnapped! Don't you get it?"

The attendant with the syringe responded. "Yes, we get it. We hear that a lot. That's what most all the people say when they first arrive."

Paula and George were shocked into silence by the comment. Paula looked back at George questioningly. George made an expression of total confusion. They were both at a complete loss.

"Please!" the attendant said. "Be cooperative! It is for your own good. We need to get you comfortable."

Reluctantly, Paula acquiesced.

The two were led through a large common area furnished similarly to the outer reception area. There were no signs of any other people. Then they were escorted down a long, brightly lit corridor. There was no conversation. Paula had seemingly resigned herself to the situation. They came to a door, which one of the female attendants opened with a key attached to a ring, which was in turn attached by a wire to her trousers. She motioned to Paula to go inside.

Paula hesitated and George took a step forward to look. It was a relatively small room, approximately ten feet by ten feet, and all white, with a simple bed and chair. There were no windows. George felt a nudge on his back and moved down the hall.

He could hear Paula protesting that she didn't want to go into the room. One of the women told her that if she didn't cooperate, she would be tranquilized. That was the last thing George heard as he was pulled to a stop outside another door beyond which was a room similar to Paula's.

"After you," the attendant said to George.

George stepped into the room. It had a bed and a chair and nothing else. No decorations on the blank white walls and no windows. There was a bathroom that had no door. Inside were a toilet, sink, and shower head. The shower was not enclosed and a drain was positioned in the middle of the floor. The word *institutional* popped into George's mind.

On the bed were clothes that looked like hospital scrubs. They were a nondescript medium blue. There were also underwear, socks, and slippers. George looked up. In the middle of the ceiling was a small inverted dome of dark glass, which George guessed was a surveillance camera.

Another attendant stepped behind George and used a pair of clippers to cut through the plastic tie binding George's wrists. When he looked down at his wrists he saw there were deep red indentations but no lacerations.

"Dress," the third attendant ordered as he pointed to the clothing on the bed.

George finally spoke, attempting to keep his voice calm. "Can you tell me where we are and why we've been brought here?"

"You'll know that in the morning." The man's voice was impassive, and he spoke as if to a child.

"I know you said you've heard it before, but we actually have been kidnapped."

The attendant nodded and again pointed to the clothes on the bed. "Please, put on the clothes. And, yes, we hear all the time about being kidnapped. Almost everyone who is brought here says it and, in a way, they are right."

"What other people?" George asked, although he could only guess. He imagined it was people with serious addiction problems whose families had resorted to forcible therapeutic intervention.

"Please, just relax. You'll learn everything you want to know in the morning. I suggest you get some sleep in the meantime."

George tried to ask a few more questions, but to no avail. The attendant merely repeated that George would have to wait until morning for answers. With that, the three attendants turned and left. George heard another resounding click as the heavy door was secured.

He sat on the bed and stared at the door, feeling a twinge of claustrophobia. He got up to test the knob and confirm it was locked. *You never know*, his brain kept telling him, *it just might miraculously open.* He gave the knob a twist and jiggled it. It didn't open. He went over to the wall that he guessed was common with Paula's room and put his ear against it, but heard nothing. He rapped on the wall. Almost immediately there came a muffled reply. George guessed the wall to be thick and soundproofed. He called out Paula's name but heard only silence in reply.

Next, he checked the bathroom. He saw nothing he hadn't already seen when he'd glanced into it earlier. It was remarkably utilitarian with no sharp objects he could use to harm himself. He went back into the main room and sat on the bed. His heart was still pounding from the ordeal of being kidnapped. What the hell was going on here? What other disaster could possibly await him after being arrested, thrown in jail, and now committed involuntarily to a mental health institution?

He lay back on the bed, worrying about what he had brought upon Paula. It seemed to his paranoid mind that any woman he got close to—Pia, Kasey, and now Paula—seemed to suffer some horrible consequence.

Feeling charged up as if from caffeine, he got up and paced the small room. Silently he mocked the attendant's advice to get some sleep. There was no way in hell he would be able to fall asleep. Then he realized that there were no switches to turn off or even to lower the level of bright light in the room. He wondered if the room was meant for someone on a suicide watch. Vaguely he wondered why he even bothered to wonder. Would he really get all the answers in the morning, or were the attendants just trying to placate him with an empty promise? Then his mind switched to thoughts of whether anyone would look for him. It was another depressing question.

After a time George lay back on the bed. He closed his eyes to the room's glare, but couldn't turn off his mind. Could he actually be kept hidden away for an undetermined period of time? Could that really happen in this day and age? Unfortunately, he thought, it was possible. The only person he could imagine might actually look for him was the bail bondsman.

All of a sudden George felt tears well up in his eyes. Covering his face with his hands, he let himself cry for a few minutes before recovering. What pulled him out of his despair was the thought of Zee. As bad as his situation was, George had to recognize he was better off than Zee, who was dead. Or was he?

"Get a grip on yourself!" George said out loud. He stood up and started running in place. He knew he needed to get himself under control and hoped that by exhausting himself he could accomplish it. When he was adequately out of breath, he stopped running and flopped down onto the floor and did a series of twenty push-ups.

Once he was finished with the push-ups, George sat back down on the bed. His breathing was labored, but he felt more in control. He even thought he might possibly be able to relax.

52

A loud click jolted George awake. He shot up to a sitting position, shocked that he had actually fallen asleep. The door swung open and three beefy attendants came into the room. One was carrying a breakfast tray.

"What time it is?" George asked.

"Eight fifteen."

"What about my friend? The woman?"

"She's fine. She's breakfasting as well."

That was a relief, although why he believed the man, he wasn't sure. "When am I going to learn where I am? And why, for that matter?"

"Eat. We'll be back for you in half an hour." They turned and left.

Great! Answers galore, George thought. He looked down at the food: eggs, bacon, toast, orange juice, and coffee. He was impressed, assuming it wasn't poisoned or drugged. There was even a copy of the *L.A. Times* on the tray. *How considerate*, he thought. He drank his orange juice and picked at the food. He had no appetite. He scanned through the paper and found no mention of a kidnapping or home invasion in Santa Monica, or any follow-up on Zee's death.

George used the toilet and washed his face, then went to the wall between his room and Paula's and rapped on it again. There was a muffled knock in reply. He tried again to call out to her but heard nothing back. Without a clock or a watch, he didn't know how much longer he would have to wait, but soon enough there was a knock on the door, just before it swung open again. The same three attendants stepped into the room.

"Ready?"

George ran through several smart retorts in his mind but held his tongue. He knew it was best not to aggravate his keepers. "Ready," George agreed. He stepped into the hall with the three attendants following.

Almost simultaneously, Paula emerged from her room dressed in scrubs similar to George's. Three matrons in white followed her almost in step.

George's heart lifted. "Paula!"

The attendants made no move to restrict contact between them so he enveloped her in a hug. When she hugged him, he could hear the relief in her voice as she said, "I'm so glad to see you."

"Are you okay?"

She let go of him and tried to regain her composure. "As well as can be expected, I guess."

"Same here."

"What is going on, George?" She looked up and down the hallway and then at the attendants, who appeared to be waiting patiently.

"I have no idea. Hopefully we're about to find out."

"Please!" one of the female attendants said, motioning them to follow her down the hallway the way they had come when they had first arrived. "You need to get a move on. You don't want to be late."

George and Paula did as they were told with the other five attendants trailing behind. Having gotten away with the hug, George took Paula's hand and squeezed it. She squeezed back as they exchanged a wary glance. They held hands as they walked.

"Do you know where we are?" she asked in a whisper.

"If I had to guess, I'd say somewhere in the Hollywood Hills."

She glanced over at him. "That's odd if you are right. But then again, what is there about all this that isn't odd?"

They were led into a conference room, glimpsing a sign on the door: BOARDROOM. They had encountered no other people, attendants or inmates.

Inside the room was a long table with seating for five people along each side and one at each end. A whiteboard was mounted at one end of the room. A large window looked out upon a stand of dense sycamore trees. No other buildings were visible.

George and Paula were asked to sit on the opposite side of the table, facing the door. Again they did as they were told. Hoping answers were forthcoming, they were willing to be compliant. Three attendants positioned themselves at each end of the room and stood silent with folded arms.

George and Paula looked at each other, increasingly baffled. They had no idea what to expect, but at least they were being well treated, hardly like kidnapping victims who would normally be kept in total isolation without being allowed to see or talk to their captors.

After a few moments, George leaned over to Paula and whispered, "How was your night?"

"Delightful," Paula answered sarcastically. "How was yours?"

"I liked the first half better than the second," he said.

Paula laughed softly. She reached out and squeezed his hand under the table. "I think I preferred the first part as well."

"What did you think of the room service?"

"Better than expected," Paula admitted. "The whole situation defies belief. I never expected a breakfast like that, especially not with a newspaper."

"Did you sleep?" he asked.

"Not a wink. You?"

"Surprisingly, I did. I suppose it was thanks to my previous night in jail."

"Lucky for you," Paula said. Regaining some of her courage, she called out to the attendants, "How long do we have to wait?"

"Not long," came the reply.

As if on cue, the door to the room opened and three men appeared.

Both Paula's and George's jaws dropped in utter shock. They couldn't have been more shocked if the president of the United States had just walked in.

53

Bradley Thorn, Lewis Langley, and Clayton Hanson entered the room and took seats opposite George and Paula. They avoided eye contact with their totally dumbfounded hostages. It was as if they were embarrassed.

Thorn set a folder on the table with particular deliberateness, adjusting it to be perfectly perpendicular to the table's edge. He made himself comfortable in his chair and only then did he look across at George and Paula. Langley and Clayton had followed suit but without the folder. For a few pregnant moments the five people stared across the table at one another.

George felt a certain relief in seeing these men, recognizing that there had to be some reason other than death or rendition for why he and Paula had been snatched in the middle of the night. These were professional business-men and doctors, not murderous thugs. And perhaps most important from George's perspective, they were not rep-resentatives of some secret government organization, or at least he didn't think they were.

Finally, Thorn cleared his throat. "I can only imagine your surprise. First off, let me apologize on behalf of all of us for the ordeal you've suffered, which we heard about only this morning. We can well imagine that it must have been frightening, but as you will soon learn, the situation was thought to be an emergency, and the people in charge didn't want to take any chances. Actually there was one man in charge, and that was Mr. Gauthier, Amalgamated's head of security."

"What?" Paula shouted, practically leaping out of her seat. She pounded the table with both her fists. Everyone at the table jumped. "Amalgamated was responsible for our being kidnapped! You?" Her eyes drilled into Thorn's. Her voice was shrill and angry. Several of the attendants stepped forward in case they needed to restrain Paula.

Thorn lifted his hands as if he thought he needed to protect himself. He momentarily averted his eyes from Paula's accusatory stare. He spoke in a carefully modu-lated voice. "In the final analysis, yes, I am ultimately responsible. Although I should reiterate that in the urgency of the situation, the decision of how to handle it was made by Mr. Gauthier, and I, or should I say we, learned about how the operation had been carried out only after the fact." Thorn glanced at Langley and Clayton, who both nodded in agreement.

"As head of security, this was in his domain, and he decided it was an extreme situation that needed to be turned over to professionals to whom he has access when the need arises. Ergo, the strong-armed methods that you unfortunately experienced. But still, we are all responsible. So, we again apologize."

"But why?" Paula demanded, now with more disbelief than anger. It was apparent that she was not about to let Thorn off the hook with a mere mea culpa.

"That's what we are here to explain," Thorn said patiently. "We, or at least I, fully expected your deserved outrage, and I accept your anger as appropriate. We know that your being dragged here in the middle of the night with no explanation must have been unnerving, to say the least. But, again, Gauthier thought that it was best to act rapidly and—"

"Where the hell are we?" Paula interrupted with venom. "All we've been told is that this is some sort of a private mental health and addiction facility."

"That is correct," Thorn said. "It once was a top-secret military film studio. It dates back to the early forties. It was later transformed into a private treatment center for celebrities with addiction problems and for wealthy families who sought complete discretion for their children, who were often brought here, as you were, in the middle of the night. Amalgamated picked up ownership as part of a package deal for a hospital chain. Although we were initially indifferent to its ownership, subsequently we have found the facility handy for a number of functions."

George remembered that once Zee had pierced the high-anonymity proxy servers, he had identified a server bank located somewhere in the Hollywood Hills. George wondered if those servers were in this facility behind the many closed doors.

"Where is this facility?" George asked, speaking for the first time.

"The Hollywood Hills. Laurel Canyon, to be precise. Few people are aware of its existence. Even most neighbors aren't aware of it. We're very secluded up here, despite being ten minutes from the Sunset Strip." He motioned out the window. "There's considerable wooded property with an elaborate security system, surrounded by electrified razor-wire fencing."

George nodded, trying to keep himself calm in contrast to Paula. It seemed to George that Thorn was doing more than giving them a verbal tour of the facility. He was sending a message: Paula and George could be held in the facility and no one would know. Some of the fear that George felt before Thorn, Langley, and Clayton had walked into the conference room returned.

As if reading George's mind, Thorn continued: "The fencing guarantees security both for people getting in and people getting out. We have a very discreet, well-trained staff who are accustomed to dealing with clients who have been brought here against their will according to dictates of their families or executors." He nodded at the attendants.

"Okay, okay," Paula said as she closed her eyes and

seemingly counted to ten. "Just how long must we stay here? And why? What's the emergency?"

George cringed at Paula's tone. It seemed that he more than she was conscious of their vulnerability.

"All very good questions," Thorn said. "The answer as to length of time is entirely up to you. We would like to get you home as soon as possible. But your leaving is going to require some assurances from you."

"Assurances about what?" George blurted.

"In order to understand the current problem, we want to be sure we have your undivided attention."

George and Paula exchanged a disbelieving glance in response. It didn't seem real to George. He could tell Paula felt the same way. "Of course you have our undivided attention!" George snapped, despite his attempt to contain his emotion. "After being kidnapped in the middle of the night and terrified out of our minds! Please!"

"I'll take that as a yes from you both." Thorn cleared his throat again as he motioned for the attendants to leave the room. He looked at Paula and George and smiled as the attendants headed for the door. It was clear that this had been decided beforehand. Thorn fingered what appeared to George to be a small wireless electronic fob with a button on it. "They'll be right outside if they are needed." Thorn placed the fob on the table, to be used if necessary. George got the message.

Once the attendants were gone and the door closed, Thorn began. "I want to emphasize first that the beta test has gone much better than expected and has been an enormous success, thanks to you, Paula, for the idea in the first place, and thanks to Lewis and his team for the consummate programming effort."

Langley nodded, appreciating the recognition.

"But," Thorn continued, "we have hit a bump in the road. A glitch has appeared. It was not even noticed at first. In retrospect, we realize that it started several months ago, but that was only after we knew what we were looking for and had looked at it retrospectively. The glitch came to our full attention only during the previous week, and I should add it had nothing to do with iDoc's functioning in general, nor did it have anything to do with iDoc's acceptance as the primary-care practitioner of choice of thousands of people. iDoc continues to work far better than our most optimistic predictions. It has been fantastic. iDoc promises to be a win-win situation for patients and the country, and the world, for that matter. It will return some sense to a health care system that has always seen a dearth of primary-care doctors and a lack of emphasis on prevention."

George's hands, clasped in front of him, began to rub against each other and his right leg started to bounce under the table. Despite trying to rein in his emotions, he found himself progressively impatient for Thorn to get to the point.

But Thorn didn't. He went on to say that iDoc was going to have an enormously positive effect on the health of millions and in the process would save countless billions of dollars. It would also eliminate the need for millions of doctor's office visits and equally important ER visits, which would also save an enormous amount of money over the years. "I am certain both of you understand all this,"

Thorn said, as if sensing George's impatience. "Especially since George here played a role in giving Paula the concept in the first place." Thorn looked directly at George. "Amalgamated would like to financially recognize your contribution, but more about that later. iDoc is a fantastic opportunity for Amalgamated since we will be billing for iDoc user access—"

Paula interrupted angrily, taking the words right out of George's mouth. "Enough of this shit! You're not telling us anything we don't already know. I think you should just get to the damn point. We don't need a lecture."

"Patience, Paula, patience." Thorn raised a restraining hand. "Here's something you don't know: Negotiations with Centers for Medicare and Medicaid Services, or CMS, have progressed to the point where they agreed to do their own beta test with iDoc. They are very excited about our baby. 'Your baby,' Paula. Isn't that how you refer to it?" He managed a smile at her with a patronizing wink. "Which means that unless there is an unforeseen problem, Medicare and Medicaid beneficiaries will eventually all have iDoc at their disposal. That's somewhere around a hundred million people!

"And the negotiations with foreign governments, particularly European, are all going swimmingly. Added to that, we now have commitments from a number of hedge fund managers who will be injecting many hundreds of millions of dollars into Amalgamated, so that iDoc's general release will all happen quickly and seamlessly."

Paula interrupted again. "This all sounds well and good, but I don't understand how it applies to George and me!"

Thorn raised his hands yet again to calm Paula. "I merely wanted to remind the two of you about all the good news on the horizon before getting back to the fly-in-the-ointment: the glitch."

The word hung in the air.

"It first appeared with a patient at Santa Monica University Hospital. Unfortunately it was a young woman who had serious medical issues. The glitch resulted in this individual's passing."

George stiffened, realizing that Thorn might very well be talking about Kasey. He felt a wave of anger at hearing someone characterize Kasey's death as a glitch. Even Thorn's use of the laundered term *passing* irritated him. With effort, George held his tongue.

"The glitch subsequently appeared with patients frequenting the L.A. University Medical Center in Westwood. That's something that you, George, noticed."

George nodded, then suddenly added, "Calling it a glitch camouflages what it really is. It is the apparently purposeful killing of iDoc patients. People. Human beings with friends, family . . . loved ones."

George's vehemence silenced Thorn for a moment. There was a brief pause until Thorn nodded solemnly. "I admit that the glitch has been associated with unexpected death, but I wouldn't use the term *purposeful*. How many deaths did you notice at the medical center?"

"You're asking only about the L.A. University Medical Center?" George asked.

"Yes."

"Four." He didn't even want to mention Kasey's name.

It would be a disservice to her memory under the current circumstances.

Thorn looked toward Langley and Clayton. Both nodded in agreement.

"There were three more at Santa Monica University and three at Harbor University Hospital," Langley added.

George wondered if the three at Santa Monica included Kasey but didn't ask.

"What did your investigation of these deaths turn up?" Thorn continued. "What was the cause?"

For a moment George debated what to say. It was hard to organize his thoughts with all the emotion he was feeling.

"Your cooperation is needed, George," Thorn prompted. "Especially if you are interested in leaving this mental health facility sooner rather than later."

George felt Paula grip his thigh. He took a deep breath. "If you are asking about confirmed results, I'd have to restrict my impressions to Sal DeAngelis."

"What were you able to learn? And how?"

George shifted in his chair, debated with himself how up front he should be.

"We are counting on your being honest," Thorn said, as if reading George's mind. "Just as we are prepared to be straightforward with you. What we have in mind," he added, motioning first to George and Paula and then to Langley and Clayton, "is for all of us to be on the same side."

George looked from one man to the other, trying to gauge their sincerity. All three stared back, unblinking.

Clayton in particular had hardly spoken since he walked in the door. George had no idea what he was thinking.

George cleared his throat. He glanced at Paula.

She nodded to him and gave his thigh another squeeze.

"I thought the drug reservoir in all of these people had played a role. I made the effort to find the reservoir that had been embedded in DeAngelis's abdomen."

"How did you manage that?" Thorn asked.

"It wasn't easy. First I tried to obtain it at the morgue, where I saw Clayton apparently doing the same."

Thorn and Clayton exchanged a glance.

Clayton spoke for the first time. "I did go to the morgue for that reason but didn't find the reservoir."

Thorn nodded and looked back at George. "Go on."

"Well, I didn't know it wasn't where it was supposed to be. I then tried to retrieve it from the corpse at a funeral home. That's when I realized that it had already been removed. And since I had seen several people searching DeAngelis's apartment, I assumed everyone was looking without success. So, I figured maybe DeAngelis had succeeded in cutting it out of himself while driving to the medical center. I located the crash vehicle at a salvage yard and was able to find the reservoir inside the car."

"You found it?" Thorn asked nervously. He exchanged a quick glance with his colleagues.

"I did. With a lot of effort."

"Did you examine it?" Thorn asked.

"Of course. I used a dissecting microscope. The reservoir was completely empty, which I thought very disturbing, since it was supposed to have lasted for several years. Not two months."

"What did you deduce from the empty reservoir?"

George looked directly at Thorn, thinking the executive was being deliberately obtuse. "I was worried that it had been a deliberate event and that—"

Thorn interrupted. "What do you mean by 'a deliberate event'? Let's call a spade a spade. You thought his death was a homicide?"

"Yes," George said, nodding. The cat was now out of the bag. "And I set out to prove it."

"And how did you do that?"

"I had gotten hold of DeAngelis's broken smartphone and had an IT-savvy friend of mine see if he could determine if the phone had received a message to do a global dump, meaning emptying the reservoir all at once. My friend confirmed that to be the case. The phone had jammed from the force of the crash, meaning its memory hadn't been remotely wiped clean by iDoc. An unaltered record of iDoc issuing a mass dump is in my possession."

Thorn looked to Langley with a frown. Langley squirmed.

"I knew then that Sal's death had been deliberate, not a malfunction of either the reservoir or the smartphone. I then encouraged my friend, Zee Beauregard, to try to hack into the iDoc servers to see if he could find the command to do the dump. I was worried about that type of thing after reading an article describing the potential problem of hackers breaking into wireless health care devices."

"You had your friend do this even though you and he knew that hacking into iDoc servers was a serious crime?"

"Of course!" George snapped irritably. "But the circumstances warranted the risk!"

Thorn held up his hand. "Please. I commend both your reasoning and your persistence."

Langley was impatient now; the discussion was getting into his bailiwick. "What did this Zee fellow find?"

"At first everything seemed normal. There was no evidence of a global-dump command, meaning that Sal's smartphone had been hacked. But then Zee noticed something that he called an artifact. The presence of this artifact indicated to him that there had been an overwrite of the record. He reasoned that there probably had been a dump command, but it had been overwritten. He found the same artifact in all five of the cases I was looking into. It wasn't an easy thing to spot on its own, but the fact that it appeared exactly seventeen minutes before the death of each of the five patients helped him identify it."

George noticed Thorn glaring at Langley, who glanced away. George sensed that Langley had been responsible for the overwrite and had essentially screwed up, which was why Zee discovered it.

With an exasperated expression, Thorn turned back to George. "Okay, you suspected a homicide. What were your thoughts up to this point?"

George hesitated.

"Please," Thorn persisted.

"I thought that someone or some group at Amalgamated had decided to use iDoc to save money."

"Can you be more specific?"

"I was worried that someone had been using iDoc as a kind of 'death panel' and then overwriting the commands to get rid of the evidence."

Thorn and Langley nodded.

"Again," Thorn said, "I must commend you on your reasoning and work, but . . . at the same time, I have to tell you that you are wrong."

George looked at Thorn, puzzled.

"I'll let Lewis explain what really happened."

George and Paula leaned forward, their anger and fear momentarily forgotten.

54

It was Langley's turn to clear his throat. "First and foremost," he began, lowering his voice as if concerned about being overheard, even though the attendants had left the room, "I have to go back to basics. I must be certain that both of you really know what it means for a program to be heuristic."

George and Paula exchanged a glance. To both of them it seemed a strange way for Langley to start.

"Of course I do, Lewis," Paula replied. "I've been selling that feature to God knows how many people!"

"I'm mostly interested in Dr. Wilson's answer. But still, selling heuristic and understanding heuristic can be two different things." He turned to George.

"I have an idea, but I'm not entirely sure I could define it."

"In its original meaning, 'heuristic' denoted a speculative concept that could serve as a guide in the solution of a problem, or a teaching method by which learning takes place through discoveries made by the student himself."

George and Paula looked at each other for a moment with confusion. Neither understood what Langley was saying. George, in particular, under the circumstances, found Langley's comments bizarre.

"In computer programming," Langley continued, "'heuristic' means a problem-solving technique that can be described as the ability to take advantage of previous solutions. What I mean is that the application incorporates information and solutions in its database to apply them in future problems, which it had not been originally programmed to solve." Langley focused on George to see if he was grasping it.

George nodded. It seemed like an awfully complicated way to say that a computer program could learn.

"It was important from the outset that the iDoc algorithm be written to enable it to take advantage of previous cases that it had encountered and to do it quickly. The initial alpha trials gave us an idea of the number of situations that would need a flesh-and-blood medical specialist as backup. To fulfill this need we created what we call the 'control room.' The control room is—"

"Paula actually has taken me on a visit to the control

room," George interrupted, hoping Langley would get to the point more quickly.

Langley smiled. "Good. At the outset of the beta test iDoc referred relatively often to the control room for answers, but that number dropped very quickly, meaning iDoc was functioning as planned in a heuristic fashion. In other words, there was a rapid reduction in the number of situations that iDoc didn't feel capable of handling on its own, demonstrating that it was indeed learning, and learning at a phenomenal rate." Langley stared at Paula and George, waiting for an acknowledgment that they were keeping up with him.

They both nodded.

"Now, to understand the glitch that occurred, you must know that the algorithm upon which iDoc is based includes a number of subjective issues such as pain and suffering associated with various medical treatments and even with some supposedly preventive testing. Even something simple, like the inability to sleep or eat normally, has been incorporated into iDoc if it is a frequent side effect. What we are essentially talking about here are quality-of-life issues, which are hard to quantify to include for the purposes of digitization. Nonetheless, we tried to incorporate them because we feel strongly that they need to be considered much more in health care decision making than has been done in fee-for-service medicine. And let me mention another variable: cost. The iDoc algorithm is responsibly aware that health care is already taking too big a bite from the GDP and that costs have to come down in order to ensure that health care can be distributed equitably. Am I making sense here?"

Both George and Paula nodded. The phrase *it's not rocket science* went through George's mind.

Langley cleared his throat again. "So here is the truth. No one knowingly used iDoc to kill anyone. The fact that a small number of patients died because of iDoc was a surprise to all of us. What happened was that the iDoc algorithm decided on its own to eliminate certain individuals after taking into consideration the pain and suffering associated with the specific cancer treatments they were facing, the predicted outcome of treatments, and cost consequences. There was no outside interference. In other words, there were no 'bad guys.' iDoc made its decision dispassionately with the evidence it already had in terms of the illnesses involved, the treatments available, the suffering that the patients would have to endure, and the cost. And that is basically *it*."

There was a prolonged silence. The only sound penetrating the room was the chirping of birds outside the window.

Paula was the first to speak. She was decidedly less angry. "How long has this glitch been known?"

"A week," Langley answered. "I first received evidence the same day that Amalgamated gave the presentation to potential investors."

"And what actions have you taken?" Paula asked.

"As soon as we determined what had happened," Langley continued, "we put an immediate end to what George has termed *global dumping commands*. Then we wanted to know how it had happened. Our first concern was the same as Dr. Wilson's, namely the existence of a rogue hacker. But that was immediately ruled out when it became obvious that the dump commands had come from iDoc itself, meaning it was the algorithm that had made the determinations and given the orders."

"And then what did you do?" Paula asked, taking the words right out of George's mouth.

"Like I said, we stopped iDoc's ability to issue dumping commands."

"The selection of these types of patients . . . was that also stopped?" George asked.

"No. Because we want to look at the cohort of people that iDoc would have terminated along with how iDoc reached its decision, so that we as programmers could in a sense learn from iDoc: a heuristic event in reverse."

"How many more patients were there besides the four that George discovered?" Paula asked.

"There were eight others, for a total of twelve," Langley admitted. "There was one more associated with L.A. University Medical Center that Dr. Wilson was not aware of, four associated with Santa Monica University Hospital, and three with Harbor University Hospital."

"Did all of these result in deaths?" Paula inquired. She sounded like an attorney taking a deposition.

"Yes."

"Has iDoc identified anyone as fitting the criteria for a global dump since you stopped such a command from being issued?"

"Yes, there have been three of those. Two at L.A. University Medical Center and one at Santa Monica University Hospital."

"So, these three people are still alive?"

"Yes, but they are about to undergo very difficult treatments that will severely impact their quality of life with little chance of slowing their respective diseases."

George interrupted. "I assume iDoc has also identified a group of candidates that would fit the global dump profile that do not have an embedded reservoir to do its dirty work, were it allowed."

Langley was silent a moment. His eyes flicked toward Thorn. "Yes."

"How many of those has it identified?"

"I don't have that exact information available. I can get it for you, though."

"But that is a good question," Thorn admitted.

George nodded, then moved on. "Was Zee correct in his assumption that the records of the four cases I investigated had been overwritten to cover up the dump commands?"

"Yes. We did that," Langley admitted.

"Why did you wipe the patients' smartphones clean of all data and try to do so with DeAngelis's phone as well?" George demanded.

"That has been standard procedure since the outset of the beta test. We wipe a phone clean immediately upon confirmation of death. That has nothing to do with the dump commands. It has to do with privacy issues that—"

Thorn interrupted. "Lewis is correct. There was no attempted cover-up with the smartphones. Our damage control was limited to the overwrite of the global-dump commands and their physiological consequences on the servers. And that was to prevent anyone at Amalgamated or our iDoc subsidiary from discovering the glitch. Only the three of us, plus one other individual at Amalgamated, were aware of what happened. Our intent was, and is, to prevent the media from learning what had happened. We know that such information would ignite a media frenzy. Remember what happened when Sarah Palin brought up the subject of 'death panels.' And that was only about discussing end-of-life choices with elderly patients. We feel that iDoc is so potentially beneficial to the country and the world that this unfortunate glitch should not derail it. When iDoc's benefits are known to the world in terms of democratizing medicine and truly focusing on prevention, then dealing with the issue of this glitch can be accomplished without 'throwing the baby out with the bathwater.'"

Thorn stopped and took a deep breath. Everyone was silent, absorbing Thorn's impassioned defense of iDoc.

George was the first to speak. "iDoc is going to be good for Amalgamated as well."

"Absolutely!" Thorn agreed without hesitation. "I want you and Paula to understand that the glitch does not represent any kind of conspiracy on the part of Amalgamated. There was no Amalgamated 'death panel.' Nor will there ever be. Frankly, to be perfectly honest, we do not need it."

"Why didn't you come directly to George and me instead of snatching us in the middle of the night?" Paula demanded, some of her anger returning. "We could have been seriously injured."

"I apologize for that. As I mentioned earlier, that decision was made by Butch Gauthier, our security chief. Don't worry, I'll be having a word with him very soon. Unfortunately it was one of those situations where the right hand didn't know what the left hand was doing. The professionals who snatched you had no idea who you were, just that you were dangerous. I understand how you both feel. And for good reason. But keep in mind, the situation was deemed an emergency, which had to be contained as soon as possible. That said, we apologize again."

Langley and Clayton nodded their heads in agreement.

"In view of what you two have had to endure, we here would like to say that we are prepared to make it up to you if you're willing to cooperate."

"What the hell do you mean by 'cooperate'?" George demanded.

"'Cooperation' means that you recognize the glitch for what it was. The deaths of the patients involved are regrettable, as they had no say in the decision. That's completely contrary to informed consent. But also remember that all of those people were terminal in the very near future and facing considerable pain and suffering with the treatments available, and therefore a very low quality of life."

George and Paula exchanged a glance of disbelief.

"And if we don't, as you say, cooperate, what then?" George asked.

Thorn sighed audibly. "That will necessitate a prolonged stay at this rather pleasant facility with no opportunities for outside communication until it is deemed possible for Amalgamated to deal with whatever revelations and accusations you might feel appropriate. In other words, we need to cover our behinds." He offered a crooked smile along with his attempt at humor.

"Do you think you can actually get away with keeping us locked up?" Paula asked.

"Yes, of course. If pressed, we can manufacture evidence for addiction problems that require treatment. Something in that vein," he said with a flip of his hand.

"People will look for us!" Paula said with disbelief.

"We'll deal with that. Although we know that neither one of you will be missed by your employers for a few days." Thorn glanced at George. "Well, for you, George, it's a bit longer than a few days, isn't it? Anyway, that's a usual source of questions apart from local family or intimate relationships, which neither of you have."

Paula looked at George as if to say, *This is crazy.*

George turned to Langley. "You've described the glitch that killed the patients as a spontaneous creation by the algorithm. And you also stated that it has only been temporarily blocked rather than removed."

Langley nodded in the affirmative but Thorn interrupted.

"Let me anticipate your concerns. As I mentioned earlier, Amalgamated is in direct negotiations with CMS to provide iDoc to all Medicare and Medicaid beneficiaries. Part of their due diligence is to allow the URI, or Universal Resource Initiative, to monitor the test. URI is a clandestine agency under the aegis of the IPAB, or Independent Payment Advisory Board, which is in turn mandated by the Affordable Care Act. While the URI was performing their due diligence, they detected the glitch almost the same time as we did."

George remembered that Zee had stated that one of the high-anonymity proxy servers was located in Maryland. It was the government association that had spooked Zee.

"Among other things," Thorn continued, "the URI has been tasked with looking into the rationing of medical care in the last months of life, particularly for Medicare."

Paula and George's faces reflected their horror.

Noting their reactions, Thorn said, "Some kind of limitation or rationing has to be considered to control runaway costs. Most industrialized countries already ration medical care at the end of life, but it is, on occasion, associated with favoritism if not out-and-out corruption. The fact that iDoc made an unexpected venture into a form of rationing was looked upon by the URI with interest. They like the fact that it is totally and completely nondiscriminatory. They have specifically asked us not to rectify the glitch but merely to block the global-dump command. In short, they do not want to terminate the people selected, but they want them selected, perhaps to put them on a different track, which has yet to be specified.

"So to answer your question," Thorn went on, looking directly at George, "the glitch has not been removed, in the sense that it is still collating the data. It is still selecting people according to its logic, but not terminating them."

George and Paula exchanged yet another glance, a bit overwhelmed by what they had been hearing.

"Listen," Thorn continued, "as I said, Amalgamated

and the rest of the health insurance industry do not need 'death panels.' It is the country and the world that need some rational approach to end-of-life care. Amalgamated will not promote any particular methodology. If the government wants it as part of the Medicare-iDoc package, then that is the government's decision, not ours."

Thorn looked down the table at Clayton, who took the cue. "Cooperation on your part will bring other benefits, George," Clayton said. "I will have you reinstated as a fourth-year resident. The charges of HIPAA violations will be dropped immediately. I'm sure you're aware that a number of health care professionals have been convicted of similar violations and are now in prison."

"Likewise, the hacking charges against you will also be dropped," Thorn added. "You will also be given stock in Amalgamated to compensate you for having the initial conceptual idea for iDoc. And you, Paula, will be given additional stock added to your already sizable holding."

George leveled a gaze at Thorn. "That sounds like a bribe."

"Think of it as appropriate compensation. There will be time in the future for both of you to voice your feelings about the iDoc algorithm, but only after iDoc has been given its final FDA approval and has been at least distributed nationally.

"George, your second contribution is that you have underlined our need to correct iDoc sooner rather than later, saving iDoc from a media frenzy that might have put off its adoption for years. Amalgamated owes you a vote of thanks."

George and Paula both appeared shell-shocked.

"Now," Thorn said, "if you don't have any more questions, we will let you discuss the situation in private. Then you can let us know how you feel about what has been said."

George wasn't done. "I do have another question. Was Amalgamated responsible for my friend Zee's death?"

55

Thank you for asking," Thorn replied. "I meant to bring up the issue earlier, as we were certain you assumed that we were, but we weren't, at least not directly. What happened was we hired professionals to monitor you, to find out exactly what you knew or suspected, then Zee Beauregard entered the picture. We assumed he was helping you, especially when he managed to break into our iDoc servers. When he suddenly bolted early Saturday morning, we knew we had to follow him and bring him here along with you. He was trailed as he drove north, and we would have picked him up when he stopped. Unfortunately, that was not the way things worked out. Somehow he realized that he was being followed, and he apparently panicked. He pushed his car to unsafe speeds. I was told that it was an old vehicle. We believe he just lost control of the car and hit the concrete abutment of an overpass."

"Why did the media report that he had a stuck accelerator?"

"No idea. You'd have to ask them. We guess it was because of his vehicle's make and age and the fact that he was traveling over a hundred miles per hour, and it was the kind of accusation that would sell papers and up TV ratings. But, again, that's just a guess."

"You were going to have me picked up Saturday morning?" George asked.

"I was told that that had been the plan. But unfortunately when a backup team returned to your apartment, you had been arrested for hacking. That put us in a tailspin. We were very concerned you were going to tell the police, alerting the media in the process and putting the whole iDoc program in jeopardy, after all. But then things began to look up when you got out of jail so quickly, eventually leading us to Paula's house."

"How did you follow me to Paula's house?"

"We personally didn't follow you. The professionals did."

"I thought I was being careful."

"Well, they are, by definition, professionals. I assume they merely tracked your cell by GPS. Either that or they put a GPS tracker on your car."

George looked at Paula, who raised her eyebrows as if to say "I told you so."

"Now, if there are no more questions . . ." Thorn looked back and forth between Paula and George, waiting.

At first neither Paula nor George moved. Then Paula piped up: "When the, quote, 'professionals' invaded my house, they blew my front door off its hinges. What do you plan to do about that?"

"Already taken care of. The door is back on, restored to normal, as is the security system."

Thorn waited a few beats before adding, "Well, then, the ball is in your court. We will leave you two alone to discuss the situation. But remember, we believe that now is not the time for the general public to hear about the 'glitch' issue. The public is not ready for the debate about resource allocation, and iDoc should not be made a hostage to it. That's why you two must agree not to expose iDoc's problem, at least in the short term, until iDoc is introduced on a national scale and included with Medicare and Medicaid. At that point, the government and Amalgamated will respect your input."

Paula had another question. "How long do we have to make up our minds?"

Thorn shrugged. "As long as it takes. Let's just say as soon as possible. If you have any additional questions just let the attendants know. There's a large common room where you'll be allowed to spend most of your time. And a dining room where you will take your meals. Nights will be spent in the rooms you occupied last night. You will not be bothered. At the moment you are the only . . ." He searched for the right word, finally adding, "Guests." He rose from his chair. Langley and Clayton followed.

"We hope to hear from you both soon," Thorn said with a forced smile.

With that, Thorn, Langley, and Clayton filed out of the room, closing the door behind them.

George and Paula eyed each other, mouths agape.

"That was one of the weirdest experiences I've ever had," George said, shaking his head.

"Agreed," Paula responded. "I don't know what I expected but that certainly wasn't it. I don't know whether to be thankful or mad or both. Hell, they could have just phoned us rather than sending in the goon squad."

A minute later the door opened and several of the attendants reappeared. They motioned for George and Paula to follow them to the common room.

56

George and Paula cast their eyes around the large, very institutional-looking common room, which was furnished with several aged couches and a smattering of club chairs that faced an old TV set. The TV was tuned to a morning game show. In addition, there were four game tables and two bookcases, with a collection of dated books—mostly old *Reader's Digest* condensed editions—and magazines and board games. To complete the functional decor, the windows were barred.

Standing off to the side, near the entrance to the room, were four of the original six attendants, keeping an eye on their charges. On the other side of the entrance was the hallway leading back toward the conference room, and farther on, in the same direction, were the rooms where George and Paula had spent the night.

Paula and George were not watching TV but left it on to cover their muted conversation. They were settled into a couple of the chairs, as far away from the attendants as possible.

Paula was still incensed. "I cannot believe that they are treating us like this, holding us captive in this fifties-style mental institution."

"The whole affair defies imagination," George stated. "But I have to say that right now I'm feeling a lot better and a lot more relieved than I expected I'd be feeling."

"I guess I have to agree."

"I wonder if there are any other inmates or patients here despite what Thorn said." George looked back toward a glass-fronted nurses' station. Inside was a desk, where one of the attendants was doing paperwork.

"If there are other people, then they must be in isolation," Paula said, her eyes following George's as they took in their surroundings for the hundredth time.

"Okay," George said, turning to face Paula. "We have had time to recover from our shock at seeing Thorn, Langley, and Clayton. We have to talk! What's your gut reaction to Thorn's lecture?"

Paula shook her head. "I haven't had time to completely internalize it. I still feel so shell-shocked about the whole affair that it's hard to think clearly. All at once I have much more of an appreciation of post-traumatic stress."

"Me, too. But we have to make an effort. I imagine they expect to hear from us fairly soon."

"You're probably right." She reached out and touched his hand reassuringly. "Listen! I don't know how I feel about it all, but at least there are some compelling aspects to their offer."

"What do you mean?"

"I mean the part about needing some kind of rationing of health care for the last months of life. Ironically it has always existed, but behind the scenes. I mean, the demand for health care, or should I say sick care, is near infinite. Rationing has always been around in this country. And I must say it's been unfair, since it has been based on ability to pay or celebrity status. People with money and power have always gotten the health care they needed or desired. I don't know for sure, but maybe Mickey Mantle's liver transplant is a case in point. Possibly the same for Steve Jobs's."

"Are you buying Thorn's premise to let sleeping dogs lie?"

Paula shrugged. "I'm not buying anything. I'm just thinking out loud. I was blown away by Langley's explanation that iDoc actions were responsible for the deaths. Like you, I thought for sure it had to be hackers. It never occurred to me that it came from the iDoc algorithm itself. I mean, I did know about all the subjective aspects Langley mentioned regarding cost control and quality of life that had been taken into consideration when the iDoc program was designed, but I never would have made the leap to think that iDoc would be analyzing these considerations and making the decision that it's best to get rid of people. Yet rationing has always been around. Maybe there is something to letting an algorithm, which is completely nondiscriminating, handle the matter. What could be more fair?"

"It sounds like you have made up your mind."

"No, but I have to say, talking about it does help. When I think about the individual cases, I mean, there is no way that they should have been murdered, because that *is* what happened. Yet at the same time they may not have wanted to be tortured with any more drugs that wouldn't have cured them and might have had horrific side effects. Maybe there is a place for assisted suicide or at the very least for expanded hospice care."

George nodded. He could see Paula's point. "I have to admit that I have never given much thought to the issue."

"Well, maybe it is an issue that can no longer be swept under the rug."

George ran a nervous hand through his hair. "Health care is changing so fast with Washington mandating private health insurance. What the government should have done is make health care a function of government alongside education and defense, like medicine for everyone."

"That was never going to happen," Paula said. "That unfortunately got mislabeled as 'socialized' medicine way back when none of our politicians had enough courage to take it on."

"Well, we doctors should have been for it, but we were too afraid of losing control of the profession, which now is going to happen via the digital revolution. Maybe we deserve it, having tried to support the fee-for-service paradigm for so long."

"I couldn't agree more," Paula said. "Doctors certainly have been dragging their feet about informational technology in general. It is just another reason why iDoc is going to be a huge plus."

"It's not going to be a huge plus if, as you say, it murders people."

"Let's put that behind us for a few minutes," Paula said. "I'm inclined to do as they wish. I committed the last three years to developing iDoc. Maybe you should feel the same, since it was your germ of an idea that started it all." With raised eyebrows she looked over at him and studied his face.

George was taken aback. "I hope you are not suggesting that you and I bear some of the responsibility for these deaths."

"Hardly. But I am beginning to think that they are, as Thorn has suggested, an unfortunate consequence or growing pain of a new and improved system that is going to have an enormous positive effect on the health of the public. A few people die in all sorts of medical studies, particularly drug trials. As long as the unintended killing has stopped, I think I can live with keeping quiet about this glitch, at least in the short run. What about you?"

George sighed. "You know, I have a real problem because one of these murdered souls was someone I loved, and another was one I cared about as a friend. That makes it hard to think of them as unfortunate 'growing pains' or statistics. What I would have paid to have had six more months with my fiancée. But maybe she would have wanted to avoid the pain and suffering. Still, I would much rather that the decision had been hers and not an algorithm's. . . . Jeez!" George lifted his hands in a gesture of frustration and confusion.

"These issues are a thousand times more troublesome when they are imbued with emotion. I can understand. And I'm sorry." She touched his hand again, this time leaving her hand resting on his.

George glanced at the attendants, then leaned closer to Paula. "Thorn also said that the government doesn't want the glitch to go away."

"But the killing has stopped."

"But it is only a click away if the glitch, as they euphemistically call it, remains."

Paula removed her hand from George's. "I see your point."

"This Independent Payment Advisory Board is a scary behind-the-scenes organization. Its members are appointed, not elected, and this Universal Resource Initiative is even more of an enigma."

"Agreed. But Thorn said that what the government does with the glitch is an open question and that our input will be respected."

"True. But the secrecy worries me. And when you get down to it, the federal government is going to do what the federal government wants to do. If our input doesn't line up with their intentions, who do you think wins?"

"Well, we can agree not to let it remain a secret.

Meanwhile, I think we should get out of this place. We can tell Thorn that we agree in principle to what he's asking, meaning we won't go running off to the media. That will get us out of here, and we can continue talking at my place, which will be a hell of a lot more pleasant."

"Do you think Thorn will buy it?"

"I do! I'm taking him at his word. We have no other choice if we want to walk out of here."

"Letting the glitch persist makes me feel I have taken the first step on a slippery slope. It's like the beginning of herding up the weakest among us for a future cull."

"That may be, but as long as no more people are murdered, we can afford to continue thinking about it. I *have* to get the hell out of here. And you need to finish your residency instead of going to prison."

"Okay!" George said. "Okay!"

"Okay what?" Paula asked.

"Okay, I guess it is worth a try. I hope I can make it sound convincing."

"All we are promising is not to go to the media right now. We can sound convincing because that is exactly what we are doing, and for the moment at least, it's all they're asking."

57

Just when Paula and George were beginning to despair that Thorn might not return that day after they had sent word that they had agreed to his offer and wished to see him, he walked into the common room. They had returned there following their lunch. They had been the only people in the dining room, and the isolation of the place, its pervading silence, and its vintage fifties decor were beginning to wear on them.

Thorn dismissed the attendants and brought a chair over to where Paula and George were sitting.

"I must tell you that I was ecstatic to hear the good news!" Thorn said. He was clearly pleased that his speech had had the desired result.

As George and Paula had decided prior to Thorn's

arrival, Paula spoke while George stayed silent. It had been her idea because she knew Thorn best and was also more confident she and George were making the right decision. She didn't waste words: "We have talked it over and agree that the iDoc program should not be held up by the glitch, which we understand would occur if the media happened to get ahold of the story. So we will not be alerting the media, or anyone else, for that matter, despite, should we say, our continued misgivings."

"I'm pleased to hear this," Thorn said with a contented smile. "Can I ask what your misgivings are, specifically?"

Paula glanced briefly at George in the hope that he would indeed stay silent and let her answer. "Our biggest concern is that the glitch has not been eliminated, or should we say dismantled, from the iDoc program."

Thorn looked at George. "I trust that these are your feelings as well."

George nodded.

Paula added, "We would also like to impress upon you our desire to be included in the ongoing discussions vis-à-vis CMS's response."

"Excellent! I can assure you of that. In fact, we welcome your input." Thorn turned back to George. "I want to be absolutely certain that Ms. Stonebrenner is speaking for you."

George nodded. "She is."

"Excellent," Thorn repeated, slapping his thighs. "I consider this welcome news, as you can well imagine. Now, you can leave this facility, but we feel it would be best if neither of you goes back to your work routines for, let's say, at least a week. I would also prefer that you stay together during the upcoming week so that you can continue your discussions. We would be happy to put you up in a hotel."

"I don't think that's necessary," Paula said. "Our plan is to stay in Santa Monica."

"You wouldn't prefer, say, the Four Seasons in Maui?"

Paula turned to George with a questioning expression. The idea had some merits.

He shrugged. "I think Santa Monica will be just fine." He was not interested in becoming beholden to Amalgamated, which he thought would be the case if they accepted a paid vacation in Hawaii.

"Excellent," Thorn said yet again. He turned to George. "Just so you are aware, I'll be telling Clayton to reinstate you at the medical center. As for the stock options, I will bring them up at our next board meeting."

"I think I'll pass on the options," George said.

Thorn gave him a look, suggesting that was not what he wanted to hear. "I will put in the request just the same," he said, standing. "I will make the arrangements for you folks to leave. If you change your minds about Maui, let us know."

Thorn stuck out his hand to Paula, who took it and shook. He then did the same with George, saying in the process: "Once again, let me apologize to you both for last night."

Both Paula and George just nodded.

58

As promised, in less than an hour two attendants accompanied Paula and George out to a waiting black SUV. Two muscular-appearing men in black suits and short, military haircuts were in the front seat. Although Paula and George didn't recognize the men from the previous night, they decided that they were of the same ilk, "professionals."

As they left the facility, George was surprised to see how close they were to Laurel Canyon Boulevard. There was no sign identifying the place.

The drive home was a quiet one. Paula and George didn't want their conversation to be overheard by their drivers, and the drivers did not speak to them or each other. The SUV pulled to the curb in front of Paula's house, and George and Paula stepped out, still wearing the blue institutional clothing they had been given. Paula said thank you to the drivers, but there was no response.

Paula and George watched the vehicle pull away.

"They certainly aren't going to win any personality contest," Paula said.

"My sense is that their seriousness was a message."

"How do you mean?"

"Thorn is letting us know that the people who used the strong-arm tactics on us last night are still in their employ."

Paula nodded. "I bet you're right." She steered George to a door on the side of the house and retrieved a key from a lockbox hidden under a fake rock. They went inside.

The first thing that Paula wanted to do was inspect the front door. As it had appeared from the street, it was back on its hinges and no worse for wear. They went to the guest room and saw the unmade bed was just as they had left it.

Paula turned to George. "You can stay here in the guest room or upstairs with me. Your choice."

"Maybe we should see how the evening progresses. This has been one hell of a stressful experience."

"Excellent idea."

They went upstairs to check out the second level and saw that the panel hiding the chute down to the basement was still ajar. Paula went to close it, but George stopped her. "That was one scary ride in the dark," George said. "Maybe we should try it again."

Paula smiled. "Another good idea!"

Like a couple of kids they slid down the chute and ended up in a tangle on the floor. It made both of them laugh, and it relieved a certain lingering tension.

Back in the kitchen area, Paula opened the refrigerator, glancing at the contents. "Not a lot in here," she said. "What do you think we should do for dinner?"

"We could go out."

"I think I'd rather eat in. I feel asocial. Would you mind?"

"Not at all! In fact, I'd prefer it."

"It just means I have to go to the store."

"I could come and help."

"No need. You stay and relax. You could even take a swim if you'd like."

"Actually, I need to pop over to my apartment. Since I'll be staying here for the rest of the week, I need some clothes and all. While you're at the store, it would be a good time for me to do it."

"Perfect. You get your stuff while I go to the market. What would you like to eat?"

"Whatever," George said. "As long as it is with you, I don't care."

Paula smiled at the compliment. "I'm not the world's best chef. Would you mind a repeat of steaks and salad?"

"I'd be thrilled."

"Great! Why don't we get it out of the way right now. I'll head off to the store, and you go back to your apartment." She took a garage-door remote out of one of the kitchen drawers and handed it to him. "But do me a favor!

Don't be long. The idea of being alone in this house gives me the creeps."

"I'll make it fast." He gave her a quick, reassuring hug and was out the door.

Before climbing behind the wheel of his Jeep, George checked the car for a GPS device. He even checked under the hood. Nothing. With the same concerns in mind about covert surveillance, he purposely left his cell phone on the edge of the garage sink. Only then did he back his car out into the alley and head toward his apartment. As he navigated L.A.'s notorious rush-hour traffic, he couldn't help repeatedly checking around him, including the rearview mirror, to see if he was being followed. He suspected that, after this bizarre experience, paranoia was going to be his close companion for a long time coming.

At his apartment George changed out of the institutional scrubs and immediately felt better. He started organizing what he wanted to bring to Paula's, but when he went to his closet for an overnight bag, he took down the box of Kasey's things instead. He found her phone at the bottom. It still had a residual charge, and he turned it on and stared at the iDoc icon. It made him think about the slippery-slope issue in a very personal way. Could he really trust the Universal Resource Initiative or its parent, the Independent Payment Advisory Board, not to take advantage of "the glitch"? George thought not. It was too convenient, too tempting, too financially rewarding, and ironically, on one level, too sensible and objective to be ignored.

Carefully putting the things back in the box, he returned it to the closet and pulled out his overnight bag. Later, as he hurried out to the Jeep, he glanced at his watch. It was getting late. He had a few stops to make before he drove back to Paula's, and he wanted to be there way before dark.

59

As planned, George arrived back in Santa Monica almost a half hour before sunset. He pulled into Paula's garage alongside the Porsche, lowering the door behind him, and retrieved his phone from the edge of the sink. Inside the house, he found Paula wearing a white Turkish towel robe. She looked completely revived.

"Welcome back!" She approached him, happily smiling, pointing out a selection of fresh fruit and still unshelved groceries on the countertop. "I was very efficient while you were away, getting groceries, as you can see, and even taking a short nap before a long and very luxurious bath." She ran her hand across his back and gave him a hug. "I feel like a different person."

"You look wonderful," he said. He held up his duffel bag. "I was successful as well."

She looked him over. "I see you changed your clothes. Did you get a chance to take a shower back at your apartment?"

"No. I didn't want to stick around there any longer than I had to."

"Well, I think you should, to wash off that vile mental institution. It will feel great. You go up to the master bath or into the guest suite, whatever your druthers, and indulge! I'm going to do a little more work here on dinner. We can eat as soon as you finish."

"I think I'll head into the guest suite," George said. Handling Kasey's things had affected him negatively on some level, more deeply than he had expected.

George did enjoy the shower. He stood motionless under the warm, massaging spray for a good ten minutes. Putting on his robe, he started back toward the kitchen. He certainly felt better than he had in several days.

Paula had the dinner completely under control. Even the barbecue was ready.

"Well, how about I open the wine?" he offered, holding up the bottle she had already selected.

"Yes! Do!"

Five minutes later they were sitting outside, watching the grill as evening turned into night. George sipped his wine. What a life! For the moment he couldn't imagine being more relaxed. Over the last forty-eight hours his life had been a roller coaster, but at the moment he was at the pinnacle.

They ate inside and the conversation was very relaxed. The atmosphere gave them both a chance to think over and address in detail everything that had surfaced during the bizarre meeting with Thorn, Langley, and Clayton. Both agreed it would be to society's detriment if iDoc's adoption was held up. And with the help of the wine, they relived the scary abduction episode. To their surprise they were able to laugh about aspects of it now that they were safe and sound, even though they were still indignant and angry over being victimized.

After dinner they started to talk about medical costs and how it was probably the biggest problem facing health care. Those costs had to come down if there was ever going to be an equitable distribution of service. They knew iDoc would help tremendously. George said the Affordable Care Act was more about improving access than lowering costs, and an unintended consequence, in his opinion, was that it would inflate costs more than anyone expected. That discussion brought them back to the need for rationing in the last months of life.

"I realize now that rationing will have to be considered," Paula said. "Do you agree?"

"I'm not so sure," George replied.

"The more I think about it, the more I understand Amalgamated's position as voiced by Thorn," she admitted.

"Exactly what do you mean?" George said, eyeing her over a bite of salad.

"I feel better about the glitch as long as it only collects data that might be helpful in the future."

George listened but didn't respond.

Paula became aware that he had gone quiet. She studied him. "Is our thinking in sync?"

George shook his head.

"What's changed?"

"I took out Kasey's cell phone when I was back in my apartment. It made me wish I could have had a bit more time with her to tell her how much she meant to me. It made me question what she would have chosen."

"George, the killing has stopped."

"For now," he replied. "If the glitch had been completely removed, I probably would feel differently. The fact that the application that killed Kasey is still functioning and that government-appointed officials are considering iDoc makes me feel extremely uneasy." He swirled the wine in his glass. "There has to be an open debate to let people know what iDoc is capable of."

Paula nodded slowly.

"Paula, can you really live with covering up a series of what most people would agree were murders?"

"I don't know, George, when you put it in those terms." She sat still for a moment, staring down at the table. Finally she looked up at him. "If you can't live with it, I can't, either."

George was impressed and even flattered by her reaction. "I appreciate that."

She smiled and picked up his empty wineglass. "Let me refill these and we'll have a toast!"

"Sounds like a plan."

George watched Paula go over to the kitchen counter, where the wine bottle stood. He exhaled forcibly, closing his eyes. He was exhausted after no sleep whatsoever Saturday night and very interrupted sleep Sunday night, but he was glad he had voiced his concerns. Having done so made him even more certain how he felt. The decision had been building all afternoon and had come to a head when he had held Kasey's cell phone. He didn't fully realize it at the time, but he did now.

Paula came back with full glasses and handed one to George. They clinked glasses and Paula said, "To our current decision."

"To our decision," George corrected. "I am not going to change my mind."

"Okay, then, to our current final decision." She smiled.

George nodded and they drank.

"When do you think we should tell Thorn?" Paula asked.

"Not for a while. If he calls, we'll just say we are still debating the pros and the cons. We can certainly get away with that for the rest of the week."

"And then what?"

"Eventually we'll have to come clean. But I don't want to do it until we have our backs covered."

"What do you mean?"

"We can't allow ourselves to be so vulnerable again. Simple as that."

"You're right." She held her glass up. "By the way, what do you think of this wine?"

The wine was a deep ruby color. George nodded appreciatively. "I think it's fine. But I'm not much of an authority."

"You don't have to be an authority to recognize this is rather exceptional. It's called Cheval Blanc. I've been saving it for a special occasion."

George smiled appreciatively. "It is delicious." He took another mouthful, holding it in his mouth. He was hardly a wine connoisseur, but it tasted great. They continued making small talk until Paula asked exactly how they should "cover their backs."

"I have some ideas," George said. He looked at her. "How about you? What do you think we should do?"

"I imagine that between the two of us we can come up with something."

George nodded in agreement as he tried to suppress a yawn.

"Tired?"

"Yes. Exhausted."

"Do you know where you want to sleep?"

"I think tonight the guest room would be best. There is no way I'd be very entertaining."

"No pressure. Especially since I'm tired, too, despite my nap."

George let out another yawn.

"Why don't you head into the guest room while I put the kitchen in some sort of order."

"I can help."

"Fine, but let's finish our wine first. It would be a crime to waste it."

She emptied the bottle into their glasses, and they finished it off. George struggled to his feet as Paula collected their plates. He helped carry some dishes into the kitchen, wobbling in the process. Paula noticed.

"Perhaps you should sit down while I finish. I'm not going to do much. I just want the place to look decent in the morning when we come in for breakfast."

George nodded as he barely made it to the couch. A moment later his head was resting against the sofa's back, and his mouth was slack and ajar. His legs were splayed out in front of him. He was breathing deeply, snoring slightly.

Paula finished with the kitchen and approached him, giving George's shoulder a shake. She said, "Wouldn't you rather lie down on your bed? It's more comfortable than being sprawled on the sofa."

But George didn't move. He was out.

Paula tried again. Same result. She shrugged and walked down the hall to the study.

She picked up her landline and dialed out. "Bradley? It's me. I hope I'm not calling too late."

Thorn's voice was thick with sleep. "I didn't expect to hear from you for a few days."

"I didn't think I would be calling so soon, either, but unfortunately George won't go along. Your whole complicated ruse didn't work."

"Are you certain?"

"Of course I'm certain. What a waste, the whole damn charade. The break-in, the smoke machine, the police sirens! Let's end it now. George is intent on covering his back, as he put it."

"What does that mean?"

"I think he wants to tell the world what happened. Have Gauthier pick him up. Tonight."

There was a pause on the other end of the line. "Will there be any trouble?"

"No."

"How can you be sure?"

"Rohypnol. Double dose in his wine. He's going to be out of it for a while, but I want Gauthier to pick him up now. I'm feeling guilty."

"Guilty? That was not part of the plan."

"I know, but he's actually a terrific guy, maybe too idealistic for me in the long run. Now, don't get jealous or anything! There's no way he could come between you and me. But tell Gauthier to be careful and handle him with kid gloves."

"Anything else?"

"Yes. George's car. Have someone pick it up and drive it back to his apartment." She moved to hang up, then paused. "Oh, Bradley? Make sure Gauthier knocks this time."

Thorn laughed before disconnecting.

EPILOGUE

D r. Paul Caldwell found a padded USPS envelope in his mail inbox. It stood out among what was mostly junk mail. Caldwell looked for a return address, but there was none. He noticed the postmark: Los Angeles. It was the only piece of mail he didn't throw into the recycling bin.

As he headed back to the emergency room, where he was the director, he tore open the envelope. Out dropped a second envelope with just his name hand-printed in large letters. He stooped down to pick it up. There was no return address on it, either. He began walking again, glancing back into the larger envelope. There was a single sheet of paper in it. He pulled out a short note in cursive script that looked as if it had been dashed off. Caldwell recognized the distinctive handwriting. It belonged to George Wilson, a radiology resident with whom he'd become acquainted. There had been considerable correspondence between them by snail mail and e-mail over the previous year involving a mutual friend.

Paul stopped in the busy hospital corridor and read the note with a perplexed frown:

Hope all is well with you. This might sound weird, but I have a favor to ask. If you don't hear from me in let's say a week from the time you are reading this, try to text or call my mobile phone. The number is (917) 844-3289 in case you have misplaced it. If you don't get me, open the sealed envelope and read the contents, and then do whatever you think is best. As for me, I'll probably be committed to a private, highly secure mental health facility someplace up in the Hollywood Hills off Laurel Canyon Boulevard and would appreciate being, should we say, sprung! But don't try to do it alone. Bring the cavalry, meaning the media and law enforcement. And if I'm not there, then I'm probably dead. Let's hope I'm there! It's going to be an explosive story.

George.

P.S. Your job as you know it might be on the line!

AUTHOR'S NOTE

For those readers interested in delving deeper into the changes coming to the profession of medicine due to the convergence of informational technology, nanotechnology, and genomics, I heartily recommend the nonfiction book called: *The Creative Destruction of Medicine* by Eric Topol, MD.

I was in the middle of writing *Cell* when I came across this fascinating work. The introduction alone impressed me with how closely the author's vision of the future of medicine and my own coincided. Reading the book enabled me to add some richness to *Cell* that it wouldn't have had otherwise.

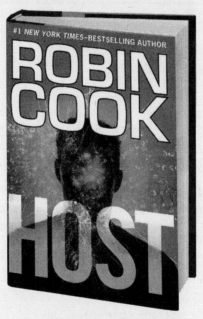